Destiny's Path

The vortex yawned before them. A searing streak of lightning shot out and caught Neil full in the chest, flinging him into the air. The wreckage of The Separate Collection whirled as the powerful forces spun him and Ted around as though they were feathers. Then he felt the terrible might of the gateway dragging and clutching at him, drawing him ever closer to the shimmering brink. With a clap of thunder, the flaming coils gaped wide and suddenly he was inside—rushing relentlessly down the twisting helix, shooting deep into the absolute blackness. Both Neil and Ted vanished from the Wyrd Museum.

WYRD MUSEUM

The Woven Path
The Raven's Knot
The Fatal Strand

WYRD MUSEUM

The Woven Path

Robin Jarvis

CONTENTS

8:47 P.M.

Death and horror flooded the night. In the fog-filled street, as the awful, clangorous rumor of German bombs grew gradually closer, an American airman stumbled to his feet and gazed down. The ground quivered as a parachute mine exploded three streets away.

Suddenly, two circles of light came sweeping through the mist, accompanied by the fierce rattle of a military jeep that plowed through the fog, its hooded headlights straining to illuminate the way ahead. A gruesome sight unexpectedly caught in the soft beams.

Standing over the lifeless body of a soldier was an American Air Force lieutenant. The Military Police saw the murder weapon in his hands, and the face he turned to them was wrung with guilt.

"Frank's dead," he called desolately.

"The knife!" the driver hollered. "Drop it!"

"You got it all wrong!" the man cried.

"Reach!" the other MP shouted, sliding the white truncheon from his belt.

Lunging forward, the lieutenant pelted into the mist.

Darting past the soldier's corpse, the driver pulled out a gun and bawled, "Hold it, Signorelli!"

The airman's running figure shuddered as a burst of white light flared behind him.

With the gunshot still resounding through the fog, he

glanced down and saw a blossoming circle of red soaking through his shirt.

The pistol blazed three more times, and the man screeched as the bullets blasted and ripped clean through his flesh.

Gasping, the airman toppled backward to the ground, clasping his hands to his perforated chest.

"No!" he choked, convulsing with shock. "Oh Lord, no—I ain't ready. Hell, I *weren't* ready."

His frantic movements began to slow and the man rolled onto his front.

A blackness closed over his eyes.

Before the darkness took him, the lieutenant's fingers clenched, tightening around the soft body of a toy bear.

Then it was over.

CHAPTER 1

NEW ARRIVALS

In keeping with the festive season, the twenty-seventh of December began beneath a stark covering of bitter, bristling frost. The previous night had been intensely cold, and long icicles now speared down from the gutters, glittering as the pale sunlight edged over the rooftops.

As morning crept toward midday, the shuddering cold showed no sign of relenting. Instead, its grip seemed to tighten, and the treacherous ice that had been dispelled from the roads by the salt spreaders stealthily returned.

On the Mile End Road, a trail of exhaust pipes spluttered and their foggy fumes hung thick and acrid on the freezing air. Delicate frosted masterpieces sparkled over every unprotected windshield, and a chorus of coughing vehicles crawled through Whitechapel toward Bethnal Green. Among this sluggish congestion, a small blue van laboriously wheezed and whined, protesting at the grueling journey it had been forced to endure.

Joshua Chapman scrunched up his eyes, gave a prolonged bored yawn, then wriggled and dug an elbow into his brother's side. The front seat of the van was not very wide and it was a tight squeeze to fit both boys onto it. The four-year-old shuffled uncomfortably. They had been in the van for some hours now and had not stopped once. Josh's bottom had gone numb and his growing unease about the quantities of lemonade he had drunk were soon confirmed.

"I have to go," he said abruptly.

Brian Chapman gave a nervous sideways glance at his son then fixed his eyes back on the road ahead.

"It isn't far now, Josh," he promised. "Can't you hang on a little bit longer?"

"No," came the firm reply.

Mr. Chapman stooped over the steering wheel and looked desperately on either side of the busy road. "I don't know where there is one," he mumbled, beginning to get flustered.

With an annoyed "tut" the elder boy looked up from the book he was reading, glared at his brother, then stared in annoyance at their father.

"Don't give in to him!" he said emphatically. "By the time you manage to find somewhere we could be there. Serves him right for guzzling so much lemonade anyway—I said you shouldn't have given him yours as well!"

Mr. Chapman lifted his glasses and pinched the bridge of his nose—the familiar sign that he was getting anxious. "I don't want him to make a mess, Neil," he muttered.

"He won't," the boy answered, giving his brother a warning glare.

Wedged between them, Josh pulled a sullen face and stubbornly folded his arms. "I have to go," he repeated.

"Ignore him," Neil told his father.

By the time the van turned off the main road, Mr. Chapman's nose was a deep shade of red from the continual pinching. He forced himself to concentrate on the way before them, squinting up at the street names fixed to the renovated and newly built buildings on either side. He had made this journey only once before, and although that had been a short three weeks ago, he was finding it difficult to remember the exact route.

With growing impatience, Neil watched the man's thin face cloud over as he peered down at the map propped on the dashboard. Mr. Chapman was a ridiculous and disheveled sight. He didn't seem to care how he looked, and his shabby appearance irritated his son. Lank brown hair hung long, unkempt, and greasy over the collar of his rumpled shirt. Although he had made an effort today by shaving, Neil wished he had also spared the time to trim the wiry tufts of hair that sprouted from his nostrils. And he was wearing those dreadful beige chinos that were an inch too short and flapped about his ankles.

Morosely, Neil recalled how his father's appearance used to make him laugh. Since his mother left, however, his incompetent parent had become merely a source of embarrassment.

Neil was a serious-looking boy of eleven whose hair was the same dismal shade of brown as his father's—but there the similarities ended. Mr. Chapman's eyes were a mottled green, set slightly too close together on either side of a bony, ill-shaped nose. Neil's eyes were soft and gray, and thankfully he had inherited his mother's pleasant, if unstriking, features.

"Darn!" Mr. Chapman suddenly exclaimed. "I think we took a wrong turn. I don't recognize this at all . . . no, hang on . . . it's down that backstreet and left—I think."

The van trundled on, past the towering, graffiti-covered apartments, then down a narrow, cobbled way that wound between deserted warehouses and a derelict factory.

"You sure this is right?" Neil asked doubtfully. "It's the middle of nowhere."

His father gripped the wheel a little tighter and nodded with uncharacteristic conviction. "Oh, yes," he affirmed, "this is definitely the right road."

"Who'd want to stick a museum around here?" the boy murmured.

A high wall tipped with broken glass reared up to their right, and the afternoon appeared to grow dim as they traveled beneath the wall's crumbling fastness. Facing it, and seeming to huddle over the roadway, was a rundown group of dark, Victorian houses—cramped, cheerless dwellings with untidy window boxes trailing withered plants and dead, twiglike weeds. Some of the houses were empty, and wooden planks had been nailed over the doors and windows. A collection of bulging garbage bags formed a lopsided mountain on the sidewalk, and Neil saw that a foraging animal had torn into the plastic, snouting for chicken bones and disgorging the rest of the rotting contents in the process. It was a horrible, squalid place, and he wished they were back in Ealing and that his father had never accepted this new job.

"It's getting dark," Josh abruptly announced,

forgetting about the call of nature as his fear of the night welled up inside him.

"No," his father assured him, "it's these old buildings and that high wall, they're just blotting out what light there is. Nearly there now, anyway—Well Lane should be just . . . ah!"

The van had lumbered around a corner, and the narrow way was barred by three thick iron posts. Beyond these, the road shrank into a litter-filled alley, bordered by the high wall on one side and a curious building on the other.

Mr. Chapman stared out at the stout posts that blocked the way, and he pouted as he rubbed the bridge of his nose. "Blood and sand!" he said sharply before opening the door and stepping out onto the frosty cobbles.

While his father glowered at the iron posts and gave them a few tentative and frustrated kicks, Neil leaned forward to gaze up at the strange building before them.

It was large and squat and grotesque. An uneasy tangle of architectural styles jarred and fought with one another, combining to make a discordant whole that lacked all symmetry and grace—mocking the historic periods that it had leeched into itself. It was impossible to say at which point in history the place had been built, for all of them seemed to be featured there.

Bizarre pinnacles and turrets spiked up from the lichen-encrusted roof, and their rusting points gleamed dully in the frostbitten air like the upturned spears of some forgotten, medieval army. Beneath them, nuzzling just under the eaves and a buckled length of clogged gutter, was one tiny, leaded window. Besmirched with the soot and pollution of many years, the dark diamond-shaped panes peeped slyly down at the alleyway far below—watching every movement of the few souls who ventured there.

Square Georgian windows gazed blankly from the two lower stories, but these were too large to sit comfortably around the moldy old building. They made it appear startled and amazed, as if abruptly woken from a sound slumber.

As Neil stared at the somber, sinister-looking place, the cold seeped through his clothes, crawled over his flesh, and sank deep into his bones. Quickly, he averted his eyes and drew away from the windshield.

"I don't like it," he muttered in revulsion, "and I definitely don't want to live there."

Beside him, Josh shivered. "Is it a castle?" he whispered. "Are there ghosts?"

At that moment their father opened the door of the van and peered inside.

"I'll just ring the bell," he said. "You stay here for a minute."

Before his father closed the door, a wild, unreasoning panic erupted within Neil, and the boy shouted to him urgently.

"Dad!" he begged. "Don't! Let's go! Leave this place—*please!* It's horrible!"

Mr. Chapman looked at his son in surprise. Neil was always so levelheaded and practical, it wasn't like him to be scared of a funny-looking building. Mouthing useless phrases like "there's nothing to worry about" and "it'll be fine, you'll see," he rummaged for the meager vestiges of capable fatherhood that so often eluded him.

But he failed as Neil's implorings grew steadily louder. Burbling still more inane words, Mr. Chapman grew impatient with himself and vexed at Neil's continued pleadings to return home.

"Look!" he snapped. "Get off my back! I need a job where I can keep an eye on Josh during the day—and this is it. We're lucky I managed to get this one. I don't need you whining. Get a grip on yourself."

Slamming the door, Mr. Chapman stomped toward the alleyway, fuming at his son's unusual reaction and at himself for letting it affect him. Perhaps it was because Neil's unaccountable fears were so similar to his own when he first set eyes on the forbidding building three weeks earlier.

Now he was approaching that monstrous doorway again, and although he thought he knew what lay beyond its threshold, he couldn't help catching his breath. Of all the additions made to the architecture of this hideously unique edifice, the entrance was the most unusual. Framing the arched, wooden door was an ogre of Victorian sculpture and design.

Fashioned in bronze, this elaborate creation snaked over the brickwork with great festoons of carved, flouncing material weaving in and out of the various images that cluttered and pressed close to the entrance.

The figures of women flanked both sides of the doorway, and each was dressed in a richly textured fabric that draped over her slender form in luxuriant and generous swaths down onto the tiled steps. An expression of supreme calm and serenity had been captured on the faces of these beautiful statues. Though the bronze was stained both black and putrid green, their loveliness glimmered through these ravages of the weather like the moon through the leaves.

Surmounting them, a third figure cast down her gaze from a mass of folds carved above the arch. The face of this creature, however, was stern and proud. The artist who had wrought and molded this folly of ostentation had blessed this final character with no humanity. Unlike the others, the sculpted face was grave and haughty; about the languid droop of the half-closed eyelids were traces of arrogance, and around the corners of the narrow mouth was the shadow of cruelty and callous disregard.

In her outstretched hands this figure held an unfurled banner, and written upon a field of tarnished gilt were the words WYRD MUSEUM.

Chapter 2

The Webster Sisters

Mr. Chapman's eyes passed quickly over the clumsy, imposing grandeur of the entrance. The uncompromising resolve he had shown to Neil was already evaporating, and he wondered if it might be possible to return to Ealing after all.

Apprehensively, he looked back at the small blue van and the faces of his sons staring out at him. With the bitter wind tugging the hem of his chinos and biting into his exposed ankles, he felt as small as Joshua. Clearing his throat he nonetheless managed to give them what he hoped looked like a hearty wave and made a determined stride up to the doorway.

Concealed beneath a sculpted ash leaf fixed to a hinge was a small brass button, and Mr. Chapman gave this a couple of furtive stabs. Within the museum there echoed a faint, tinkling noise, and the man waited on the middle step for the call to be answered.

Several minutes passed, and as he grew colder he

wondered if he had been mistaken about the entire situation. It didn't take much to confound or confuse him, and people were often taking advantage of this, devising what they considered to be hilarious practical jokes at his expense. What if this was just an elaborate hoax?

"Don't be silly," he told himself. "I had an interview, saw the premises."

Yet even as he thought this, Mr. Chapman couldn't help but doubt the whole business. Everything had happened so very quickly, from the time he had answered the advertisement to the subsequent brief interview and the immediate acceptance of his application. If he hadn't been so desperate for work he would have found the unnatural haste suspicious—but now it was too late to begin worrying. Everything was settled.

He was just about to press the bell again—but even as he raised his hand to do so, he heard the rattle of a heavy bolt being drawn back. Swiftly, he swept his fingers through his greasy hair as the iron-studded door opened.

Brian Chapman found himself looking into the face of an elderly woman whose steely eyes fixed accusingly upon him as she studied him with a sour expression on her pale, gaunt face.

"We are not open," she stated acidly. "If you desire to view the collections then you must return on the last Thursday of the month—before luncheon. Good day."

The lady was obviously very old, yet she was not like some elderly people who, with an imbecilic, faraway look, shuffle around in sloppy slippers, lost in a large cardigan. No, this woman retained all the frosty dignity that had ever been hers, and her wits were as sharp as her words.

An abundance of fine white hair was piled on her head in exquisite curls, and a string of black beads threaded its way between them, dangling in darkly glittering loops just above her ears, which were adorned with pendulous diamantine earrings.

Her bluish, almost translucent skin was stretched over a fine-boned skull that sat erect and high upon an elegant, if somewhat scrawny, neck.

She was dressed in a faded black evening gown, trimmed at the neck and sleeves with black beads matching those that snaked in and out of her hair. Arrayed in this dimmed finery, she looked like a once-regal duchess who had come upon hard times. She was a remarkable sight, and she reminded Mr. Chapman of a dried flower that had once been fair and beautiful but was now fragile and withered—a poorly preserved semblance of the glory it had once known and reveled in.

"Wait!" Brian called out as the elderly lady moved to close the door in his face. "Mrs. Webster, I've come about the job—remember? You interviewed me. I'm the new live-in caretaker, Mr. Chapman."

A flinty sparkle gleamed in her eyes as she nodded, and he suspected that she had known who he was the entire time but enjoyed making people feel uncomfortable.

"You will remember that I am *Miss* Webster," she smartly informed him. "Neither I nor my poor sisters are married."

"Ah, yes," he answered apologetically, "you told me that last time."

Opening the door a fraction wider, she gestured for

him to enter, and the taffeta of her faded gown rustled softly with her movements.

"You had better come in," she said curtly, in a tone that commanded absolute obedience. "You may as well begin at once. What is it, man? Why do you hesitate? Speak!"

Brian pinched his nose. "My children," he uttered, cowed by her brusque and scornful manner. "Do you recall I mentioned them at the interview?"

"Young man," she began with disdain ringing in her clipped voice, "I am not senile. I recollect all that was said on that occasion. If this is your blundering attempt to tell me that they are here with you, then I suggest you bring them in before they catch their deaths."

In silence, but with a curious smile traced on her face, Miss Webster disappeared into the darkness that lay behind the entrance as the new caretaker scuttled over to his sons.

"Neil!" he called. "Give me a hand with these bags, will you?"

It didn't take long for the Chapmans' possessions to be unloaded from the van, forming an untidy pile beside the iron posts, ready to be carried indoors.

With a backpack full of clothes slung over one shoulder, a medium-sized suitcase in his left hand, and a bulging duffel bag in the other, Neil trudged toward the building and looked for the first time at the grandiose entrance to the Wyrd Museum.

"Looks like the doorway to a tomb," he muttered under his breath. "A great big, hungry tomb just waiting to be fed and swallow us whole. This entire place is foul!"

Frowning, he climbed the three steps and cautiously passed into the shadows beyond.

The moment he crossed over the threshold, Neil coughed and dropped the suitcase as a horrid, musty smell assailed his nostrils. It was like opening a closet that had been sealed for years and inhaling in a single fetid breath all the damp rot that had accumulated.

"Are you ailing, Child?" snapped a brisk voice.

Neil looked up. There was Miss Webster standing before him with her thin hands clasped primly in front of her.

"It's just the smell," he explained. "I wasn't expecting—"

"Smell?" she archly interrupted. "I smell nothing. Is this a schoolboy joke? I have had little or no experience with your generation, Child, so you would do well to keep out of my sight while you are here and refrain from any more of this idiotic humor. I have never tolerated nonsense, and frivolity of any sort repels me. Have I made myself clear?"

"Very," Neil answered, bristling indignantly at her severe and unjust tone. "This slum probably hasn't been cleaned for years," he observed in a grim, inaudible whisper as he surveyed his dingy surroundings.

No interior could hope to live up to the Victorian façade that framed the entrance to the museum, but the poky room he found himself in was exceptionally disappointing.

It was a cramped and claustrophobic hallway, stuffed with ornaments—from a tall and rather spindly specimen of a weeping fig planted in a stout china pot, to an incomplete suit of fifteenth-century armor that leaned drunkenly against the dark oak paneling that pressed in on all sides. To the right of where Neil stood and just beyond the entrance, a small arch had been cut into the oak panels, and traced in letters of peeling gold leaf were the words TICKETS FOR ADMITTANCE.

A flight of stairs covered in a threadbare red carpet, and mostly hidden by a solid wooden banister, rose steeply to the other floors. On the landing, one of the Georgian windows let in a pale ray of dirty brown light, weakened by having been filtered through the grime of centuries—and this tinted all it touched a melancholy sepia. Under the ghastly influence of this light, the dim little watercolors that hung on the far wall seemed to have been daubed from mud, and where it touched the weeping fig it was as if the leaves cringed and curled in revolt.

Stepping into the province of the pallid beam, Miss Webster glanced uncertainly upward, and her white hair was sullied and transformed into a filthy gold color.

"As you are to live here, Child," she said, addressing Neil once more, "know now that you may wander where you will in this museum, *if your courage allows.*"

A secretive, almost teasing tone crept into her voice as she gazed about the hallway and inhaled deeply as if savoring the rank atmosphere of the place.

"You see, Child," she told him, "there is an ancient and fundamental belief among some people that assigns to certain sites or buildings a particular mood, a spirit— or heart, if you wish. It is a belief that I am wont to share most wholeheartedly.

"In the days that are to come, when you are roaming within these venerable walls and learn the little you can of what they have to offer, pause a moment and think on that. What manner of heart might you suppose beats here? What will be the nature of the force that watches you and feels your footfalls traveling and moving inside it as a whale might feel a shrimp wriggling deep in the caverns of its belly?

"Perhaps the answer to that lies within yourself, but many are those who have blanched and fled when they became aware of the presence that abides here. Older than the soil wherein the foundations of this museum lie it is. For an eternity has it pulsed, this shadow-wrapped and mysterious heart. Yet, whatever its nature may be, it is most certainly not a comfortable one. I make no apologies for it—or what it may choose to do with you. In many ways it is out of my control."

Her words hung ominously in the air, and Neil wondered if the terse old woman was trying to frighten or intimidate him. To show that she had not succeeded, he folded his arms and stared back at her with as bored an expression on his face as he could muster.

"This you will discover for yourself," Miss Webster stated. "Until then all you need to know is that the private apartments of myself and my poor sisters are located on the third floor and that area is forbidden to you. I must also tell you that my sisters are not as . . . strong as myself and sleep much during the day, therefore you will make no disturbance of any kind in case you awaken them. Now, who is this?"

Neil turned to see that Josh had walked in the door carrying a small bag of his own clothes in both hands. Immediately, the four-year-old screwed up his face and let out a loud "Eerrrrkk!" followed by "It stinks!"

Miss Webster eyed the fair-haired child caustically and pressed her lips so tightly together that they turned a bloodless white.

Under the glare of this cold contempt, Josh moved closer to his brother and caught hold of his sleeve.

"Don't like her," he murmured honestly. "She's got a face like a camel."

There was an awkward silence. The old lady breathed deeply through her nose but said nothing until the boys' father reappeared bearing two cardboard boxes.

"Mr. Chapman," she began in a wooden voice, "I will now show you to your rooms."

"I haven't finished bringing the rest of the stuff in," he said. "Won't be too long. I can't leave it on the road—"

Miss Webster's lips parted as she turned on him a chilling smile, revealing a row of mottled brown teeth. "My time is precious to me, Mr. Chapman," she interrupted with an assured finality. "Let your belongings remain where they are for the moment."

"But someone might—"

"Out of the question!" her crisp voice snapped before he could finish the sentence. "The folk who dwell around here are no doubt aware by now that you have been made welcome in this place. They would not dare tamper with or take anything that belongs to a guest of mine. Only once has my hospitality been violated, and by the likes of one that shall never be seen again. For who now could withstand those nine nights hanging from the ash? Besides, it was so very long ago, so very long, when I was green enough to . . . well, let us say that I have never allowed myself to be so vulnerable again."

She licked her discolored teeth and sneered scornfully. "But this is not the hour for such ancient histories. Mr. Chapman, I swear to you that your possessions have never been safer, not ever."

"If . . . if you're sure?" he said doubtfully.

"Decidedly," came the insistent reply. "There are many, many affairs of which I am most certain. Now, follow me to your quarters."

As Miss Webster turned to open a door in the far wall, Brian put down the cardboard boxes and pulled a wry face at Neil.

"Old bag," his son mouthed silently.

The father nodded hurriedly, then looked across the room to where Josh had wandered. A strangled gurgle issued from Mr. Chapman's mouth as he stared at his youngest son in disbelief.

"Josh!" he cried.

The little boy was staring at the suit of armor and, before anyone could stop him, gave it a none-too-gentle nudge.

With a snap and a rattle of rust, the spear broke free, toppling headlong into the paneled wall, where it scraped and gouged a frightful, deep scratch in the wood, inscribing a perfect arc all the way down to the parquet floor. Thrown off balance by the violence of the weapon's descent, Josh tumbled backward against the armor. For an instant the helmet quivered, then it flew through the air like a cannonball and punched a great dent into one of the cardboard boxes, buckling it and sending it spinning against Neil's legs. Promptly, the boy fell into the box, then with a tremendous, resounding crash of clanking metal, the rest of the armor collapsed, and a riotous clamor rang throughout the dismal hall.

With flurries of dust flying about him and in the midst of this clanging destruction Josh scrambled to his feet, a scared expression on his face.

"I didn't mean it!" he gasped. "I only wanted to take a look and play . . ."

His voice died in his throat as he beheld the stony face of Miss Webster. The old lady was awful to look upon. Medusa-like, she glared for several moments at the four-year-old then advanced menacingly toward him, picking her way through the debris of scattered gauntlets, cuisses, and pallettes that now littered the floor.

"I will not have this!" she seethed. "For only a moment have you been here but already you have caused grievous harm. What right have you to despoil the armaments of the glorious dead? Have you performed deeds equal to his—he who fought in those forgotten wars? Would you reward such valor by this wanton destruction? How dare you raise your hand to this memorial of one whose renown is greater than your baseborn house ever shall be?"

Terrified of this stern apparition, Josh skipped over the upturned breastplate and ran wailing to his father.

"I'm . . . I'm awfully sorry," Mr. Chapman stuttered. "I'm sure he didn't mean that to happen."

"Then he ought not to have touched it!" Miss Webster roared back in a shrill, shrieking voice that made the man blink in astonishment and shrink away from her.

"If I catch him meddling with anything else," she began threateningly, "then it will be the worse for him.

All I have to do is withdraw my protection from you all. You would not like that—I swear!"

Struggling out of the cardboard box, Neil placed himself between the old lady and his brother.

"Leave him alone!" he yelled. "He's only four. That thing wasn't supported properly. You're lucky Josh wasn't hurt."

A peculiar glint flickered in Miss Webster's eyes as she regarded Neil, then a mocking smile curled over her face as she stepped back toward the door, the hem of her beaded dress brushing softly over the dismembered armor.

"We shall say no more about it," she stated simply. "It was perhaps an honest mistake. I am unused to company—I have been confined in the museum for too long. I only hope that the noise did not awaken my poor sisters. I would not wish them to be disturbed. Now follow me, if you please."

Neil glanced at his father, who shrugged and took hold of Josh's hand. Suddenly, the four-year-old let out a cry of surprise and alarm.

"Dad! Up there!"

Both Mr. Chapman and Neil looked up to where Josh was pointing.

Peering down at them from the landing, with their chins propped on the banister and grinning like a pair of naughty children, were the faces of two elderly women.

"Veronica!" Miss Webster called out. "Celandine! You know you were not to come down. Go back upstairs at once!"

Childlike dismay spread over the faces of the other women and they both groaned in protest. "Oh, Ursula!"

they complained in unison. "Don't be beastly. Let us come down and meet the strangers. We're so excited, we've even managed to dress ourselves—wasn't that clever of us?"

Before their sister had a chance to refuse them, Miss Celandine and Miss Veronica came pattering down the stairs like two great flapping geese.

"How darling!" Miss Celandine squealed when she saw Josh. "See, Veronica—what a bonny baby boy! Is he the one?"

The two old ladies reached out to tweak Josh's cheeks, and though he growled and tried to fend them off it was no use.

Neil stared at them in bewilderment. These two old bags were even odder than the first.

Miss Veronica's hair was dyed an unnatural coal black and hung down her back in a wild tangle like the ungroomed tail of a horse. The color contrasted starkly with her pale complexion, accentuated by the way she had applied huge quantities of white powder to her face that crumbled when she grinned and fell in fine, dusty trails upon her clothes. It was as if she was a small girl playing with her mother's makeup. A pair of finely arched eyebrows had been painted high up on her forehead, so that she looked perpetually startled and astonished. A vivid stripe of vermilion lipstick obliterated her twittering mouth so that it resembled a viciously bleeding wound.

Her sister, however, was as unlike her as it was possible to be. Miss Celandine's face was tanned and crabbed like an overripe apple. Her small eyes were as dark and glittering as the beads on Miss Ursula's gown. Below her upturned, bulbous nose she possessed a wide mouth that always seemed open, displaying her protruding and goofy teeth. Miss Celandine's hair was just as long as her sister's but it was the color of dirty straw, shot through with wisps of gray and twisted into two enormous braids that hung on either side of her head.

Both women were dressed eccentrically. Miss Veronica wore a loose-fitting garment of billowing silk that had once been white but was now gray and peppered with small spots of black mold. Dancing slippers of creamy satin embroidered with gold thread were on her feet, and in her hand she carried a pearl-handled walking stick, for her left leg was rather stiff and she limped when she walked. Stooping over Josh, enveloped in the voluminous folds of her frayed silk gown, she looked like some frail and geriatric goddess.

Velvet of an intense ruby red was the main theme of Miss Celandine's outfit. Her bare, freckled shoulders were draped with a tasseled shawl, and she had squeezed herself into a tight-fitting evening dress of the same material. But the pile of the velvet was worn, and the vibrant color had faded to a muddy orange in places, so that it looked as if she had been splashed with bleach.

"Oh, we're so delighted!" they cooed in jubilation. "How exquisite, what fun we shall have."

Miss Ursula eyed her sisters with impatience and clapped her hands for their attention as they fussed over Josh.

"Veronica! Celandine!" she commanded. "Stop that at once! The child does not like it."

Miss Veronica's hand fluttered to her garish mouth and disclosed that she had painted her nails a deep shade of violet. "But it's been so long," she trilled into her palm. "We've been so terribly anxious these past weeks."

"Yes, we have," chimed in Miss Celandine. "So don't be cross, Ursula, and tell us what we must and mustn't do. You're just as eager as we are, admit it."

"I assure you, I am nothing of the kind," her sister corrected.

"Pooh!" Miss Celandine argued as she adjusted the shawl, which had slipped from her shoulders to reveal an expanse of sagging, blue-veined flesh. "I know what you think before you do, most of the time. You can't fool me and never could."

"That will do," Miss Ursula scolded, and both her sisters drew their breaths as if she had slapped them. Turning to Mr. Chapman, the old lady made some brief introductions.

"This is Mr. Chapman. He is to be our new caretaker. I was just about to show him his apartment."

Miss Veronica buried her face in her hands. "Splendid!" she prattled, peeping coyly between her fingers at the unfamiliar, gangly man with the greasy hair. "And will he truly take care of us, like the beautiful white stags used to, so long ago?"

"Not us," Miss Ursula replied with a weary shake of the head as if she had labored through this conversation many times before. "He is employed to look after our museum."

"Oh," Miss Veronica murmured, unsuccessfully trying to suppress a pang of regret in her voice, "the museum, of course. I had forgotten about the museum. Have the mists abated and the valiant guards perished? Do we still have all the collections? Is that where we are now?"

It was Miss Celandine who answered. "Of course it is, darling." She laughed. "You remember Ursula's little design, don't you?"

Miss Veronica's troubled look of confusion cleared almost immediately. "Why indeed!" She giggled. "Then this is the man who is to be caretaker."

"Just so," confirmed Miss Celandine before she turned her attention to Mr. Chapman. "We are overjoyed that you are here," she greeted him. "I hope you will be most comfortable." With that, she held out her hand evidently expecting it to be kissed, but the man was so bemused and flustered that he merely shook it.

Snatching her hand back, the old woman let out a high-pitched cry, as though she had been scalded, but the noise quickly turned into a giggle and she focused her black, sparkling eyes upon Neil and his brother.

"Such delicious children," she murmured. "They really are quite enchanting—aren't they, Veronica?"

"Mouthwatering."

"I know we shall have fun together," Miss Celandine promised, bringing her nutty brown face close to Neil's. "You will be surprised."

Neil coughed, partly from nerves but mostly because of the pungent whiff of mothballs that wafted from the red dress.

These three old women were completely cracked. Why had his father accepted this job? Of all the incredibly miserable blunders he had ever committed, this had to be the worst. Who, in his right mind, would willingly agree to be cooped up in a museum that reeked of mildew with three crazy senior citizens who ought to be locked away in padded cells?

"Celandine," Miss Ursula called, "why don't you take Veronica upstairs? You both look tired."

Miss Celandine nodded readily. "Yes," she agreed, "excitement is so very draining. Do you think we might see the children again another day?"

Miss Veronica let out a shrill cackle. "When the hurly-burly's done!" she gibbered.

"But that may be too late!" complained Miss Celandine. "Please, please, do let us see them again. We would relish their company so much before we have to—"

"Be silent!" Miss Ursula commanded.

Her sister's wrinkled face seemed to cave in on itself as she sucked in her bottom lip and screwed up her eyes. "I never said it," she sheepishly whispered through the top row of her large, gravestonelike teeth. "I wouldn't give it away, you know I wouldn't!"

"Get you both upstairs," warned Miss Ursula.

Abashed, Miss Celandine and Miss Veronica ambled back to the stairs with downcast faces. Then, with one trembling and withered hand poised upon the banister, Miss Celandine glanced anxiously back at their formidable sister.

"Ursula," she uttered in a meek and plaintive voice, "does this mean that you won't permit me to begin knitting? You did promise. It's been an age or more since I last—"

"Of course you can begin," came the calm reply. "Now begone."

Miss Celandine's shriveled face brightened immediately, and she turned to the raven-haired and chalk-faced woman at her side. "Then you must cast on for me, my pet," she squeaked. "Let us begin at once. Quickly, we must be swift."

"I wanted to remain with the children!" moaned Miss Veronica.

"Well, you can't. You heard Ursula."

"But I don't want to measure the wool and cast on for you. It's been too long. I mightn't remember how."

"Of course you will."

"But there are so many things I do forget, so many faces I cannot recall, and the museum crowds in so, it confuses me on purpose!"

"You're being a silly."

"I am not!"

"Are too!"

And so, squabbling, they made their way back up the stairs until they were out of sight, but their voices continued to drift down for many minutes.

Alone with the Chapmans, Miss Ursula Webster allowed a wan smile to steal over her gaunt features. "Alas for my poor sisters," she sighed. "They have so few excitements, your arrival is a great occasion. I would repeat, however, that they are not strong and tire easily. Kindly bear that in mind."

With that, she gave both Josh and Neil a steady, chastising stare, then briskly opened the door. "Follow me," she instructed.

Neil nudged his father in the back. "Are you serious about this?" he asked in disbelief. "Dad, these nutters could be dangerous. What we're doing is crazy."

Mr. Chapman let out an exasperated snort. "Do you really think I'd put you and Josh at risk? Give me some credit, Neil. They're just harmless old ladies."

"Well, they give me the creeps," the boy answered, "'specially the head witch over there."

"Don't lag behind," his father said, turning to follow Miss Ursula. "Come and see where we'll be living from now on."

Beyond the hallway was a large, rectangular room. Great glass display cabinets crowded much of the space, but here and there a marble statue peeped above, around, or below them. The walls were painted a dusky blue, and on them were hung many drab oil paintings depicting various unrecognizable landscapes and even more unrecognizable people.

Neil's footsteps resounded on the wooden floor even though he trod cautiously, glancing around the strange surroundings and conscious the whole time of the old woman's remarks about the heart and spirit of the museum. He felt terribly small within it.

"Do hurry along," she barked, spinning on her heel and striding resolutely to the far side of the room toward a second doorway.

"What's that?" Josh asked, pointing to the tall display cases.

"Boring stuff," Neil told him. "Dull, dusty history. Old papers, old books, old trash."

"Oh."

Through this room the dignified elderly woman led them, and next they found themselves traipsing through a smaller area jam-packed with fossils and countless mineralogical samples, from fragments of bubbled lava to myriad different-colored quartz. Decorating the walls was a frieze of a prehistoric landscape in which dinosaurs chewed lush vegetation and savagely attacked one another. Josh especially liked this room and would have lingered to gape at the exciting pictures, but Neil warned that he would get himself lost and hauled him briskly away.

Into one room after another Miss Ursula marched, sometimes turning right, then left, or straight ahead, until Mr. Chapman lost all sense of direction and began to feel that he would never find his way out again.

Finally, they came to a dimly lit passageway and were shown to a door covered in peeling green paint.

"This suite of rooms is to be yours," the old lady told them, turning a key in the lock and ushering the Chapmans inside. "It hasn't been lived in for some years now, but I'm certain you will find it to your liking."

The apartment was small and consisted of a living room, one double bedroom, a kitchen, and a bathroom.

Standing in the shabby living room, Neil surveyed the drab, flowery wallpaper and the few pieces of old furniture. There was a brown couch, the arms of which were black and shiny from years of use; a fold-down table with two unmatching chairs; and a bookcase that was empty save for a dead spider plant and a chipped mug. In one corner stood an ugly pole lamp covered with a dusty turquoise shade, and hanging over the narrow window was a net curtain that had yellowed with age.

The disgust was plain on Neil's face, and he glanced briefly into the bedroom to see if that was any better. It wasn't.

"Dad," he muttered, "where are Josh and I going to sleep? There's only one bed."

Mr. Chapman began to get flustered, and he pinched his nose as he stared miserably into the room.

Wearily, Neil shook his head and folded his arms. "Do you mean," he hissed at his father, "that you took this job without even looking at our rooms? I don't believe you sometimes."

"Is there a problem?" inquired Miss Ursula.

"No, not at all," Mr. Chapman hastily lied before Neil could say anything. "This will be fine. Once we get our belongings in, it'll be cozier than our old place. Thank you very much, Miss Webster. I'm very grateful."

The old lady smiled icily. "Then I shall leave you to settle in," she said. "If you can begin work first thing tomorrow, Mr. Chapman, I shall inform you of your duties."

Closing the door behind her, Miss Ursula left, and Neil turned a belligerent face on his father.

"Before you start," Mr. Chapman protested, holding up his hand to halt the torrent of blame and criticism that was about to be unleashed, "I don't want to hear it! You know I couldn't afford the mortgage on the house since your mother left. Okay, maybe I should have checked out this apartment, but I never expected to get the job. So what if it's a bit small? It's only for eating and sleeping in. You can wander around the whole museum when you want to. Look out there. There's a yard for you both to play in. As for the sleeping arrangements, I'll take the sofa. You and Josh'll have to share the bed until I can get another one. Cheer up, Neil, it isn't that bad."

Neil said nothing but stared at his father reproachfully. They had left everything—their home, his friends, his school, and for what? For this tiny box of a place in the middle of nowhere with three crazy old loons for company.

At that moment, Josh began to cry, and though Mr. Chapman tried to comfort him he would not be silenced.

"You'll soon get used to it, Josh," he burbled. "A coat of paint'll brighten this place up, and once you've unpacked your toys—Oh, stop crying for pete's sake!"

Standing by the window, Neil gazed out at the dreary walled yard, feeling thoroughly bleak and miserable. As his brother's wailing continued, Neil turned toward the little boy and gave a pitying groan.

"I think he's wet himself," he muttered.

CHAPTER 3

IN THE SEPARATE COLLECTION

In the days that followed, the new caretaker and his family did their best to make the small apartment more comfortable. The walls were given several coats of canary-yellow paint, and although here and there ghostly images of flowers were still visible, the living room appeared bright and brimming with sunshine. The shabby sofa was covered with a colorful check blanket, and their old television was given pride of place in the corner, where the pole lamp had stood. Mr. Chapman filled the bookcase with his own precious volumes on bird-watching and steam trains, and since they could not afford any more paint, Neil covered the somber bedroom wallpaper with football posters.

During this hectic time, the boys had little opportunity to explore the rest of the museum and saw nothing of the strange Webster sisters. Mr. Chapman was kept extremely busy for, as Miss Ursula pointed out, the general upkeep of the place was now his responsibility.

Floors needed polishing, as did the glass cabinets; the statuary had to be dusted, and it was his duty to ensure that the potted plants were well watered. He also had to be on call during the rare occasions when the museum opened to the public.

The first such opening took place on the second day after the Chapmans' arrival, and Brian became extremely nervous when he realized that he would be quite alone. Miss Ursula instructed him in the plainest of terms that she had no intention of assisting in the supervision of the visitors. When the day came, however, Mr. Chapman's anxieties proved foundless, for though the doors were open from half past nine in the morning until midday, not one single person wandered into the premises. When he remarked on this to Miss Webster the following morning, she expressed no surprise and said that it was an unusual event when someone did stray into the museum.

When Neil and Josh finally left the confines of the apartment, they ignored the dubious attractions under their father's care and decided instead to venture out to the grimy yard.

The concrete-covered area was a sad and gloomy place. Hemmed in by the back of the museum on one side and twelve-foot-high brick walls on the other three, it was like stepping into the exercise yard of a prison. The lofty walls were tipped with iron spikes, and although there was a wide opening in the side wall it was barricaded by a padlocked metal gate that was covered with sheets of wood.

In this colorless courtyard, Neil and Josh kicked a ball around, using a spare plank and a drainpipe to mark out the goalposts. For a little while, the thud of the ball resounded around the four walls, joined with Josh's happy laughter. But eventually the claustrophobic and melancholy atmosphere of the place began to affect them, and Neil was soon glancing nervously up at the blank windows of the museum.

"There's someone up there," he murmured, "watching us. Maybe we've woken those nutty sisters."

Unsettled, Josh shivered in spite of the warm scarf that came up to his nose and the woolen hat he had pulled low over his ears. Leaving his brother to continue the game alone, he shuffled despondently about the yard like a mouse in a cage.

Fixed to the wall, beside one of the windows, was a porcelain drinking fountain, and Josh stared long and hard at it. The glaze of the bowl was chipped and covered in a livid green, slimy moss that he touched with the tip of his mitten and sniffed gingerly.

Giving the ball a final kick into the air before catching it, Neil turned his face to the museum and glared defiantly at each window, trying to catch a glimpse of whoever was spying on them. Only the dull gray light of the leaden sky was reflected in the glass, and the boy's unease mounted.

"It's as if the museum itself is watching me," he breathed. "All those windows are its eyes—it didn't like having a ball kicked against it. It doesn't like me . . ." His mouth dried as this unwelcome thought took menacing shape in his mind. Then abruptly he shook himself and managed a deriding laugh.

"Don't be crazy," he scolded himself. "I'm letting this dump get to me. It's just a smelly old heap of bricks."

Disgusted at his childish imaginings, Neil called to his brother that it was time for him to prepare their father's lunch and they'd better go back inside.

"Neil," Josh piped up, "why is this toilet out here?"

"Dimbrain," his brother chuckled. "That's not a toilet. It's one of those drinking things—my old school had one."

"What does it drink?" came the fascinated response.

"The blood of little boys," Neil teased.

"Doesn't!" Josh moaned unhappily, taking a step backward.

"'Course it doesn't—you're supposed to drink from it. I wouldn't drink anything that came out of that horrible old thing, though. It's all green, and I bet the water would be stagnant, probably full of germs."

"How does it work?"

"You push this lever down and . . . oh, nothing. The one at school didn't work either. Come on, I'd better open a can of soup for Dad—he'll be finishing his rounds about now."

Together they headed for the door to the apartment, but just as Neil was about to follow his brother inside, a faint trickle of laughter floated down to the courtyard from somewhere high above.

The boy threw his head back but saw no one. "It was one of those nutcases," he muttered to himself.

* * *

On New Year's Day, Neil finally decided to explore the museum. Josh had been listless all morning after having dreamed about their mother, and he kept asking questions about her. Thankfully, it was a Sunday and Mr. Chapman was there to deal with his son's confusion, albeit rather clumsily and with much shaking of the head, because he didn't fully understand either. Josh was too young to grasp that she had made a new life for herself and that they would probably never see her again. Yet his continual harping on the subject, combined with his father's inept and faltering explanations, made Neil irritable. Leaving Josh drawing a picture of her, with Brian looking glumly on, Neil left the apartment and wandered into the Wyrd Museum.

The first of the large rooms now smelled strongly of floor polish, and the cabinets sparkled in testament to the diligent labor of the new caretaker.

Above each doorway was a large brass plaque denoting what was housed in that particular room. Neil spent some minutes in The Fossil Room but was too eager to roam through the rest of the building to take much interest in individual exhibits.

It was a peculiar sensation, knowing he had the entire place to himself. According to what his father and Miss Ursula had told him, the three sisters hardly ever left the third floor, so he was not afraid of bumping into one of them. Through room after room he went, a lone figure intruding upon the unending solitude that lay heavily over the whole museum.

In his mind, Neil likened his slow exploration to an insect crossing the surface of a deep, dank pond. Before him all was calm and still, but his progress caused rippling swirls of disturbance that eased only when he had left and the timeless peace gradually returned.

It was a perfect place for thinking, and after nearly an

hour of this idle meandering, his thoughts soon drifted back to Josh's preoccupation with their mother. He wished she had been able to put up with his father for a little while longer. If he hadn't driven her to distraction, she wouldn't have sought refuge in evening classes and would never have met *that* man. Sorrowfully the boy wondered what she was doing now and found that he missed her far more in this strange, eccentric environment than he had when they still lived in Ealing.

Unexpectedly, Neil discovered the door that opened into the main hallway, and this reminder of that first day jolted him from his preoccupied thoughts.

The suit of armor was now reassembled and leaned, once more, against the wooden paneling. Idly studying the rusting figure, he wisely refrained from giving it even a tentative prod and instead directed his attention to the staircase.

With one hand on the banister, Neil craned his neck to see the second-floor landing as he began to climb.

It was obvious that his father's efforts had not yet extended to the upper floors. The brass plaques above the doors were dull and unburnished, the floors had not been waxed, and layers of dust had settled upon the cabinets.

The museum was much larger than he had imagined. Perhaps it was the layout of the galleries and rooms that tricked him, for there was always another door to pass through. Unless he looked out of the windows, he had no idea where he was in the building.

Several rooms were boxed within others and had no windows at all. These relied on electric light for their illumination and were in total darkness when Neil came upon them. They were often filled with deep shadows that no amount of electric light could disperse, and the hairs on the back of his neck prickled when he walked among the exhibits.

One of the windowless rooms was called The Egyptian Suite, and when Neil found the light switch he discovered that it contained three large sarcophagi, complete with mummies lying in long glass cases.

"Well, those 'mummies' won't be going to evening classes," he muttered grimly. But despite these glib words, Neil shuddered. He had never liked horror films where the embalmed and bandaged dead came back to life to throttle everyone who disturbed their rest, so he hastened through and snapped the light off as quickly as he could.

By then it was late in the afternoon, and just as he decided to return to the apartment, he came across a room called The Separate Collection.

The musty smell was stronger here than anywhere else, and when Neil entered he wondered if one of the windows had been left open, for it was intensely cold. Goose bumps crawled over his skin.

At first glance, the room appeared the same as the countless others he had wandered through. But when he looked a little closer, Neil realized that the exhibits were totally different than those in the other rooms, and increasingly bizarre.

He noticed the statues first. Where before they had been competent but boring examples of reclining figures or tame representations of classical gods, here they were startling shapes with twisted expressions contorting their faces. Several sculptures were incomplete, and near the door, he saw a grand plinth covered with a relief of golden, scrolling ferns. All that was left of the statue it had once supported was one shapely foot carved from ivory and snapped off at the ankle.

A grin spread over Neil's face when he saw this, and he bent down to read the small inscription written around the base of the plinth.

THE REMAINS OF THE FIRST IMAGE FASHIONED BY
PUMIYATHON, WHICH ASHTOROTH DID ENTER
AND WHICH CAUSED MUCH TERROR TO THE
PEOPLE OF PAPHOS.

"Weird," he mumbled. Yet as he cast his gaze around the oak paneled room, Neil discovered many more peculiar artifacts.

Within the nearest cabinet, suspended on woven threads like a ghastly display of ghoulish bobbing apples, was a row of shrunken human heads. The boy studied these macabre items closely and shuddered with delight at the shriveled features. Beneath each of them was a lengthy description of who the person was, how he had died, and the names of those who had ritually murdered him.

Neil's fascination ebbed as he started to read the detailed text, and he began to feel slightly sick. A shrunken head was just a shrunken head, an object so alien to him that he never connected it with a real living person. Yet when he learned the names of those tribesmen—how they had lived and the name of each member of their families—he turned away, ashamed of his previous mawkish interest.

Instinctively, he walked toward the windows, for the

daylight was beginning to dim and he couldn't bear to be lost in the shadows that were welling up in the corners of the room.

Passing another display case, he paused and frowned when he peered within.

The exhibit was a large, irregular globe of ancient and crackling leather. It resembled an old-fashioned soccer ball, only three times the size.

THE EYE OF BALOR THE FOMORIAN, SLAIN BY
LUGH IN THE BATTLE OF MOYTURA THE
NORTHERN. MAY THE SALVE REMAIN LOST AND
LONG MAY THE EYE BE AT SLEEP.

"What a load of old junk," he said to himself.

The next cabinet was much smaller and contained a golden necklace, its unwieldy locket claiming to hold the heel bone of Achilles.

"This is getting loonier," Neil breathed, moving on to a neat array of frog skeletons with silver bells tied about their legs, lovingly laid out upon a cushion of emerald velvet.

Then the boy noticed a tall cabinet set slightly apart from the others, its three glass sides draped with a black cloth. Curious, he ambled over to this new find. He parted the material carefully and peered inside.

On a bed of straw was a small wooden casket, and the sight of it both repelled and enthralled him.

It was black with age and intricately carved with esoteric, Oriental-looking letters twining around the sides. The curved lid was sealed tight with lumps of brown wax, but sprawled across the top was the image of a hideous creature with a large head in which two narrow eyes glittered, inset with tiny red stones. Sharp slivers of bone created needlelike teeth in the widely grinning mouth, and rising from the low forehead was a pair of silver-pointed horns.

Neil grimaced and pulled more of the curtain aside as he searched for the caption that accompanied this new horror.

FINAL RESTING PLACE OF BELIAL—
ARCHDUKE OF DEMONS.

"Is that all?" he said to himself, disappointed. "Isn't there anything else?"

Apparently there was not, and he let the black drapes fall back into place, feeling cheated.

Suddenly from outside the building there was a fervent clanking, and he raced over to the window to discover the cause.

Below him, Neil could see the cheerless courtyard he and Josh had played in, but he was surprised to discover that the boarded gateway had been thrust open and a procession was trailing inside.

"What's going on?" he murmured. "I wonder if Dad knows about this?"

His first thought was that the museum was being robbed, but there were too many people for that to be the case—criminals wouldn't march around in great gangs. Besides, everyone was walking very slowly.

They were certainly an odd-looking gathering. It was almost as if a double-decker bus had pulled up outside and was pouring out its passengers into the courtyard. Nobody appeared to belong with anyone else, and Neil couldn't understand what they were doing down there.

They were from all walks of life: businessmen in pinstripe suits, a window cleaner, two ordinary-looking housewives, and even a traffic cop and an airline attendant. Yet there was one thing they all had in common—they were all bearing flowers.

"Looks like a funeral," he muttered, "or like when someone dies in an awful accident and they put floral tributes on the spot where it happened."

Intrigued, he watched as the last of them trailed inside—all but one solitary figure, who remained in the street beyond, wrapped in a light-brown raincoat, staring at the unusual company through the thick lenses of his glasses. There was something furtive, even sinister, about this grizzly-haired man, but before Neil could spend any time guessing who he was, his attention was distracted elsewhere.

One member of the crowd was pushing to the front, and Neil smiled in amusement at the outlandish costume this character was wearing.

He was a short, gypsy-looking man, dressed in an old-fashioned and very worn frock coat. Patched at the elbow and around the pockets with squares of ill-matching cloth and studded with hundreds of decorative pins, it was far too big for him and the tails almost dragged on the ground. In one hand he carried a battered top hat and in the other a bouquet of white carnations. The unusual man strode up to the drinking fountain, where he reverently laid the flowers across the chipped porcelain bowl.

In a single file, the rest of the silent assembly stepped forward to lay down their tributes, and when the area at the base of the fountain was a mass of color, the gypsy stood before them and raised his hat in the air.

"See, mighty Urdr!" he bellowed. "There are still those who remember! We do not forget! We do not forget!"

As one, the entire group lifted their heads and repeated his words over and over until the yard rang with their chanting.

"Keepers of the well!" the gypsy cried. "That sacred and most hallowed of springs, font of every destiny, where once Nirinel, the final root of Yggdrasill, the mighty world-tree, was nourished, from whose branches were forged the loom of thy omnipotence, that which yoked both men and gods—accept this our tribute and be appeased. Reveal to us, the last descendants of Askar—the ancient ash land—your will and purpose. Is not the time that was set down when the world was young now upon us?"

Gazing reverently up at the windows, he seemed to be searching for a sign, for some acknowledgment of his words. Around him the crowd grew silent as the chanting died on their lips and they all waited.

Peering down at them, the boy thought the motley group appeared rather nervous, and their anxiety mounted until he could almost feel their tension filling the courtyard.

Then it was over. With a shake of his head, the gypsy averted his eyes.

"Again there is no word," spoke one of the women. "Always we are ignored."

The gypsy looked at her sharply. "The time will

come," he told her with absolute certainty. "The day that we and our ancestors have long awaited fast approaches."

"You've been saying that for the past seven years, Aidan," she said, "and not once have we, or those who preceded us, seen anything."

"Then will you not be making the pilgrimage next year?" he asked coldly. "Would you abandon them as have so many others? You know that they are our only hope, the only hope of everyone."

The woman looked ashamed. Staring at the ground, she sniffed and answered, "I will be here. Always have my family served the blessed weavers. I would not desert them now."

"Come then!" the gypsy cried to everyone. "Let us be gone. Our part is done." With a final bow to the museum, he called, "As ever, we are ready and shall await the time when your resting is over. Till that glad day, may the waters guard and keep you."

At this, the crowd murmured their agreement. The gypsy placed the top hat on his head and led the way through the gates. Each of them drifted away until the street beyond was empty—except for the grizzly-haired man in the raincoat, who stared at the museum for several minutes before turning and disappearing from sight.

"Maybe everyone around here is cracked," Neil whispered to himself. "Either that, or they're related to the weirdy sisters."

"Yes, they are delightful!" cried a voice directly behind him. "But no relation, I'm afraid."

With a yelp, the boy jumped and whirled around.

"Oh, my dear, did I startle you?"

CHAPTER 4

A VOICE IN THE DARK

There stood Miss Celandine Webster. Arrayed once again in ruby velvet, with her faded golden braids hanging on either side of her walnut-like face, the old lady was almost overcome with joy.

"Did I creep ever so silently, like a teeny beetle?" she asked Neil, hissing through her goofy teeth. "Did you not hear my feet tapping over the floor?"

"No," Neil answered, disconcerted to observe that the balmy woman was not wearing any shoes and that her pale lilac stockings were full of holes. "I didn't hear a thing. Who were those people?"

"I am so glad!" she confided, ignoring the question. "I'm not supposed to be down here, you see. Ursula doesn't let me; she says I mustn't, but I can't help it."

Lowering her voice and padding a little closer to Neil, she let her bright black eyes roam around the room to see if anyone was listening, then added in a conspiratorial whisper, "I like to dance through the galleries. I simply cannot stop myself. It's so stuffy upstairs, you see, and Ursula bullies us most dreadfully."

Running her fingers over a case containing jars of pickled snakes, she stretched out like a sunbaked cat and dreamily laid her head upon the glass.

"I adore this place," she confessed. "I know every corner, every surface, every dark chink. Much more than Ursula. She thinks that just because she's the eldest she knows best—but that isn't always true, is it? I know lots of things, lots of secret things that she doesn't. Sometimes I come down here at night—I do, really I do, and she isn't any the wiser. Never caught me yet, and I've been doing it for ever so long now."

She giggled wildly, then straightened and began to slowly dust the case with the end of one braid, her glittering eyes fixed intently on Neil.

The boy began to feel uncomfortable. He wanted to get away from this alarming old crone—there was no knowing what was ticking away in her jumbled-up mind.

"They look different in the dark," she said abruptly.

"They?" Neil repeated. "Who does?"

Miss Celandine spread her arms wide and danced around in a tight circle. "Everything does. My friends— I have friends in the night. They speak to me. Ursula would be very cross if she knew—she would, I know she would. She doesn't want me to have any friends, she never has. Poor Veronica and I have never been able to have any callers, not a one."

A self-pitying sob choked her speech, and she stared morosely down at her dirty big toe, which was poking through her stocking.

"There hasn't been a gentleman here for ever so

long," she warbled. "No kind nobleman or gentle knight, no hero to climb the wall or slay the dragon. Not since the tapestry was ended, not since Ursula broke the loom and our labors were over."

Neil looked at her dubiously. Miss Celandine didn't seem very well. She had begun to sway and was constantly turning her head from side to side. "Are . . . are you all right?" he asked. "Shall I fetch someone?"

The old lady put a hand to her wrinkled temple. "That was it," she uttered in a fretful moan. "That was the end. I was supposed to be the mother, wasn't I? Red for the mother, white for the maiden, and black for the crone. That's how it was supposed to be, and yet we all remained maidens, not just Veronica. The child I was supposed to bear, she who could assume the terrible burden and cast off our threads, was never born, so we too are doomed—just like the rest. But if Ursula had never used the loom, then the root would have been destroyed, and the end of light and life would have come all those years ago.

"Now look at us, such is the price we have paid. The tapestry was never completed, you see, and now I'm afraid it's too late. We have withered alongside the root. Ursula's waited too long—she has, she has. What if the child refuses to come to us? What if Ursula is mistaken and she isn't the One?"

Neil began to edge toward the door. She had pulled a face that suggested she was about to cry, and he'd had quite enough of her. "I'll just go and see . . ." he began, but Miss Celandine gave a dismissive cry, then ran past him and squashed her nose flat against the window.

"Did you see it?" she demanded excitedly. "Did you see them?"

The boy halted by the door. "The people with the flowers?" he ventured, trying to fathom where her derailed train of thought had leaped to now.

"Yes!" she cried, whipping around and holding out her hand for him to join her.

Neil remained where he was.

"Wasn't it grand?" Miss Celandine gurgled, chewing the now dusty end of her braid. "I knew they'd be here. Ursula said they wouldn't; she said they'd have forgotten, but I knew they would. I told her so, I did, I did."

"Why did they do it?" Neil asked, doubting if he'd be able to get a sensible answer from her. "Why put all those flowers down there? What does it mean?"

With her nose pressed firmly against the glass the old lady peered down at the mass of flowers in the yard below. "Because they remember," she said simply. "Ursula always says they won't be here, and I always say they will. She thinks I don't know anything, but I know enough to get away from her when I want to. You've seen me, you know I can."

"What does your other sister say about those people?"

"Veronica?" she cooed, tilting her head to one side. "Veronica says nothing; Veronica never even looks out of the window to watch them. She'd rather eat jam and pancakes—she adores jam and pancakes. I say they're too sweet but she won't listen—oh, no, and Ursula lets her eat far too many. If I want anything, I have to stamp and cry before she'll allow it, and even then . . ."

A soft chuckle shook her velvet-covered shoulders as she tenderly stroked the windowsill. "But I watch them," she admitted. "I do, and I know Ursula does when she thinks we're not looking. I've seen her smile, I have, I have. Do you know who those goodly folk are?"

The direct question startled Neil. "No," he replied, hesitating for an instant, "but I should like to."

Miss Celandine left the window and hugged herself smugly. "Then I shan't tell you," she teased, "except to say that they were all . . . well-wishers, yes, that's it, ha ha! But this isn't why you are here, no, it isn't—not that.

"First things first, you know. Another little task lies in wait for you, a most vital one. A long time has Ursula spent hatching and planning, oh, yes, and now she's ready. Oh, but without me you couldn't do it and we would all be lost. Celandine is to be important again, like she was when the rhyme of the ash was first sung and the lords of ice and dark had been dispelled, when the first terrible strand was measured and spun and the four white stags still roamed near the pool. A new path is to be woven, the first web since the days of the encircling mists, and you shall be a part of it—enmeshed within the unyielding threads of—"

"Celandine!"

The old lady gave a horrified shriek and threw up her arms in fright.

Neil turned his head and saw that Miss Ursula had entered through another doorway at the far side of the room and was striding sternly toward them.

"She can't find me!" Miss Celandine wailed, brushing past the boy and fleeing through The Egyptian Suite. "She never finds me—I'm upstairs with Veronica, I am, I am. I never told him about it, did I? I never breathed a word. I wouldn't do anything like that—oh, no."

As the old lady's woeful voice trailed off into the distance beyond the next room, her sister approached Neil with an expression of severe reproof upon her gaunt face.

"What did she say to you?" Miss Ursula demanded. "Why did you not hold her?"

"She didn't say anything!" Neil protested. "Nothing that made any sense anyway, and I'm not catching hold of anybody!"

The reproach faded on Miss Ursula's face, and she managed a feeble smile. "Poor Celandine," she said almost compassionately. "She thinks I don't know that she flits about down here like some kind of ghost. By now she will be back upstairs cowering in her bed, trying to pretend that she has not been out of it all afternoon, and by nightfall that is what she will believe. I suppose it does no harm, but I still worry. She is not strong."

"She ran off pretty quickly," Neil commented.

The woman pursed her lips and smoothed the creases that had formed in the black taffeta of her gown. "So, Child," she began briskly, "I see you have found The Separate Collection. Does it interest you? It is the pride of the museum. In the old days children were not allowed to enter here and few adults could stomach it."

"Why? It's a bit odd but there's nothing too awful in here."

"Ah, it was larger then, and the exhibits were more impressive. They were . . . fresher."

Neil didn't understand what that meant, but then he had come to expect that with the Webster sisters.

"How old is this place?" he suddenly found himself asking. "How long have you been here?"

Miss Ursula allowed her gaze to fall upon the courtyard before answering. "The museum is very ancient," she drawled. "There has always been a building here of one kind or another over the years, but it has not always been a museum, you understand. No, this has known a legion of uses. My family has owned it for quite some time now, and my sisters and I are very proud of it. Although architects despise the place because of its imperfections, they are the reasons for our unshifting devotion. It has been added to, you see. The building has changed with the ages, growing another room here, adding a window there, until it is as you see it now. I doubt if it will change much more, but we shall see—perhaps that will be after my time. Who knows?"

"You speak of it as though it's a living creature," the boy breathed.

"I'm certain I gave no such impression," she retorted. "Now, I must go to my poor sisters. It is growing rather dark, Child. Should you not be making your own way home?"

"I was just about to."

"Then be quick about it."

Neil walked toward The Egyptian Suite but wavered at the entrance. "Miss Webster," he began, "who were those people outside before? Your sister said they were well-wishers. Who were they wishing well?"

"Were there people?" came the crisp reply. "I saw no one. Perhaps the gate could be made more secure. I must speak to the caretaker."

Neil shrugged. It was pointless trying to ask these nutcases anything; one was just as crazy as the other. He stepped into the room containing the Egyptian relics, but Miss Ursula's voice called him back.

"Child," she said, with a look of concern on her face that was quite foreign to her. "You must beware of any who wait without these walls. There are many dangers in this world, and not all of them are born of it. Should you meet anyone beyond those gates, do not speak to him, do not tell him your name or why you are here. Harm comes in many guises, remember that."

"I will," he answered, wondering if she was telling him not to speak to strangers. "I know all about that, thanks."

The concern vanished from the old lady's face, and she assumed her stern aspect once again. "Then you had best begone," she advised. "This is no place to be after night falls. It is not safe—I mean, of course, that you may fall and injure yourself."

Neil gave her a humoring nod and set off through the darkening rooms.

Making his way homeward, he suddenly realized he hadn't eaten any lunch and was ravenous. A growl from his stomach confirmed this and he quickened his pace, retracing his steps to try and find the landing and the stairs once more.

But Neil didn't find the landing. Soon the rooms he found himself in appeared strange and unfamiliar.

"Must be the shadows making them look different," he told himself. "The sun's getting low, that's all, it's the change of light. I must have been in here before—I came through that door there."

For a quarter of an hour his search for the landing continued, and he tried to convince himself he was going the right way. But when he came across a corridor filled with stuffed exotic animals—from leopards to chimpanzees—Neil knew he was lost.

"This is stupid!" he scolded himself for not being able to find the way back to the landing.

It was like being lost in a maze that continually altered and changed as he moved through it, and a growing fear spread within him. There was no way he wanted to be stuck on the second floor all night. He wasn't afraid of the dark like Josh, but his courage had its limits and he had no desire to test them.

Anxiously, he quickened his pace and hurried into the next room. Without warning he found himself in the corridor filled with the dusty results of the taxidermist's art again, and a hundred blank faces watched him snarl in frustration and kick the doorjamb.

Neil was becoming afraid; this wasn't natural. A wild, crazy suspicion was forming, and he didn't like it. "The building," he whispered. "It's deliberately misleading me, trying to trick me. It knows where I am, it can feel my movements."

Realizing how foolish this sounded, he tried to laugh but only managed a thin squeak. "Get a grip," he told himself firmly. "There's got to be a perfectly reasonable explanation. I turned off wrong somewhere. Just go back and . . ."

Running frantically, he sprang into a completely new room that contained nothing but an old armchair. Giving a dismal howl, the boy spun on his heel. Panic had seized Neil entirely, and flying blindly through door after door, he blundered into the mounting shadows with terror filling his heart.

Some evil intelligence was behind all this, some

malignant mind controlling the interior of the museum, leading him deeper and deeper into its heart, watching his movements as it had watched him playing in the yard. Was it guiding him to itself? If so, what for? What would he see? At the end of his stumbling search, what crouching horror would confront him? He would be too tired to fight the creature off, that was why it was doing this. When the end came he would be utterly exhausted, too spent to defend himself.

His eyes stinging with anguished tears, Neil burst through the gathering darkness and yelled at the top of his terrified voice.

"Stop it! Let me out! Let me go!"

From the gloom, something rose up and caught hold of his foot. Neil screamed as he fell and crashed to the floor with a heavy thud.

"Get off! Get off!" he bawled, tugging his foot free.

The sweat was streaming down his face as he stared fearfully into the dim shadows before him. He gave a choking cry as he saw that it was only the corner of a rug that he had tripped over.

"I'm getting as nutty as those three upstairs," he muttered. Then he realized where he was and his spirits plummeted lower than ever.

He was in The Separate Collection, and above him was the cabinet containing the Eye of Balor. Neil shuffled backward. Either it was his imagination or a trick of the failing light, but in a deep crevice that scored the leathery surface of the eye, he thought he saw a glimmer of red.

"Let me out of here!" he called again. "Stop—please!"

The silence in that eerie room almost deafened him, but he was too petrified to get back on his feet. Sinister shapes crowded behind the cabinets, a terrible silent throng that waited for its moment.

Then, from an unseen point beyond the cases, there came a voice.

"Hey, kid," it yelled. "Cool it, will ya? It's jus' this heap o' bricks toyin' with ya 'n' havin' its fun."

Neil slid across the floor as he scrambled to his feet. He hadn't a clue who had spoken, but it was muffled—as if it had come from inside one of the display cases.

"Hey! Leave the kid alone!" the voice yelled again. Emitting a high-pitched screech, the boy hurtled from the room, and then, three minutes later, found himself standing on the landing.

With his knees trembling and the breath wheezing in his chest, Neil hurried down the stairs as the awful question flashed horribly bright in his mind: Who had spoken?

CHAPTER 5

TED

When Neil finally returned to the apartment, he made no mention of the disturbing experience on the second floor. When his father asked what he had been doing, he merely shrugged and mumbled that he had only been wandering around. Now that he was safe and surrounded by everyday, normal objects, with the television droning away in the background, his fears seemed foolish and absurd.

Later, when Josh was fast asleep, his young face turned to the glow of the nightlight that shone feebly by the bedside and his arms wrapped tightly around Groofles, his toy polar bear, Neil lay on his back staring up at the dark ceiling. Had he imagined it? Had his own terror blinded him to the correct route to the landing? Yet what of the voice that had spoken? That was no figment of his frightened mind. He had heard it, there was no doubt about that—none whatsoever.

Resolving to return to The Separate Collection the

next morning, he murmured to himself, "There has to be a simple explanation."

Before long he fell into a wretched sleep troubled by disembodied voices, and when morning came he felt as though he hadn't had any rest at all.

After preparing his father's breakfast and leaving Josh stubbornly attempting to dip a toast soldier into a hard-boiled egg, Neil quietly slipped out of the apartment.

Into the museum he went, glad of the brilliant wintry sunshine that streamed through the windows. There would be no murky pools of shadow for his imagination to work upon today, and with this comforting thought at the forefront of his mind he quickly made his way toward the hallway, then hurried up the stairs.

Through particles of swirling, floating dust that gleamed and scintillated in the morning rays Neil went, incredulous that he could ever have lost his way the previous night. Everything appeared so completely ordinary, and his fears seemed more ludicrous and unfounded than ever.

Only when he approached The Egyptian Suite did a momentary pang of disquiet return as he fumbled for the light switch. Yet the electric light was not necessary, for the daylight around him was so bright that it spilled in through the open doorway in a welcoming and almost friendly manner.

He was beginning to wonder why he had bothered to investigate last night's events at all; the entire incident seemed so silly to him now.

"I suppose I might as well while I'm here," he decided, stepping briskly into The Separate Collection.

The room appeared smaller in the stark, unforgiving

glare of morning. The oak-paneled walls were riddled with woodworm, the varnish on the paintings was cracked and flaking, and the glass panes in several of the display cases were fractured and held together by masking tape. One of the cabinets was missing a leg, and the damaged corner was supported by three fat books. Like the Webster sisters themselves, the place had the air of faded elegance—a thing once fair and lovely carried too far beyond the span of its natural life.

Neil gave a faint embarrassed cough as he recalled the terror that had been so convincing and real to him.

"Still, I'm not surprised," he consoled himself, "not with all these grislies. You could believe anything here." But this did not explain the voice that he was certain he had heard. No matter how frightened he may have been, he had not dreamed that up.

Neil walked among the cabinets, casting his gaze this way and that, searching for an answer to this perplexing and disturbing riddle. A theory had occurred to him early that morning that the answer might lie in some mechanical device hidden in the room. Perhaps there was an old intercom system here, or maybe someone had left a radio behind, and this was the sort of evidence that he hunted for.

Peering beneath the tables and cases, he looked for a telltale wire and listened for the faint crackle of a radio signal, but there was nothing.

All that was in the room with him was the collection, and however much Neil tried to be rational and dismiss the horrendous possibility of a supernatural answer, the prospect would not be subdued and kept returning to the surface of his thoughts.

It was impossible not to think of it, for he was surrounded on all sides by macabre and gruesome artifacts, and that morning he discovered many that he had not noticed before.

Beneath two glass domes, set upon either end of a stout table whose legs were carved into the scale-covered claws of a huge lizard, were the preserved and ancient remains of two ravens. Neil stared at them and looked for an accompanying label but there was none, and he wondered why these mangy specimens had been kept at all.

Whoever had stuffed them hadn't done a very good job. Their plumage was patchy and the bottoms of the domes were covered in fallen feathers. No glass eyes gazed out from their balding skulls; instead there was a sunken knot of papery skin stretched and torn over the fragile bone.

One of the birds had fallen from its artificial perch, and a shriveled eye socket was pressed against the curving glass as if it was squinting lecherously at the outside world. The beak of this ogling imp was hanging wide open, for the flesh that had once kept it in place had crumbled. So not only did it appear to leer, but this chance imitation of a hearty grin suggested that the creature was enjoying itself immensely.

Neil scowled at the raven, which looked as though it was laughing directly at him. He gave the dome a flick with his finger that made the glass chime like a fine crystal bell.

"Well, beakfeatures," he said, "it can't have been you I heard last night. Or maybe you had a parrot friend around?"

With a dismissive grunt, the boy moved through the

room, then paused when he remembered the row of shrunken heads. "No way!" he scoffed. "Those things are dead. Whatever I heard, it certainly wasn't any of them."

Despite this, Neil wandered over to the chilling display and took another look at the ghoulish tribal heads hanging there.

"All right," he began with mock sternness, "own up. Which of you was it? Who likes frightening people half to death? I won't be mad if you just tell me. Is it because you've got nobody to talk to?"

He managed a weak chuckle at the pathetic joke, then really laughed at how stupid all this was.

"I'm glad I never mentioned this to anyone," he sighed. "Dad would have put me upstairs with the rest of the crazies. Neil Chapman, you're losing it."

Still laughing, he gave the shrunken heads a farewell wave. "Probably couldn't speak English anyway," he chortled before his stomach began to growl and his thoughts turned toward the breakfast he hadn't eaten. "Sorry, guys, got to go—don't want to waste away like you, do I?"

"Hey! Pipe down, will ya!"

Neil froze, and his previous terror came crashing in on him in spite of the glorious sunshine that filled the room.

"Who . . . who said that?" he spluttered.

"Aw, it's getting so ya can't get any peace, not nowhere, these days."

The voice was muffled, irreverent, and, to his surprise, spoke with a broad American accent. It sounded ordinary enough, but Neil could not keep his hands from shaking. Whoever was speaking was definitely in the same room—but where?

He could see only the display cases. There was no one else present, at least no one visible.

"Where are you?" he called, nervously eyeing the doorway and longing to sprint over to it.

"Quit bawlin', will ya? If there's one thing I can't stand it's noisy kids. Didn't you make enough racket last night?"

With hesitant steps, Neil began to move in the direction of this belligerent voice. It appeared to be coming from within one of the cabinets, and the boy steeled himself for whatever he might find.

"Bad enough hearin' them screwy dames," it continued, "now I gotta put up with you. I didn't think the neighborhood could get any worse. I shoulda known better."

Past an array of pickling jars that contained repulsive examples of serpents and small mammals all drowned in alcohol, Neil drew ever closer. Before him, rising tall and forbidding, was the draped cabinet that held the casket of Belial.

"So, kid—what ya doin' in this shack? It's a heckuva day. Get out there an' throw a few pitches."

Neil stood in front of the black curtains, then abruptly he turned aside. The voice wasn't coming from in there, so where? . . .

Nearby, beside the arrangement of frog skeletons, was a plain case that he had previously overlooked. Inside, according to the label, was a grouping of articles found in the trunk of an Air Raid Patrol Warden from World War II.

There was a stirrup pump, a corroded flashlight, a bundle of yellowing leaflets, a ration book, a small shovel propped up in a metal bucket, a gas mask, and, sitting incongruously in the corner, a grubby-looking teddy bear.

Neil stared through the glass thinking that he had been correct all along. Somewhere in all that junk there had to be a concealed speaker. One of the Webster sisters had been playing a game with him, disguising her voice to sound like a man and no doubt tittering her dotty head off.

Huffing in disgust, he ran his eyes over the walls. She was probably hidden behind a secret panel, watching him through a tiny hole or through the eyes of a painting.

"Very funny," he said aloud, stooping to look for the incriminating cable running from the back of the cabinet.

When he failed to find it, he cupped his hands around his face and leaned against the glass, peering inside.

"It must be in there," he muttered, glaring at the suspiciously bulky pile of papers. "You'd think senior citizens would have something better to do with their time."

Groaning wearily, Neil shook his head. "Okay," he called to the unseen old woman he was sure was hiding in the wainscoting, "you win. I was fooled."

At that moment, he caught sight of a movement out of the corner of his eye and stared into the case once more.

Something had moved. Over there in the corner, near where that ragged bear was sitting.

Neil hunted for a logical explanation. Perhaps it was a mouse. Shuddering, he hoped it wasn't a rat—this old place could be overrun with them. He shivered at the thought, then a slow smile spread over his face as he regarded the lonely looking toy.

"They'll be making a nest in your stuffing next, pal," he chortled.

The teddy bear was old. Its grimy fleece and the faded red ribbon tied around its neck told Neil that much, yet there was also an endearing, homemade quality about it. The face was a little understuffed, and coupled with the patch of leather that served as its nose, a wry smile was stitched into the fur. Two large ears were sewn onto the sides of its head, and the left one drooped amusingly just above one of the round glass eyes.

Neil smirked. The eyes were fixed directly on him as if the bear was staring back with as much curiosity as his own.

Suddenly, all expression drained from the boy's face as the fur at the edge of the bear's mouth puckered and twitched. Then, as Neil watched, incredulous and disbelieving, the toy broke into a broad grin.

Neil fell backward and cringed away from the cabinet, terrified that now his mind was deceiving him, conjuring up insane and impossible illusions.

Behind the glass the leather nose wrinkled and folds of dusty fur blinked over the round eyes. With a shake of the head, both ears gave a sharp wriggle, and the bear craned his neck to see what the boy was doing. Then the toy's mouth opened.

"What the heck you scared of?" he cried. "Yer ten times bigger'n me!"

Dumbfounded, Neil could only answer with a choking splutter that gargled deep in his throat. Then the teddy bear raised one of its arms and signaled for him to rise from the floor where he had fallen.

"Ya look like a real jerk down there, kid!" he scoffed.

"We ain't got time for you to stay gawkin' down there."

The glass eyes almost disappeared beneath a furrow of fur as the bear scowled with irritation. Throwing his head back, he glared upward and shook his paws furiously.

"This ain't gonna work!" he raged. "Geez—the kid's a geek! What the heck am I supposed to do with him? Fifty years I've been kept hanging around—an' fer what? He ain't got no guts; he's yeller'n the rose o' Texas! I want outta this right now! Pronto!"

Neil didn't know who the bear was shouting at. He seemed to be ranting at the ceiling, then abruptly he halted and flinched as though a voice the boy could not hear had thundered back at him.

"You gotta be jokin'!" the bear snapped up at the empty air. "You tellin' me I ain't got no choice in this? After all this time? It ain't right I tell ya. I don't want the kid—let him stay here! If that dope's the only chance I got, I might as well give it up now. Yeah, I know he's the one. I'm not sayin' he ain't, but look at him for cryin' out loud! He's useless, and I ain't takin' him!"

The bear winced once more and raised his paws defensively to the ceiling as if warding off a terrible onslaught of abuse, but the anger that burned in his eyes was wild and horrible to look at.

Then the furry arms were lowered and the wrath on the toy's face was gradually replaced by weary resignation.

"All right, all right!" he apologized. "I hear ya; if it's gotta be, it's gotta be, but jus' remember what I said. I ain't gonna take the rap if he don't come outta this in one piece—okay?"

Throughout this one-sided argument, Neil had stared at the living toy transfixed by a mixture of horror and fascination. His initial shock had faded, and a fierce indignation at the insulting names the creature had called him now burned within him.

A great sigh puffed from the bear's mouth when he turned his attention to Neil again. A sheepish grin spread over the fleecy face and the bear shrugged meekly.

"I tried, kid," he said. "You heard me. I tried, but they won't listen."

Finally Neil found his voice.

"What . . . what are you?" he asked.

"Hang it all!" the bear cussed scornfully. "Are you blind or what? What in Sam hill d'ya think I am?"

"You look like a teddy bear."

"Give him a hand!" the creature cried, clapping his paws together in sarcastic applause. "Had me worried fer a minute, kid. Any more brilliant questions?"

Neil didn't care for the toy's mocking tone, but it was all so extraordinary and preposterous that he couldn't help asking stupid and obvious questions.

"Teddy bears don't speak," he said plainly, "or move their arms."

A loud groan came from the cabinet as the creature fell backward.

"Lordy!" he wailed. "The kid's a genius. Wire the president, it's front-page news!"

Neil's face became stern, and he finally picked himself up from the floor.

"Well, they don't!" he shouted.

Slowly, the creature lifted his head, then rolled over. Placing a paw on the pile of old newspapers, he lumbered to his feet and took three shambling steps toward the front of the case.

"You better wise up, kid," he warned in a threatening voice, "and do it quick, 'cuz there ain't room for no morons in this outfit. You got that?"

Before Neil could answer, the creature continued. "Okay, you wanna know what I am, right? What I'm doin' here? How? Why? When? All the usual junk? Well, listen up 'cuz this'll be the only time I'll tell you."

"I'm listening," the boy answered.

Placing his paws behind his back, the bear began to pace up and down inside the case.

"Sure," he droned, "I'm a teddy bear. Yeah, I can move, I got intelligence—more than most folks around here by the looks of things. I can talk, I swear like a trooper, and I love the smell of coffee. I've been stuck in this daffy place way too long an' I want out—now. What else you wanna know?"

"But how can you do all that?" Neil asked. "I don't understand . . ."

"Dang it, kid!" the bear snarled. "What is there to understand? You ain't supposed to know why, just accept it. I think, therefore I'm a bear—is that too difficult? When was the last time you asked yourself why *you* could get off your butt and walk around? It just is, that's all."

"That's different."

"No, it ain't. Look, you gonna spend the rest of the day arguin' or what? Does it matter if I'm a teddy bear? You got a problem with that? You prejudiced against speaking to me? Think yer better'n me?"

"Of course not, I . . . I don't even believe I'm having this conversation. Have—have you always been like this? Are there other—"

The bear let out an exasperated wail and pulled on his furry ears. "This ain't no kindergarten story!" he snorted. "What, you think on the stroke of midnight, when the grownups have gone to bed, the nursery comes to life? The only one here visited by the fairies is you, kid. You been watching too much Hollywood crapola. Plug in your brain. I'm gonna say this once and for all. There ain't no Santa Claus, the Easter Bunny's a load of hooey, cartoons ain't real life, I don't care who says so but Eddie Cantor just ain't funny, and you're lookin' at the one and only bear with a hankerin' for Betty Grable this side o' Mars. Before you think it, I ain't no alien either! Geez, but you're dumb."

He folded his arms and waited for the boy to respond, but the only remark Neil could manage to utter as he fought to accept the strange sight before him was, "You've got a foul mouth, whatever you are."

"Hey, I ain't no Joan of Arc either."

Neil chewed his bottom lip. "Have you got a name?" he asked.

The bear seemed taken aback by this, and the stitched mouth opened as if he was about to tell, then he checked himself and with a self-conscious cough said, "You, er . . . you just call me Ted, okay?"

"Ted?" Neil repeated. "That's not very original."

"Best I can do, kid. Now, you finished asking questions?"

"Not really," the boy replied, "you still haven't explained anything—"

Shrieking at the top of his voice, the bear flew at the glass in a rage of frustration, but he immediately reeled backward when one of his stumpy paws gave the pane an impotent kick. A soft thud vibrated the cabinet as the toy fell among the papers, where he remained motionless.

"Are you all right?" Neil eventually asked when there was still no sign of movement. "Are you hurt? Hello?"

The bear remained absolutely still, and the boy's concern mounted. Taking a step closer, he stared into the case, but Ted looked like any ordinary stuffed toy. Neil began to think he really was going bonkers.

"Hello," he said again. "Can you hear me? What's wrong?"

The limp body gave a jerk as a mournful laugh burst from the bear's mouth.

"'What's wrong,' he asks!" Ted cried, sitting upright and gazing sorrowfully out at the boy.

"Can't you see?" he muttered with a forlorn sniff as he waved a paw around the display. "How'd you like to be cooped up in here year after year? I'm goin' stir-crazy, kid. If I have to spend one more week locked up, I'll go bananas."

The anguish in the bear's voice was unmistakable and genuine. Neil had heard it once before, when his mother left home, and this unpleasant memory flustered him.

"You listening to me, kid?"

Neil blinked, then nodded. "Well . . . well, why don't you get out of there?" he murmured.

The bear pulled himself to his feet. "'Tain't that easy," he admitted, looking the boy squarely in the face. "I can't do it on my own, I need help. So, I'm asking you, let me outta here—please."

"You want me to do it?"

"I'd prefer Veronica Lake, but she ain't available. C'mon, lemme out."

Neil ran his hands over the cabinet, searching for a catch to release the front panel. "How does this thing open?" he asked. "I can't find—"

"What the devil you doin'?" Ted shrieked impatiently. "There ain't time fer that! Those dippy dames keep all the keys, and there's no way they'll give them to you. Just break the glass!"

Neil stared in at the bear for a moment then backed away. "Oh, I couldn't do that," he said. "My dad's the caretaker here, I can't go smashing things."

"Oh brother!" Ted cried. "I must have the only responsible kid in the world here. Who made you so old? Look, if you knew what I was goin' through, you wouldn't be standing there gawkin'—this glass'd be spilled all over the floor and yours truly'd be gone."

"Where would you go?"

Ted hit a woolly fist against the pane and hung his head. "Mebbe you should ask me 'when,'" he muttered darkly. "Aw, kid, trust me, I just gotta break out."

Neil considered all he had been told, but finally he shook his head. "I'm sorry," he said. "I can't. My dad needs this job."

"A job!" Ted yelled, growing more and more impassioned. "There's more at stake here than a measly janitor's job, kid! Your father can get work someplace else."

"You don't know my dad," Neil put in.

But Ted would not be placated. "I gotta get back!" he screamed, hammering on the shuddering glass. "I gotta! You're my only hope! The one chance I've been waiting fer since who knows when. Please, I'm beggin' you, just do it."

The bear buried his face in his paws and looked like such a pathetic figure that Neil gently put his hand on the glass that separated them and promised to think about it.

"Don't cry," he said, surprised that he should feel so sorry for Ted and his predicament. "I'll think of a way to get you out without smashing anything."

Ted turned a sullen face to him. "I'm a teddy bear, kid," he muttered defensively, "as in, made from fur and stuffed with kapok. I don't eat, never go to the john, and I certainly don't cry. Got it?"

The sound of footsteps suddenly interrupted them, and a man's voice called the boy's name.

"Neil?" The recognizably uncertain tones of Mr. Chapman echoed through The Egyptian Suite. "You there, son?"

"That's my dad," Neil said. "Let's ask him if he can wangle a key out of Miss Webster."

He turned toward the doorway, but a hiss from Ted brought him sharply back.

"You crazy?" the bear cried. "Don't you go sayin' nothin'. You say one word about me and you get yourself a rubber room with a half dozen shrinks starin' in at yer."

"But you can show them," Neil insisted. "Once people see you—"

"I ain't no freak show, kid," Ted hissed out of the corner of his mouth, smartly sitting down as Mr. Chapman entered. "I only do my act fer you. Now keep quiet, here's your old man."

"Neil," Mr. Chapman called, dragging a reluctant Josh behind him, "what happened? What did you go off for? I've been looking for you for ages. I've got work to do, you know. If you want to wander around, take your brother with you."

"Er . . . sorry, Dad," the boy began, glancing quickly down at the motionless stuffed toy in the cabinet. "I just wanted to—well, it won't happen again."

"I'll leave Josh here with you then," Mr. Chapman said. "I've got to see Miss Webster at ten, then make a start up here."

"Look, Dad!" Josh squealed with mawkish glee. "Baby heads on strings!"

Neil desperately wanted a final word with Ted, and it was obvious the bear would say nothing with anyone else present. "Dad," he piped up, "could you take Josh back to the apartment? There's something I want to do here first. I'll be along in a second, I promise."

"What are you up to?" Mr. Chapman asked. "You haven't broken anything, have you? These things might look shabby, Neil, but they could be worth thousands— oh, no, don't tell me you've broken something!"

"I haven't!" the boy assured him. "Honest. I was . . . I was just reading about . . . about these frog skeletons. They're really interesting. I won't be able to concentrate if Josh is here."

His father's nose-pinching ceased and he breathed a grateful sigh of relief. "All right," he agreed. "There's certainly a lot of rubbish in here, isn't there? Still, be careful, and I'll see you downstairs in five minutes."

Mr. Chapman left, dragging the unwilling four-year-old with him.

"I want to see the skellingtons, too!" Josh complained.

When he was alone again, Neil turned back to Ted.

"Nice family," the bear chuckled. "Yer pa sure knows how to dress. Great hair, too."

"You leave my dad alone!" Neil warned.

"Hey, I'm sorry, okay?" Ted cried. "I've been out of touch for fifty years, what do I know about fashion? Yer old man's a great guy—a little funny lookin' but swell all the same."

Neil stared at the animated creature angrily. "Shut up!" he demanded.

"Cute kid, though," Ted continued. "Was that half-pint your brother? Let's hope he don't end up like your pa—or you, even. Poor little runt. Don't stand much of a chance, do he?"

"Why am I listening to you?" Neil cried, stepping back from the cabinet. "I don't need this right now. You just leave me and my family alone. You were right. Santa doesn't exist, and I'm too old to play with teddy bears, so you can forget it. I don't know what I'm doing here. You want to get out? You do it without my help. I've had enough of you."

Ted leaped to his feet in alarm. "What you doin'?" he called as Neil hurried to the door. "Don't run out on me, kid! Hey, I thought we had a deal, you were gonna let me out! Don't go! Don't go! I got a big mouth. I'm sorry. Stop, will ya?"

Sternly, Neil glanced over his shoulder at the glass case. "If you're as smart as you think you are, then you don't need me!"

"Kid!" Ted yelled. "You come back here! Hey! Let me out! Let me out! You gotta do this—it's all worked out!"

With the bear's shouts ringing in his ears as he

stormed from The Separate Collection, Neil swore to himself that he would never enter that room again.

"Aw, kid!" Ted whimpered, sliding miserably among the newspapers. "Ya shouldn'ta done that."

Dejected and heaving melancholy sighs, the bear tugged at the ribbon around his neck and blew a forlorn raspberry. What could he do now?

Then, very slowly, a dangerous glint flickered in the glass eyes and a soft, roguish snigger gently shook his shoulders. "Didn't leave me no choice, did he?" Ted chuckled to himself.

CHAPTER 6

UPON THE MOONLIT STAIR

Neil spent the rest of that day in the apartment with Josh but was too preoccupied with his own thoughts to take much notice of what his brother was doing. Only later did he discover that the little boy had mischievously scrawled on every football poster he could reach. Fortunately for him, Neil was too busy thinking about Ted to be annoyed, and this unexpected, yet welcome, lack of concern spurred Josh on to greater crimes.

Brimming with malicious delight, he took several of his father's books from the shelf and scribbled indelible expanses of black crayon inside them. When Mr. Chapman finished work, he was surprised at first that Neil hadn't started making dinner—then he noticed what Josh had done.

"Neil!" he yelled, snatching his favorite book on steam trains from Josh and staring at the defaced treasure in horror. "What on earth do you think you were doing? Couldn't you see what he was up to? Blood and sand, boy—it's ruined! Why didn't you stop him? Do you know how much this was? I can't afford to get another one."

Brian Chapman stomped around the poky living room, waving his gangly arms in the air and pointing accusingly at his eldest son. Meanwhile, Josh slunk into the bedroom and waited for the storm to pass.

Up till then, Neil had borne the censure in silence. Now he glared at his father and shouted back at him so fiercely that the man was astonished.

"Stop it!" the boy roared. "Why are you blaming me? Josh was the one who did it. You never yell at him though, do you? No, if anything goes wrong it's my fault! You're always relying on me! Why can't *you* do something for a change? Other fathers do! No wonder Mom ran out. She said she couldn't stand you anymore. I wish she'd taken me with her. I'm sick to death of it, too. I don't want to be relied on. Why can't people find someone else? I've had enough!"

Angrily, Neil stormed from the apartment, only to find himself inside the museum. With an irritated grunt, he realized that this was the very last place he wanted to be.

* * *

Two days passed in which Mr. Chapman continued to sulk and brood, while Neil tried to forget all about the strange creature in The Separate Collection. He had almost managed to convince himself that it was a peculiar hallucination when a chance remark from Josh compelled him to think otherwise.

For most of the morning, he had entertained his younger brother. First they played in the yard, and Josh immediately ran to the drinking fountain to inspect the masses of fading flowers placed beneath it.

"Look!" he cried. "A garden, a garden!"

Into the mound of bouquets he waded, grabbing handfuls of petals and thrusting his nose into the heart of the brightest blooms. Neil couldn't help laughing; most of the flowers were wilting, and they drooped sadly when the child brandished them in his mittens, but this didn't deter him. Shrieking joyously, he danced and jumped, twirling them over his head like sparklers and flinging them as high as he could manage.

"You're making a mess!" Neil chuckled. "Get out of there."

Josh traipsed out of the colorful chaos he had created. Broken stems dangled limply from the collar of his coat, fallen leaves were tangled in his fair hair, and when he shambled from the wreckage, the soles of his shoes dragged a number of bedraggled bouquets after him.

Pulling the floppy stalks from his clothing, he peered at the large image of a tree made solely from petals and turned an excited face to his brother.

"Neil," he whispered, "is that a magic picture?"

Neil tapped him on the head with a bunch of browning daffodils. "Don't be silly, there's no such thing."

"Yes there is," Josh told him with a superior air. "This place is full of magic."

"If you say so."

"It is!"

Neil wiped his forehead where a splash of water had landed. "It's starting to rain," he grumbled. "Come on, you, back inside."

Josh glowered at him mutinously. "There is, too,

magic," he breathed. "I seen it."

Back in the apartment, Neil read a book while his brother emptied a bag of toys on the floor and quietly began to play with them.

After half an hour, Neil laid the book down and looked around to see what Josh was up to.

The four-year-old was sitting behind the sofa with the fluffy polar bear he usually took to bed propped up on its hind legs before him. Unaware that he was being observed, Josh whispered and beckoned to the stuffed animal, staring at it the entire time with unusual concentration on his expectant face.

Neil had never seen him play like that before.

"What are you doing?" he asked finally.

Josh raised his eyes, pouting with impatience and confusion. "I wanted to show you," he burbled. "Why won't it work?"

"What won't?"

"Groofles," came the perplexed reply. "He won't wake up."

Neil groaned and tried to remember if he had been as childish as this when he was Josh's age. Picking the book up once more, he gladly abandoned Josh to whatever nonsense he was playing.

From behind the sofa the child's plaintive voice resumed speaking to the polar bear.

"Say 'hello,' Groofles," he instructed, "you can do it. Go on, like the other one does. Say 'hello.'"

Neil threw his book to the floor as he raced around to grip Josh by the shoulders.

"What did you say?" he demanded. "What 'other one'? What do you mean, Josh?"

The child gazed at him in bewilderment. "Let me go!" he squealed. "That hurts. I'll tell Dad."

But a dreadful suspicion had stolen over Neil, and he grasped his brother's arms even tighter and shook him. "Tell me," he shouted, "has someone been telling you that toys can talk? Who was it? It's important, Josh, you've got to tell me. Was it when you were with Dad yesterday?"

Josh nodded.

"What happened, did someone speak to you?"

"Might've."

"Did they?"

"You'll make fun of me."

"I won't, I promise."

"Will!"

"Honest. Tell me, who was it? What was it?"

The child stared straight into Neil's eyes and in a tiny, yet defiant voice he said, "It was a teddy bear!"

Neil released him and looked away.

"It's true!" Josh insisted. "It was an old teddy with a ribbon. He said he was magic and wanted to play with me. Said I could wish for anything, but Dad came and he said I wasn't to tell!"

By now Neil's head was in his hands and he was thinking wildly. When he next turned his face to Josh, it was scared and his voice was trembling and anxious.

"Listen," he said frantically, "you're not to go into that room where you saw that thing again. Do you understand me?"

"Why?"

"Because it's dangerous, Josh. You've got to swear not to go there!"

"'S only a toy."

"Don't argue, just do what I say."

"But . . ."

"Promise me!"

"I promise," Josh said solemnly, but as he spoke he hid his hand so that Neil couldn't see his crossed fingers.

When Mr. Chapman returned, Neil hurried up to The Separate Collection and stormed over to the cabinet that contained Ted.

The bear was sitting in his usual corner with a blank expression on his fleecy face.

Neil gave the case a sound thump with his fist that rattled the contents and made Ted jiggle from side to side.

"How dare you speak to my little brother!" Neil fumed. "You leave him alone! Do you hear me? I don't know what you're up to, but there's no way I'd ever help you now."

The bear made no response. He remained motionless and stared fixedly ahead like any other stuffed toy. Neil found this even more infuriating, and he slapped the cabinet's sides.

"Fine!" he bawled. "If you want to play dumb, go ahead! But believe me, if I find out you've spoken to Josh again, I'll have you out of there so fast you won't know what's happening, and I'll shove you straight into the nearest fire. You got that?" he shouted at the top of his voice. "Answer me! Answer me!"

"What is the meaning of this?" rapped a grim voice suddenly.

Neil whirled around, and there was Miss Ursula Webster advancing toward him.

The old woman's face was flushed an indignant and angry purple. "I will not have this!" she cried, bearing down on him, the nostrils of her long nose flaring like a snorting horse and her lips curling back over her brown teeth. "You are a vandal, Child—nothing more. I cannot begin to comprehend what you were trying to do. I am thankful that my mind does not plumb such iniquitous depths."

"I wasn't going to break anything!" Neil told her.

"Liar!" she rasped back. Without warning, her bony hand flashed out and caught him by the hair, which she tugged and twisted in her grasp. "I saw enough to satisfy me that you were about to smash your way into this case and destroy one of the exhibits. Is that any way to repay me for giving your bumbling fool of a parent an honest position?"

Neil struggled to be free of the old woman's clawlike grip. But her fingers were as strong as iron, and no matter how much he squirmed she would not let go. It felt as though she was trying to tear the scalp from his skull.

"Little boys always bring trouble and heartache!" she snapped vehemently. "They are dirty, lying, filthy beasts—no better than disease-carrying flies. That's what you are, Child, a germ-ridden fly who requires swatting. No, you are far beneath that—you are the maggot the insect carries in its belly. A lowly, creeping, crawling worm, that's all you are; a filament of putrid flesh writhing and burrowing within its own slimy phlegm."

"Get off!" Neil called, having to stand on tiptoe to ease the torture of his hair. "I wasn't going to break the glass, I swear!"

"But you did break it!" Miss Ursula snarled. "You trespassed and entered where you were forbidden to tread!"

Neil looked back at the cabinet. The woman was un-hinged; the glass wasn't broken. To make matters worse, he saw that a smug grin had appeared on Ted's face.

"Deny it if you dare," Miss Ursula badgered, "but if I find you smashing any more windows or if you so much as touch another pipe, let alone rip it from the wall, I will have to take the most severe of measures. Is that understood, my little maggot?"

"You're mad!" Neil shouted. "I don't know what you're talking about."

Scorn and disdain twisted the woman's face as she shoved him roughly away from her. "Get you home," she spat, wiping her hand on her coal-black gown, "and be assured that I will speak to your father about this."

Neil rubbed the top of his sore head. Unable to bring himself to say anything more to the insane baggage, he stole one final, warning glance at Ted and ran from the room.

* * *

When Mr. Chapman finished work that afternoon, Miss Ursula sought him out and told him that she had caught his son in an act of wanton vandalism. The caretaker could hardly believe it, but she was so emphatic that his faith in Neil began to waver. As soon as he returned home he accused his son of doing all that she had said and would not listen to any of his protestations.

Neil was sent to bed early, even before Josh, and he lay there cursing Miss Webster and the whole wretched museum. His entire life had been turned upside down during the past week, and he was startled when he realized how extremely sorry for himself he was feeling.

Presently, Josh crawled in beside him, gloating that his older brother had been punished. Neil gave an irritated grunt as he tried to ignore the little boy and sulkily turned on his side.

Maliciously, the four-year-old giggled into Groofles's ear and pointedly repeated their father's scornful tirade with the utmost satisfaction.

"Shut it, squirt!" Neil rumbled, aiming a swift kick under the bedclothes.

Josh gave the polar bear a gleeful squeeze, then threw himself against the pillows.

Outside, the moon was swollen with ghostly radiance and ringed with a bright and frosty halo. Yet the heavens were crowded with thick clouds that hugged and pressed around the wintry disk, scurrying before her face and causing deep voids of traveling shadow upon the world below.

Lost in the ever-changing gloom, the Wyrd Museum sat silent and watchful. The turrets and spikes that speared from its roof knifed and jabbed at the blackness, then gleamed icily in the silver moonlight as the empty night slowly deepened.

The room was dark when Neil awoke. Several disoriented moments passed as his vision swam in the gloom, and he rubbed his eyes wearily. His sleep had been fitful and haunted with nightmare images of Miss Ursula Webster, who dragged him around the whole of the museum on a short leash and beat him with a stick before each exhibit.

His scalp was throbbing. That nutty old woman was dangerous. It wasn't safe for her to be loose. Well, she wouldn't get a second chance to attack him. He was absolutely determined to keep out of her way from now on.

Warbling a great yawn, he tried to recapture the fleeting fragments of sleep. Snuggling deeper into the warm bedclothes, he waited for the inevitable drowsiness to conquer him, but it was no use, and the harder he tried, the further away the elusive slumber slipped.

After ten minutes had dragged by, Neil was wide awake, and an uncomfortable, sickening chill began to prickle along his spine.

The room was uncannily silent, and with a jolt, he understood why.

"Josh?" he murmured. "Josh?"

The soft sound of his brother's gentle breathing was completely absent, and worried, Neil reached out for him.

The far side of the bed was empty.

* * *

Neil sat up in the bed and reached down for his slippers. His brother never got up in the middle of the night, not even to go to the bathroom, and a dreadful suspicion was forming in Neil's mind.

Pulling on his robe, he reached for the flashlight he kept by the bed and crept into the living room.

Erratic, piggish snorts regaled him from the sofa, where Mr. Chapman lay curled beneath a comforter. When the boy switched on his flashlight he was careful not to shine the beam in his father's face. Sweeping the small circle of light into the corners, then through the doorway into the kitchen, Neil could see that Josh wasn't there, and after a brief examination of the bathroom, his fears were confirmed.

"He's gone into the museum," he breathed, marveling at the youngster's courage. "But why? What could have persuaded him to go there in the dead of night? He hates the dark."

But Neil had already guessed the answer, and in a fierce hiss he spat out the name.

"Ted!"

Wasting no more time, he opened the door of the apartment and closed it silently behind him, leaving it unlocked.

The narrow corridor was black as tar, and even the flashlight beam made little difference in the dense darkness. Neil had never been inside the Wyrd Museum in the middle of the night; the early evening had proved to be bad enough. Now there was no telling what might be lurking in wait for him. He thought of all the macabre exhibits—what if Ted wasn't the only one that came to life? There could be many more terrifying creatures roaming the deserted building.

Swallowing nervously, and with these unsettling fears seething within him, he forced himself to take the first step down the corridor.

Before him, the flashlight bobbed and trembled unsteadily as his hand began to shake. It was almost worse being able to see glimpses of the way ahead, and if there were any horrors wandering through the museum, they could not fail to see him. The flashlight would act like a beacon to draw them close. Every ghastly, unnamed specter would flow silently and unerringly through the gloom—sailing toward him with bloodless talons reaching for his throat. Even now, a host of unclean spirits could be thronging around him, lured by the light and the scent of his pulsing blood. Perhaps these demonic fiends were skulking behind him, keeping well out of the feeble light, letting him blunder deeper into the museum's heart, where they could all pounce and feed upon his tender flesh.

Neil uttered a cry of dismay as these frightening thoughts got the better of him. He whirled the flashlight wildly around, shining it into the thick shadows of the corridor until he was satisfied that it was empty.

"Get a grip," he scolded himself. "Josh has come through here in total darkness. I can't think how he . . ."

The thought of his small brother pushed some of his fears aside and Neil pressed onward.

Through the ground floor rooms he went, the beam of his flashlight picking eerie glints from the displays around him and flinging grotesque shadow shapes onto the walls.

Occasionally, the pale moonlight burst in through the windows as ragged clouds blew across the sky, and the rooms were abruptly flooded with a deathly glow that made everything it touched appear wraithlike and otherworldly. It was like being in the middle of a painfully slow lightning storm as the Georgian windows sluggishly brimmed with radiance, glimmered for a moment, then faded back to the dismal dark.

In a small but determined voice Neil called Josh's name, but he heard no response, and his instincts told him he would not find him on this floor. His only hope was to reach The Separate Collection before Josh did.

Whatever Ted wanted from Josh, Neil was sure it was

evil and dangerous. The bear hadn't been sealed in the cabinet for nothing. Neil was convinced that if Ted was ever released, something dreadful would happen.

"Maybe everything here is treacherous," said a voice in his head as he hurried for the hallway. "Perhaps that's what this place is for. This is where all the nasty stuff is kept, all the bad things. That's why no one ever comes. It's like a dumping-ground of horrors—all that's foul and gruesome eventually manages to find its way here."

This new and unwelcome thought panicked him, and when his light finally fell upon the paneled hall and the staircase, he tried to quell the terror rising to the surface once more.

"Stop it!" he snarled as he reached the stairs. "It's only a creepy ruin; there's nothing to be scared of. Just find Josh and go back to the apartment!"

Suddenly, caught in the beam of his flashlight, Neil saw a long, glittering knife blade come slicing toward him.

The boy screamed and stumbled down the steps, flinging his hands in front of his face as a gnarled claw flew from the shadows to clutch at him.

"No-o-o!" he yelled. "Help—Dad!"

The flashlight clattered on the floor as it fell from his grasp, and a flickering pool of light went spinning across the room. Towering above his prostrate form was a ghostly figure swathed in robes.

"Keep away from me!" he bawled as the nightmarish apparition shambled closer and crouched over him, filling his nostrils with an overpowering reek of damp and stale decay.

Then it spoke.

"Do you think *she* will like it?" the phantom cried. "I do hope she will, I really do."

Neil recovered himself and stared upward. At that moment, the moon emerged from the shrouding clouds and the staircase was bathed in a pallid splendor.

"M—Miss Celandine! . . ." he gasped.

With the moonlight shimmering over her braided hair, Miss Celandine Webster jerked her head sideways and blinked her tiny bright eyes.

She was dressed in a nightgown of antique and moth-eaten lace that twirled and billowed around her like tattered shreds of mist caught on thorny branches. As she moved, a large silver-winged insect fluttered in a drunken spiral above her head before zooming down to crawl inside a deep fold once more. A bemused and preoccupied look was on her face and the air squeaked in through her buck teeth as her gaze roved around the hallway, before finally coming to rest and settling on Neil.

Then, sucking in her cheeks and fizzing with excitement, the old woman showed him what she had clasped to her breast.

In her withered hands Miss Celandine flourished a square of knitted wool. What Neil had mistaken for a weapon was actually one of a pair of knitting needles.

"I haven't lost my touch, have I?" she asked, holding it close to his face. "It took Veronica simply ages to wind it and cast on, but not me. I've forgotten nothing. My fingers never were as fickle as hers. Ha! They both thought I wouldn't be able to manage, that I wouldn't have the strength, but look—see how the threads are enmeshed ever so tightly with one another. That is how it should be, a blissful binding of one line into another. A splendid raveling together to create the perfect weave. I'm so happy with it. I am, truly I am! Oh, to lead the willing and drive the stubborn—how glorious it was!"

Neil stared at the scrap of wool she waved in his face. It was made from different shades of green and shot through with fine strands of bright silver tinsel that sparkled and gleamed in the moonlight. Miss Celandine was obviously proud of her handiwork and pressed it lovingly to her cheek.

"It's been so long," she crooned, "so very long. When the loom was broken I never thought I should make anything again, yet here it is. I've done it—another web, after all these years. How glad it has made me." She broke into a high, squawking laugh, thrusting the cherished woolen square back to her bosom, and swayed from side to side, enraptured.

Her laughter stopped when her eyes alighted upon Neil again, and the toothy grin melted from her face. "You didn't tell me!" she yelped in a wavering wail.

"Tell you what?"

"If *she* will like it? You do think she will, don't you? Oh she must, she simply must, that's what it's all for, isn't it? Nothing else matters—only her!"

"Do you mean your sister? Is that who you're talking about?"

Miss Celandine buried her blobby nose deep into the wool and gave a low chortle. "Oh, this isn't for Ursula!" she tittered. "How silly you are! Why, if it were, how could she cast off for me? Don't you know anything? I'm talking about the One who is to come after, the daughter who should have been mine—the mother's offspring.

Ursula says that at last we can fetch her. We must, we must, for if we don't bring her here then we are all lost. The cold ones we banished will return, and we are now too weak to halt them. They shall maim and wither the final root just as they did the tree."

"Please, Miss Webster," the boy began, "have you seen my brother, Josh?"

The old woman ignored him and continued to examine the knitting in her hands. "How could she not like it?" she gabbled. "We have thought of everything. Ursula has been so very clever; she can be quite brilliant when the need arises. Of course, she doesn't know where I am now. I'm not supposed to be here, you see—but I cannot disappoint my friends now, can I?"

"Er, no," Neil told her, not understanding a word she had said. "I'm sorry, I can't stay here. I must find Josh— I'm sure whoever 'she' is will love what you've made."

"Oh, it isn't finished yet!" Miss Celandine clucked. "There's still so much to be woven into it. I've a long way to go before the battle is over, as have you. Your path may be the most deadly of them all."

"Right," the boy muttered dubiously. "I'm going then."

A gurgle of amusement issued from the old woman's wrinkled lips as he brushed past her on the stairs. "Good luck!" she called after him. "Good-bye, and remember, *we favor the bold.*"

With that she skipped from the bottom step and twirled her ragged nightgown around her as if it was a ball gown.

With her precious knitting clutched tightly in her other hand, she let the empty darkness lead her into the middle of the hall, where, with her head tilted whimsically on one side, she slowly began to dance.

Neil watched in fascination. The woman was obviously reliving some joyous moment from her youth, and his heart went out to her. Once, an age ago, she must have been pretty enough to warrant many men coming to court her, and yet she never married.

Flitting in and out of the shadows below, turning from one imagined admirer to another in her tatty nightgown, Miss Webster's tired figure now looked like a swirling bundle of dirty wash.

"O you sea captains and heroes of old," she murmured, spinning around and around, clutching desperately at the vacant air as she hummed snatches of half-remembered tunes, "whence did you depart? Why was I left to fall under the yoke of that infernal device? Where are the children that should have been born unto me?"

Reeling out of control, she lost her balance and fell against the wooden panels, where she dug her nails into the splintering grain as hot tears coursed down her time-ravaged face.

"All are gone," she whimpered, sliding to the floor, where she sprawled in a sorrowful and wretched heap. "Age has taken them and I am lost and barren. I have nothing, nothing at all! There is n-nothing. Why have I not died? Let me perish with the rest . . . please . . . pleeeeeaaase!"

On the stairs, Neil looked away as her bitter sobs echoed pitifully from the shadows, and he hastened to the landing with his hands over his ears, more anxious than ever to find his little brother.

CHAPTER 7

THE FIERY GATEWAY

Enveloped by the murky gloom of The Separate Collection, Josh stood before the cabinet that contained Ted and stared in through the glass.

The little boy was both frightened and excited. He had dared the extreme darkness and found his way back to this most fabulous of places. It had been a breathless, exhilarating night quest, something he had never dreamed he could accomplish, but the bait that spurred him had banished his terror of the dark, and now here he was, face-to-face with it again.

"Knew you'd come back, kid," that incredible voice said from the shadow-filled display. "Now that's what I call gutsy."

Josh's already goggling eyes shone eagerly as a small furry shape emerged from the darkness and came swaggering toward him, pressing a leather nose against the glass.

The moonlight was weaker in The Separate

Collection, but the little boy could see the toy's face quite clearly. The round ears were waggling at him and the corners of the mouth had wrinkled, forming a pleased and benign smile.

"Gotta congratulate you, Shortstop," the bear said. "You kept your part of the bargain."

A jubilant grin split Josh's face. "You *are* magic!" he rejoiced, jumping up and down. "I knew it—I told Neil, I did!"

"He ain't as smart as you, General. Older brothers don't know it all."

Josh could only gaze at the creature, enamored of every movement he made and every syllable he uttered.

"You an' me know what's cookin', don't we?" Ted continued, rubbing his paws together. "Of course there's magic in the world. Didn't I tell you I was good at all this hocus-pocus stuff? Didn't I promise I'd do some for yer?"

The boy nodded keenly. "Can you?" he cried. "Can you do it?"

Ted wagged a reassuring paw. "Relax, kid," he replied. "I gave my word, and you know that magic teddy bears always keep their promises. Why, I'd be drummed right outta Toyland if I went back on my word. You do trust me, don'tcha?"

"Yes," Josh breathed.

"Then all ya gotta remember is to do exactly what I tell ya. Unnerstand? Swell! Now, what'll happen might look a little kooky and strange, but ya gotta put some jazz into this kinda stuff."

Josh could hardly contain himself. "I love you, Mr. Teddy!" he cried. "Quick, do it now!"

The bear stared for a moment at Josh's upturned,

trusting face, then wrinkled his nose and coughed uncomfortably. "'At's a smart kid," he eventually muttered. "You just do what I say an' you'll get all I promised."

Josh beamed at him, and Ted raised his stubby arms into the air. As he sneaked a sly glance at the doorway, a peculiar, knowing smirk stole over his fleecy face before he looked back at Josh and winked encouragingly.

Then the bear threw back his head and in a surprisingly loud voice yelled, "You hear me? I've done it—the kid's here. Open up! Tear it apart—let me go back! Let me go back!"

Ted lowered his arms and peered cautiously about the darkened room. "C'mon," he whispered impatiently, "where is it? Them dames better be fast."

Beside the cabinet, Josh followed the enchanted toy's gaze around The Separate Collection but could see nothing.

"Where is it?" he murmured in disappointment. "I can't see—"

"Hey!" Ted roared, glaring up at the ceiling. "All I see is a fat load o' nothin'. Cripes! If you don't make it soon this whole show'll be wasted. Stop foolin' around! Where's the gate? Where is it? I ain't been wastin' all these years fer you to louse it up now!"

"Mr. Teddy . . ." Josh began, but even as the words tumbled from his lips the young boy's hair was ruffled by a faint breeze, and when he saw this, Ted leaped up and gave a cheer.

"That's it!" he crowed. "She's on her way. Oh baby, she's on her way!"

Josh looked around for the window that must have

been left open. The breeze was growing stronger. It tugged at his pajamas and streamed in his eyes. The black drapes that covered a nearby case began to flap like great dark wings, and the paintings on the far wall swung on their chains.

"What's happening?" Josh howled as the unseen forces whipped about the room, growing stronger with every second. Now the breeze had become a gale, and it charged fiercely between the cabinets, thundering through the winding aisles and battering against the panels.

"C'mon!" Ted shrieked. "Open her now!"

A terrified whine squealed from Josh's mouth and he screwed up his face, grimly holding on to the display case as the furious storm plucked and tore at him. The uproar had become deafening, and the violence of the unnatural tempest raged uncontrollably around The Separate Collection. Quaking cabinets slid across the floor. With a crash and an explosion of splintering glass, one of them toppled over, spilling its contents into the greedy wind.

The flapping black drapes were snatched up and sent thrashing through the tormented air, churning the shadows and swarming into the gloom.

Josh screamed in terror and closed his eyes to the chaos that engulfed him, but Ted's voice rang above the din, exultant and triumphant.

"Look, kid!" he bellowed, hammering on the glass and pointing to the far corner. "Do you see it? Just there!"

The boy dared to open his eyes and peer into the darkness.

"You wanna see hocus-pocus, kid—well, here it comes!"

High above the tops of the tallest cases, the darkness was shimmering. Like muddy black water, turgid ripples wound out through the storm, whirling and lashing the very air itself.

"This is the magic, kid!" Ted declared. "This is what you wanted to see. Take a good long look, this is what I been waitin' fer. It's been a long time! Ain't it beautiful?"

As Josh watched, the disturbance grew, forming a spinning whirlpool in the tumultuous atmosphere that hovered high overhead.

With a deep, forbidding rumble, the spiraling vortex quivered and began hurling itself against the walls, flinging paintings, spears, and trophies to the ground as its flailing might beat mercilessly upon them.

"Hey!" Ted yelled at the ceiling. "Hold her steady. Can't you control this thing?"

Suddenly, the madly spinning rim of the ferocious vortex burst into flames and a wheel of purple fire spluttered into crackling life, dripping amethyst-colored sparks onto the floor, where they sizzled and singed the wooden boards. Like a vast and lethal Ferris wheel it revolved insanely, then, within the livid blaze, the throbbing air seemed to buckle and warp until it actually began to stretch backward. Swiftly it penetrated the shadows, drilling beyond the panels, spiraling out of the room, deep into the farthest expanse of the dark black night.

A searing flash of violet lightning streaked abruptly from the immense depths of the swirling vortex's heart and snaked viciously about the ceiling, blistering huge gashes in the plaster. Jagged bolts of energy rampaged around the paneled walls, lacerating and mutilating the varnished oak, gouging deep into the blasted wood ugly, smoldering scars that glowed with intense purple embers. Pillars of green smoke spilled from these charred wounds, then the panels shuddered. Out of the cinders grew large buds that sprouted and branched into the room, smashing through the nearby cabinets until The Separate Collection resembled a wild forest caught in a hellish maelstrom.

"There you go, kid!" Ted bawled as vivid lightning flared all around them. "What are you waitin' fer?"

Josh's face was white with fear. Holding on to the display case, he stared at the devastation the whirling portal had caused, then up at the dreadful, blazing horror itself.

A desolate wail blared from his mouth, but his petrified shrieks were drowned in the calamitous roar of the storm. Overhead, the lightning boiled and rivers of flame gushed down around him. The boy shivered in fright and threw his hands before his face to hide from the terrible sight.

Ted glared at him, his impatience boiling into anger. "Don't just stand there!" he screeched fervently. "The gateway's waitin'!"

"I can't!" Josh gibbered. "I—I scared."

The bear snarled in frustration and gave the glass a terrific thump. Throwing the entrance a nervous glance, he barked at Josh all the more harshly.

"Don't you want adventure?" he cried.

The boy nodded.

"Well, it's just through there! Listen! If you don't go, then the gate'll vanish!"

Through his blubbering tears Josh gazed at the whirling, fire-ringed vortex, and his sobs eased.

At that moment a figure burst into the tempest-battered room and stood stock still as it beheld the dreadful devastation and the churning, lightning-brimmed portal above. Neil stared at the awful scene, aghast. The Separate Collection was filled with purple flame and putrid smoke, yet through the reek he could see his brother standing by Ted's cabinet. The youngster was looking intently at the fiery eye of the evil storm.

"Josh!" he yelled. "Get away from there!"

The little boy glanced around at him, but Ted's voice rang loud and defiant in his ear.

"Listen to me!" he raged. "Just run to the gateway and you'll be slap-bang in Toyland Square. Trust me, kid!"

To his dismay, Neil saw his brother move away from the cabinet out toward the blistering heat of the spinning whirlpool.

"No!" he screamed, leaping over a fallen case and dodging a column of dripping flame.

"Go, kid!" Ted commanded. "If you don't, then you'll never see the panda acrobats or the flying elephants. This is your only chance!"

As Josh edged closer to the center of the tumult, his face was lit with the livid fires and his eyes were filled with wonder. Then, as he stepped beneath the dazzling wheel, the room flashed and a bolt of energy leaped from the curdling depths and streamed toward him.

Neil stumbled and froze as he saw his little brother hurled violently across the room by the lightning. The crackling energies flung the screaming child high into the air, slinging him from corner to corner, casting his small body through blinding sheets of withering flame.

The savage lightning wrapped itself around Josh's arms and legs, bearing him ever upward to draw level with the twisting gateway. Soon his eyes were staring straight down into the vast, immeasurable depths of the spiraling chasm. It was like looking down a gigantic dark throat. The fathomless coils gurgled and gaped before him, and the child could feel them pulling him closer.

Now the electric flames that circled the burning portal were all around him, and he was powerless to resist the almighty forces that dragged him on.

With a final shriek, Josh was snatched over the blazing threshold and flew headlong into the consuming darkness.

Beneath him, Neil cried out—but it was no use. Already, Josh's tiny figure was spiraling far down the whirling tunnel. In a moment he had disappeared from view, then his howling voice faded, and he was lost.

"JOSH!" Neil screamed. "JOSH!"

"No use squawkin', kid!" Ted thundered. "That won't do him no good."

Neil spun around and glared at the bear still trapped within the cabinet.

"You killed him!" he shouted. "You killed my little brother!"

"Hogwash!" Ted snorted. "The runt ain't dead."

"Then where is he? What have you done?"

"You should'a listened to me the other day. I didn't wanna involve him like that but ya left me no choice. I hadda get you here somehow. The kid's gone a long way back, but if you don't go in after him then he won't be comin' home."

"What do you mean? Back where?"

The bear gave a casual shrug and shook his head.

"Ain't got time fer all that. If you don't go now, the gateway'll close and that really will be the end."

Neil glared at the spinning entrance to the yawning tunnel that had swallowed Josh and prepared to launch himself at it.

"Oh, no, you don't!" Ted growled. "You ain't goin' nowhere without me! Listen, kid, the only way you can save little Joshy is by takin' me with you! I know where he's gone and how to find him—so set me free!"

"No!" Neil snapped.

"Then your brother's already dead! Get me outta here quick! The gateway won't stay open long!"

Neil stared at the dreadful creature as he wildly considered what he should do. Then his doubts ceased and he wrenched free the splintered leg of one of the destroyed cases and, shielding his eyes, threw it with all his might at the glass.

With an explosion of sparkling slivers, the cabinet rocked backward and the front pane cascaded onto the floor.

Ted picked himself up out of the gas mask where Neil's violence had knocked him and popped his head through the jagged hole.

"Pick me up!" he demanded, then his mouth dropped open and a look of panic burst upon his furry features. "No!" he yelled in alarm. "The darned thing's collapsin'!"

Neil stared up at the crackling portal. Ted was right. The flames that had blazed about its rim had dwindled and were now spluttering feebly. As they watched, the spinning gateway wavered in the air and went crashing into the table that held the two preserved ravens.

Feathers flew everywhere, and the ancient exhibits shot from their shattering domes, flying one last time, into The Egyptian Suite.

"Now," Ted bawled as the gateway quivered and lurched unsteadily, "before it's too late!"

Without wasting another second, Neil snatched up the bear and charged straight for the shuddering, glowing circle.

The fiery ring shrank even as they raced toward it. Shivering and throbbing, it careened wildly from side to side, smashing into one thing after another.

"Hold it steady!" Ted shouted to the ravaged and blasted ceiling. "We ain't through yet."

With a dying spurt of energy, the vortex yawned before them. A searing streak of lightning shot out and caught Neil full in the chest, flinging him into the air. The wreckage of The Separate Collection whirled as the powerful forces spun him and Ted around as though they were feathers.

Then he felt the terrible might of the gateway dragging and clutching at him, drawing him ever closer to the shimmering brink. With a clap of thunder, the flaming coils gaped wide, and suddenly he was inside— rushing relentlessly down the twisting helix, shooting deep into the absolute blackness. Both Neil and Ted vanished from the Wyrd Museum.

For several moments the gateway continued to whirl, but its strength was spent and the flames were extinguished. The hellish storm that had ripped the room to pieces was ebbing, and soon only the fragmented debris would be left.

A shower of white sparks spat from the shrinking

vortex as the torment drained away. But before the portal disappeared, the air convulsed and a finger of energy escaped into the room. Over the broken cabinets and cases it licked and danced, ricocheting off the bitter shards of glass that reflected its dazzling purple light a thousand times over. Then, even as the gateway turned in upon itself, the snaking bolt seized one solitary object and sent it racing down into the closing gulf.

A resounding crash roared through the room, and the Wyrd Museum was rocked to its foundations. Then all was dark, and the soft, pervading moonlight streamed in through the windows once more.

CHAPTER 8

INTO THE BLACKOUT

Rivers of burning light burst into the heavens as the distant report of antiaircraft guns hammered through the sky. Into the dark awning of the night, the powerful beams of the searchlights performed an endless dance, tirelessly scanning for the reviled enemy.

Another raid was afflicting London. German bombs sang out of invisible clouds, and the pulse of their destruction rifled ominously over the stricken city. For an instant the sky was as bright as day, then all was plunged into the gathering dark, awaiting the next punishing strike. Fires were burning now, scorning the blackout and blazing a perfect target for the German aircraft. Rooftops were aflame, and huge palls of smoke drifted up through the searchlights, like the rising souls of the destroyed buildings below.

It was late February in the year nineteen hundred and forty-three. Almost two years had passed since the horrific bombardments of the Blitz, but recently the

German air force had returned, and tonight's visit was one of the most brutal and tenacious. Already there had been many dreadful casualties, and throughout the capital, in every shelter, the silent, huddled people wept and waited, praying for the welcome sound of the All Clear siren.

As the skies flared and the fires rampaged, a small child tore frantically through the chaos, scrambling over mountains of rubble and panting desperately.

Below, clambering up the fallen timbers and piles of shattered brick, the figures of three men, dressed in black uniforms and wearing tin hats, gave chase.

Fearfully, the child looked down and saw that the fattest of them was drawing dangerously near. With her heart thumping furiously, the child picked up a stone to fling at the hated figure.

"Blimey!" he cried, as the missile bounced off his helmet. "She's throwing things at us!"

"Don't let her escape!" another of them called. "We've got to get her this time!"

The third man uttered a dismal howl and slithered down the slope as a fist-sized slab of cement smacked the side of his neck.

"She's gone and got Joe!" the fat one complained, wheezing from his exertions. "What with her an' the Nazis, I just don't know—watch out, Pete!"

The second man leaned to one side as another stone whistled from above. "'Sall right, Arnold," he shouted to his comrade, "she missed."

Fat Arnold glowered up at the child he had come to loathe and plowed his chubby hands into the rubble to drag himself farther up the great mound. "I'll teach that kid!" he puffed, straining in his suspenders. "The little beggar'll feel the back o' my hand—I'll—"

Too late, he saw the girl stoop and take aim. Before his plump body could swerve aside, a hail of grit and stones hit him full in his flabby face. With his short arms flailing around his plump bulk, Arnold Porter bounced and bumped back down, squealing all the way like a piglet.

Only Peter Stokes remained. Ignoring the wails of his fellow wardens, he darted on, scaling the steep slope and keeping his head well down as the stones drummed on his tin hat.

"Edie!" he shouted in as friendly a voice as he could manage, given the circumstances. "There's nothing to be scared of, love, it's only me—Mr. Stokes. I won't hurt you."

At the summit of the shattered ruins, the girl cast about her wildly. This one was tricky. She needed more than stones to ward him off. Desperately she looked for an escape route. Behind her, the rubble pile dropped almost vertically, and she knew she could not jump it without breaking her legs.

The man was closing in on her now. Another moment and she would be completely cornered.

"There's a good girl," Mr. Stokes told her. "You stay just where you are. Don't move."

She waited until he had almost reached the top, then nipped nimbly to the right and scurried straight past him.

"No, you don't, young lady!" he cried, reaching out and catching hold of her coat. "Gotcha!"

Peter Stokes yanked the struggling girl closer and grabbed her tightly by the wrists.

The child threw back her head and twisted it madly in

all directions as she vainly pulled on her captor's grasp.

"Stop that," he said sternly. "Stop that! Well, well, a fine time we've had runnin' after you these past weeks. What's got into you, girl? We was only tryin' to dig you out."

The child glared up at him, her dirty face screwed into a mask of hatred. She opened her mouth as if to scream, but her tongue was silent and the harsh words failed to emerge.

"Poor little urchin," Mr. Stokes said gently. "Must've been frightened half to death in that house o' yours. What you need is somethin' hot inside you. Come on, we'll get back to the post."

Taking one of his hands from her, he waved to the two men below. "I got her!" he shouted. "She's safe 'n'—Aargh!"

Seizing her advantage, the child had sunk her teeth deep into the hand that held her. Immediately he let go and she bolted swiftly down the slope.

Peter Stokes sucked his bleeding hand and thrust it under his arm. "She got away!" he howled to the others. "Catch hold of her!"

But it was no use. Fat Arnold had had enough, and although he was nearest as she scooted down, he let Joe Harmon follow her.

"Nah!" Joe cursed moments later. "She's gone farther into the bomb site. Never find her there—not in blackout. In any case, you know what they're sayin' 'bout that place."

"No."

"Folks reckon it's haunted—pretty strange things been seen in there. The kids won't play there no more either."

"Pah!" Arnold Porter coughed in disgust and began shaking the dirt from his coat while they waited for Peter to rejoin them.

"Bit me," Peter explained as he stumbled down. "Lord, thought we really had her this time."

Fat Arnold gave a snort that made his jowels shake like jelly. "Wasted a good hour on her," he grunted. "Well, I won't be doin' it again. There's many folk only too glad of our assistance. She can take off wherever she likes."

"You don't mean that," Peter told him.

"That I does. She's bonkers. Did you see what she had around her neck? Madder than old Phyllis Wharburton, who kept all them cats an' made pies with the kittens."

"But she's only a kid. Eight years old, same as your Doris."

"My Doris ain't no loony," Arnold said flatly. "I've done enough chargin' around after head cases. Bad for my health, all this gallopin'. I ain't no bleedin' racehorse, you know."

"More like an elephant," muttered Joe Harmon.

"I heard that," Arnold rumbled.

Winding his scarf around his neck, Peter peered into the flaring darkness and sighed sadly. "Well," he said, "she's gone now. There's more important business we can attend to this night."

Abruptly, the expansive bomb site flickered as a stick of bombs fell close by. Briefly, all three men glimpsed the silhouette of a small girl outlined against the flashing explosions.

"Sixteen days she's been loose now," Fat Arnold murmured. "How the heck has she managed to stay alive? What can she be eatin', fer Gawd's sake? That luck o' hers can't last. Sweet Lord, look after the poor mite. Next time, Peter, count me in—I'll help catch her."

Suddenly, the ground shifted beneath their feet as a house two streets away took a direct hit. All thoughts of the girl were instantly forgotten as the three air-raid wardens raced off toward the already burning building.

With the planes droning overhead, it seemed as if the world was on fire. The sky was now a wrathful red, and death poured from the heavens in an almost constant stream. The night was alive with pieces of red-hot shrapnel that whizzed and whistled onto the bomb site, glimmering like fiery hornets through the smoke-fogged air.

In this strange, unearthly landscape, Edie Dorkins spread her arms out wide and danced around and around, staring up at the marvelous fireworks display above. She was a peculiar-looking child; her face was pinched and pale from lack of food, for she had not eaten properly in many days, having to scrounge and forage what she could like a wild animal. Beneath the accumulated grime, her features were sharp and oddly angular. The silvery-blue eyes were almond-shaped and her nose was pointed and upturned, sticking out from her narrow face like a sprouting root from a thin potato. A woolen pixie hat covered her tangled blonde hair, and this, coupled with a pair of skinny legs in dark brown, hole-ridden stockings, made her resemble some untamed woodland sprite lost in the city.

Around her neck, on a length of string, she wore an incendiary bomb that had failed to detonate. As she capered around, reaching for the glowing heavens, the lethal talisman swung madly.

With a serene smile on her face, the deranged girl danced over the rubble, tripping spryly through the debris and gurgling happily. This was her kingdom and she was its unassailable queen. Nothing happened in her ruined realm without her knowledge. She knew every inch of its barren devastation and loved it all.

Presently, the smile faded as a weird yet familiar spectacle illuminated the caved-in roofs and teetering chimney stacks nearby.

Behind the crippled remains of a high wall, the night was lit by streaks of purple lightning, and as she watched, a cloud of dust was hurled into the air as a ferocious gale blustered into existence.

Then a delighted grin appeared on the girl's dirty face, and she scurried toward the wall with the greatest speed and urgency. Edie's almond-shaped eyes were gleaming with excitement as she quickly scaled the juddering brickwork, not caring that the scabs had been scraped from her knees.

Hauling her scrawny self up to the top, she craned her neck to peer quizzically into the dark and debris-filled alleyway below, catching her breath as a furious gale blasted into her face.

Down in the dim alley, swirling just above the ground, a circle of fire was crackling and ripping the air to shreds, forming a twisting tunnel of night. Livid jags of lightning spat out of its heart, and from her vantage point, Edie beamed in wonderment as the flaring bursts of purple light played over her features.

In the center of the whirling ring a tiny figure was glimmering in the remote distance, growing larger with each passing second.

The delight melted from the girl's face as she glared down at the strange form traveling within the fiery gateway. It was the shape of a boy wearing pajamas and a bathrobe and grasping something tightly to his chest.

Now she could hear his terrified yells echoing from the spinning entrance. How he howled and wailed, kicking his legs wildly and tumbling head over heels through the farthest reaches of the dark, coiling helix.

Then he was free. With a frightened shriek, Neil Chapman was thrown clear of the tunnel and rolled helplessly over the uneven ground, yelping as he struck each and every stone.

Dismay and disappointment clouded Edie's grubby features. She had hoped the wondrous spectacle was going to give her another great treasure, but she could not help smiling at the unfortunate boy when he finally came to rest against a splintered sideboard. He looked so comical, sprawled among the rubble in his nightclothes, and at last she could make out the object in his hands. It was a teddy bear. Secretively, she lowered herself behind the wall with just the tip of her upturned nose resting on the topmost brick as she continued to watch the strange newcomer.

Neil uttered a painful moan. He was covered in scratches and ached all over. A little distance away the gateway was still boiling but the flames were diminishing. As the boy lifted a reluctant eyelid, he saw the vortex implode into the tortured ether with a tremendous flash of dazzling sparks.

Neil felt sick—his stomach was still lurching and turning over. He felt as though he had been through a clothes dryer, and his head was pounding. Groaning, he attempted to rise and winced at the sharp, stinging pains that prickled all over his body. His robe was torn, and in his pajama bottoms gaped long rents through which he could see nasty cuts and bruises.

"Ow . . ." he grumbled, not knowing which wound to attend to first. "Aahh!"

In his hands, Ted jiggled and pulled himself free. "Bumpy ride, eh, kid? Ya didn't have to hold so tight—ya rearranged ma stuffin'."

Quickly, he scampered onto Neil's shoulders, then hopped onto the broken sideboard, where he gazed around as if trying to get his bearings.

"I feel awful," Neil murmured. "What happened, where are we?"

"Aw, geez!" Ted hissed to himself. "This ain't good, not one iota. Mighta guessed this'd happen."

Neil's jangled thoughts were gradually beginning to reshape, and with a shiver, all his anger and fear returned as he remembered.

"Josh!" he blurted. "Where is he?"

Jumping to his feet, the boy seized hold of the toy bear and shook him roughly. "What have you done with him?" he demanded. "What's happening?"

Ted's voice burbled strangely as he tried to explain. "W-we . . . we ain't in . . . in y-your . . . time no m-more. Hey! Cut that ou-out! If I'd e-eaaten any lunch I'd be l-looosing it r-riight now!"

"Don't talk nonsense!" the boy spat. "What do you mean, 'my time'?"

"This is nineteen forty-three, kid," Ted told him, glad that the shaking had ceased. "I said we had to go a long ways back—well, here we are."

Neil raised his eyes from the loathsome bear in his hands and looked around.

At first he had thought they were in the middle of a building site, but now, under the glare of the orange sky, he could see that what he had mistaken for half-finished houses were in fact ruined homes. Overhead, he heard the distant engines of planes and saw the searchlights desperately trying to pierce the billowing plumes of black smoke. The whine of plummeting bombs rang in the boy's ears, and a horrible cold feeling washed over him as he realized Ted was speaking the truth.

"Blimey," Neil whispered, "what have you done?"

Ted cocked an ear upward and shuddered. "This ain't my fault," he cried. "We weren't supposed to arrive in the middle of no air raid. Look, there ain't time for this, you gotta find shelter. We're sittin' ducks out here."

Neil shook his head defiantly. "We're not going anywhere," he said, keeping a tight hold of the wriggling bear, "not until you tell me where Josh is. Why isn't he here?"

"If you'da entered the gateway when I told you," Ted shouted, "he would be! Time is a funny gizmo, kid. You start tinkerin' with it an' all kindsa things go wrong. Your pigheaded delay back there in the museum throwed us a little outta whack. This ain't where Joshy is supposed to turn up, an' if we don't find that place then his chances o' makin' it through are zero. I know I ain't your best pal right now, but we gotta stick together in this place 'cuz I'm all you got and vicey-versa. You got that?"

"Just tell me where to go," Neil muttered.

The bear tapped the boy's hands indignantly until he

loosened his grip to let him climb onto his shoulder once again.

"First, we gotta get outta this bomb site—they say lightning don't strike the same place twice, but that don't apply to no German bombs. We ain't gonna be no use to no one if one of them heels up there gets lucky. You ever seen the bits left over after a bomb explodes, kid? Sometimes there ain't enough to fill a bucket. Get movin'!"

"I can't see where I'm walking," Neil said as he blundered through the rubble, stubbing the toes of his slippered feet. "Hang on, I've got a flashlight in my pocket."

"Get a move on, will ya?" Ted hissed in his ear. "Them planes are getting closer."

Moving as fast as he could, shining the flashlight before him, Neil navigated through the fallen lintels and shattered beams until at last he was standing on the pavement of a dark and narrow street.

Everything, except for the sky, was swallowed in a hollow darkness. No street lamps shone and not a chink of light glimmered from behind the curtains of the houses. Neil had never experienced anything like it before, except two years earlier when his family had gone on a camping trip in Dorset, where the absolute night of the countryside had startled and amazed him. But this was not the middle of nowhere. There were homes and shops, yet it was completely deserted—as if all human life had vanished from the face of the earth.

Ted glanced keenly from right to left and rubbed his furry chin thoughtfully. "Damn!" he cursed. "I ain't gotta clue where this is. Hurry to the corner, kid. Ya oughta spot a shelter sometime soon. They was everywhere."

Neil obeyed, for the droning aircraft were directly overhead now. Over the rooftops of the far end of the street a fountain of bricks and slates shot into the night, and Neil stumbled as the pavement shuddered beneath his feet. An acrid, burning smell hung on the air, and the tension in the bear's voice mounted as he spurred the boy on.

"That was too close, I can smell the cordite. Listen, kid, you gotta climb over the back wall of one of them houses. There'll be a shelter in the yard. Hammer on the door like there's no tomorrow."

Neil hurried around the corner of the street and breathlessly shone the flashlight beam on a low fence.

"Over there?" he cried.

"Now!" Ted urged, clinging to his collar.

"Oi!" a deep voice suddenly roared.

Neil whipped around, and the light glared in the face of a large man wearing a tin hat.

"Air Raid Patrol," Ted breathed with relief in the boy's ear. "Stick with him. He'll take care of us."

Arnold Porter stormed over to them, his fat face quivering with rage. "Put that light out!" he trumpeted, snatching the flashlight from Neil's hand. "Pete's sake, that's too bright for the blackout. Why ain't there no tissue paper over the bulb?"

He shone his own smaller light into the boy's face and scowled, making his blubbery chins wobble. "Now who might you be?" he declared. "Know most o' the young ones around 'ere, I do. Ain't seen you afore. What you doin' out in the middle of the raid? Where's your house, who's your mum and dad? What they thinkin' of—lettin' you sneak out?"

Before Neil could answer, the corpulent warden took hold of his arm and sternly frog-marched him into the next street.

"Back to the post with you, my lad," Fat Arnold said. "I reckon your dad'll be fumin' when he learns about this. You want to get yourself murdered out here? I've a mind to give you a good hidin' myself—bloomin' perisher."

Wriggling in the man's grasp, Neil twisted and turned, then over the warden's shoulder he saw a sight that made him stumble and come to a halt.

Clearly defined against the burning heavens, a large, dark shape was gracefully floating down through the wisps of smoke—almost directly over their heads. It was so big that Neil thought it could only be a car, but his mind rebelled against such a preposterous idea.

Arnold Porter turned to see what he was staring at, and at once his chubby jowls dropped in dread.

"Bleedin' Ada!" he spluttered. "A parachute mine!"

With a crunch, the lethal device disappeared behind the chimney stacks of the house opposite, splintering straight through the roof and crashing through the ceilings of the rooms below. It was followed by a vast, flapping tarpaulin that twirled briefly over the rooftop before it was dragged downward with a clatter of slates and tiles.

Suddenly, once again, Neil's world was flung into chaos, and it was a moment that remained with him for the rest of his life. Arnold Porter roared like a wounded lion, scooped Neil up in his great hands, and charged like a maniac into the nearest doorway.

The breath was forced from Neil's lungs as the heavy

man flattened him against the door, but while he was gasping for air with his face squashed into the buttons on the warden's coat, there came a loud rushing noise and a flash of brilliant light from inside the house where the mine had landed.

Neil felt the force of the explosion before he actually heard it, but the sound hit him a fraction of an instant later. The world was torn apart and his head crashed violently against the wooden door as the ground leaped under him. It was the most awful moment of his life, and he clenched his teeth as the shock wave blasted through his bones. It had taken only a moment, but to Neil the experience seemed to last forever. Eventually, the doorstep stopped shivering, and though his ears continued to ring, he knew that it was over.

Choking, he struggled to breathe, but the full weight of the warden was pressing down on him and his arms were trapped beneath the man's heavy stomach.

"Get off," his muffled voice implored, but still the man refused to budge.

Crushed and frantic for air, Neil used all his strength to move him. After several attempts, fat Arnold shifted and the great, flabby man slumped limply to the porch floor.

Neil staggered to his feet and leaned against the building, gladly gulping down the fume-filled air.

Across the street, a mere twenty feet away, there was now a large crater, but the house that had once stood opposite the very doorway in which he coughed and spluttered was nowhere to be seen. All that was left was a cloud of dust and a scattering of timbers that were strewn over the street like gigantic straws.

Neil knelt beside the warden and shook him gently. "Are you all right?"

But Arnold Porter did not move.

In the doorway, Ted pulled his paws away from his ears and tottered unsteadily from the step. Then he saw the warden and scooted around to the man's plump hands to check his pulse.

The bear let the hand drop from his paw, and Neil swallowed in horror as he beheld the ghastly expression on Ted's furry face.

"The guy's dead," Ted muttered. "Musta absorbed most of the shock. A body can only take so much. You was lucky, kid. He done saved your life."

Appalled and distraught, Neil reeled away from the warden's body, covering his mouth to keep down the rising bile.

Ted gave Arnold Porter one final glance, then looked grimly up at Neil.

"We can't stay here," he uttered fearfully. "We gotta find somewhere safe till the raid's over."

Without saying a word, Neil picked him up, and together they fled into the darkness.

* * *

Edie Dorkins carefully picked her way over the ruins. Her jumbled mind was bewildered. She had witnessed something exceedingly strange that night. The boy's teddy bear had walked and talked with him, and she had to return to her beloved sanctuary to try and figure it out.

This time, the marvelous window had disappointed

her—she thought it had appeared for her and her alone. Where had that boy come from, what did he want here? He'd better not try and recover the first gift she had seen spinning from the fiery circle. What if he had already found it and was even now stealing the lovely thing?

Hastening through the desolate acres of the bomb site, the scraggy girl drew near to the skeletal remains of three buildings that jutted starkly from the ravaged landscape and reared before her like the twisted crown of a titanic and fallen god.

Deep wells of shadow were spread before the entrances to her secret refuge. She was safe there. Not one of the iron heads had found her—they thought it was dangerous and all had heard the strange rumors that were circulating about it.

Pattering up to her fortress's central door, which was hanging off its hinges, she ducked smartly beneath and entered the dark kitchen beyond.

The shattered fragments of a broken sink winked and shimmered in the reflected light of the ruddy glare that poured in through a gaping window. A perpetual, solemn drip from one of the taps disturbed the silence and trickled a meandering trail over the dust-covered linoleum. Shards of crockery were strewn everywhere, and on the corner of a buckled table a battered metal teapot balanced precariously.

Edie paused. There was a movement in the hallway, and from the murky shadows an indistinct shape shambled toward her.

The misty figure of an old man, dressed in a glimmering gray shirt with trousers hitched up almost to his chest, shuffled to the sink and halted by the leaking tap, moving his gnarled hands into the line of drips. But the water poured straight through him.

The old man did not seem to care and rubbed his phantom hands together in a ghastly pretense. Then he turned and smiled kindly at the small girl.

"Evenin', Miss Edie," came the hollow rasping of his dead voice. "You been gone a tidy while; the others will be pleased to see you. They was all askin' after you and when you'd be back. It gets so . . . so very lonely on our own."

He stood before her, blinking in the pulsing, garish glow that streamed in through the broken window, the fiery light passing clean through his spectral form. Turning toward the back door, the ghost stared at the devastation as if for the first time and struggled to remember what had befallen him. But pitted against the fierce will of the small girl, his faded mind was powerless. Pressing his fingers to his forehead, the spirit trembled, then looked up falteringly.

"Is it nice out?" he finally murmured.

With a triumphant grin, the girl considered him for a moment then nodded.

"Does the garden still look lovely?" he asked, his pale, corpselike face wrung with worry and confusion. "I do hope so, my pride and joy that is."

Edie ignored the question and bustled past him into the hallway.

"I think the others are coming," he called after her. "Listen, Miss Edie, there's more tonight . . . Miss Edie? . . ."

Broken stair rods hung from the damaged banister

like bent reeds, but the girl was short enough to walk beneath them without having to stoop over.

In through the parlor door she trailed, and sat down on a pile of cushions she had salvaged from various houses. The room was extremely drafty, for all the windows had been blown out and most of the ceiling was missing. Tossing her head back, Edie looked beyond the walls of the room above and the few remaining rafters of the roof, up to the troubled sky. The bombers were passing now; soon the raid would be over.

Lowering her eyes, she leaned forward to a low table and gazed enchantedly at the treasures heaped upon its dusty surface.

This was her personal hoard, a splendid collection of cherished trinkets she had abstracted and rescued from nearly a hundred decimated homes. There was a bronze figurine of a dancer with ivory hands and an eternal smile molded on her gorgeous face, the cut-glass top of a decanter, a small traveling clock, a gilded picture frame, four silver teaspoons, two fox stoles, a pair of black high-heeled shoes, a blonde wig complete with fake ringlets, three lipsticks, a pearl-sequined dress, and a dented cookie tin that contained a fantastic wealth of costume jewelry.

Edie reached across and let the riches run between her fingers. Taking up one of the fox furs, she draped it around her shoulders then wiped a lipstick over her mouth. Delving into the cookie tin, she grabbed handfuls of diamante earrings and bracelets, then spent the following minutes decorating herself with them. Finally, she pulled the wig on over her pixie hat and reclined on the cushions like some miniature and grotesque goblin countess.

A piece of broken mirror hung on the blackened wall, and the girl sauntered over, treading like a tightrope walker to keep all of her booty in place. Admiring herself in the glass, she pulled a succession of faces before the fussy wig slipped down over her eyes.

Edie returned to the cushions and carefully removed the adornments. The jewels had always been her favorite treasures, and she had enjoyed hunting through the ruined houses to find them—until, that is, the latest marvel arrived.

At one end of the table this new dainty had pride of place. It had arrived three nights ago, tumbling from a ring of fire, just like the one the boy and his teddy bear had emerged from.

The girl knelt before this lovely addition to her collection and stroked it lovingly. The object was a small box of black wood, carved with mysterious symbols and surmounted by the image of a hideous demon with glittering red eyes.

An adoring expression spread over her face, and her enchantment increased a thousandfold as the box began to move.

As if it were filled with angry wasps, the Casket of Belial twitched and jerked upon the table, almost as though the horror it contained could sense the violence and destruction happening in the outside world and was eager to break free to savor it to the full. Then the erratic movements subsided and it was still once more.

Elated, Edie fished into her jewel tin once more and brought out glittering brooches and twinkling bangles, which she placed around the box in a gleaming circle, as tribute to the in-dwelling deity. Then, her handiwork done, she frowned and glanced distractedly at the parlor door.

Taking a final look at her latest treasure, she hurried into the hall and saw that the kitchen was now crowded with shadowy figures.

In the deep gloom, over a dozen shapes were standing with downcast faces, shifting aimlessly from side to side and whispering to themselves in soft, mournful words.

At the sound of Edie's approach, the specters lifted their heads and murmured faintly.

"Edie has returned," the rippling voices chanted. "The child is come back to us."

Slowly, the dark crowd raised their shadowy hands and reached out to her, beseechingly.

The girl chuckled as she gazed at each troubled face. By the power that was steadily growing within her she was holding and keeping them in the living world. These forlorn, earthbound souls were now her family, and she was both their captor and their fierce guardian. Then an exultant cry sprang from her lips as she recognized a morose, bulky figure that was staring around uncertainly.

The shade of Arnold Porter looked blankly at his surroundings before uttering a pitiful sob. "What the bleedin' heck happened?" he murmured. "Why am I here? I should be someplace else, why can't I leave? How did I get here?"

Edie only laughed in reply and danced before the distressed specter of the dead Air Raid Patrol warden.

With every raid her ethereal family grew. No longer would she be alone, no longer would the darkness be silent. They would remain with her forever, and in that, her scrambled thoughts found comfort.

Then her peculiar, disjointed mind jumped like a scratched record, and a new thought gripped her.

With her giggling laughter rising into the night, she pushed through the congregating souls as if they were nothing more than clouds of vapor, and she hurried out into the bomb site.

CHAPTER 9

THE STOKES FAMILY

Into a sky that was filled with winding threads of wood smoke, a bleary dawn was edging, gilding the ghostly shapes of the barrage balloons that floated way in the distance and climbing decorously up the church steeples that towered over the small terraced houses of the East End.

Barker's Row was one of the few streets that had as yet escaped the bombing. It was a quaint, almost unreal place whose inhabitants took great pride in the appearance of their homes. Doorsteps were swept every morning, and although crosses of masking tape covered the windows, the panes gleamed like crystal.

In a tiny bedroom at number twenty-three, Neil Chapman watched Mr. Stokes partially close the door behind him, then turned to the bear in his hands.

"Now!" he demanded. "You tell me exactly what is going on here!"

Ted glanced at the door and cocked an ear as he heard heavy footsteps descend into the hall.

The past few hours had flown by in a confusing whirl, and the bear blinked in a daze as he tried to gather his usually sharp wits and sort them into order.

After fleeing from the corpse of Arnold Porter, he and Neil had been found by two of the dead warden's colleagues and taken to an Air Raid Patrol hut until the raid was over.

It was there, in the dim light of a naked, low-wattage bulb, surrounded by official posters and first-aid kits, that Ted had recognized one of the men and stifled a gasp of surprise at the sight of him.

When the All Clear siren sounded, that same man had brought the boy back to his home. It was here that Ted now found himself, and he didn't like it, not one little bit.

"Well?" Neil snapped. "What's got into you? Why did you tell me to keep quiet and act dumb back at that hut? Now this Mr. Stokes thinks I've been bombed out and hit my head in the process. What are we doing here? This is crazy. We ought to be out there looking for Josh! Where is he—where's my brother?"

But the bear wasn't listening to him. Ted's glass eyes were roving around the small bedroom, gazing mournfully at the collection of old toys arranged carefully on the chest of drawers and the stack of movie magazines piled below the window.

"It wasn't supposed to be like this," he murmured despondently. "It was meant to be easy an' quick, that's all I agreed to. What are they playing at? Them daffy broads have got somethin' cookin' of their own. I shoulda guessed they weren't doin' this outta the kindness of their hearts!"

His dismal voice trailed off as he spotted a crumpled

telegram on the floor, and he covered his face with his paws.

"I dunno if I can take this a second time," he whimpered. "Why do this to me? Son of a—do they wanna torment me or what? If I'd known this was gonna be so tough . . ."

Puzzled by the bear's morose behavior, Neil sat on the bed next to him. "Something's gone wrong, hasn't it?" he said. "Back there in the hut, you saw something, didn't you? What happened? Does it have something to do with Josh?"

Ted stared at the boy keenly and in a grim voice told him, "We're too early, kid. We popped outta that gateway ahead of schedule. Seeing that Stokes guy was the first clue, then I saw the date on the paper the warden was readin'. Yesterday was the twenty-sixth of February. That's no use to me nor no one—leastways, I hope it ain't."

"I don't understand," Neil said. "Too early for what?"

Staring down at his stumpy feet, Ted wrinkled his nose and wondered how much he could reveal to the boy.

"Okay," he finally began. "If it's gonna keep you happy, I'll say this much an' no more. If you don't like it then it's just too bad—I got my orders. I'm sorry if this has been tough on you, but I figure it'll get a whole lot worse before we're done. All I can say is that, for the moment, your brother is fine and safe.

"I told ya time is a tricky gizmo to tinker with. Well, that hocus-pocus we went through was a shortcut to the past—don't ask me where it came from 'cuz I won't tell ya. All you need to know is that them babies ain't easy to rustle up. Takes years of plannin' to get the right dispensations, and a whole mess of one vital ingredient, which is in mighty short supply where we come from. Anyhow, these time gadgets gotta be approached right—the longer you wait before jumpin' in, the farther back they go. Think of it like a drill—the more you drill, the deeper the hole. That plain enough fer you?"

"I haven't a clue what you're talking about."

The bear gave an irritated grunt. "Little Joshy went through first, right? Well, where he'll pop out is now bound to be somewhere in the future 'cuz you took so long debatin' what to do. All that while the gateway was boring farther back, past the point where it dropped off your kid brother."

"It's very confusing."

"An' highly specialized. They can't have just anyone punchin' holes in the cloth of time, you know. You gotta restrict that kinda stuff."

Neil chewed the inside of his cheek thoughtfully. "So all we have to do is wait until Josh turns up. When is that going to be?"

The bear sniffed and looked away. "He's due on the third of March," he answered.

"But that's five days away!" Neil protested. "What are we supposed to do until then? We can't stay here all that time!"

Ted shrugged. "We don't have much choice," he admitted. "Believe me, kid, I ain't lookin' forward to it either, but it looks like this is where we're supposed to be. I sure wish I'd been briefed a whole lot better on the whys and wherefores myself.

"The next few days ain't gonna be no picnic, fer you or me. This house has seen a whole lot of grief, and it's gonna know a helluva lot more before the end if we fail in what we have to do.

"All you gotta remember is that, if you ever wanna see Joshy again, you better stick with me. I'm your only ticket outta this situation. I'm the only one who knows exactly when and where the gate'll appear to take you home.

"Face facts, kid, you need me. So you better take good care of yours truly, 'cuz if anything happens to this cuddly critter, then you can whistle good-bye to your brother and you can bet your boots you won't never see your own time again. Well, not till you're sixty. Hey, that might not be such a bad idea. You could take one of them screwball dames to the movies—maybe all three if you take your vitamins."

"But I still don't know why you did it," Neil said. "I mean, why make Josh enter the gateway in the first place?"

"I hadda get you in there somehow," Ted groaned apologetically. "You wouldn't help me any other way. You sure made that plain enough."

"But why?" the boy insisted. "What do you want me in the past for? What is it you want me to do?"

"Just do your best," Ted murmured, "that's all we ask. You can't do more than that."

"Who's 'we'?"

Ted ignored the question and jabbed a paw at the pillows. "Didn't that Stokes guy tell you to get some shuteye?" he asked. "That ain't such a bad idea, kid. 'Sides, you don't know what an honor it is for him to let you into this room."

With his mind spinning from all he had witnessed in the few hours since he had emerged from the gateway,

Neil lay back on the bed and in a matter of moments was snoring soundly.

Ted waited until he was certain the boy was really asleep. Then, quietly, he hopped from the bed, crept toward the door, and slipped out of the room.

* * *

Jean Evans lifted her arms to the early sunshine and stretched thankfully. Yawning, the young woman shook her auburn hair and gazed around the garden that, before the war, had been one of the most beautiful in the district. But now the flowerbeds were filled with the woody remains of last year's vegetables. Dead stalks of runner beans climbed the side wall of the outside toilet, behind which two chickens clucked in a homemade run, and most of the lawn had been given over to potatoes and turnips.

The only daughter of Peter Stokes, the warden, was a lovely woman—even dressed in a plain blue siren suit, her beauty was not diminished. Her eyes were as green as a cat's and sparkled in the sunlight, contrasting strongly with the red glints that danced and gleamed in her shoulder-length hair.

A whiny cry made her spin on her heel. She stepped back into the trench that her father had dug by the far wall and stooped through the low door of the Anderson bomb shelter.

Wrapped in blankets, up on one of the bunks, was a small child, and she picked him up in her arms to stop his tears.

"There, there," she said lovingly, "come on, Daniel, Mommy's here. Don't cry, angel. Did you think I'd gone and left you? Silly boy, I won't never leave you. Let's go out in the fresh air, shall we? See if Grandad's come back yet."

Peter Stokes was stripped to his T-shirt and suspenders and washing his face in the sink when his daughter entered the kitchen.

He was a tall, middle-aged man whose most striking feature was his shining bald head. In fact most of the locals joked that his ARP helmet had more hair on it. Set beneath a care-lined and bony forehead were a pair of steely blue eyes that were both piercing and gentle, situated on either side of a beaky nose he had inherited from his mother. Beneath this, as if to compensate for the deficiencies of his scalp, Mr. Stokes wore a gray mustache that was kept neatly trimmed at all times. "Mornin', Dad," Jean said as she laid her son into a great black tank of a carriage that dominated the small kitchen. "Heavy last night, weren't it? Much damage done?"

Before he replied, Peter wiped a towel over his bald head and screwed the corners into his ears.

"A tidy bit," he answered. "Five dead two streets away, an' I don't know what happened to Arnold Porter— didn't report back this morning."

"Fat Arnold prob'ly went home for his breakfast." Jean laughed, and the sound of her fluting voice rang into the hallway and up the stairs to where Ted was standing with his head pushed between the rods of the banister.

A dreamy, yearning expression haunted the bear's face as he listened to the snatches of conversation that drifted up to him.

"Nearly caught that Dorkins girl, too," Peter said, "only the tyke bit me."

"I'll put some iodine on it for you, Dad."

"No, it looks worse than it is. We got a guest stayin' with us now. A young lad—found him wanderin' around last night. I reckon he was bombed out. Can't remember a thing, poor kid. Thought I'd try an' find out who his folks are today. I . . . er, I've put him in Billy's room."

"You put him in there?" came the girl's astonished voice. "Well, there's a nice surprise."

"A shrine's no use to no one, is it? 'Sides, the poor lad was exhausted and sufferin' from shock."

"You're an honest-to-goodness saint, Dad. I reckon Bill'd be glad."

Peering through the banister, Ted stretched his neck out a little farther until he could glimpse the figure of the young woman in the kitchen. His glass eyes seemed aflame with a light all their own when his gaze fell on her.

"I better get off to the factory," she said, making for the hallway. "I don't want to be around here when Gran gets back and finds out she's got another mouth to feed."

Peter's weary chuckle floated up from the kitchen, and Ted swiftly withdrew his head from the banister as Jean strode into the hall and glanced upstairs. Scrambling over the landing with only seconds to spare, the bear shot nimbly into the bedroom once more, just as the woman came climbing up to her own room.

Leaning against the bedroom door, Ted puffed and panted, moaning woefully. "Fifty years I been wishin' fer this," he breathed in despair. "Fifty years of waitin' and hopin' I'd see that face one more time; she's twice as beautiful as I ever remembered. This is more torture than a soul can take. After all the lonely years of prayin', it sure is strange to learn that right here is the last place I wanna be."

Staring across at Neil's sleeping form, the bear rubbed his woolly chin and his ears drooped sadly. "This is a real mess I've dumped you in, kid," he whispered guiltily, "but it's too late to turn back now. I just gotta pull this stunt off!"

* * *

Later that morning, Neil was awakened by a pernicious dig in the back from the tips of two bony fingers.

"Stir yourself, boy!" barked a gruff female voice. "I haven't got all day to hang around while you dream. Get up. I'm warning you, I won't tell you again!"

Neil blinked the drowsiness from his eyes and stared up at the wizened creature hunched over the bed. At his side, Ted was also gazing at the old woman, and a look of disgust spread over his face.

Irene Stokes was an elderly, birdlike woman who squinted suspiciously through a pair of round, gold-rimmed spectacles. The lenses of her eyeglasses were very thick and magnified her roving, distrustful eyes to a startling degree, while casting generous pools of light over her shriveled features. Yet that was the only generous quality about her, and to have those ocular-enhanced points fix accusingly on you was a disconcerting and unpleasant experience. "Old Mother Stokes," or "Ma Stokes" as she was unpopularly known, enjoyed spreading such discomfort.

Now those exaggerated eyes were trained and focused spitefully on Neil, and the boy blinked under their baleful scrutiny as though they were harsh spotlights.

"Who are you?" he asked.

"You might well ask," rapped the reply as her long, beaky nose twitched to let Neil know she detested the very smell of him. "I'm only the one whose roof you're sleeping under, only the one who'll have to cook and wash for you as long as you're here."

Ted eyed her warily. She was dressed from head to toe in black. Sitting squarely upon her wiry hair was a voluminous hat of the same shade. From this, two long feathers pranced and jiggled as she huffed and drew herself up to her full height, which, as she was rather small, wasn't very much.

The bear disliked her intensely. The old woman's voice, which was cracked and squeaky, was filled with enmity. He shuddered involuntarily, hoping that she wouldn't notice.

Thankfully, her attention was entirely taken up with Neil.

"I—I thought this was the warden's house," he mumbled, also taken aback by the old woman's venom.

"That's my son you're talking about," she rattled back, "though most times I despair of it! I warn you, boy, this is my house, not his, so you'd better be on your best behavior. I'm old enough to speak my mind and I don't like strangers under this roof. It was bad enough Peter bringing Jean back when the baby was born. At least she's family. Though I can't stand her. . . . No, he's really gone and done it this time."

Her pinched features brimming with malice, she peered long and hard at him then moistened her lips. "Who are you?" she commanded bitterly. "Out with it, you can't pull the wool over my eyes. You can say what you like to Peter, he's always been too soft. Well, I'm not."

"My name's Neil."

"He told me that much!" she spat, carefully prodding the boy as if to check how much meat there was on him. "Well, I've got my eye on you, so watch out! Now, get ready. Shopping doesn't get itself, you know, and I won't leave you here in the house. You look as though thievery comes natural. I ain't leavin' no robber in my house to steal my valuables."

Neil realized it was useless to protest to this flinty old crone, but he looked down at his pajamas and said, "I haven't got any clothes."

Mrs. Stokes made a peculiar low bleating sound then turned to the chest of drawers, where some garments had been placed on top of the magazines.

"You can borrow these for the time being," she grudgingly consented, "though if you dare get them dirty, or should you so much as fray the cuffs, it'll be the worse for you."

Mumbling unpleasantly to herself, she handed over a large white shirt and a pair of gray shorts.

"That shirt's Peter's second best," she told him, "and the shorts belonged to his son, William."

"I'll be sure to thank them."

"Can't thank Billy," Mrs. Stokes snorted with a matter-of-fact shrug of her narrow shoulders. "He joined up and was killed in North Africa four months back. There's the telegram down there."

"I'm sorry."

"Billy was as stupid as his father," came the cold reply. "Hurry up and get dressed, boy. I heard there might be some sausages going today, and if I don't get in the line, well, you'll be sorry."

When Neil was dressed he was far from comfortable. The shirt was stiff and full of starch, and the fabric that the shorts were made of was coarse and scratched his legs. He tried not to dwell on the macabre fact that he had slept in a dead person's bed and was now wearing his cast-off clothes. It was just another grisly detail on the growing list of horrible events that had happened to him since he and his family had first entered the Wyrd Museum. But the one thing Neil was certain of was that the list would undoubtedly be even longer by the time he saw Josh again, and he wished he was back home with him and their father.

As neither shoes nor socks had been offered to him, the boy pulled on his slippers once more, and Mrs. Stokes opened the door for him to go down the stairs before her.

"Wait a minute!" Neil cried, running back into the room. "I can't go without Ted."

"You put that back, you little burglar!" she squawked when he returned clutching the bear. "Rob from babies, would you? I told Peter this would happen. Robbed blind, that's what we'll be."

"I haven't robbed anything," Neil shouted. "This is mine!"

Mrs. Stokes leered down at the bear in his hands and pinched it between her twiglike fingers.

"Umm," she relented. "Daniel's got a teddy like this, only his is much nicer," she hissed, nearly skipping down the stairs and trotting over to the baby carriage that was already in the hallway. She peeked in at the two-year-old to make sure that he really did have his own teddy bear.

"You better keep quiet today, too!" she told the baby, jabbing a warning finger at him before placing a folding stool across the top of the carriage, along with a large umbrella.

Before joining her, Neil looked down at Ted. The bear was rubbing his fur where she had pinched him.

"Do we have to stay here?" Neil asked. "Why can't we just hide until Josh appears?"

"We're stayin' put," the bear growled softly. "It's meant to be!"

"What are you doing up there?" Mrs. Stokes squealed up at Neil. "You keep your thieving hands off, do you hear?"

"Off what?" Neil cried, trailing down the stairs.

"Off everything!" she snapped.

The old woman finished buttoning herself into a fur-collared black coat that reached down to her ankles and took a key from the pocket as she opened the front door.

"Bring the carriage out here," she ordered.

Neil obeyed, and she immediately locked the door behind him before wrenching the handle of the carriage from his hands.

"Don't you think you can push my grandson," she warned him. "You might run off and sell him to the Nazis."

Delving into her pockets a second time she brought out a quantity of small pamphlets and flicked them through her fingers. "That's mine, Peter's, and Jean's. You 'aven't got no ration books, I suppose. Didn't think about findin' them when your house was blowed up?"

"Er . . . no."

"Useless!" she exclaimed in disgust. "Well, if that butcher doesn't have no sausages left, he'll rue this day. Come on!"

And so they set off. Down Barker's Row they went—

and a bizarre spectacle they made. Mrs. Stokes seemed to waddle relentlessly along like a clockwork toy, and the seemingly immovable bulk of her thick overcoat added greatly to the illusion. With her face set and stern and her hands glued to the handle of the baby carriage, her only movement was the trundling rotation of her feet as they flicked in and out beneath the hem of her coat.

Behind her came Neil, with Ted under one arm. His hands were lost in the long sleeves of the white shirt, the tail of which had worked free of the shorts and was now flapping after him as the soles of his slippers made slapping noises on the pavement.

Bouncing the carriage over the cobbles, Mrs. Stokes turned toward the main street, pushing the tanklike vehicle down a narrow lane, where a group of three boys sat slouched on a low wall. They must have been a couple of years younger than Neil, but they possessed old and hardened faces, as if their childhood had been stolen from them because they had seen and experienced too much.

One of them had lit the stub of a cigarette, and the precious item was dutifully passed around the trio for everyone to have a puff on it. When they heard the rattle of the carriage wheels, they turned their dirty faces toward the comical sight and cupped their hands over their mouths as they began to jeer.

"Look at him!" one of them bawled. "What does he think he is? Ah, the big baby's got a teddy."

"You got a diaper on under there?" shouted a second.

The third boy said nothing—he was taking full advantage of the cigarette before the others realized.

Mrs. Stokes turned her shrewish gaze full on them, and the boys were silenced immediately.

"I know who you are, Reginald Gimble—you, too, Johnny and Dennis Fletcher. I know your mothers and what they are. I know where your father spends his nights and who he spends his money on. Your father ain't no better, always out of work and too much of a coward to join the fighting. He ought to be ashamed, boozing what little he does get and falling behind with the rent man. I know all about it.

"Don't you dare go shoutin' at decent folk. I'll be havin' words with your scummy mothers about this, you see if I don't! Why aren't you at school, this ain't no holiday! You'll all end up the same as your dads, you mark my words. Bad ends, that's what you'll come to. So keep your tongues quiet and stop botherin' honest bodies in the street. I never heard such disgraceful, filthy talk. I'd take a bar o' soap to the mouth of each one of you if it weren't rationed!"

Stung by her lashing, viperish tongue, the boys jumped off the wall and shuffled away, mumbling unhappily.

Mrs. Stokes glowered after them. "Should've been evacuated," she complained, "leastways then they might never have come back. They might've been eaten by wild animals or trampled to death by cows. Hope the next bombing finds their houses."

Neil was too astonished by her outburst to say anything. The woman was horrendous and the exact opposite of her kind son.

Taking hold of the carriage once more, she continued on her way to the butcher shop.

At that moment a slim woman in her late fifties—and dressed rather more smartly than anyone Neil had yet seen—appeared at the end of an alleyway. She sauntered airily toward them with a superior smirk on her face.

Her face was rather spoon-shaped and her delicate features were lightly dusted with makeup. A dainty felt hat nestled on top of her meticulously styled hair, and her spotless clothes looked as though she had just bought them that morning. Under one arm she carried a plump dachshund, and in her other hand she held a parcel of newspaper that contained her purchase from the butcher.

When Mrs. Stokes saw her, the old woman bristled with resentment and a scowl that was fiercer than normal settled over her face.

"Hello, Irene," the stranger said in an irritating, nasal voice. "How are we this morning? Down in the Underground again last night, were we?"

"What if I was?" Mrs. Stokes replied through tight lips.

The other woman gave a thin and haughty laugh. "I really don't know how you can bear it," she droned. "All those sweaty people cooped up down there."

"I like their company," came the pointed and arch response.

"Well, I couldn't manage it, and poor Tommy would hate it," she added, giving the dachshund's head a kiss. "Are you off to get something nice for your son's dinner? There wasn't much left in the butcher's, I'm afraid, just some scraps of mutton and bacon."

"I heard he was goin' to have some sausages in."

"Ugh, there were. But oh, I wouldn't have given them to Tommy. You know how sensitive he is. A morsel of anything untoward and he's off his food for days. Heaven knows who'd want those nasty-looking articles. I'm surprised at Mr. Rogers, he's usually so particular in his standards. Still, I expect there are some around here who won't object, and we mustn't waste anything, must we? I was lucky enough to get a lovely couple of chops, one for Tommy and the other for Kathleen. Yes, you'll like that, won't you, laddy?"

Mrs. Stokes's face became terrible to look at; before her, the irritating woman fluttered her eyelids for a moment at Neil, perplexed as to his identity, then she decided it was wiser to leave.

"I'd love to chat," she blithely lied, "but I must return to my sewing machine. You'll be at our next meeting, I trust? I'll make a seamstress of you yet. You mustn't give up on your first few attempts, you know. I've been working on something rather spectacular. I can't wait to unveil it to the rest of the ladies."

Mrs. Stokes would have liked to bite both her and the dog, but she nodded woodenly and waited until the younger woman had gone out of earshot.

"Who was that?" Neil ventured warily, for it looked as though Mrs. Stokes would explode at any moment.

"That's Doris Meacham!" she festered. "Lives at number thirty. Thinks she's so much better than anyone else. What I'd give to bring her down a peg or three. I hope her Krautish dog gets gassed or worse. Her and her Make-do-and-Mend classes. Oh, she loves telling us how clever she is and showin' off the latest bit of rubbish she's made and all the things she's managed to salvage for the war effort. A bin for this, a bin for that! She's nothing but an empty-headed, barren-bellied woman with too much time on her hands. One of these days I'll learn her. She'll get hers, and I hope I'm there to enjoy it."

Her cracked voice faltered as a cruel and wicked idea hatched in her spiteful, jealous mind, and she chuckled callously as the plan took malignant shape in her thoughts.

"Oh, she wouldn't like that now, would she?" Mrs. Stokes sniggered, tottering back to have a conspiratorial word with the three boys she had just chastised.

Unexpectedly leaving Neil to tend to little Daniel, she spoke in a hushed whisper to the boys, nodding her head continually so that the feathers in her hat bounced a wild jig above her head.

Neil was confused by the change that had come over her. "What's the old witch up to now?" he muttered.

To his surprise, Ted answered him. "You better watch out for her," the bear hissed. "She's about as friendly as a rattlesnake, only without the personality. A hunk o' pure granite grinds where her heart oughta be. When she heard her grandson was dead, she never shed one lousy tear."

"How do you know that?"

"I seen it all before," he said mysteriously, keeping an eye trained on Mrs. Stokes, who was already trundling back to them. "You better get plenty of rest this afternoon, kid. Tonight you an' me have gotta be someplace. This whole business is about to begin."

CHAPTER 10

FRANK AND ANGELO

Plodding wearily through the factory gates, Jean Evans dragged the head scarf from her hair and thrust it into the pocket of her overalls. It was already growing dark. Another shift in the munitions factory was complete, and she had had enough. Her pretty face was streaked with oil, and all she desired at that precise moment was to soak in a bath that was overflowing with hot water and foaming with bubbles. But all they had at home was a small tin bath, and even its meager pleasures could not be enjoyed in private, for it had to be filled in the kitchen and her grandmother was continually traipsing in and out to assert that it was still her house.

Around her a crowd of similarly tired women doggedly made their way homeward—women who before the war had never seen the inside of a factory, much less worked in one. Now they could weld, rivet, strip engines, and operate heavy machinery as well as any man. Some had already begun to wonder if they could ever settle back into domestic roles once the war was over and they had to surrender their jobs.

Pushing through a group who had lingered by the gates for a smoke before returning home, an eager, fresh-faced girl with dark, chestnut-colored hair and ice-blue eyes hurriedly made her way forward.

"Jean," she called, waving her hand in the air, "wait for me."

Kathleen Hewett was a sprightly younger woman whose boundless energy at work disgruntled her fellow employees. Since her arrival in the district nearly a year earlier, she had come to be regarded as a flighty girl, always ready to enjoy herself despite the scorn she received from certain quarters. She took immense delight in the company of the opposite sex, and there was usually at least one member of the armed forces with his arm linked through hers.

For most of the war, Kath, as the troops called her, had apparently moved from one house to another, having been bombed out so many times that she had lost count. An orphan, she was something of an enigma and rarely mentioned her origins. At the moment, she was living with the snobbish Mrs. Meacham, and it gave Jean's grandmother great joy to see her reviled neighbor saddled with such a frivolous creature.

"Ooh, you look like a wet Saturday," the girl giggled as she drew level with Jean. "I couldn't let any fella see me with a face like that, I'd frighten him off. I'm gonna go down to the pictures tonight, do you wanna come, too? *The Man in Gray*'s showin' at the Gaumont. Ooh, I adore that James Mason. Doesn't his voice make you go all pimply?"

"Fellers are the last thing on my mind," Jean assured her.

"No wonder you look like that, then." Kath laughed.

"Do you mind? I am married."

"No you're not," Kath said bluntly. "Your Sandy's bought it and you know it."

Jean glared at her. "He's listed as missing!" she said forcefully.

"Same difference. One of these days you'll be gettin' a telegram like your dad did about your brother. Least then you'll be able to mourn him proper, 'stead of moping about the way you do. It's a shame your Sandy never even saw little Daniel."

"I don't believe you sometimes, Kathleen Hewett," Jean blurted as tears sprang to her eyes. "For someone I've only known four months, you go too far!"

"What've I said now, Jean?" the other girl cried in astonishment.

* * *

Neil hurried up the dark flight of steps leading to the ticket area of the Bethnal Green Underground station, until he burst into the night and took great lungfuls of the sweet, fresh air.

Sitting on his shoulder, Ted wiped his leather nose with his paw and nodded vigorously. "The smell of the great unwashed is something ya gotta experience to unnerstand," he choked. "Boy, I wish my eyes could water!"

They had just escaped from the scrutiny of Mrs. Stokes. At her son's insistence, the old woman had reluctantly taken them to the shelter she frequented every night, after giving Neil a meager and distasteful meal consisting of half a gristle-filled sausage and a dollop of sloppy mashed potato.

The platform of the Underground was packed with people and had a noxious odor borne of primitive toilet facilities and the unquenchable pungency of countless stinking feet. With his hand over his mouth, it had not been difficult for Neil to lose himself in the crowd and evade the old harpy's sight.

Now he stood in the gloom of the blackout, breathing deeply in an effort to dispel the memory of the awful smell.

"I can't stand this," Neil complained. "Why do we have to stay with that family? That old bag has made my life a misery all day. I hate her! Can't we just hide until Josh turns up?"

"Not for four whole days, kid," Ted told him. "Anyway, they're not all bad. Mr. Stokes is pretty peachy, and as for his daughter!" The bear gave a soft wolf whistle.

Neil sighed. "I suppose they're all right," he confessed. "Jean was nice to me. She even gave me some of her dinner when the old witch wasn't looking."

Ted grinned. "Glad you approve, but we better take off now. There's someone I gotta see tonight, and I wouldn't miss it fer the world."

Neil glanced around them and shivered. It was a cold night, but there was something more to it than that and his nerves were all on edge.

The bear felt the boy's shudders and he viewed the darkness curiously. "There's a bad feeling tonight," he murmured. "Dunno what it is. Somethin' downright nasty in the atmosphere an' I ain't talkin' about dirty socks. I don't like it. Sooner we take off the better. Start walkin' thataways, kid. Right now is when it all starts."

Down a pitch-dark road Neil made his way, with Ted urging him on and tapping his shoulder like a jockey on a horse. Presently, they came to the main street, which Neil recognized as the place Mrs. Stokes had taken him to that afternoon, to stand for hours on end in the lines outside shops as she waded in, brandishing her ration books like weapons.

"Whoa!" Ted hissed, reining the boy to a standstill by pulling on his ear. "Just wait a minute, kid. Man, I hope we're on time."

Neil stared up at a great, dark shape outlined against the black sky, taller than the surrounding shops. "What's that?" he asked.

"Don't you have movie theaters in your time?" Ted replied. "Hold on, look—just there!"

The foyer of the Gaumont Picture Palace was dark to accommodate the blackout rules, but inside it thrilled and flickered with silvery life and high adventure.

Striding determinedly from the double doors came the figure of a woman, who hastened past the shuttered shop fronts, heading in the direction of Barker's Row.

"Jean!" a voice called out behind her. "Hold on!"

Out of the cinema came Kathleen Hewett, her high heels clattering awkwardly over the pavement as she endeavored to catch up with her neighbor.

"'Ere," she cried, pressing some coins into Jean's hand, "compliments of the manager, with sincerest apologies. I told him that we had to leave early on account of an old man sitting behind us burping all night. Well, I weren't goin' to pay for a flick I never saw."

"You should have stayed," Jean told her. "I'm just not in the mood for watching no film. I only came out tonight to spite Gran. I should never have left Daniel with her. I couldn't sit there all evening."

"He'll be all right. The old misery guts ain't so bad as she'd let anything happen to him. I'll walk back with you, but hang on, these heels are murder."

As the two women made their way through the deep darkness, Neil turned his head to look at Ted.

"What are we spying on Jean for?" he asked. "We knew she was coming here. She said so at the dinner table."

The bear merely prodded his shoulder and pointed behind them.

Neil peered into the darkness, where he saw two figures emerging.

"This is swell, Frank! Real swell! We're here in London—the only interestin' place in this blasted hick country—and you go and get us lost! I told you we shoulda got a cab. But no, who hada get a limey bus?"

"Hey, I'm sorry, but I p-promised my mom I was g-gonna ride one o' them double-decker jalopies. I can't wait to write home an' t-tell her, though I'll leave out the shutters on the windows. Beats me how the folks around here see where they're g-goin'."

"Frank, Frank, you do not write to your mother on a weekend furlough—it's un-American! Boy, I really gotta take your education in hand. You, Private, are sadly lacking in the ways of this oh-so-wicked world."

"Is London wicked? The little I saw looked pretty g-good to me."

"I ain't showed you some o' the joints I know. I tell you, pal, there are places in this town that are really jumpin'."

"Aw I d-dunno, Voo. I only been here three weeks an' I wanna see more than the inside of some bar. D-do you know how much history there is here?"

"History? Who wants to be surrounded by a museum? This is life, kid, you gotta get out there and live it."

From the gloom the two Americans came, and Neil eyed them curiously while Ted seemed lost in a half-forgotten memory and a sorrowful expression stole over his face.

The one called Frank was tall and gawky, reminding Neil of his father. He was young and awkward in his movements, like a freshly hatched baby ostrich, but his voice and manner were painfully sincere and he apologized to his buddy for having brought him here and wasting his time.

"G-gee, I'm awful sorry," his soft, buttery voice stuttered. "You shoulda g-gone with the rest of the guys. I ain't cut out for no high life."

"You will be by the end of this furlough, farm boy. That's a Signorelli promise."

Frank's companion was a foot shorter than he was. He had a pleasant, handsome face, Latin features, and jet-black hair that was swept back over his head, glistening with tonic. Eyes like dark diamonds flashed and glittered with infuriating impudence whenever he saw a pretty face, and his brash, incorrigible speech had already won him many a heart.

He was extremely liberal with his aftershave and doused himself in it all too frequently. Wherever he went, an overpowering, fragrant odor drifted after him, much to the distaste of the conductor of the bus they had recently been riding.

"Hey," he cried to his buddy. "You gotta see this new trick—it's a doozy."

Delving into the sheepskin-lined flying jacket that swamped him, he brought out a well-thumbed deck of cards. He fanned them before Frank's nose, jumping around him like a boisterous puppy while his unceasing banter rattled along.

"Choose one!" he yapped eagerly. "Any at all, go on. This'll slay ya—I swear."

"But I can't even see the d-danged cards!" the other exclaimed.

The men were drawing near to Neil now, but as yet, neither of them had seen him.

Ted's glass eyes gleamed in the gloom, and the ghost of a smile twitched the corners of his mouth. Then his furry body shuddered and he whispered quickly into Neil's ear.

"Move into that doorway. I don't want them guys to spot us."

Without arguing, Neil obeyed, and presently the Americans passed them by.

"We gotta find a cab an' snappy," the shorter one cried. "I might as well be back at base as here. Least there I know where to find some action. Do you think this is where all the undertakers live? Frank, old buddy, I figure we've stopped off at Morgueville. I bet the stiffs have more of a riot than the folks livin' here. I ain't even seen one measly pub. I wanna be back in Piccadilly. Did you see those dames hanging around outside Rainbow Corner?"

"I'm not certain they was all that n-nice," Frank drawled,

shaking his head thoughtfully. "I heard all 'bout g-girls like that. I'd rather go straight back to the Red C-Cross Club."

"You nuts? The night is young, and who wants to meet 'nice' girls anyway? I got a reputation to live up to. The guys are countin' on me—they're runnin' a book on Signorelli conquests this weekend. Hey, I been thinkin' 'bout growing one o' them teeny little mustaches like Errol Flynn or Gable. Do you figure the broads'll go for it big time?"

Frank gave a good-natured laugh, and his companion shrugged his shoulders.

"Ah," he said, "you're right. I oughta stick with the Valentino image. He had real class, same as me. 'Sides, if I change now it might break the charm."

In the shadows of the shop doorway, Ted peered out at the retreating backs of the airmen.

"Would you just look at that no-hoper!" the bear said scornfully. "What a jerk! The boob don't realize what a geek he is. Does he really think he looks like Rudolph Valentino? He ain't as pretty as he likes to think. Look at him in that flying jacket—it's way too big. A pint-sized Romeo is all he is. Geez, it's embarrassin'."

"You know them?" Neil muttered.

"I did once, kid," he replied darkly, "but that was a lifetime ago, and a lotta things've changed since then. You mind if we follow them a little ways more? I promise this won't take long."

"I'm in no rush to go back to old lemon face," Neil answered glumly. So, keeping well out of sight, he set off up the main street.

* * *

Halfway toward home, Jean Evans was still angry at herself for letting her grandmother goad her into leaving Daniel that evening.

"I tell you, Kath," she rumbled, "one of these days I'll walk out and won't never come back. That woman gets right up my nose."

Tottering behind, finding it difficult to keep up with Jean's bracing pace in her high-heeled shoes, Kath was in full agreement.

"Can't you do something really horrible to her?" she asked mischievously, following her friend around a corner and off the main road. "Like putting sawdust in her porridge or mouse droppings in her tea?"

"Wouldn't make any difference, she'd wolf it down anyway."

"What about sprinkling water in her bed? She might get pneumonia and kick the bucket."

"No, she never sleeps in that . . ." Jean halted in her tracks and slapped her forehead. "I must be going crazy!" she cried. "What am I doing heading for home? She'll be at the Underground by now!"

Whisking around, she barged past Kath and hastened back to the main street.

Teetering on her heels, her friend scurried after, shouting, "You'll never get to Daniel now. There'll be a big jam of scruffy louseheads in the way, an' I won't go down there—it smells awful! Jean—I got me best dress on!"

"No one's askin' you to come, Kath. Go back to Mrs. Meacham's and I'll—oohh! . . ."

Plowing heedlessly through the blackout, Jean had rounded the corner sharply and blindly collided with the Americans.

Frank threw his arms wide and regained his balance just in time, but his buddy let out a startled wail, fell off the sidewalk, and sprawled to the ground.

"Son of a—why don't you look where you're goin', feller?" he yelled, scrambling to his feet and brushing himself down. "You coulda made me rip my pants. I hope the creases ain't all crinkled up! I'm in a bad enough mood already. Why, I oughta knock you down and get even."

In the darkness, Jean strained her eyes to peer at the blustering airman. She was going to apologize, but the man's rudeness canceled all thought of that.

"You do and I'll punch you right back," she warned.

Hearing the female voice, the American's attitude changed immediately and he mellowed at once.

"Hey, baby," he said smoothly, trying to make out the woman's figure in the murk, "I need my head tested. What can I do to make up for what I said?"

"Don't bother," she told him. "No harm done."

The man reached out a hand to her but she shook it off. "Now I've gone and done it," he said in an injured voice. "You got the wrong impression of me."

"I doubt that."

"Anyone told you we're supposed to be allies, honey?"

"S'pose next you'll be telling me you're goin' to win the war for us. I'm not your honey, and if you don't mind, I've got to get somewhere."

"Wait up. Don't you even wanna know the name of the guy who fell at your feet?"

"No."

The man made an elaborate bow before her. "Lieutenant Angelo Signorelli from the mighty Eighth," he grandly announced. "And this is my buddy, Frank Jeffries. Don't stand there like a dummy, pal, say hello to the lady. He's a bit shy with the fair sex."

Frank shuffled uncomfortably. "Pleased to m-meet you, ma'am," he murmured.

With a clip-clop of her heels, Kath blundered up to them, having overheard most of what had been said and agog to meet the Americans.

"Jean," she said in a demure voice, unlike her natural one, "it's so dark tonight, I can't see my hand in front of my face. Oh, are you talking to someone? Who is it?"

Angelo introduced himself and Frank once more, and the girl instantly slipped her hand through the arm of the tall airman.

"I sure am glad we ran into you," Angelo said. "You must be heaven-sent. Would you believe we was lost?"

Jean pursed her lips. "I wouldn't believe anything you told me," she said dryly.

"Aw, honey, don't be like that. Is there one of your quaint British pubs near here? What say we go for a few beers and talk this over?"

"Not on your nelly," came the flat answer.

At this point Kath extricated herself from Frank's suddenly wooden arm and pulled Jean back around the corner. "Excuse me, gentlemen," she said through a fixed grin, "would you mind if me and my chum had a quick word?"

"Heck, no."

Kath thanked them, then turned frantically to Jean.

"You owe me, Jean Evans," she hissed. "I could've been swoonin' for James Mason right now if it weren't for you."

"I'm not going into no pub with them bigheaded Yanks!" Jean stated emphatically.

"Oh, please!" Kath begged. "Just this once. When was the last time a Yank showed his mug around here? I don't want to miss the chance of getting some nylons."

"But Daniel!"

"I told you, you won't get near him at this time. Go on, just for me. They sound so nice."

"They do not," Jean began, until she realized how excited her friend had become. Guiltily reflecting that she had already spoiled part of the evening, she grudgingly relented. "Oh, all right," she said, "but just one drink."

Around the corner, a similar discussion was taking place.

"I d-dunno about this, Voo," Frank murmured. "I'm just not cut out for sweet-talking the way you are. Heck, when that girl took my arm I plum froze up. I'd really like to catch a cab an' go back to the city."

"That's just what I was sayin' before," Angelo replied, "only you didn't take no notice. Now I want to stay."

"I'll just get laughed at. G-girls always laugh at me. I go all klutzy around 'em and my brain turns to mush."

"You're with your uncle Voodini now—Lady Luck's favorite soldier. What could go wrong? Anyway, I wanna see what this doll looks like. How else am I gonna describe her to the boys? Mind you, if these dames turn out to be a pair o' mooses, we make our excuses an' head back west, okay?"

"I wish I were someplace else."

"Think of it as your first lesson," Angelo assured him, "and relax, will ya? Hush up, here they come. Well, ladies, you decided?"

"Oh, yes," giggled Kath, "we'd love to join you brave

men for a drink, wouldn't we, Jean? There's The Ring o' Bells just up the road. I believe it's supposed to be quite nice."

"Lead the way, toots," Angelo declared, and with that they strolled deeper into the shadows.

Walking a little distance behind them, Neil saw a wedge of light suddenly slice through the coal-black street as the pub door was pushed open, then the darkness sprang tightly back.

From behind the closed door, he heard Kath's muffled voice squeal in rapture. "Oooh! He's got prettier eyes than I have!"

"Whoa, kid," Ted muttered sorrowfully in his ear. "I seen enough now. Yeah, that's the way it was, that's how it started."

"You're doing it again," Neil commented.

"Doin' what?"

"Not explaining yourself. What was the point of coming here to see four people go into a pub? It's hardly earth-shattering, is it?"

A grave and empty chuckle issued from the bear's stitched lips. "Do you wanna know the real reason I brought you here, kid?" he asked.

"Outside the pub?"

"To nineteen forty-three!"

Neil turned his head and looked at the black silhouette sitting on his shoulder. The bear appeared forlorn and weary. His furry shoulders were hunched as though a tremendous weight was pressing down on them, and his little chest heaved up and down as he battled to fight back the sobs in his throat.

"Tell me," Neil breathed.

Ted lifted a paw and pointed at the blacked-out windows of the bar.

"Those people in there," he said, his voice splintering with remorse, "they're why we're both here."

Staring hard at the dark entrance as if trying to see through the wooden door and glimpse the scene within, Ted groaned wretchedly.

"Right now they'll be checkin' each other out. Angelo'll be gawkin' at the warden's pretty daughter and she'll be lettin' him know she's off limits, while that other girl'll be chattin' up Frank and makin' the poor guy blush to his toes."

His voice faded into silence, and then, in a cold, grief-filled breath, he added, "In a matter of days, three of them will be stone dead."

"You mean I was dragged back here to help you save them?" he demanded.

Ted hung his head. "I been promised I can save them, kid," he said with a determined growl. "I got one chance an' I ain't gonna foul it up. That's why I'm here. You gonna help me or what?"

"You risked both Josh's and my life!" Neil muttered. "You never said a word what for, and now you tell me it's to save three total strangers!"

"Hey!" the bear fumed. "I ain't interested if you like it or not. You're gonna help me, or little Joshy won't last five minutes where he's headin'!"

"I don't believe you!" Neil cried incredulously.

"You'd better," Ted answered somberly, "'cuz the fate of your kid brother, and I do mean fate, is tied up with theirs."

CHAPTER 11

THE BROKEN SEAL

As the hours melted into the early morning, Edie Dorkins bounded over a jumble of pulverized brick and roof slates, clutching a small bundle close to her chest.

It had been a peaceful night. No German planes had appeared in the skies, and though she was sad that the beautiful lights were not dancing and plummeting from above, she had been extremely busy.

Scavenging like a ravenous wild dog, she had capered into the gardens of the hated houses that fringed the bomb site, rooted in their garbage cans, and scrabbled at the earth for the potatoes that had been planted there. Summoning her courage, she had forced herself to enter one or two kitchens and looted the cabinets, slurping the cold stew left on the stove and tearing great, jaw-breaking mouthfuls out of the bread left on the table.

Now, with her stuffed stomach burbling inside her and the splattered evidence smeared and staining her face, she hopped and hared back to her refuge.

The jagged bulk of her adopted domain was already in sight, a tall, skeletal blackness deeper than the surrounding night. Wiping her mouth on the sleeve of her ragged coat, Edie paused to admire this solitary fastness, her most marvelous bolt hole that contained all her treasures. Set amid the rolling wasteland, rising like a gothic enchanted castle centered in a country of the unquiet dead, it had become her new home and she loved it dearly. With a power as old as the foundations of the world now coursing through her veins, she was certain that no one could ever take this delicious abode from her.

Then a puzzled scowl stole over the child's face—the ruins looked different. The building in the center seemed smaller than usual, and Edie's frown turned into a look of shock and anger. The rafters that had pointed starkly upward from the demolished roof were no longer there.

At once, the girl's thoughts flew to her hoard of precious salvage, and letting the bundle of cabbage leaves and soil-covered potatoes fall into the dust, she flew swiftly toward her home, clinging to the incendiary bomb about her neck to stop it from swinging into her face.

In the gloom that gathered around the rear door, a throng of whispering figures called out as she hurried forward.

"Miss Edie," their spectral voices cried, "are you safe? Something terrible was here. A shadow shape is loose—it frightened us and fled into the dark. We are very afraid. Help us, stay with us. We always feel better when you're here. We don't like it on our own."

Not listening, the child tore past them and scurried in through the damaged back door. Mewling with sorrow, her phantom family flowed after her, wringing their hands in despair.

Through the hallway Edie plunged, but when she tried to open the parlor door it refused to budge.

"Don't you go in there, Miss," the plump shade of Arnold Porter warned. "The roof just caved in suddenly. Shook the whole house, it did."

Edie glared at the dead warden for daring to give her orders.

"I didn't mean to speak out of turn, Miss," he said. "I wouldn't do that. I was only voicing my concern, so to speak. The roof made such a noise, and you shoulda clapped eyes on the nasty whatsit that came tearing out of there."

Edie hesitated and glanced over her shoulder. Behind her, the hallway was crowded with wraiths. Horror was written on their ghastly faces, and a vague, startling notion fluttered at the back of her garbled mind.

Squealing violently, she suddenly flung all her fury against the blocked door, and with a lurch, the barrier gave way.

A cloud of dirt billowed into the girl's eyes and she spat the grit from her mouth as she waded into the room and stared miserably around.

The collapsed roof timbers had scored and scraped the blasted walls when they came crashing down, gouging a vicious vertical trail of destruction down the length of the house. Now they stabbed in through the shattered floorboards, dividing the demolished room with dangerous diagonal posts that creaked and groaned, threatening to wreak more havoc by falling like dominoes through the remains of the bay window.

A wreck of lath and plaster, torn from the already tattered ceiling, obliterated much of the room, and Edie darted recklessly beneath the treacherous beams to forage among the rubble.

Clawing away the debris, her fingers cut and bleeding, she frantically sorted through the choking dust, hurling aside razor-sharp slates and chunks of crumbling mortar. Brimming with tears, she found the bronze figurine, but the head had been sheared from the shoulders and one of the ivory hands was missing. Edie hugged the dancer desperately, then scrabbled for the rest of her treasure.

The wig was caked in filth, and sadly she put it aside as a pale gleam caught her almond-shaped eye. She fished out one of her bracelets and rammed the trinket into her pocket. Then she found a fragment of the gilded picture frame buried next to the bent face of the traveling clock, but her efforts became increasingly anguished and frenetic and she began to rip through the dirt, howling like a maniac.

Then, to her delight, she found it. Sobbing with fatigue and gladness, she pulled the small wooden box from the wreckage and clasped it lovingly.

But her joy was short-lived, for the prize of her collection was broken. The wax that had kept it sealed for thousands of generations had cracked away and the carved lid was nowhere to be found.

Edie thrust her hands into its black interior, but whatever the box once contained was no longer there. The Casket of Belial was empty.

Turning to face the frightened ghost of Arnold Porter, the girl was suddenly aware of the change that had occurred. The very atmosphere was charged with fear, and for the first time in many days she felt uneasy as the darkness seemed to press all around. Something horrible was loose—something ancient and evil had escaped into the unsuspecting night. No longer would her sanctuary be safe. Something final was approaching, and though she would protect both her kingdom and her spectral family, she sensed that soon everything would change.

* * *

"So why does Frank call you Voo?" Jean asked as Angelo walked her home. "Is that a technical term like MP?"

The man at her side laughed. "Nothin' like that, babe. It comes from me being such a kook. I got this real bad fault in my character."

"Just the one?"

"Did I tell you I know Clark Gable? I could get you his autograph."

Jean groaned and quickened her pace. The man's pathetic pick-up lines were beginning to grate on her nerves. Every negative trait she had ever heard about American men seemed to be true.

Sensing that he was beaten, Angelo scuffed his heels dejectedly and glanced around at Frank and Kath.

In the company of that lively girl, his buddy had started to come out of his shell. After the first ten minutes of awkward, stilted responses, he had really opened up to her, speaking of his life in Ohio and the family farm there. Now the pair of them were strolling dreamily along, arm in arm, talking easily.

The sight pricked Angelo's pride and threatened his renowned reputation, but he was generous enough to be pleased for his buddy.

When they reached Barker's Row, Frank saw Kath to her door and Angelo's discretion forced him to look elsewhere.

Jean was already opening the gate to number twenty-three when he caught up with her.

"If you're about to try any more lines on me, you'll be wasting your breath," she advised.

"A guy can only take so much cold shoulder," he replied. "I'm not dumb, I know when I'm licked. Say, can we haul up a flag of truce here? I was angling up the wrong tree, and I'm sorry."

"You don't really know Clark Gable, do you?"

"Nope."

"Good night, cowboy."

"Yep," he muttered when she closed the front door behind her, "another red-letter day for Signorelli. I really struck out that time."

Reaching into the pocket of his flying jacket, he took out a knitted toy dog with large glass eyes and kissed it.

"Where were you when I needed you, Tex?" he mumbled. "Never mind, you got all day tomorrow to make up for it."

Returning the toy to his pocket, he sauntered over toward Mrs. Meacham's house.

Standing on the porch, Frank held Kath gently in his arms, having just arranged to meet her the following evening.

The grin that divided Frank's face shone white in the blackout, and he looked around to find Angelo.

"Aw," he said, "Voo d-don't look happy at all. I think he liked your friend Jean more than he realized."

"Well, he was wasting his time there."

"It'd b-be swell if you could persuade her to come along tomorrow. I hate to see him so miserable. Say you'll try, Kath."

"Okay, but I'm not promising nothing."

The couple kissed once more. Feeling as buoyant as a cloud, Frank ambled down the street after his buddy, while the high-pitched yapping of Mrs. Meacham's dachshund greeted Kath as she let herself in.

So wrapped up were they in their separate thoughts, none of them noticed how cold and dark the night had become. Within the dense blackout, an ancient horror was prowling, and already the first chill tendrils of its sinister power were threading through the gloom.

* * *

The next morning dawned bright and surprisingly warm for so early in the year. A straggling line of bleary-eyed people slowly poured out of the Bethnal Green shelter, squinting under the white glare of the sky as they wound their way home and to work.

In one of the streets that ran off Barker's Row, Reginald Gimble and the Fletcher brothers—Johnny and Dennis—were giggling and snorting raucously.

"Howzat, yer bleedin' Nazi!" Reg crowed, releasing the elastic of his catapult.

Whizzing through the air, a sharp stone zinged into the derelict garden of a burned-out house.

"Missed it!" Dennis squawked, stooping to pick up a larger rock and hurling it with all his might. "Good riddance to the German dog!" he yelled.

"If Hitler were here now," Johnny fiercely chirped,

"I'd do this!" and he threw a charred plank into the garden, his face twisted with malicious glee.

"Yeah!" shrieked Dennis madly. "Let's get Adolf!"

Chanting bloody slogans and war cries, the three boys threw a hail of stones and bricks at their target. Shaking with hatred and sweating ferociously, they seemed possessed by some feverish, evil deity. Their harsh calls echoed through the empty streets and out over the desolation of the great graveyard of the bomb site.

Abruptly, Reg gave the others a warning shove and pointed to the end of the road. All three dropped whatever was in their hands and ran in different directions, laughing shrilly under the diabolic influence that afflicted them.

Sniffling into the back of her hand, Mrs. Meacham came tripping into the road. Immeasurable concern was ingrained on her face, and her bottom lip quivered piteously. The normally well-dressed and superior neighbor of the Stokes family usually looked impeccable in public and never so much as answered the door if she still had curlers in her hair. But today, Doris Meacham had blundered from her front gate still in her slippers and wearing her housecoat.

In a whimpering, fragile voice, she called aloud, craning her spoon-shaped head over garden walls and hedges.

"Tommy!" she whined. "Here, darling, where are you? Mommy's here—Tommy!"

Clutching a gatepost for support, she stared wildly around. Her little dog had never roamed off on his own before, and she couldn't begin to think how he could have escaped from her back garden.

"Oh, where are you?" she snivelled. "What did

Mommy do to make you run away? I'm sorry, dear!"

Stumbling onward, she glanced left and right, despair rising in her palpitating bosom.

And then she saw it.

A grotesque gargle constricted her throat, and for Doris Meacham the bright sunshine perished.

Lying in the weed-choked garden was the limp body of her beloved pet and companion. The devoted friend in times of empty dismay, gentle comforter and silent champion of the past seven years, was lying in a pathetic, broken heap on the bare ground.

The dachshund's head was battered and grazed from countless cruel blows. His silky tan-and-black fur was now matted with blood, and both back legs had been crushed beneath a slab of stone that Dennis had dashed against him.

But Tommy was not quite dead. A heartwrenching whimper squealed from his mouth as the tongue he had bitten in his terror dabbed and licked his scarlet gums that were now bereft of teeth.

Doris Meacham balked in anguish and dropped to her knees before him.

Shivering with agony, the dachshund gazed mournfully up at her with his remaining eye and gave a fretful bleat.

"No-o-o!" the woman howled, gingerly reaching out to calm him.

The moment she touched the dog's fur, he let out a hideous scream and twitched uncontrollably.

Doris fell back, but her tears did not blind her to the pink froth that foamed from the dachshund's mouth. The dog's tormented suffering was awful to witness, but she could do nothing to end it.

Like one demented, she staggered from the derelict garden, screaming until her lungs ached, her housecoat smeared with Tommy's blood.

Out of the surrounding houses the neighbors hurried to see what was the matter.

"Help him!" Doris shrieked. "Help Tommy! Oh dear! Please—someone put him out of . . ."

From the direction of Barker's Row a young woman came running.

"Mrs. Meacham!" Kathleen Hewett cried. "What is it? What are you doing out here?"

She halted when she saw the red streaks across her landlady's front and looked questioningly around at the concerned neighbors.

"What happened?" she asked them.

"I don't know," one of them answered. "I think she found somethin' in there."

Mrs. Meacham nodded but was too distraught to speak.

Warily, Kath stepped into the garden, covering her mouth when she saw the mutilated dog twitching and whimpering on the ground.

"H-h-help him!" Doris finally blurted through her choking sobs.

By now the neighbors had flocked behind Kath and uttered loud tuts of sympathy.

"Only one thing you can do for the poor love," one of them told the girl. "I'll go an' get my gun."

At Kath's feet Tommy flinched, and his streaming, bewildered eye stared imploringly up at her.

"No," she said quickly, "I'll do it."

Grimly she picked up a large chunk of cement and,

looking directly into the dog's trusting face, raised it high over her head.

Doris Meacham's scream drowned out any other sound, and she fled from the scene with her hands over her face.

In Barker's Row, Neil and Mrs. Stokes were just returning from the Underground when they saw the distressed woman gallop around the corner and go wailing into her house.

A sly, secretive smile crept over Ma Stokes's callous face, delighted that her little suggestions had been acted upon but as yet unaware of the drastic and extreme lengths Reg and the Fletcher boys had been driven to.

"Make do and mend that!" she spat malignantly.

* * *

Neil spent the rest of the day outside, and as soon as he left the house, Mrs. Stokes lumbered upstairs and snatched a surprised Ted off the bed.

Down to the front room she tramped, and threw the bear at little Daniel with the words, "'Ere, play with that one for a change, and make sure you're rough with it. That's all we'll be getting out of that scrounging little devil."

To Ted's dismay, he endured a whole day of mauling and chewing from the two-year-old, who dribbled on him and pummeled his belly until he was squished out of shape. Yet there was nothing the bear could do to escape, for not once did Ma Stokes leave the room. She was engrossed in cutting up an old curtain and cackling contentedly to herself.

"Well," she sniggered to herself, "that's the last we've

seen of that uppity Meacham—at the classes, at any rate. Bossin' folk around, thinkin' she's better at everything. 'Don't feed the squander bug, my dear'—hah! That mangy cur got all it deserved, and good riddance, I says. Least it won't be yap, yap, yappin' at all hours—ugly, deformed mutt."

* * *

After wandering around for a little while, Neil found that his footsteps were leading him to the park, and wrapped in a cloud of despondency, he strolled inside.

"You're that mystery lad, aren't you?" called a voice directly behind him.

Neil turned. Sitting on a bicycle, with one foot on the ground and the other poised on a pedal, was a round-faced and eager-looking teenager. His mousy hair was shaved close to his head, and a square of gauze and cotton was fixed to his temple with a wide bandage.

"My dad told me about you," the boy rattled on. "He said you don't know who you are. I read about this man who had the back of his head blowed of by some shrapnel. He could only make noises like a startled chicken and ate Spam straight from the can for five years, until he was bashed on the head by a cricket ball. He was right as rain then, well, for about half a day, 'cuz he dropped dead soon after. Do you collect shrapnel? I got a lovely collection. Found some beauties yesterday after the raid."

"Hang on," Neil said. "Who are you?"

"Michael, but I get called Mickey. My dad's Joe Harmon, the baker. He does ARP with Mr. Stokes. Is it true then, have you lost your memory or are you pulling a fast one? I wouldn't tell if you were, I'm only askin' 'cuz I like to know what's goin' on, not to tell no one else. I know lots of things. I know how much water the landlord of the pub puts in his beer. 'Ere, don't you tell that I said that. Mind you, no one'd believe you anyway, if you are a genuine head case."

Neil looked quickly at the talkative lad's forehead and wondered if he had suffered a blow to the brain like the man who ate Spam.

Mickey saw what he was looking at and patted it cautiously. "Not fallin' off, is it? Good. I got this firewatchin' the other night—got too close to an incendiary. It only frazzled my hair and scorched my skin a bit, but my mom's makin' me wear this. Do you think I should say it's a war wound? I got it on active duty so to speak, so it's the same thing. I'll be able to join up in two months, anyway. I like firewatchin'. I got a whole street to look after, and when Albert Fletcher can't manage, I ride around an' keep an eye on yours, too."

"Oh," was all Neil could find to say, flabbergasted by the adolescent's constant jabbering.

"I know what your name is," Mickey babbled, "my dad told me. If you really can't remember anything, apart from your name, of course, what does it feel like? Is it like havin' a piece of bread with no jam on it but you know there's jam in the house somewhere only you can't lay your hands on it?"

"Er . . . no," Neil chuckled, amused by Mickey's idiotic chatter and trying to keep up with his lightning flashes of thought. "None of those—more like a bun without a hot dog in it, and no relish neither."

"I've never had a hot dog. You going anywhere special?"

"What, now? Not really, why?"

"I'm just a bit bored, that's all. Mom said I shouldn't do the deliveries today 'cuz of my head, but there's nothing else to do. There's no one my age left around here."

"You can't even watch TV," added Neil.

Mickey's eyes blazed excitedly and he pushed the bicycle forward to draw alongside his new friend.

"Did you have a television set then? You must've been rich. I'd love to see what one's like, but they stopped transmitting when the war started. Is it like having the Gaumont in your own living room? Wow, unbelievable. Hey, you just remembered something, didn't you! Is there anything else? What was the house like—were it a big 'un?"

Neil hastily shook his head. "No," he said, "that's all there is."

"It's a good sign though, ain't it?" Mickey cried. "Maybe it'll all fall into place and you'll wake up one day and know exactly who you are!"

"Can't wait. Feel like a walk? I'd probably get lost on my own, being such a head case."

"'Course!" the other replied with gusto. "Did you see what happened before with that dog? Weren't it 'orrible? Them Fletcher lads are downright nasty. Albert's not so bad but his brothers stink. My dad says they did that and worse in Germany. He's glad he got out when he did. I ain't never seen them Fletchers do anything so completely awful before though. Dunno what got into them."

"Your father's German?"

"Yes, but he hates the Nazis and he'd been here five years before I was born. He thought our government was gonna intern him when it all started, but my mom's English so it were all right. We was all worried at the time though, an' my dad said it was getting like Germany, although don't tell anyone I said that, either. I don't know what he meant by it actually, but he's worried about the family he's still got over there. I can't wait to get drafted and fight the Nazis. I was real envious when Billy Stokes went—until he died, o' course."

"What else do you know about the people around here?"

And so, talking at a rapid rate, Mickey regaled him with one doubtful story after another, and together they passed out of the park, dawdling through the streets beyond.

When nearly an hour had gone by, the lad on the bicycle was still nattering merrily.

"You seen that Dorkins girl yet?" he asked. "Golly, but she's a funny 'un. That's why the Fletchers and Reg Gimble hang around the streets now. Those kids're too scared to go into the bomb sites like they used to—not that they'd admit it."

"Why, what's so frightening about her? I heard Mr. Stokes say she's only eight."

"Oh, she is, but she's stark raving mad an' all! Used to be such a quiet little thing—always hanging on to her big sister's sleeve and not sayin' boo to a goose. But that was before her house was bombed. Four days Edie was trapped down there, four whole days and nights. They hadn't gone into their shelter, see, and were all in the parlor when it happened. Imagine, all that time trapped in the dark, buried alive. The rescue workers had given up hope of findin' anyone breathin', it took 'em so long to dig their way through the rubble. But when they did, she was lying squashed under her mother's body, not able to move, and her big sister's dead hand was restin' on her face—just her hand, the rest of her had been blown by the stairs."

"Yuk! You're a bit bloodthirsty. That's gross!"

"Huh? Well, as soon as they lift the girl's mom off her, she leaps up and legs it deeper into the bomb site, after all that time trapped an' all. That's why some don't reckon it was her. They say that she was really blown to bits in the explosion. I seen that happen, too."

Mickey looked disconcerted for a moment as the gist of what he had been saying eluded him.

"The girl in the rubble," Neil prompted.

"Oh, yeah. Well, some say, an' I know for a fact that it was Reg Gimble said this, that what sprang from the rubble was really Edie's ghost."

"You don't believe that rubbish, do you?"

"No, no, of course not," he blustered. "But I was on firewatch last week, an' cycling around on my bike just about here, when I saw her. Runnin' like a scared rabbit over the road. I reckon she'd been stealin' from someone's house."

"Well, that proves she's no ghost. I bet . . ." but whatever Neil was about to say was lost on his lips, for at that moment he suddenly realized exactly where they had wandered to.

There were the iron posts at the entrance to the narrow alleyway, and rising to the left was the great, squat, pinnacle-spiked fastness of the Wyrd Museum.

Spluttering in disbelief, he rushed into the alley, crying, "Why didn't I think of it before? Of course it'd be here."

Astonished at his new friend's inexplicable behavior, Michael Harmon rode after him.

Neil was staring at the entrance and breathing hard.

The ornately sculpted figures that stood on either side of the door were hidden and enclosed within a sturdy wooden framework to protect them from flying shrapnel. The entrance itself had been boarded over.

Excitedly, Neil charged up the steps and pulled on the wood.

"Need a crowbar to get in there," he muttered in disappointment.

"What you interested in that place for?" Mickey called.

Neil whirled around. "Do you know anything about the three sisters?" he asked. "They'd be in their thirties or forties now."

"Three sisters?" Mickey repeated. "No, but my dad has a chum who lives out in the Seven Sisters."

"This is serious!" Neil insisted.

"You remembered something then?"

"What?"

"About where you come from?"

Neil laughed wearily. "Something like that. I—I think I lived here once."

Mickey's eyes rolled in their sockets and he giggled helplessly. "Then you really are a head case!" he hooted. "That place used to be an infirmary for the loonies. No wonder Edie Dorkins is attracted to it—being so balmy."

"It's a museum," Neil retaliated. "I know it is."

"Lunatic asylum," came the blunt correction, "least it was before they closed it down."

Neil gazed back at the boarded entrance and kicked it

bitterly. "This isn't funny!" he roared at the building. "I know the answer is in there—it has to be!"

"Calm down!" Mickey cried. "It's only an empty old place. They should open it up again if you ask me, 'stead of it lyin' idle. Could make a useful warehouse. Come on, let's go. You'll get the cops on you if you keep kickin' that door. They might think you're a looter."

Neil gave the entrance one final disgusted shove, then trudged down the steps. Holding his head back he stared up at the Georgian windows covered with crossed tape and he let out a rebellious shout.

Before Mickey could stop him, Neil grabbed a stone from the ground and flung it upward.

A ponderous crash echoed over the alleyway as one of the mullioned panes shivered into a hundred pieces.

"Oi!" Mickey yelled. "Stop that or I'll go an' tell the law. You'll be locked up if you carry on like that!"

Unable to take his eyes from the windows in case he caught a furtive movement, Neil murmured, "I've got to get inside that place. I'm positive that's it."

Mickey shook him gruffly. "You better go back to the Stokeses'," he suggested. "I think you need to lie down."

"Mmm," the mesmerized boy answered, "I think you're right. I want to have a word with my teddy bear."

Together they walked back down Well Lane, and the dark, tape-crossed windows of the Wyrd Museum watched them disappear into the distance.

CHAPTER 12

THE SQUANDER BUG

By six-thirty, fourteen women of widely differing ages had gathered in the church hall. They carried copious bags of clothes that were either too small or too worn to wear, together with assorted scraps of wool left over from scarves and hats and old sweaters waiting to be unpicked. A strident, staccato percussion struck up briefly as tobacco tins filled with odd buttons were dumped on the trestle tables, followed by the clatter of spools of thread being pulled from sewing baskets.

During working hours, the church hall had been taken over as an administration center, catering to those bombed out of their homes and needing emergency blankets and clothes. While religious posters and colored prints of biblical scenes were once pinned to the wall, they had been either replaced or covered over by charts and government posters advocating everything from Digging for Victory to trapping sneezed germs in handkerchiefs.

Two racks of donated garments were pushed into one

poorly lit corner, behind a large chalkboard covered with a list of names and the rota of the local Women's Voluntary Service. Next to this was a teacher's desk—positioned opposite the two rows of trestle tables where the attendees of the Make-do-and-Mend class were already heaving out their latest projects.

Leaving Daniel—who was feeling grouchy because his mother had gone out with Kathleen Hewett once more and had taken that nice teddy from him—behind the chalkboard, Mrs. Stokes rifled quizzically through the articles dangling from one of the clothing racks and grimaced scornfully before marching to her usual place among the assorted wives and mothers.

She detested these weekly meetings and had only joined in the hope that she could sabotage Doris Meacham. As yet, however, her neighbor had proved to be a competent instructress, albeit a haughty one, and the old woman found it impossible to fault any of the articles and ideas she had come up with.

"I think we'll be on our own tonight," Mrs. Stokes informed the others, her face contorted by a sickly grin. "Doris had a nasty shock this morning, doubt if she'll be well enough."

A greasy-haired woman, wearing a peculiar blouse made from an old tablecloth that was stained with beetroot juice around the back, looked up from a pair of her husband's trousers she was repairing and nodded vigorously. "Ooh," she said, eager for the gory, gossipy details, "I heard a bit about that. What happened exactly?"

Florrie Jenkins, Mrs. Stokes's plump bunk mate in the Underground station, was sucking her one tooth and listening keenly. "Stoned to death!" she interrupted.

"The poor lamb, I was there, I saw it. That Hewett girl put it out of its misery. I gave them Fletchers and that Gimble a real talkin' to when I saw them after. Little devils, they are. What could have got into 'em?"

"I don't like dogs, anyway," the greasy-haired woman replied. "They only make a mess on your floor an' get into your garbage cans."

Peeved at being thwarted in spreading the news, Mrs. Stokes rummaged inside her bag and pulled out the skirt she had been working on that day.

"Oh, Irene!" Florrie exclaimed. "That will be nice. Such a useful brown, won't show the dirt. Did your Jean help you with the pattern?"

"I wouldn't ask her," the old woman retorted huffily. "It's all me own work."

"Well, it's lovely. If you carry on like this you'll be the one taking these . . ."

Everyone's face turned toward the door, and Florrie Jenkins was stunned into silence. Beside her, Mrs. Stokes let the skirt drop on the floor, and her beaklike nose twitched with supreme annoyance and loathing.

Walking unsteadily toward the chalkboard with puffy, raw-looking eyes and dabbing away her sniffles came Doris Meacham.

The recently bereaved woman looked gray and drained, but she held her head erect and placed a large shopping bag on the desk before her. She may have been a snob, she may have been irritatingly condescending, but Mrs. Meacham was religiously patriotic. Though her heart was still bleeding in her breast and her life was empty without her yapping companion, she knew where her duty lay.

"Ahem," she began, needlessly giving the desk a tap with a piece of chalk as she already had their undivided attention. "Good evening, ladies."

Everyone responded, except for Mrs. Stokes, who glowered through her spectacles and ground her teeth together.

"I must apologize for my tardiness," Mrs. Meacham continued in her nasal whine. "I'm afraid that I have suffered a very sad loss today, and if at any time during the course of this evening I should be a trifle distant or indeed tearful—yes, ladies, tearful—I trust you will understand."

Her opening speech did not elicit a great deal of sympathy from the audience. Most of them had endured real grief since the beginning of the war, and few had time for the woman's absurd lamentations.

Nevertheless, Doris thanked them for their support in her bleak hour and the Make-do-and-Mend class began in earnest.

"Remember, ladies," she said, "we must be as ruthless and disciplined in the home as our gallant menfolk are overseas. Every shirt you patch, every tear you stitch, helps us to win this terrible conflict. Yes, Mrs. Sproggit, that old, shabby cardigan you are unraveling could bring the end of the war that tiny bit nearer . . . I beg your pardon? You're knitting it, not unpicking? Well, the point is the same. 'Raw materials are war materials.' We cannot shrug off this tremendous responsibility. Every day, in every way, we can spare vital supplies needed for the greater purpose."

Now in her stride, Mrs. Meacham bustled over to her favorite poster, the one she pointed out at every meeting.

The level of fidgeting rose sharply while at the same time her audience's interest waned.

Giving vent to a deliberate yawn, Mrs. Stokes stared coldly at the picture that so captivated her annoying neighbor.

Depicted on the poster was a crudely drawn cartoon of an outlandish, cockroachlike creature. From a dumpy body that was covered in swastikas waved a devilish, forked tail, and upon the imp's ridiculous and jug-eared head were two pathetic horns. A burlesque caricature of Adolf Hitler, complete with the recognizable black mustache, formed the insect's face, and Mrs. Meacham gave the drawing a resounding slap.

"We know who this is, don't we, ladies?" she preached to the women, who were already beginning to talk among themselves and admire one another's handiwork.

"Oh, yes," Doris intoned, "the wasteful squander bug! He's the one who whispers in your ear and tells you to waste your coupons on a new dress when there's a perfectly decent one at home just waiting to be renovated and given a whole new life. Remember, patches are patriotic! What are we to do with this fiendish monster, ladies? Crush him! That's right, we must all shun his vile temptations. My one aim in this dire time is to be certain the loathsome devil does not succeed. We shall not fritter away our resources as he dictates. That is my mission—don't throw that old pot or kettle away, they can be made into tanks and planes. Save those scraps of paper to make gun cases. Don't consign to the trash those boiled bones from the humble stew, they too can be turned to good use. Let us stamp out this infernal squander bug completely, ladies. Recycle and we shall be victorious!"

"Bet she didn't put that dog's carcass in the bone bin," Mrs. Stokes commented to Florrie Jenkins.

With a final, disparaging glance at the poster, Mrs. Meacham returned to the desk and opened the bag she had brought along.

"Here is the item I have been toiling on for the past two weeks," she declared with pride, "my most ambitious experiment yet!"

Deftly, she trawled out a mass of lemon candlewick and brandished it gloriously in front of their eyes.

"A winter coat!" she announced, slipping her arms into the sleeves and twirling brazenly.

The assembled women gasped with envy at her ingenuity, and Mrs. Stokes seethed with impotent malice.

"See how an old coverlet can be magically transformed!" Doris exclaimed as she sauntered among them, vaunting her cleverness. "Tonight I will show you how this minor miracle can be achieved. Let your needles be your weapons, ladies. We must not shirk from this most noble fight."

Unable to stand any more of this detestable, boastful woman with her lofty, superior ways, Mrs. Stokes scowled at the lemon candlewick creation as it pranced by, searching vainly for a stray hanging thread integral to the garment's constitution that she could accidentally tug at. To her dismay, no such ripcord was evident, and she decided that she could not trust herself to remain in the same room as Doris.

"I've had enough," she told Florrie Jenkins. "Something stinks in here."

"You going to the shelter?" the gummy woman asked. "Save me a bunk, I'll be along later. I want to know how to make that coat. There's a spare piece of tarpaulin at home coverin' the holes in the shed roof. I've been savin' it for something special—ooh, that'd be perfect."

Grumbling under her breath, Ma Stokes rose from the table and crumpled the unfinished and outshined brown skirt in her hands as if punishing the cloth for its lack of lemon candlewick.

Shuffling to the baby carriage, she roughly pushed the material inside and began wheeling it to the exit.

"Leaving us so soon, Irene?" Mrs. Meacham cried. "But I haven't had a chance to look at your little effort!"

Hurriedly, Mrs. Stokes evacuated the church hall before blows were exchanged, and she plodded broodingly toward the Underground station.

"Makes her look like a lanky canary, anyway," she sourly consoled herself.

When she reached the shelter, the platforms were buzzing with rumor—a dark shape had been glimpsed scuttling through the bomb site and heard snuffling in the ruins. Whatever it was had not been human, and the people nervously speculated on what this new addition to the desolate, haunted region might be.

Mrs. Stokes scoffed when she heard the worried whispers discussing this nonsense. There was always some sensation to gratify their thirst for excitement, scandal, and unfounded hearsay.

"Perhaps it's a Nazi secret weapon," she cackled to frighten them even more.

Resenting her derision of the matter they had been discussing so solemnly, the old woman's fellow shelterers refrained from talking to her. This suited Mrs. Stokes perfectly well for, as she lay down on the bunk, a hundred convoluted and dastardly plots involving the downfall and lasting humiliation of the lemon coat's creator unfurled within her embittered brain. With these charming images and designs dancing behind her eyelids, she slipped into a peaceful and contented slumber, blissfully innocent of the actual and ghastly doom that truly awaited her unsuspecting neighbor.

* * *

Mrs. Meacham lingered in the church hall to fastidiously put the chairs back in their correct places and sweep up fallen threads and specks of frayed cloth.

The meeting was over for another week. She indulged her vanity and conceit by letting her eyes drink in the wonderful sight of her creation that was now hanging from a prominent hook on the wall, reveling once more in the praise and acclaim her ladies had awarded it.

"Oh, Tommy," she murmured mournfully, "you would have been so proud of your mommy."

Before the magnitude of her dreadful loss could overwhelm her again, she hastened to pull on the delicious candlewick and turned a triumphant face to her favorite poster.

"We won't listen to your imprudent ways, Mr. Squander Bug!" she grandly declared. "I shall foil you at every turn."

With a swirl of her lemon coattails, Doris Meacham turned off the lights and trotted primly from the hall.

In the absolute darkness of the blackout, she rooted in her bag for a small flashlight and waited until its insipid beam was shining on the ground before setting off.

Through the empty streets she toddled, wretchedly

reflecting that no welcoming bark would greet her return, and tonight the shelter in her backyard would be a cold and lonely place.

As she wallowed in this melancholy and carefully picked her way in the pitch gloom, her coat seemed to shimmer and, for a brief instant, appeared to sparkle with flashes of silver tinsel woven into a field of swirling green.

But Mrs. Meacham noticed none of this. The night was bitterly cold and she shivered, pulling the collar of her new garment tight about her throat.

Crouching within the invisible dark, something was watching—its foul breath gurgling softly and polluting the night with horror. In mounting anticipation, it waited as the woman crossed the road, waving the pathetic flashlight before her. Then, gloating hideously, the evil shape stole after her.

Unaware of the terror that stalked her, Doris Meacham continued on her way, wrapped in thought and wondering what to do with Tommy's things. Of course, she knew that it would only be right for her to donate them for recycling. But, no matter how fervent her zeal for salvaging all she could to help the war effort, somehow she could not bear to part with these intimate mementos of her beloved pet.

Suddenly, a faint hiss floated through the night toward her, and Mrs. Meacham turned around quickly.

"Hello?" she said. "Is there someone there?"

As she shone the flashlight into the blackness, a hunched, deformed shape scampered deeper into the shadows.

Unperturbed, the woman resumed her journey—there were many sounds in the night. When she had first slept outside in the shelter, she had been alarmed how noisy the garden was under cover of dark. If it had not been for the company of her dachshund she . . .

This time the sound was closer. It was a guttural, burbling grunt, and Doris Meacham whisked around a second time.

"Who is that?" she demanded nervously. "Show yourself. What do you want?"

Again she could see only empty darkness, and walking more briskly, she hastened down the street.

Across the road the unseen shape scampered, its claws scraping over the pavement in its fiendish hurry to overtake the solitary woman. With its eyes fixed solely upon her and its nostrils thrilling with the scent of her life, it sped onward, then turned around and waited, its mouth watering in gruesome expectation.

Straining to catch the slightest sound, Doris stumbled fearfully along. Perhaps a wild animal was loose. When the war started, most of the dangerous creatures in the zoos had either been put to sleep or evacuated, but what if one of them had escaped? A lion or leopard might be prowling after her. She pressed her lips together to stop herself from crying out at this awful prospect.

"Don't be foolish!" she tried to tell herself. "Be rational. It couldn't have survived this long without someone spotting it. Really, Doris, you're like a child sometimes."

Then she saw them—two fiery slivers of brilliant red shining malevolently in the darkness before her—and the blood froze in the woman's veins.

A snorting, repulsive laugh issued hungrily from the invisible creature's gullet, but that was immediately drowned out by Mrs. Meacham's screams.

Screeching in panic, she fled back the way she had

come, her sensible shoes pounding over the pavement. The small flashlight was still gripped firmly in her hand, but so desperate was her terror that she plunged through the blackout not heeding where she was going. To get away from those ghastly eyes was her sole intention, and blindly she stumbled, her arms thrashing the night to ward off the evil that menaced her.

Now the rasping gurgle growled to the right of her, and Mrs. Meacham shrieked all the louder. She blundered down a narrow alleyway, calling for someone to save her.

Without warning, a blank wall reared from the darkness in front, and she struck her hands upon the coarse brick, scraping the skin from her sweating palms. Waving the trembling flashlight around, she realized too late that she had taken the wrong turn and staggered into a dead end.

With her heart in her mouth, she whirled around to escape into the main street—but it was too late.

From the entrance those narrow eyes gleamed at her, burning with unhallowed hatred.

A vile laugh mocked her as the shape advanced, and finally the pale beam of her flashlight fell upon it.

Mrs. Meacham's mind recoiled from the repellent sight, and the light dropped from her hands. Her jaw lolled open, but now she was too petrified to scream.

With its lobster-red hide glistening in the feeble light, the horrendous, malformed creature crawled forward, thrilling to the tantalizing fear that flowed from its victim in an endless, overpowering stream.

Six gangly limbs sprouted from the leathery flesh of its repugnant segmented body, each ending in two barbed claws that scratched and scrabbled over the ground as it dragged itself closer.

Trailing behind its unclean torso, the monster lashed a three-pronged tail that scored fierce scars in the bricks of the enclosing walls and arched high above its head like the sting of a scorpion.

Yet it was the face of this nightmare that was branded upon the brain of Doris Meacham. Though her flashlight now lay beyond her reach, she could not forget what she had seen.

Mounted above the ugly ridges of the misshapen thorax and crowned by a pair of twisting horns, the face of the apparition was unmistakable. Shielded from behind by a steel-strong shell was a mass of pale, rancid flesh that rippled and bulged to form foul parodies of all-too-familiar features.

A wide gash sliced open to create a grisly mouth, behind whose bloodless lips were row upon row of razor-sharp teeth that chattered and gnashed at the cold air, dribbling a river of saliva down the knobbly chin. A piggish nose pushed itself from the flabby, wrinkled skin above, and tufts of coarse, bristling black hair snaked out below it. An insidious cackle echoed in the alleyway, and the fiery eyes grew round and insane, and a clammy forehead quivered into place as more clumps of hair flicked out, forming sweeping bangs.

The undulating flesh of the hateful face pulsed and throbbed before the stricken woman as it tried to control and retain the ghastly shape it had chosen. Then, as a finishing touch, a bloom of reviled markings abruptly peppered and crept over the crimson hide.

The grotesque travesty of a real, animated squander bug burned into Doris Meacham's fainting soul as the loathsome semblance of Adolf Hitler's face taunted and mocked her. Beneath the wiry mustache its white lips curled back over pale gums, and a bloodcurdling growl rose from its black throat.

Like a cornered mouse, Mrs. Meacham pressed herself into the walls, hiding her face in her hands.

Then it sprang.

With its limbs flailing wildly, the squander bug pounced on her, hurling the woman to the ground as it laughed demonically. Doris Meacham's struggles were brief; the light from her flashlight threw the desperate contest against the wall as she screeched in torment. But the sound was lost when the tremendous blare of the air-raid siren suddenly warbled through the streets.

Reaching upward, the evil, distorted cockroach gave a gruesome chuckle. Snapping and crunching, the claw that curled from one of its spindly legs began to stretch and straighten as the skin flaked away to reveal a gleaming spear of burnished metal.

Where its talon had been, there was now a huge sewing needle that winked and flashed in the flashlight beam. For a moment it continued to glitter, then its rapier point came knifing down.

In the narrow alleyway, Mrs. Meacham's terrified screams abruptly ceased.

Gurgling with delight, the squander bug scuttled over the body of its slaughtered prey and lowered its already blurring face.

A vile lapping sound drifted out into the jet-black night, and then there was silence. Belial, Archduke of Demons, had claimed his first victim.

CHAPTER 13

BEARNAPPING

Jean Evans sat at the small table and shuffled along the seat as Angelo came to join her.

"You tired already?" he asked.

"I'm not really in the mood for dancing," she replied.

Sitting at the edge of the dance floor, they watched as other couples gracefully sailed by in time to the lilting strains of the dance band. Somewhere among the milling throng, Kath and Frank were holding each other close, but it was impossible to see them.

The dance hall was full tonight, and not one person had bothered to leave when the siren sounded. GIs, glamorous and debonair in their pink-and-green uniforms, greatly outnumbered the few local boys, who stood together in a resentful group, unable to compete with the allure and dash of the Americans.

It was baking hot in the packed hall and the air was misty with cigarette smoke. In spite of the pleasant music, there was a tenseness in the air. The atmosphere was charged and electric, as if at any moment tempers would erupt.

Feeling edgy and uncomfortable, Jean looked at Angelo. "Don't you ever take that flying jacket off?" she finally asked him. "I should think you'd be roasting by now."

Angelo slicked back his hair and shook his head. "I'd take a shower in this, baby, if I could," he told her. "It's my protection. Nothing can happen to me while I got it on. It's one of my lucky pieces."

"Superstitious, are you?"

"Hell, every airman is—though not as much as me, maybe. I got enough charms to open a store."

Shifting in the seat, he turned away from her so that she could see the design painted on the back.

Jean studied the colorful and highly exaggerated figure of a beautiful woman reclining in a provocative pose and arched her eyebrows.

"A friend of yours, is she?"

"She better be," he replied. "That there is Lady Luck. Hey, read what it says underneath."

"*The Kismet,*" she said aloud.

"That's the name of our bomber," Angelo told her, quickly turning around once more, "as in Fate. The guys let me christen her. She's a beauty—you ever seen a B-17?"

"No."

"Ah, everyone should see one of them honeys in flight. They got a grace about 'em—even when they ditch there's a spooky kinda elegance, like a ballet. Understand what I'm sayin'?"

"Not really."

Angelo shrugged, then snapped his fingers. "You wanna see some magic?" he asked, taking a cigarette from the pack in his pocket. "Here, duchess, put your kisser on there."

"I beg your pardon?"

"I want your lipstick on the paper. Trick won't work otherwise."

Jean complied, and along the side of the cigarette was a perfect print of her lips.

"Ah-h," Angelo cooed, "that's one lucky smoke. Now, watch—this is so great."

From his wallet he took a one-pound note and rolled the cigarette inside it.

"OK, sweetlips, you ready? Here she goes."

Flicking open his lighter he thrust the paper tube into the flame and the money fizzled between his fingers.

Angelo dropped it into the ashtray and waited until there was nothing left but ash.

"Now!" he cried, reaching behind the woman's ear and pulling out a cigarette. "Hey presto! Look, see, it's the same one, there's your lips. Ain't it a scream?"

Jean looked down at the ashtray then glared at him angrily. "Do you know how much money people earn a week?" she snapped. "Have you any idea what I could have bought for Daniel with that?"

Taken aback by the ferocity of her outburst, Angelo fished out his wallet again.

"Don't you dare offer me money!" Jean raged at him. "What do you think I am? Do you have to keep showing off?"

Angelo rammed the wallet back into his jacket and threw his hands into the air in defeat.

"I give in!" he cried. "Maybe I'm losin' it. You done nothin' but gripe and drag that long face around with you ever since we met. I can't do anythin' right, an' lord knows I tried, lady. What you doin' here anyways? I thought you'd changed your mind 'bout me when I saw you'd come out tonight."

Jean folded her arms stiffly and gazed at the passing dancers. "I only came 'cuz Kath begged me all day to keep her company," she said. "It certainly wasn't to see you again."

"Oh, gee, babe, thanks a bundle!" the American muttered, rising from the table and sulkily pushing his way through the couples.

Jean watched as the painted figure on the back of the flying jacket disappeared in the crowd, and a wave of guilt flowed over her.

"That was a cruel thing to do, Jean Evans," she scolded herself. "You've really hurt his feelings now. He was only trying to be friendly."

Springing out of her seat, she hurriedly chased after him, hoping that he hadn't already left.

Outside the dance hall, Angelo leaned against the wall and lifted a cigarette to his mouth, then, realizing it was the one marked with Jean's lipstick, he scrunched it up and cast it to the ground.

Lighting a second, he took a deep lungful of smoke and blew a continuous stream from his lips.

It had turned into a beautiful night. The obscuring clouds that made the blackout so bleak and impenetrable had cleared to reveal a radiant full moon, and London was dipped in a pool of silver.

Inside the building, the band began to play "Stairway to the Stars," and Angelo raised his eyes to gaze at the glimmering lamps of heaven above.

"Penny for them?" a voice said behind him.

Angelo drew on the cigarette. "I'm not gonna take your money, either," he answered, but there was a lightness in his tone that showed he didn't bear any grudges.

"If I stay in there a minute longer, I'll punch someone," she confessed, shaking off the tension.

"You got a pretty sky here," he marveled as Jean came to stand beside him.

"No sign of the planes yet, then?" she asked, scanning the night. "Maybe it was a false alarm."

Angelo smiled. "Didn't mean it that way," he said gently. "Can't see stars like that in Brooklyn. It gets you thinkin', a sky like that. Would ya just look at that old moon blazin' so cold an' frosty up there?"

"I hate the moon," the woman bluntly replied. "I dread nights when it's full. It makes it easier for the Germans to drop their bombs."

The American lowered his eyes for a moment. "Yeah," he slowly agreed, "it does."

"What's it like?" she asked.

"What's what like?"

"Dropping bombs on people."

Angelo stared at the glowing end of his cigarette as he considered her question.

"Weird," he answered. "We hurl ourselves into the backyard of heaven, hoping all the while that whoever's up there can hear us, 'cuz we're all prayin' like crazy. And, you know, I get to thinkin', what makes our prayers better'n the Germans'? I don't know how many civilians our bombs have killed. Not every German's a Nazi, an' that's somethin' that'll hit me when all this craziness is over. Don't reckon them faceless people'll ever leave me. I gotta carry them around till I die."

Jean shivered, staring up at the brilliant, swollen disc. "I don't know what it is," she said, "but for some reason it seems worse tonight. It feels as though there's something out there prowling under that bright moon. It's horrible that something so lovely could be the cause of so many deaths."

"Hey," Angelo murmured, "if you really think that, then there's no point fighting this war. What victory would there be if beauty's gonna be feared and cursed? I wouldn't wanna live in a world like that, would you?"

"I think I already am," she breathed.

"No crime in havin' fun, Jean," he told her. "You scared you might like it?"

"You called me Jean," she said in surprise, "not 'babe' or 'honey.'"

"Maybe I decided I like Jean better."

Within the dance hall the band began to play "Moonlight Serenade," and the woman laughed, finally dispelling all traces of her earlier stress and unease.

"You wanna go back inside?" Angelo asked. "It's mighty cold out here, an' my footwork ain't as bad as my personality."

Jean shook her head. "No," she replied. "Dance with me out here, just once, under that bright moon. Maybe I won't hate it no more."

* * *

"Yer wasting your time, kid," Ted had said, back in Billy Stokes's bedroom at number twenty-three. "Won't do

• 198 •

you no good goin' to that museum, not in this time. It's just a heap o' bricks. All it ever had goin' for it was me."

"You mean you won't come with me?" Neil asked. "Mr. Stokes is taking me to the wardens' hut tonight— we can slip away when he goes out."

The bear shook his head and primped the red ribbon about his neck. "Snoopin' around that place is the last thing I wanna do right now. I told ya, we got three more days till the gateway appears an' you meet up with Joshy again. Goin' to that museum is just a waste of time. 'Sides, I gotta stay in to see the look on that lieutenant's face when Jean snubs him. Right now, they've got a truce goin', but it won't last long. That jerk'll step outta line pretty soon. I gotta stick around to see that."

"I'll go on my own then," Neil decided.

Ted eyed him cautiously. "You just be careful if you're really gonna do that. You oughta know by now, that museum ain't no amusement park. It might not take kindly to any intruders. There's a helluva lot you don't know and can't guess about it. That building ain't no ordinary place."

"I've got to go," the boy answered. "Apart from you, it's the only link to my real time and Josh. I've got to feel as though I'm doing something. I wish you'd come with me."

The bear rubbed his furry chin. "I can't," he said.

"Why?"

"Just believe me—I got a reason to be here tonight. It ain't just to see the lovebirds when they come back. Oh, kid, I don't want you wanderin' around that kooky museum on your own, but believe me my place is here tonight. I'm sorry."

With this exchange ringing in his ears, and determined

to visit the Wyrd Museum that very night, Neil left the house and accompanied Peter Stokes to the wardens' post.

In the sandbagged hut, Peter gave the boy a copy of the *Magnet*—a comic for boys—to keep him occupied while he was on his patrol.

As soon as he was alone, Neil waited ten minutes then darted from the post and into the moonlit night.

To avoid bumping into another warden, he had decided to cut through the bomb site. In a matter of minutes he was standing at the edge of the large expanse of ruined houses and wasteland.

Before crossing over the rubble-strewn threshold into that eerie devastation, Neil held his breath. It was not the most inviting place in the world. The baleful moonglow cast great gulfs of shadow below the irregular broken walls that jutted from the landscape, and the tapering black chasms were pointing at him like accusing fingers.

"There's nothing to be scared of," he whispered. "It's not as bad as when I followed Josh up to The Separate Collection. That really was creepy."

Heartened by this recollection, the boy clambered over a mound of bricks and passed into the bomb site.

Bathed in a ghostly radiance, the desolation was startling. It looked as though an avenging spirit of destruction had stormed over the land, leaving nothing but decay in its wake.

Yet this strange, barren country was starkly beautiful. A dusting of frost sparkled on the wreckage of a hundred homes, and a profound, graveyard silence lay heavily over all.

Scrambling across the uneven ground, warily keeping a sharp eye where he stepped, Neil made slow progress, and he began to wish he had kept to the roads.

Into the hollow between the burned-out husks of two houses he went, swallowing nervously as he ventured through their deep shadows.

"It's like walking in a city of the dead," he reflected grimly, and at once regretted giving voice to the macabre thought. "Brilliant," he muttered with a frown, "that's just the right frame of mind to be in. I'll be seeing bogey men in every shadow now."

The sooner he left the ravaged area behind the better. He could already see the dark perimeter of the bomb site where it butted onto a row of terraced houses, and he knew that the preternaturally strange Wyrd Museum lay in that direction.

Moving as quickly as he could, he journeyed deeper into the cold heart of the demolished realm—and then the voices began.

At first they were indistinguishable from the slight breeze that blew icily into his ears, but it was not long before he could discern actual words floating through the night. The boy stopped dead in his tracks as the hairs on his neck prickled.

"Boy!" a plaintive, melancholy voice whispered. "Boy!"

Neil glanced around to see who had spoken but could spot no one. Surrounded as he was by the ramshackle remains of blasted buildings, the countless shadows provided innumerable places to lurk unseen. He longed to be back in the wardens' hut.

Then the voice spoke again. "Come to us," it called softly. "Be with us."

In the gloom the darkness was stirring, writhing with dim shapes that stealthily crept out into the deathly moonlight.

"We see you, boy," came a bleak, chanting chorus. "We have watched you. We know where you are headed. We cannot permit you."

From the deep shadows they came. Eight misty figures with sunken eyes and ashen faces, wearing the clothes their bodies had perished in. No shadows were cast beneath them as they shambled from the dark recesses, and as one they lifted their grasping hands to Neil.

Spluttering in dread and horror, the boy fell back into a clump of weeds, and with faltering steps, the murmuring phantoms crossed the stony ground that separated them.

"Get away!" he yelled. "Keep back!" But his terrified voice was thin and without force, dissolving feebly into the freezing air.

"You must not go," their empty, lifeless voices called as he dragged himself up and lunged away from them. "Come and join us!"

But Neil did not listen. He sprang over the ruins, not daring to look back.

Behind him, one of the wraiths let out a terrible shriek, and to his dismay, Neil heard answering calls all around the bomb site.

"They're everywhere!" he cried.

From the consuming night that pressed and smothered the haunted wasteland he saw more shapes drift toward him. Four indistinct forms were already melting from the shadows ahead, and to the left he could hear many discordant wails growing louder with every instant.

Nervously he glanced to his right, where the rolling devastation reared and dipped toward the chimney-topped outline of the shops that lined the main street.

The boy sobbed in relief—as yet, that way was deserted.

Jumping a low wall, he pelted over the rubble to the welcoming, empty darkness. If he could only escape those horrific specters and reach the world of the living once more.

At once, the gathering shades sent up a frightful howl, and with an unearthly gale tearing at their ragged clothes and hair, they hastened after him.

Beyond a ridge of crumbling ruins, Neil could already see the solid black shapes of the street buildings growing closer, drawing him on and inspiring him with hope. But close behind, the wraiths' chilling, frenzied clamor was increasing, and their hideous cries now filled his ears, killing all other sounds.

Recklessly, Neil launched himself up the uneven scree of the final mountain of wreckage, scrambling over tumbled masonry and blocks of ravaged stone. With his heart smashing against his ribs, he sped on, plowing through the dirt, heedless of everything except his desperate plight.

Then it happened. With the top of the hill almost within Neil's reach, his foot slipped on a broken timber. Hurling clouds of dust out over the bomb site, the beam went crashing down the slope, and yelling for his life, Neil came slithering after.

At the base of the ridge, the phantoms were waiting. Their lifeless eyes watched keenly as the boy toppled and fell, powerless to stop himself.

Into their ghastly midst Neil plunged, and when his violent lurchings came to an abrupt halt at their shadowy feet, he lifted his aching head and saw the now silent crowd flock around him.

Their faces were awful to look upon. Expressions as desolate and lonely as the wild terrain they haunted plagued their tormented features.

A deadly cold, more biting and intense than the night's frost, flowed out from the grim-countenanced apparitions, and the boy felt his crawling flesh turn to ice as they pressed ever closer.

With twitching fingers, they stooped over him.

"Get off!" Neil screamed.

"You were warned," one of them hissed. "Why did you not listen?"

"No!" he bawled, throwing his hands before his face.

The echoing cold began to burn into his bones, and Neil thought that he was lost forever.

"All right! All right!" barked a dismal voice, pushing through the crushing throng. "Stand back, stand back. What the bloomin' 'eck's goin' on here?"

Neil recognized the voice immediately, and he stared wildly up at the phantoms that were already lumbering forlornly to one side.

Cutting a swath through the misty figures was the ghost of Arnold Porter, who stumbled to a standstill as he gazed down at Neil in confusion.

"I know you," the warden's shade muttered, his fat face quivering with doubt and stupefaction as he battled to remember. "There was something above—it . . . it!"

But the chaos of his mind was not to be stilled, for at that moment the phantoms around him gasped sorrowfully and pointed into the gloom behind.

"She is coming!" they sobbed. "You were to guard her. Why did you abandon the child? If she is harmed then we are all doomed to the dark, and oblivion shall take us. Without her spark, we are nothing."

Arnold's troubled spirit turned his face from the perplexing boy lying in the rubble and stared into the night.

"Go back!" the others chanted as a new figure came barging between them. "It is not safe, you must return."

To Neil's astonishment, a young girl thrust her way into the center of the ghostly circle and glared down at him.

Both children regarded one another suspiciously. The girl knew the boy at once as the one who had emerged from the fiery window, and though he had never seen her before, he guessed her identity.

"You—you're Edie Dorkins, aren't you?"

The girl made no reply but continued to glower at him, narrowing her almond eyes into the meanest of slits.

"I've heard about you," the boy rambled anxiously. "Aren't you afraid of these things?"

An unpleasant smile flickered on the girl's grimy face and she shook her head with slow pride.

"What are they?" Neil asked. "What do they want?"

The smile vanished and was replaced by the familiar scowl.

"Come now, Miss Edie," Arnold Porter began, looking around them in a fluster. "You know what we said. It ain't safe out here this night. Downright dangerous it is."

Irritated and annoyed by his interruption, the girl turned on him and screeched shrilly.

"I'm sorry, Miss," Arnold cried, "but there's somethin' not right."

Edie stared up at the ridge Neil had fallen from, then glanced back at their frightened and alarmed faces.

"It is out there," the shimmering figure of an old man warned, pointing a trembling finger over the steep hill. "The fiend! It has claimed that corner as its very own. We dare not tread there. And it is growing—inch by inch its territory increases. That lad was headin' straight for it. Oh, Miss Edie, can't you feel the evil? It's stronger now than it was before. You must go—before it smells you out and comes huntin'. We know what it feeds on. You must run."

Edie's eyes grew large with defiance and she bared her teeth like a possessive dog protecting a bone.

"No, Miss!" Arnold called as she paced toward the mountain of debris. "You can do nothin'! You can't control the thing, it's stronger than any of us ever were. You ain't got that kind of power, no one has!"

Upon the bitter night air, from the other side of the steep ruins, the faintest ripple of a distant, hideous laugh wafted across to them, and the sound cut through Neil like a jagged knife.

"What was that?" he cried. "It didn't sound human."

"That's it," Arnold whimpered. "I don't like that one little bit. Oh Gawd, pretty soon it'll know we're here."

A flash of understanding jolted into Edie's meandering thoughts, and a cry of dismay issued from her mouth. Pulling her pixie hat down low over her forehead, she made a grab at Neil's hand and dragged him to his feet.

The boy stared around at the empty, imploring faces.

"Go with her," they urged. "Flee while you can."

Frantically Edie tugged at Neil's arm, and he was forced to follow her, back the way he had come, back to where it was safe—away from the hungry darkness that lurked in the bomb site.

"Hurry!" Arnold's woeful voice called out to them. "Get out before it's too late!"

Swiftly Edie ran, like a hare darting over a field. It was difficult for Neil to try and keep up with her, and a hundred questions were spinning in his head.

"I don't understand," he panted, "what's going on?"

Capering over the ruins, the girl hurried to the far edge of the bomb site, and only when she was standing within sight of the road did she stop. Pirouetting upon a fallen section of fence, she danced on tiptoe until Neil came puffing alongside her.

"That . . . that shape in there," he wheezed, not wishing to say the word "ghost." "I saw him killed, he was a warden. He's dead, I saw him!"

Edie covered her mouth with her filthy hand and laughed into it.

"What does it mean?" Neil persisted. "Why is he . . . why are all of them? . . ."

The girl lowered her hand and smugly pointed at herself.

"You?" Neil asked. "You mean, you're the reason?"

Edie nodded and pranced up and down the fence.

"Can't you talk?"

Not appearing to have heard the question, or choosing to ignore it, she performed a cartwheel, then gazed back into the devastated acres of the bomb site.

Neil stared at her. The girl was certainly peculiar. The

shadowy figures that had pursued him were less ethereal and peculiar than she was. Then he noticed the incendiary device hung about her neck.

"Is that alive?" he gasped. "Edie, it could go off at any second. Take it off!"

Anxiously, the boy rushed forward to take it from her, but she gave a fierce squeal and leaped away from him.

"Don't go!" he shouted. "I won't hurt you, I only wanted to remove that. It isn't a toy, Edie."

Fearlessly, the girl lifted the bomb in both hands and nuzzled her cheek against it. Then, half closing her eyes, she stroked the tail fins and rocked from side to side, crooning to the lethal instrument as though it were a baby.

"Everyone was right," Neil said. "You are mad."

Edie opened one eye and gave an enchanted chuckle, as if in confirmation, then she skipped to the end of the fence. In two nimble bounds she jumped onto a collapsed lintel and up to a lofty wall, where she twirled dreamily and looked down upon the boy below.

"Wait!" Neil called. "Don't go. You can't go back in there. Think about what those things were saying. It's not safe."

Laughing, she pointed in the opposite direction, then gamboled sprightly along the wall, disappearing behind a tall, plaster-dusted hedge.

Unnerved by his experience, Neil hastened back to the road. If the girl wanted to stay then he wasn't going to go back in there to fetch her. Besides, he still had to get to the museum.

"That place is my only chance of getting out of this madness," he told himself. "If I don't get back home pretty soon, I'll end up as cracked as she is. She's like a younger version of Miss Celandine Webster."

Since he hadn't the slightest desire to attempt the shortcut a second time, Neil was compelled to go around the bomb site. Hoping he didn't run into anyone else that night, he hurried on as fast as he could.

The main street was deserted. Looking cautiously from right to left, he scurried across to continue the journey hidden beneath the deep shadow of the shuttered shops.

He hadn't gone far when a faint whirring made him turn. A weak, hooded lamp sailed toward him, and Neil ran to the nearest shop doorway, hoping he hadn't been spotted.

Pedaling leisurely, Michael Harmon was gliding down the street on his rickety delivery bicycle. A tin hat was jammed onto his head, and he was wearing a pair of dark overalls. Inside the large basket fixed to the handlebars, a stirrup pump and a bucket clattered and crashed together as the machine bumped over the road.

So far it had been a disappointing night for firewatching. Mickey hated these phony raids that either took ages to arrive or didn't begin at all. If the German planes took any longer it would be too late, and the embarrassing eleven o'clock curfew his mother had imposed on his duties would come into force.

Listening for the drone of planes overhead, Mickey saw a movement caught in the dimmed beam of his bicycle lamp. He was pretty certain that the retreating figure nipping into the doorway was the mysterious amnesiac boy.

"Hey!" the firewatcher yelled, stepping harder on the

pedals. "Neil—that you? What you doin' out here? I know it's you, so you can stop hidin'."

With a groan, Neil stepped out from the shadows. The last person he wanted to see was the chattering baker's son.

"See you tomorrow," he called back dismissively, hoping he would get the hint.

As Neil began to run, Mickey heaved on the pedals, wishing the bicycle wasn't so old. Clanking and jangling, the machine bounced along, and Mickey had to let go of one handlebar to keep the pump and bucket from falling out of the basket.

As he did this, Neil disappeared into an alleyway. When the cyclist next looked up, the boy was nowhere to be seen. "Neil?" he shouted, applying the brakes and shining the lamp down the street. "Where did you—"

Nearby, his friend suddenly gave a frightened cry.

"No!" Neil's voice shrieked. "Oh, no!"

In a rattling instant, Mickey had found the alleyway, and he rapidly angled the lamp around.

There was Neil, standing stiffly in the narrow dead end. Slowly, with an odd, jerky movement, he shifted around to stare at Mickey, the color draining from his face.

Puzzled, the baker's son hoisted the bicycle onto the sidewalk and glanced down at the bedraggled bundle that lay on the ground.

There was the bloody corpse of Doris Meacham. The eyes were still wide with horror, and her open mouth was locked in a hideous, petrified scream.

Morbidly, Mickey pushed his machine closer for a better look as Neil turned away in revulsion.

"Wow!" the firewatcher gleefully drawled. "What a corker!"

* * *

"Who was that wise g-guy anyway?" Frank asked as he and Kath dawdled behind Jean and Angelo. "He sure had some nerve hollerin' at you the way he did. Why, I should've slugged him on the jaw. Pity Voo stopped me."

Kath snuggled against him and in an innocent voice replied, "I told you, I never saw that chap before. I never heard of no Larry. He was upset because his friend was dead. He got me mixed up with someone else, that's all. Happens all the time. We English girls all look the same to you Yanks."

"D-don't say that, Kathy," the airman said, sounding wounded. "I ain't one o'them no g-good rats. He was just sore 'cuz I was dancin' with the prettiest girl there."

"Charmer." She giggled. "I wish we could've stayed till the end. I'd liked to have done another jitterbug."

Frank scratched his head awkwardly. "Well, I weren't no g-good at it, anyways," he admitted. "Angelo's the expert. He can d-do all that kinda stuff. Real pop'lar with the g-girls near the base, he is."

"At least him and Jean aren't at each other's throats all the time now," she said. "Oh, I wish you didn't have to go back to camp tomorrow."

"That g-goes fer me, too, but don't you worry none. Soon as I get my next leave I'll be knockin' on your d-door."

"I hope that'll be soon," she murmured. "I had a grand time tonight."

"Yeah, well, here's hopin' I make it through the n-next mission. Heck, I ain't lookin' forward to it—not one bit. Hope I can handle a raid over the Big B."

"They won't send you over Berlin, will they?" the girl cried, staring at him in alarm. "They wouldn't think of doin' that, surely?"

Frank popped a stick of gum into his mouth and chewed pensively.

"I said too much already," he answered.

"Well, if they do send you out there, I hope it won't be for a very long time—if ever."

"How's the d-day after tomorrow grab you?" he muttered.

Kath stared at him in shocked surprise. "No!" she cried. "Not so soon—that isn't fair."

"Forg-get I said that," he quickly told her. "I could be thrown into the slammer for lettin' that slip."

"But how can you be certain?" she pressed him.

"I got a buddy in Intelligence," he murmured in a hushed voice. "Come Monday mornin', we'll be halfway over Germany. I sure hope I d-don't let the rest of the guys d-down."

"A fine, strappin' bloke like you?" Kath exclaimed, as they turned into Barker's Row. "Not on your life! Here, give us a kiss."

Outside number twenty-three, Jean was saying good night to Angelo and thanking him for a pleasant evening.

"There's one thing I never did find out," she told him.

"What's that?"

"Why does Frank keep calling you Voo? You didn't tell me last time."

Angelo dug into his flying jacket and brought out his

toy dog. "Jean," he began importantly, "I'd like to introduce you to a real good pal of mine. Meet Tex."

The woman laughed. "Hello, Tex," she said.

"Likewise," Angelo barked out of the corner of his mouth. "I got him the first night I was in England. Boy, was that dame a hot tomato!"

"What has that to do? . . ."

"Hold on," he declared, pulling a silver chain from under his collar. "This is a St. Christopher's medal, and in this pocket I got a bottle top, a watchstrap, a broken lighter, a picture of the Empire State—kinda crumpled by now but that don't matter."

"What's it all for?" she asked, bemused.

"Hey, I ain't finished, there's three more pockets yet."

"Don't tell me," Jean said. "They're more lucky pieces?"

Angelo winked in affirmation.

"Most people are usually content with a rabbit's foot, you know."

"Ain't that kooky?" the American replied. "What luck did it ever bring the rabbit? Naw, I'll stick to what I got already. Every one of these charms has been with me since the first mission. I've flown out on twelve now and I'm still here, so one of them's gotta be doin' somethin'."

"Ah," she muttered in mock solemnity, "but what'll happen on the next one? That'll be number thirteen."

Angelo's face changed dramatically and he crossed himself at once. "You tryin' to put a hex on me?" he cried. "Don't fool around like that! It ain't funny."

"I'm sorry," she apologized, distressed to see the effect her words had had on him.

Sullenly, the airman looked away from her, but he

recovered quickly and even managed to turn on his mischievous grin.

"My fault," he said. "It's just that I'm kinda jumpy about the whole setup. Still, I got me the two most potent hocus-pocuses a dope could wish for. One is Tex. I put him up there above my radio when I'm in the bomber an' he keeps an eye on me. The other is the jacket—I told ya', nothin' but nothin' can happen to me while it's on my back. You wait an' see, I'm gonna come through this war."

Jean folded her arms and tutted. "I'm none the wiser," she said. "Voo—remember?"

"I was just comin' to that. All the guys call me Voo. It's short for Voodini—as in a mix of voodoo and Houdini. Some joke, huh?"

"Actually, I think it suits you."

"That's the shame of it. I reckon I deserve it."

The amusement faded from Jean's eyes as an almost imperceptible whine sounded in the moonlit sky.

"Here they are," she moaned. "I better get out to the bomb shelter. I really did have a nice time, Angelo. Thank you."

"You just gonna send me out in the middle of an air raid?" he taunted. "Real cruel, that's what you are. When they find bits of me from here to London Bridge, I hope you'll be happy. Don't I even get a cup of coffee?"

Jean considered him uncertainly. "I really don't know," she said.

"Here," Angelo declared, thrusting his toy dog into her hands, "to demonstrate that I have only honorable intentions, you can keep Tex hostage the entire time, but

I gotta have him back, okay? Don't want you two fallin' for each other."

Relenting, the woman accepted the mascot and tucked him in her belt while she took a key from her purse. "Just one cup," she warned, "and it'll have to be tea."

"Hey, any more than that an' I'll be yawnin' in Technicolor," he assured her.

Inside the house, a small, furry figure stood upon the stairs with both ears cocked toward the front door. Listening to the lighthearted conversation taking place out on the doorstep, Ted chortled to himself and prepared to clamber back up to the bedroom.

Suddenly, the door opened, and before the bear could take cover, Jean and Angelo entered.

"I'll put the kettle on," the woman said, walking to the kitchen.

"You do that," Angelo answered, gazing with interest about the hall.

Daniel's off-white teddy bear lay on the floor where Mrs. Stokes had discarded it, and there, lying inert on the stairs, was Ted.

"What d'you know?" Angelo sniggered, picking both of them up and following Jean into the kitchen. "I guess this means my oath ain't valid no more."

Filling the kettle from a spluttering tap, the young woman turned around when he entered. "Didn't catch that," she said.

Twiddling his eyebrows, Angelo dangled the two teddy bears in his hands. "Look what I found," he proclaimed.

Jean laughed. "That one belongs to my son, and a poor bombed-out boy my dad brought home owns that one."

"Kinda scruffy lookin', ain't he?" the American scoffed, failing to notice the insulted frown now furrowing Ted's fleecy forehead. "Still, you know what it means, don't you?"

Jean smiled doubtfully. "What does what mean?" she asked.

"I got me two hostages of my own!" he cried, placing the toys on the cupboard and moving toward her with outstretched arms.

"Don't be silly," she said. "The kettle won't take long."

"Just one tiny kiss, Jean," Angelo pleaded. "You wouldn't deny a man about to leave on his thirteenth mission that, would you?"

Sitting alongside a chipped cup and saucer, Ted grimaced at the man's crass stupidity. "Bozo!" he whispered scornfully.

"I think you'd better leave," Jean said, dodging Angelo's arms for the third time.

"Listen to the lady," Ted muttered. "Ugh! I can't watch."

Sitting on the cupboard, the bear pulled a face and looked away as the airman kissed her.

"Stop!" Jean cried suddenly, pushing Angelo away. "Get out. Go on!"

Grabbing a saucepan, she threw it at him, and the airman leaped back in surprise.

"What's the matter?" he yelped. "I didn't do nothin' you didn't want. You gotta face it, Jean. The guy you married ain't never comin' home. You're too young an' pretty to waste your life on somethin' that ain't never gonna happen."

"I've got three more pans here," Jean snapped

vehemently, as she reached for another. "If you don—"

At that moment, there came a tremendous thud and clatter from the garden, and ignoring the blackout regulations Jean drew the curtain aside.

A small, rodlike object had landed on the roof of the outside toilet, and already tongues of blueish-white phosphorous flame were lapping over it.

"Incendiary!" she yelled, flinging open the back door and running outside. From his position on the cupboard, Ted watched as she vainly tried to extinguish the device with a bucket of water. But it was no use and the flames grew ever brighter on the toilet roof.

"Just look at that guy," the bear mumbled as Angelo raced out to help. "What a hero."

With the aid of a garden rake, Angelo maneuvered the incendiary into the empty bucket and threw fistfuls of soil on top of it.

"Poor sap don't realize the big brushoff is coming," Ted groaned. "Well, what'd he expect?"

Standing by the smoldering bucket, Jean thanked the lieutenant and said that he had better leave.

"What?"

"Just do it!" she demanded.

Angelo wavered, not understanding what he had done wrong, and he took a step closer to her.

"No!" Jean cried, suddenly desperate to be left on her own and searching for a way to make him see that she was serious. Taking Tex from her belt, she held the dog in her hand and lowered it dangerously close to the fizzing and crackling bucket.

"If you don't go now," she threatened, "I'll drop him right inside."

"You wouldn't."

The woman nodded earnestly. "Yes, I would," she told him. "Please, Angelo, my life is too complicated already. The last thing I need is to make it worse. Just go. I know how much Tex means to you."

"That li'l fella's my lucky piece," Angelo said, confident that she was bluffing. "He's gonna see me through this awful war. Without him, I'm finished. You ain't gonna do nothin' to old Tex. You wouldn't be so cruel."

Jean stared at him, hating his conceited arrogance. The American grinned, but too late realized that he'd pushed her too far.

Sobbing with emotion, Jean threw the dog on the charred, glowing soil within the bucket, where it immediately began to smolder.

"Hey!" Angelo roared, lunging forward, but it was too late—eager flames were racing up Tex's body.

"Get back!" Jean cried. "Just get out!"

Horrified at what she had done, Angelo stared at the flickering bucket and watched helplessly as the fire consumed his mascot's body.

"You—you got a real problem, lady," he uttered huskily. "I never meant no . . ."

With the sleeve of his flying jacket, he roughly wiped away the tears that sprang to his eyes. Without Tex to protect him, he was certain this thirteenth mission would be his last, and the horror of that crushed him absolutely. Unable to say another word, Angelo turned on his heel and stormed back into the house.

Shortly afterward, Jean heard the front door slam, then she pushed the rake into the bucket and fished out the burning toy dog. She hastily smothered it with dirt to quench the flames.

Gingerly she picked the blackened remains of Tex off the ground and ran back into the kitchen with them.

Only the large glass eyes were worth salvaging. The rest of the unfortunate mascot was blackened and incinerated beyond redemption.

"You can be a witch when you want to be, can't you?" she chastised herself. "What'll he hang above his radio now? What's wrong with me tonight?"

Then she noticed that the place where Angelo had put Neil's and Daniel's teddy bears was empty.

"He couldn't," she cried. "He wouldn't do that!"

Still clasping the remains of Tex, the young woman hurried to the front door and peered down the street, where she saw Angelo's figure already disappearing in the dark distance.

Standing on the porch of Mrs. Meacham's house, Frank stared across at her.

"What d-did you do to him?" he yelled.

Jean made no reply. She was too ashamed. She ran tearfully back into the house feeling wretched and despicable, wondering how on earth she could face both Neil and her son.

Frank hugged Kath tightly. "I gotta g-get after Voo," he said. "I ain't never seen him like that before. Listen, Kathy, I'm gonna write as soon as I get back to base, an' you just wait till I get my next pass!"

Giving her one last kiss and pressing a pair of nylons in her hands, the tall American leaped over the gate and vanished into the night after Angelo.

When she could no longer see him, Kath gave a curious smile and stepped into the house.

"Mrs. Meacham?" she called. "You in?"

Assuming her landlady had retired into the bomb shelter out back, Kath trudged upstairs to the room that had been allotted to her and threw her coat on the bed. Then she walked over to the wardrobe and unlocked it. Kneeling on the carpet, the dark-haired girl pulled open a drawer and snorted with mirth at its silky contents.

"Crammed to overflowing," she observed.

Taking her newest pair of nylons in her hands, she stuffed them roughly in among the dozens of others as an ugly sneer transformed her features.

The sneer spread into a smirk as she pulled a large wooden box out from under a pile of clothes. She lifted the box out with extreme care and gentleness and placed it delicately on the dressing table.

CHAPTER 14

THOSE THREE OF MORTAL DESTINY

In the early hours of the morning, heavy clouds crept across the clear sky, and when the daylight finally glimmered above the horizon, a dismal and steady rain was drizzling over the East End.

The news of Mrs. Meacham's murder shocked and horrified everyone, and the local police lost no time in interviewing those present at the Make-do-and-Mend class.

Arriving back from the Underground slightly later than usual, Mrs. Stokes was aggravated to find a police inspector with spiky eyebrows and an officer who looked like a beaten wrestler, complete with cauliflower ear and broken nose, standing in her front room, waiting to take a statement from her.

When she first heard the distressing news, not a twitch nor a blink betrayed the old woman's thoughts. She merely peered at the two men through her spectacles and, with a face like a gargoyle, ruminated over what they had just told her.

"Did you understand what I said, Mrs. Stokes?" the inspector asked. "Your neighbor, Doris Meacham—"

"I heard!" she rapped sharply. "Don't you talk to me as though I was ripe for putting in a nursing home!"

"Er . . . I'm sorry," the poor man replied, gazing around at Peter Stokes for support.

That morning the warden looked unusually weary. It had been a bewildering night, having first returned to his post to discover that Neil was missing, then learning that the boy was at the police station, describing how he had stumbled across a dead body.

Unwilling to sit down while so upsetting an incident required the presence of the police in the house, Peter stood tense and rigid in front of the fireplace and looked across the room to where Neil was now sitting.

Dark circles ringed the boy's eyes. He was incredibly tired and his head kept nodding onto his chest.

"Why don't you go to bed, lad?" Peter suggested kindly. "You've finished with him now, 'aven't you?" he asked the inspector.

"Yes," the policeman replied, leafing through his notebook and licking the end of his pencil. "The boy was most helpful, very concise—unlike the baker's lad. Ghoulish little vampire he is. Kept rambling on about everything under the sun. Used up most of my pad taking down his statement. Do him a world of good, the army will—ah, beg your pardon, sir. No, no, Neil's done his bit for now. I can always stop back if there's anything else I need to know, but it's more or less routine now."

"I'll get Jean to bring you up an Ovaltine," Peter said as the boy hauled himself from the chair and plodded out of the room.

Mrs. Stokes gave a sniff and pursed her lips. "So," she chirped, her eyes gleaming and hungry for luscious details, "how did it happen? How did Doris get it? A fine state of affairs, isn't it, when a body ain't safe in the streets at night? Where were your boys when all this happened? Not doin' their job, obviously."

The inspector coughed uncomfortably and stuck out his bottom lip, which was striped by the pencil lead. "If you could just begin by telling me . . ."

"Was it murder, then?" the old woman broke in. "How was she done in—were it strang'lation or were she stabbed and hacked at, like a scrag end o' mutton? Were it a vicious, cruel, lingering end? Did the stuck-up old fool suffer with it?"

"Madam," the inspector declared, "an extremely serious crime has been perpetrated. I need to know what time you left the church hall last night and if the deceased happened to mention—"

"Typical!" Mrs. Stokes uttered in disgust. "All this fuss. Even when she's dead that Doris has to swank!"

"Mother," Peter murmured.

"What'll happen about her house and things then?" she demanded. "She didn't have no relatives, you know."

Suddenly, a loud thumping resounded through the house as Neil stomped down the stairs and came running back among them.

"Where is he?" he cried, racing around the room, scattering cushions everywhere. "I can't find him!"

Peter gently caught his arm. "What's the matter, lad?" he asked. "What've you lost?"

"Ted!" the boy shouted back, ignoring the astonished

faces of the policemen. "He isn't upstairs, what's happened to him?"

"Perhaps Jean knows," Peter suggested. "She's in the kitchen giving Daniel his breakfast."

But his daughter had heard Neil's outburst and was already standing in the doorway. "Neil," she guiltily began, "I'm so sorry—"

"What's happened?" he cried, alarmed at her ashamed tone. "What've you done with him?"

"It's all my fault," she said. "If I hadn't burned that stupid toy dog!"

Neil gaped at her. "What are you trying to say? Ted's all right, isn't he? I mean, he isn't hurt or anything?"

"Hurt?" Mrs. Stokes squawked. "What's the boy talking about? It's only a ratty old teddy bear!"

"I'm afraid it isn't here," Jean explained. "Someone took both yours and Daniel's teddy away—I couldn't stop him."

A look of fear fixed itself on Neil's face and he felt twice as sick as when he had found Doris Meacham. "Who took him?" he shrieked manically. "Where'd he go? Jean, you've got to tell me. Please, you don't realize how important this is!"

"It was an American," she answered, feeling her grandmother's eyes bore disparagingly into her. "I think he must have taken it back to his air base—I don't know where that is. I think he mentioned Essex, but I couldn't say for certain. Oh, Neil, I'm sorry. I'll make you another one, I promise!"

The boy's face had turned white, and he staggered away from her, shaking his head in disbelief. "I've got to get Ted back!" he whimpered. "Don't you understand? I'll never get home without him. In two days' time the gateway'll appear, but he's the only one who knows exactly when and where! I'll never see Josh again! How could you let it happen? How could you?"

Peter put his arm around the boy's shoulders. "There now," he said coaxingly, "what's all this then? Who's Josh? Is it starting to come back? Do you remember where you're from, lad?"

Neil stared up at the bald man in consternation. "Josh is my brother!" he muttered before turning wildly to the two policemen, who, by this time, were totally baffled.

"You can find him for me, can't you?" he babbled desperately.

The inspector glanced nervously at Peter before answering. "Do you mean your brother?" he inquired, wetting the pencil again. "What does he look like? Is he older or younger than you?"

"Not Josh!" Neil bellowed. "Ted! Find Ted! Get everyone on the radio and tell them what's happened. I've got to get him back. Oh, no, you don't have radios, do you?"

Pushing past Jean, he ran from the room crying, "I don't want to be trapped here forever!"

The inspector raised his spiky eyebrows. "Should've grown out of teddy bears at his age," he remarked firmly, as though Peter was to blame.

"He's as crazy as that Dorkins girl!" Mrs. Stokes commented. "I warned you about bringing him into this house, Peter. The boy's insane. Well, I shan't be taking him to the Underground with me no more—I might wake up with my throat cut. Wouldn't surprise me if he was the one who done old Doris in. I'd think about that very seriously, Inspector. Loonies like him need locking up where they can't harm no one. Shame that madhouse ain't open no more."

Licking his pencil yet again, the policeman dutifully jotted down what she had said.

* * *

With his nose pressed against the window beside his bunk, Angelo gazed dolefully out at the mizzling rain. Under the slate-gray sky, the airfield was lit by depressing, almost funereal light, mirroring the cheerless depths his spirits foundered in.

"Hey, Voodini!" his captain called. "You're missin' one hell of a poker game. You sure you don't want in?"

Angelo moved away from the window and stared blankly around the barracks to where a group of other officers were sitting at a table immersed in the card game.

"Count me out," he replied, flopping back onto his bunk and staring up at the hut's curved ceiling.

"What's eatin' him?" Captain Jimmy Resnick asked, nudging one of the other men.

"He's just sore 'cuz he struck out with some dame," came the cynical response. "Some Romeo—I lost ten bucks on him."

"Musta been some girl," one of the men whistled. "I never seen him so riled up before."

A timid rap sounded on the barracks' door, and the captain called out when the visitor failed to enter.

"You gonna catch your death out there," he shouted.

His head and shoulders dripping with rain, Frank Jeffries fumbled with the handle and stepped inside the officers' hut.

"Beggin' your p-pardon, sirs," he said formally, "would it be okay to have a word with Lieutenant Signorelli?"

"Dammit, Frank," the captain drawled, "when you gonna start callin' me Jimmy? Ain't no top brass around here to hear you. A bomb crew ain't like no other outfit. You gotta loosen up."

Frank nodded and looked over to where Angelo was sitting on the bunk.

"Pay no attention to them," he said. "What can I do for you?"

"B-bout them toys, Voo," the man finally muttered, "the ones you told me you took from Jean's house? I know why you did it, but that don't make it right. I think you oughta send 'em back. Don't you care what them kids'll be thinkin'?"

Angelo leaned forward and in a low growl said, "If you know why I did it, then get off my case. I figure my need is greater than some kid's. Twelve missions I been on, Frank, nearly all daylight raids, an' I ain't had so much as a scratch. That's no coincidence, farm boy, and the more times I come through, the more luck I'm gonna need. Now, tomorrow is an important run fer me—thirteen. You know how many guys make it that far? Well, this one ain't takin' no chances. I ain't goin' up in that Fortress without protection. I'm gonna be decked out like a Christmas tree on that mission. The German flak is gonna bounce off my lucky pieces."

"But you don't need both—"

"You leave it to me to decide what I need. Them bears are stayin' in my kit bag till the morning, and don't you say nuthin' to the rest of the guys!"

"What have we here?" one of the men cried, having sneaked up behind them and listened to what was said.

"Gimme that!" Angelo snapped as the man wrenched his kit bag from beside the locker.

"Hey, lookee here!" he taunted, pulling out one of the teddy bears. "Our Voodini's Santa Claus in reverse: he visits kids and takes their toys. That's a rotten thing to do."

Angelo flew at him, but the man tossed Daniel's stuffed bear across to the captain, who in turn threw it to another.

"Stop it!" Angelo ranted, leaping in the air as he darted to-and-fro, trying to catch the flying toy. "Let me have it!"

Baiting him, they raced around the hut brandishing Daniel's bear in their hands, until Angelo could stand it no longer. Thundering to his locker, he snatched up a bottle of beer and stormed from the barracks.

"Aw," the man pouted, "Voodini don't wanna play no more."

Running to the doorway, Frank stared after his buddy and rounded angrily on the officers.

"I sure d-do hope you're mighty proud of yourselves, sirs," he reproached them. "Voo might take his cockamamy hocus-pocus a mite far, but there ain't one of you, I bet, who d-don't d-do the same. I only been on one mission so far, but you can bet that tomorrow morning I'll be d-doin' the exact same thing I did last time, so as not to break the luck that brought me home safe. Ain't right you makin' fun of Voo like that, you oughta be ashamed. He's g-got enough on his mind!"

The other men stared sheepishly at the floor. One of

them opened his mouth to retaliate, but his captain nudged him into silence.

"Can it, Pat," Captain Resnick said. "I seen the way you put on your socks on mission days. You always wear one inside out. I guess you're right, Frank, we shouldn't have teased Voo like that. I'll go apologize. Did you see where he went?"

Frank looked at his watch. "It's three o'clock," he answered simply. "Voo'll be doin' his ritual now."

The officers looked at one another, abashed.

Greatly subdued, the bombardier took Daniel's bear and returned it to Angelo's kit bag. Then, in a remorseful humor, they left the hut in single file.

Out on the airfield, the squadron's bombers were lined up on the tarmac in vast, stately rows.

Despite their unwieldy size and olive-drab markings, the B-17s were oddly beautiful and possessed an indefinable, elegant grandeur that the crews of the smaller, pregnant-looking B-24s could only envy.

On the sides of these regal aircraft, a virtual chorus line of delectable and imaginatively proportioned women had been brightly painted alongside garish letters pronouncing each bomber's name. There was *Sweet Sue*, *Darlin' Daisy*, *Naughty Katy*, *Cutelips*, *Parson's Daughter*, *Flyboy Dream*, and a host of others. Several of them bore more descriptive legends, such as *Helldragon*, *Nazi Killer*, and *Flak Trap*, but standing proudly between *Big Momma* and *Li'l Honey* was *The Kismet*.

Angelo Signorelli had already clambered up onto the left wing when Frank and the officers found him.

Unaware of anything but himself and the aircraft, Angelo began the ritual he had started as a drunken joke on the afternoon before his first mission and before his superstitions had come to obsess him. Raising the bottle of beer to the leaden heavens, he threw back his head and called out the exact same words he had uttered then.

"Hey!" he cried. "Fate, Lady Luck, Kismet—whatever you wanna call youself! This is Lieutenant Angelo Signorelli speakin'. First thing tomorrow mornin' me an' my buddies are gonna be puttin' our necks out, an' we'd sure appreciate it if you could see that we come outta this in one piece."

Walking along the wing, he poured a drop of beer over each of the two engines before hoisting himself over the windows of the flight deck and dropping down the other side, where he repeated the ritual on the remaining two.

A sizeable crowd had now gathered around the Fortess. The rest of *The Kismet*'s aircrew had come out to join the officers, whose numbers were already swollen by many of the ground staff.

No one uttered a sound; only the rain, as it pattered and drummed on the fuselage, could be heard until the ceremony that had become important to all of them was complete.

"There!" Angelo yelled. "That's the libation, now don't you let us down, ya hear? Keep this baby in the skies!"

Swigging back the rest of the bottle, the American's voice dropped to a fretful murmur as he added, "Please. I got a real bad feelin' about this one."

On the ground, the whole of *The Kismet*'s crew bowed their heads, then everyone else followed suit. Angelo's ritual had become a rare fixture in each of their lives now, and they knew he invoked the powers of Fate on all their behalf.

* * *

Within the officers' barracks, the unbroken silence was disturbed suddenly by the rustle of canvas as Angelo's kit bag shuddered and jerked.

"Peeyoooh!" Ted breathed gratefully when he finally managed to pop his head out and wriggle free, past Daniel's bear. "This guy oughta wash his socks more often."

Hopping from the bunk, he walked over the concrete floor into the middle of the hut, where he warmed himself by the small, coke-burning stove and let his eyes roam sadly around the poster-covered walls of the hut.

"Geez!" he breathed excitedly as old memories came crashing back to him. "Here I am again, been a long time. I forgot how young this crew was. That's Pat Dyson's cot. That Detroit wise guy gave me such a hard time. Over there's where Artie Stewart used to keep the whole hut awake with his hog snoring, till he was killed over France—poor sucker was only twenty-one. Bob Cotterell was only nineteen when the fighter's lead found him. Here's Herb Miller's place, and old whatshisname with the sweet tooth . . ."

Ted's ears drooped sorrowfully, and his eagerness to look on the barracks once more vanished as the faces of his dead comrades floated out from the dusty corners of his woolly mind.

"You louse!" he condemned himself. "All these years I been so wrapped up in my own trouble that I didn't even stop to think and remember. You were good buddies to me, saved my neck every time we went on a mission, and this is how I pay you back—by forgetting. Sorry, pal, you're just a face that was there one day and replaced the next.

"It's good that toys can't cry, else I'd need wringing out. 'Tain't so good when all you can say is sorry. I'm sorry I'm such a selfish heel who's been too busy tryin' to free himself. I don't even know what happened to the rest of the group after I dropped out. Did Jimmy ever make it back to Myra? Did any of them get to finish their tour of duty? Prob'ly not. All of us burned bright and brief."

Returning to Angelo's bunk, Ted pulled himself up and went to stand on top of the locker, where, by stretching as high as his fleecy legs allowed, he could just peep over the windowsill.

On the airfield, the ceremony was over and the men were drifting back to the barrracks.

A regretful light shone in Ted's glass eyes as he stared at the majestic outlines of the B-17s and their returning crews.

"Ain't none of them gonna get much shut-eye tonight," he predicted, hopping from the locker and struggling back inside the kit bag, "and if they do, it'll be riddled with nightmares."

* * *

The shadows of evening spread thickly over the East End, and though the rain had ceased, it left behind expansive pools of black water that leaked across the

• 232 •

streets and formed gurgling rivers that rushed along the gutters beneath a flotilla of scum and dust.

Once Peter Stokes had gone on duty and his crabby mother had departed for the shelter, Neil falsely told Jean he wanted to go and speak to Michael Harmon in the hope that she would let him out of the house. The prospect of visiting the Wyrd Museum burned and consumed him more than ever. Without Ted, that sinister building was now his only link with the future, and he desperately hoped that there he could find all the answers.

But the young woman bluntly refused to allow him, reminding the boy that whoever killed Mrs. Meacham was still at large.

Although he appreciated her concern, Neil ignored her warnings. As soon as she went into the garden to put Daniel into the shelter, he slipped out of the front door and ran down the street.

Twenty minutes later, he was splashing through the countless puddles that swamped Well Lane, and the fastness of the Wyrd Museum, with its spear-tipped roof, loomed high above him.

A deathly quiet lay over the place. Looking up at the dark, blank windows, Neil had an uneasy feeling that it had been expecting him. Still, nothing to do with this peculiar, menacing building would surprise him anymore, or so he thought.

Striding into the narrow alleyway, he took out his flashlight and shone it up onto the boarded entrance.

"I need to find a length of pipe or a railing to get that board off," he told himself, mounting the steps to run his hands over the thick sheet of wood that barred the door.

To Neil's surprise, the wood was loose—the nails that held it in place were rusted through. Without too much effort, he was able to nudge it aside.

"No way was it like that the other day," he whispered. "What's going on here?"

Even as he voiced his doubts, the arched door before him gave a painful-sounding creak and swung wide open.

Startled, the boy leaped down the steps again and directed the flashlight beam into the awaiting blackness beyond the threshold.

"You can stop playing your little games," he snarled at the forbidding building. "They might have scared me once, but I haven't got time to care anymore."

Grimly he ascended to the entrance again, and the next moment the darkness swallowed him.

Waving the flashlight around the paneled hallway, Neil had to keep reminding himself that he was still trapped in 1943. He thought glumly of his father and wished he had not argued with him; at that moment, he would have given anything to see him again.

At first, apart from the absence of the suit of armor, everything looked exactly the same as when he and his father had first arrived and unloaded the van. Then he began to notice the subtle changes.

In place of the watercolors that he remembered seeing on the walls, there were now large notices advising visitors not to approach anyone who wasn't wearing a uniform, and under no circumstances were the patients to be given anything not authorized by the medical staff.

Where the armor had stood there was a life-size anatomical model of a human body displaying, in successive degrees and various detachable layers, the muscles, skeleton, and internal organs. Beside this was a line of primitive wheelchairs, each one stacked high with a pile of metal bedpans.

"So it was an infirmary," Neil breathed, venturing a little farther and peering into the first room.

Gone were the glass cabinets and exhibits of his time, and in their place was a row of empty iron bedframes pushed against the far wall. Suspended from the high ceiling was a complex network of gas pipes that crisscrossed the room, feeding the broken lamps above each empty bed.

A fierce smell of chemicals prevented him from exploring in detail, but before he returned to the hall he saw, to his discomfort, that each bed possessed a set of leather restraints.

Turning his attention to the stairs, he began climbing them, hesitating only when the memory of Miss Celandine Webster, dressed in her nightgown with her knitting in her hand, waltzed briefly through his thoughts.

Up to the landing he went, then he started to make his way toward the room that had held, and would still hold, The Separate Collection.

Neil plowed through ward after ward of empty beds, their damp and fusty mattresses heaped in the corners.

"They really should've reopened this. I'd have thought they'd need as many hospitals as possible."

Keeping his hand over his nose and mouth, he vainly tried to blot out the all-pervading, insidious reek that he gradually came to realize was growing stronger. The sickly laboratory atmosphere was a noxious mixture of rancid disinfectant, damp bed linen, carbolic, and spilled formaldehyde that condensed on his palate, forming a foul acidity around his tongue and stinging his eyes until they watered.

Eventually the boy reached the windowless room he had known in the future as The Egyptian Suite and found that it was empty except for a locked drug cabinet and a barbaric dentist's chair with cruel jaw clamps, a neck brace, and iron manacles to hold down the hands and feet.

Hardly glancing at the savage contraption, Neil hastened past, eager to see what changes time had wrought upon the place where he had first heard Ted's voice.

A raised platform of wooden benches running the length of three walls was the first thing he noticed. It was like standing on a sunken stage and having the empty auditorium staring down at you. The floor was covered in moldering sawdust, and in the center of this gloomy arena, he saw a long wooden table surrounded by three small carts.

Cautiously, Neil walked over to them. Each of the carts bore a selection of tools—long hacksaws, vicious-looking knives, and gargantuan hypodermic needles that looked as though they were made to pierce the hide of a rhinoceros.

Then it dawned on him that they were all medical instruments and he was in an archaic operating room. Staring up at the dark, empty benches, he imagined the awful carnage those mawkish onlookers would have witnessed.

"Mickey would love this," he mumbled.

The paneled walls must have soaked up a cacophony of screams to rival purgatory, and the floorboards must have been steeped in and awash with the hot gore that gushed and spilled from the table.

Squeamishly he wondered how many of the patients, or victims, had survived the brutal surgery. Perhaps the asylum inmates had been experimented on. Had the tops of their skulls been removed for the inquisitive students to inspect what a mad person's brain looked like?

Chilled by these unwelcome imaginings and not wishing to remain a moment longer, the boy fled back past the dentist's chair and through the echoing wards until he stood again on the landing, where he gulped down great breaths of the sweeter air.

"It's so different," he sighed. "I hardly recognize it."

Then, even as he tried to come to terms with the indisputable reality that there was no way out of this period in time, a feeble glimmer of hope began to glow in his mind. With renewed hope, Neil glared up the stairway that led to the third floor.

"That's where the answer is!" he exclaimed with a rush of understanding and comprehension. "Ted was always shouting up at the ceiling of The Separate Collection. He wasn't yelling at heaven, it was the room above—where the sisters lived!"

Vaulting the stairs two at a time, he hurtled up to where a white-painted door forbade access to any wandering patients.

Even in the future, Neil had never set foot in the Webster sisters' quarters, and as he turned the handle to admit himself, he couldn't help remembering that Miss Ursula had expressly forbidden him to go there.

Then he was inside and he turned the flashlight beam curiously about him.

Neil found himself in a large room. Heavy velvet curtains, fringed with silk tassels, were draped over the windows, and a worn Persian carpet covered the floor. But crammed into every spare inch, shouldering and jostling for space, was a multitude of different-shaped and different-sized furniture, and every piece was covered by its own individual dustsheet.

Flaring strangely in the flashlight, the shrouded cabinets, bookcases, and wardrobes looked like pantomime ghosts of themselves. The suspicion that under one of them someone might be lurking in wait occurred to the boy more than once as he pushed and squeezed his body between a cloaked cabinet and what he presumed to be a chest of drawers.

Warily he drew aside the nearest sheet and peered underneath.

"Aah!" he squealed as a tiny, withered face leered out at him, caught in the flashlight's beam.

But his fear didn't last long, and in amusement, he took a second look.

Beneath the mantling sheet was a glass case, and dangling in a ghastly row was a display of shrunken heads.

"The exhibits," Neil cried, dragging off one cover after another to reveal many of the Wyrd Museum's specimens. "This is where they are."

Hurrying between the crowded cabinets, he passed into the next room and discovered that it, too, was stuffed to overflowing.

"They're all up here!"

Moving through the whole of the jammed third floor, intermittently inspecting the displays, Neil finally came to a halt in front of a small door.

An image of a flowering tree had been carved into the panels, and the boy traced the chiseled shape with his fingertips. It was a masterly piece of craftsmanship. Every leaf was clearly defined, and an intricate pattern of bark wound over the gently raised trunk, down to each of the tree's three roots. Beneath the central, longest root, a circle of lapis lazuli had been cunningly inlaid and set within a narrow band of gold.

Studying the design in the flashlight beam, Neil chewed his lip and wracked his brain. "I've seen this before," he murmured, trying to jolt it from his memory, "or something very like it. That picture made from flowers those people put in front of the drinking fountain—it's just the same."

The door was obviously the entrance to somewhere important and, gingerly, he reached for the handle and pushed it open.

A narrow flight of steps covered by a plush green carpet lay beyond. Spanning the entire length of the wall above was a huge oil painting of a mythological landscape executed in the Pre-Raphaelite style.

Mounting the stairs, the boy paused to look at the great canvas. The scene was the edge of a forest. A titanic ash tree dominated the middle of the picture, and at the base of the trunk, positioned around a pool of blue water, were the slender figures of three beautiful nymphs arrayed in flowing robes of white, red, and black.

Each exquisite, willowy woman was holding something

in her pale, elegant hands. Neil held the flashlight very close until he could see what these objects were.

The crimson-clad figure, whose hair shone in the sunlight like a river of molten gold, was depicted performing a graceful dance, and she bore aloft a silver spindle wrapped in many different-colored threads.

Next to her, and reaching for one of the threads with her right hand, was the white-robed maiden, who carried a measuring rod in her other hand. The beauty of this woodland goddess caused Neil to catch his breath. Her coal-black hair streamed behind her in long raven tresses, and her face was lit by a heavenly radiance that emanated from within.

Turning from her, Neil brought his scrutiny to bear on the third and final female.

Standing a little apart from the others, this black-gowned woman had a sinister air about her. Lost in the tree's shadow, she stood beside a large wooden loom. A veil obscured her face, and in her hand she clutched a pair of shears that she brandished menacingly. Unlike the rest of the picture, where spring and summer flowers mingled idyllically in the warm sunshine, the ground near this cowled figure's feet was stony and barren, and the only plants that grew there were monstrous toadstools and strangling weeds.

Neil shuddered and searched for the painting's title, which he found written in gold letters along the bottom of the frame.

THE NORNIR
THOSE THREE OF MORTAL DESTINY

Then he saw, to the left of the painting, a much

smaller frame hanging on the wall. The frame contained a yellowing fragment of parchment that had evidently been torn from an old manuscript. Frowning, the boy tried to decipher the faded writing.

OF THE NORNIR

In the beginning of years when Yggdrasill still flourished, it was prophesied that while one part of the world-tree remained green and growing, then the ogres of the deep cold would never despoil the land and cover it with their ice and darkness.

Thus did the fearsome lords assail the blessed realm of Askar—the ash land—and close did they come to accomplishing their grim task. Two of the roots did they poison, and with their axes did they hack until Yggdrasill was thrown down.

Yet Nirinel, the third and greatest root, was tended by the daughters of the royal house, who fed it each day with water from the sacred pool.

Urdr was the eldest of those noble maidens, and the names of her sisters were Skuld and Verdandi.

Yet also in that sylvan place was bestowed for safekeeping the forbidden loom that had been wrought out of the first branch hewn from the world-tree. When the clamor of the dark host rang in the surrounding forest, and the royal maidens knew that this was in truth the direst moment in the brief history of the world, in their terror they took it upon themselves to operate the dreadful loom. So was set in motion a power greater than any other, unto which they too were bound and could not escape.

Thus was the doom cloth first woven, and though by its strength was Nirinel saved, the fate of the world was at last set down and all men fell under its might.

Neil looked up from the parchment and stared uneasily back at the three figures depicted in the painting. Then, leaving the canvas behind, he ascended to the top of the narrow staircase, where a thick damask curtain hung from a brass pole. Cautiously he tugged the curtain aside and stepped through an open archway.

Neil had found it at last. The musty room he entered contained no covered display cases, only the same shabby furniture that could be found in any old house.

Three well-padded but worn leather armchairs took up much of the space and were arranged around a circular table upon which was an ornate candelabra obscured by dribbles of wax. Directly over this, hanging from the ceiling, was a grimy chandelier, and smothering the faded wallpaper, together with shelves of black-bound books, were watercolors and arrangements of elaborate fans.

The only window was a small square of diamond, lead-latticed panes, and towering before it was a tall, naked hatstand. Every available surface was cluttered with a thousand tiny knickknacks and trinkets, but over all this—armchairs, table, and everything—was a thick layer of dust.

Ancient, frayed cobwebs hung in tattered wisps from the cut glass of the chandelier, and gossamer threads stirred gently as Neil's breathing disturbed the long-stale air.

"The Webster sisters can't have lived in just this one room," he declared, looking for another entrance but unable to find one. "Is this it, then? Is this where they grew up and spent their youth—in one dingy little shoebox?"

Just behind the door, a drab watercolor hung on the wall, and the boy contemplated it with interest.

The pale, washed-out sketch was of a grand manor house set within its own well-tended grounds. It was only after he had been staring at it for some minutes that Neil recognized the shape of the building. Only three pinnacles soared from the roof of this more dignified version, and the entrance was a simple arched door, but there was no doubt about it. Here was a much younger incarnation of the Wyrd Museum.

"What happened to the gardens?" he mused to himself. "Maybe the family had to sell them off. Perhaps one of the Websters' ancestors went broke or lost the fortune by gambling."

Stealing over to the bookshelves, he dragged his finger through the choking dust and speculated where the three sisters could be in this time. "No one's been here for years," he mumbled. "Perhaps they left the city and evacuated to the country to escape the bombs."

Then one of the book titles caught his eye, and Neil pulled the volume from its niche.

INVENTORY OF THE WYRD MUSEUM
AS COMPILED BY MISS URSULA WEBSTER
BEFORE THE INSTITUTION'S CLOSURE IN 1897

"That's impossible," Neil uttered in a small voice. "It can't be the same woman. Must be her grandmother."

Sliding the inventory back to its place, he removed its neighbor and put his hand to his forehead as he read this next inscription.

REGISTER OF ORPHANS 1855–1871
BEING THE NAMES AND AGES OF THE UNWANTED
CHILDREN AND FOUNDLINGS THAT HAVE RESIDED UNDER
THE CHARITY OF MISS URSULA WEBSTER, PRINCIPAL,
THE WYRD ORPHANAGE

Breathlessly, Neil studied the next book.

RECORDS OF ACCOUNTS FOR THE WELL LANE WORKHOUSE
WYRD PLACE
1839–1854

As Neil started to return the volume to the shelf, a card fluttered from its pages and landed on the floor. Retrieving it, he saw that it was a yellowing invitation and the overtly elaborate, scrolling letters had been printed in silver ink.

Miss Celandine Webster

cordially invites you to
a celebration banquet
to be held in honor of our noble Lord Nelson's
victory over the French
Wyrd Place
Well Lane

There will be dancing

On the reverse of the card a firm, flowing hand had written:

> *Yet another of Celandine's foolish ideas that I have forbidden. Fortunately I confiscated the invitations before they could be delivered. Celandine is becoming as absurd as Veronica, and as I write this, she is weeping like an infant. I shall destroy her ball gowns this very day to put an end to these fancies once and for all. There will be no parties in this house, and I shall keep this to remind her.*

In thoughtful silence, Neil slid the card back into the accounts book. But before he could examine anything else the shelf had to offer, his attention was arrested by an oval painting above the fireplace, positioned between two vases filled with peacock feathers. With a sense of foreboding, he crossed to the hearth and slowly raised the flashlight.

"No!" he spluttered. "No!"

The painting was a portrait of three women, and Neil knew them instantly.

Smiling out of the oils were the Webster sisters, but to the boy's amazement and consternation, they were exactly the same as when he had last seen them.

Standing directly behind the others, stiff in her black taffeta and looking with disdain at the unknown artist, Miss Ursula was gaunt and austere. Her sister Veronica, ridiculous with her dyed hair, smeared lipstick, and flour-covered complexion, sat below her. At her side, with her goofy teeth hiding her bottom lip, was Miss Celandine.

No bloom of youth touched them. It was a portrait of three elderly, haggard women, and each looked identical to the way she had appeared to Neil, fifty years later.

"It can't be them!" he cried. "They'd only be about thirty in this time, and the picture must have been painted ages ago. Family likeness, that's all it is—they must be the aunts of the ones I met."

Yet in his heart he knew it really was a painting of the Websters he had met, and he recoiled from it as though it had burned him.

"What's going on?" he asked wretchedly. "I don't understand—they never grew any older. Who are they? What are they?"

Staggering from the unsettling room, he stood at the top of the narrow staircase and shouted for his brother.

"Josh!" he bawled. "Josh, I'm sorry. I can't find the answer! I tried, but I just can't!"

Outside the building, engulfed in the shadows that filled the cramped concrete yard, a small figure heard the boy's anguished cries and glanced impishly up at the dark windows.

A fey smile curved over Edie Dorkins's face as the muffled shouts faded into silence. She scampered swiftly over to the drinking fountain, where she pressed the lever and gargled in the glittering water that poured from the nozzle.

As the sacred liquid tingled through her, she wiped her mouth and listened for any more voices. Then, very faintly, Edie began to hum to herself.

Chapter 15

Caught by the Light

Peter Stokes licked the neatly trimmed hairs of his mustache and placed the mug on the shelf.

"I better get goin' and see what's doin'," he told Joe Harmon. "Have to make sure everything's nice and dark out there, though I don't think the Nazi flyboys will bother tonight."

His fellow air-raid warden looked up from the copy of the *Magnet* that Neil had left behind and sucked the air through his teeth uncertainly.

Joe Harmon was a thin, wiry man with a grim face, but his dour expression could alter in a twinkling into one of jovial kindness.

"Do not place any of your bets on this," he cautioned. "We have been making many raids on Germany in the recent days. I fear the Nazis will be wanting to avenge them."

"You could be right," Peter granted. "I'll just have to be doubly vigilant. Let's see, it's a quarter to ten. I'll do my rounds and see you back here in an hour or two."

"If only Fat Arnold were still with us," Joe said sadly. "I do not like having to do his shift plus my own. Already it has made me miss Gert and Daisy on the radio—a most funny pair of English ladies."

Peter wrapped his scarf around him and pulled on his tin hat. "I always prefer 'Bandwagon,'" he said. "That Arthur Askey's even been known to put a smile on my mother's face, and if that's not proof that miracles do 'appen, I don't know what is."

Mr. Harmon looked at him for a moment and then, in his gentle accent, said, "It is good to see you like this, my friend. There was a time, not long ago, when I worried for you."

Peter coughed uncomfortably. "Takes a while, doesn't it?" he answered. "But life goes on, as my Jean kept telling me. Some days I even forget he's gone, you know, and I find myself thinkin' I must tell Billy this or that. Then I remember that he ain't here no more. 'Orrible, empty feelin', that is. Won't ever get over that."

"We are nothing without our children," Joe commented. "Many, I fear, will know that feeling by the time this war is over—and some more than most. Ah, still, you are most lucky yet to have your daughter."

Peter nodded, then sloughed off the solemn mood by saying, "I 'eard your Mickey gave the cops a hard time this mornin'."

Mr. Harmon threw his hands in the air. "All day long I have heard nothing but murder from that boy. What monster have I raised? His talk makes his mother faint. Twice already this day he has done this to her. When he goes to war he will, I think, be changed. I pray that is all that befalls him."

"Him and Neil make a funny pair."

"You are fond already of that mystery boy," Joe observed. "If you keep lucky, then maybe he will never remember where he lives."

Peter smiled but made no answer. "Time I was off," he said. "See you later."

Joe Harmon waved to him as he left the wardens' post, then picked up the *Magnet* once more and continued reading.

As Peter Stokes walked through the empty streets, his thoughts were preoccupied by visions of William, his son. He was a high-spirited boy who had inherited his pigheadedness from his grandmother. When Billy enlisted, Peter's chest had swelled with pride, glad that his son was willing to march off and fight for his king and country. It never entered his head that he might never come back—not once. Tragedies like that happened to other families, not his.

Angrily the warden shook himself. He had been through all these recriminations so many times. He knew he had to get on with life and make the best of it, that's what Billy would have wanted.

Trudging through the puddles, Peter fastened the top button of his coat and buried his face in the scarf—it was getting chilly again.

In the darkness, for a brief second, the woolen scarf appeared to glint and shimmer with a greenish hue shot through with strands of silver. Then the illusion vanished and the scarf was dark blue once more.

"Somethin' nasty about tonight," Peter grumbled, ambling past the edge of the large bomb site. "There's somethin' foul in the air. I don't like it."

Glancing suspiciously around the dark, murky street, the warden grunted. It wasn't like him to be so edgy. "It's that Joe Harmon mentioning Billy that's done it," he told himself. "I think I might stop back home for a bit and have another cup of tea. My skin's creeping like it's full of ants."

Shoving his hands into his pockets, Peter Stokes turned in the direction of Barker's Row, then he stopped dead in his tracks.

"What the? . . ."

Unable to believe his eyes, the warden blinked and stared out into the bomb site again.

Toward the middle of the bleak wasteland, behind the ruined walls and heaps of rubble, a row of three shattered houses reared into the damp night, and Peter mumbled under his breath in bewilderment.

"'Ell's bells!"

In spite of the fact that it was gutted, derelict, roofless, and deprived of heat and water, one of the buildings had suddenly burst into light. From every broken window and every splintered door dazzling shafts of radiance blazed into the night, their intense beams piercing and mocking the blackout, spiking the darkness in all directions with brilliant, blinding blades.

"What the bleedin' 'eck's going on over there?" Peter rumbled, hastening into the unearthly landscape. "What sort of idiot's doing that?"

Quickly the warden ran toward the shameless beacon, shouting the entire time for the people responsible to douse the dangerous glare.

"You want to tell the Germans exactly where you are?" he bellowed. "Put that light out! I'm warning you!"

But the building continued to gush forth with rays so fierce and bright that it hurt his eyes to look at them.

"Never seen the like!" Peter snarled. "The rain must've shorted an exposed fuse somewhere. If this is that Dorkins girl, I'll get her this time, even if she tries to bite me whole hand off."

Into the glare he ran, his stretching shadow flitting farther back as he drew ever closer to the blazing windows.

Tearing through the harsh brightness that shone starkly over the rough terrain at the rear of the empty house, the warden dashed for the back door and threw himself inside.

The demolished kitchen was unbearable. The lightbulb that dangled from the warped ceiling was like a tiny sun, and a crackling buzz chimed within the filament as it scorched and flared a thousand times brighter than it was made to.

Peter could hardly open his eyes as he fumbled his way toward the switch, squinting and shielding them with his hands as every surface reflected the unnatural brightness full in his face.

Eventually he found the switch and flicked it. But the garish bulb refused to be extinguished and steadfastly continued to burn.

"What on earth? . . ." the warden gabbled, lumbering from the intense kitchen and out into the equally dazzling hallway.

He was not able to see where he was going, and a broken banister rod smacked him in the face, cutting and gouging his cheek until a trickle of blood gleamed on the broken skin like a luminous string of rubies.

Groping his hands over the walls, Peter found the hall switch and angrily snapped it off, but still the bulbs blistered and seared.

"This ain't right," he muttered. "Not right at all—plain weird."

Opening the parlor door, he looked quickly around the glowing room with its collapsed roof timbers still thrust into the floor, but no one was there.

"Edie's got to be in here someplace," he told himself. "I'd stake my bacon ration on it."

Screwing up his face, he looked upstairs to the landing and sucked his teeth as he considered what to do.

"I'll bet that little devil's up there," he decided, "havin' a good laugh at my expense. Well, them steps better hold out, 'cuz she ain't makin' a fool out of me no more."

Tentatively he tested the bottom stair. It seemed strong enough, and so Peter Stokes began to climb.

Suddenly, the kitchen was plunged into darkness, but now he was almost halfway up and did not see the kitchen light go out. Behind him, as he neared the top, the hall light snapped out and the whole of the downstairs was lost in deep shadow.

Peter stared down into the well of blackness where the stairs descended, and a wry grin broke over his face.

"She's gettin' a bit smart, ain't she—fiddlin' with the 'lectrics? You'd best be careful, Edie," he called out, "else you might fry yourself."

Looking along the landing, he tried to guess which of the two rooms she was holed up in.

"Ain't no floor in the end one," he reminded himself. "Now then, Miss, I've got you."

Warily pressing the weight of his foot on the landing, expertly listening to the boards squeak and complain, the warden approached the nearest bedroom.

Before he reached it, the naked bulb that hung over the stairwell began to flicker, and just as his hand reached for the doorknob, it went out.

An absolute darkness crashed in around Peter Stokes, broken only by the slice of light shining from under the bedroom door.

Hesitating before he pushed the door open, the warden felt his skin tingle, and a ridiculous fear of the blackness that swamped him flared in his mind. He had never experienced such a complete darkness. Even in the worst blackout the night did not possess such a deep and somber solidness.

It was as though the dark had taken a form and substance all its own to become a tangible, suffocating enemy, an adversary in which every terror was made manifest and every nightmare became a hideous reality.

To his distress, it seemed that the pitch gloom was actually growing darker. The malevolent night crept through the hallway below, flowing up the stairs to come pouring toward him. A vile, fetid reek was borne on the advancing, blind blackness—a stench of open graves and rotting corpse flesh—and at once, Peter was overwhelmed by unreasoning fear.

Kicking the bedroom door open, he leaped inside, then sent it slamming into the frame behind him, propping himself against it to try and keep the darkness out.

As beads of sweat pricked over his forehead, the warden squinted around the bedroom. Except for himself, the only illuminated place in the derelict house was totally empty.

For a puzzled instant the warden stared around at the four bright walls, then he swallowed nervously. Whoever was trying to unsettle him was doing an excellent job of it.

Wildly he wondered if he could crawl out of the shattered window and drop down to the ground below, just to get out of this uncanny building that lured its victims with light and crept after them with unfathomable dark.

"Easy now," he panted, trying to stop the panic. "Don't be hasty, don't be hasty. You'll only go an' break your neck. What's to be scared of? Yer an air-raid warden. You ain't suppose to be 'fraid of the dark. You came here to put the darn lights out, so don't go to pieces when they do go out."

Then he heard it, a faint noise in the hallway below, a furtive, shambling tread creeping toward the stairs.

"There is someone else in the house!" he cried, and his relief at the plainly human sound banished the fears that had threatened to unman him.

But the smile soon melted from his face. There was something horrible and repellent about the purposeful stealth of those dragging footsteps.

"Hope that's Joe come to see what the lights were about," he murmured hopefully. "Hey, Joe, that you?"

He received no answer, but the footsteps continued to climb the stairs and Peter's mind flew to Doris Meacham. Perhaps her murderer was with him now, steadily mounting the steps in complete blackness, hungry for another victim.

"Right, then," Peter growled, looking around for

something to serve as a weapon and picking up the leg of a broken chair. "You come in here, chummy, you won't find me so easy to butcher."

By now the footsteps had reached the landing, where they turned and began lumbering toward the brilliantly lit room.

Peter moved away from the entrance and lifted the chair leg over his head, tensing himself for the door to fly open and the assailant to come charging in.

"First I'll knock whatever knife you've got out of your hand," Mr. Stokes assured himself, "then I'll whack you out cold."

Above him, the buzzing lightbulb abruptly dimmed, and the shock of that instilled more terror into Peter than any murderer ever could.

"Don't you go out!" he prayed. "Don't leave me in the dark."

The footsteps were right outside the bedroom now, and while the light continued to wane, Peter took deep breaths as he prepared for the brutal attack.

Nothing happened. Not a sound filtered through the door, and the perspiration turned cold on the warden's brow as he waited for the onslaught to begin.

After several minutes, with only the high buzzing of the failing lightbulb to be heard, Peter's arms began to ache, and he cried, "What are you waiting for? Come in, why don't you?"

A faint noise like a strangled sigh groaned behind the doorway, and Peter chewed his lower lip.

"What was that?" he called. "If you've got something to say, you'd best do it in here."

"Dad?" came a fevered voice. "Dad, is that you?"

Peter Stokes lowered the chair leg, and the pit of his stomach tightened into a painful knot. "Who . . . who's that?" he stammered.

"Dad, it's me. Let me in."

"No," Peter gasped, the weapon dropping from his trembling hands, "it can't be."

"Please, Dad," the voice pleaded, "it's so dark out here, it's been so very dark. I'm scared."

"Oh, Lord, help me," the warden sobbed. "Bill."

"That's right, Dad, it's me, Billy. Don't say you've forgot me, Dad. It's so cold out here. Let me in."

"That isn't you out there, son," Peter wailed. "It sounds like you, but it isn't."

"Listen to me." The familiar tones of his dead son's voice razored through his soul. "I'm going to come in now. I want to see you again, Dad."

Mr. Stokes's throat dried like sandpaper as the doorknob gave a sly twist, then turned, and with an ominous click, the catch sprang back into the lock.

Very gently, the door opened, and Pete shuffled backward as a hand came reaching around to push it wide.

With a shudder the doorknob tapped against the wall, and there, framed in the entrance but keeping well within the murky shadows, was William Stokes.

"Hello, Dad," he said. "Glad to see me?"

Only a ghastly croak passed the warden's lips as he gazed on the dark form of his dead son.

The boy appeared to be dressed in his army uniform—Peter could see the buttons glinting dully—but because the unlit figure remained in darkness it was impossible for him to discern any more.

"Billy," he finally whispered. "How can this be? I . . . I had a telegram."

"Only a wound, Dad. It was a mistake."

Peter made a move toward him.

"Don't come any closer," the young, shadowy soldier warned.

"Why not? Why won't you step into the light? Billy, what is it?"

"I don't want you to see me like this. It was a nasty wound, Dad, left some 'orrible scars. Won't be winnin' any beauty prizes."

"Son," the warden said gently, "let me see."

"Don't say I never warned you," came the chuckling reply.

Slowly, Billy stepped over the threshold of the bedroom.

In the now dim light, where the ragged edges of the uniform gaped in tattered rents, pulsing shapes glistened and quivered.

Above the right hip, where his stomach should have been, there was only a shadow-filled cavity, and above that, within the smashed remains of his rib cage, was a mass of torn flesh and ruptured organs. No arm was attached to the shreds of bone that poked from the shoulder, and hanging loose from the exposed throat, the windpipe jumped and jerked.

A vile laugh hissed and gurgled from the apparition's mouth, the right side of which was raw and ripped right down to the splintered jaw and crushed cheekbone.

The demon that had assumed Billy's shape appeared to Peter Stokes exactly the way his son had looked at the moment of his death, and it watched in grisly amusement as the warden fell to his knees in torment.

"You did this to me, Dad," it taunted. "I wouldn't have joined up if you hadn't made me. Took me six hours to die, Dad, and it was all your fault."

"No," Peter protested. "You're not my Billy."

"Perhaps not," the demon cackled, its eyes flashing with red fire.

As Belial moved in on him, the warden let out a piercing scream.

Outside, in the bomb site, Edie Dorkins stared up at the glimmering window, shivering in horror at the chilling sound of the man's dying screech. And then the failing light was snuffed out and Peter Stokes's howls were silenced.

Yelping in fear, the girl turned and hared over the ruins, fleeing into the farthest reaches of her rapidly shrinking realm.

CHAPTER 16

THE KISMET

At four the next morning, before the first gray traces of daylight climbed into the dark heavens, Angelo and the other airmen who had tied towels to the ends of their bunks to show they were flying that day were awoken by a light in their faces.

Shivering, the Americans slid out of bed, cussed at the iciness of the concrete floor, and dressed for the mission briefing.

Laying out his gear, Angelo pulled on his clothes in a careful and precise order, then he meticulously shaved his face so that there would be nothing to irritate his skin when he wore the oxygen mask.

When he was satisfied that everything had been done exactly the same as the previous twelve times, he took up the two teddy bears, just as he had carried Tex, and followed the rest of the men to the mess.

Despondently, Angelo ate his breakfast, not speaking to anyone, and conscious that he was observing another of his rituals, none of the crew tried to engage him in conversation.

"Least we g-get real eggs on mission days," Frank mumbled appreciatively, dipping his toast into the runny yolk.

When the meal was over, the airmen filed into a hut for the briefing and learned the nature of the day's mission. Frank's information had been correct—they were to destroy an oil refinery deep in the heart of Germany.

With solemn, downcast faces, the men left the hut and piled into the equipment room, where they hauled on their electrically heated flying suits, flak jackets, Mae Wests, and parachutes. Then they clambered aboard a jeep and drove to the airfield.

All through the night the mechanics had been working on the Flying Fortresses, loading the bombs and bullets, running instrument checks and refueling. Now the planes were ready for the aircrew, and as Angelo stared up at *The Kismet*, he touched the St. Christopher's medal under his shirt, muttering, "I need all the help I can get today."

With sober efficiency everyone assumed their stations. Pat Dyson, the bombardier, sat in the nose of the B-17 with the navigator, and behind them, raised on the flight deck, sat Captain Resnick, his co-pilot, and the flight engineer.

A strengthened bulkhead divided the pilots from Angelo, who made the routine examinations of the radio. The waist gunners inspected the great machine guns mounted behind the wings, which fired through gaping holes cut into the fuselage.

Beyond the bomb bay doors, the ball gunner waited

for takeoff so that he could crawl into the deathtrap situated under *The Kismet*'s belly, and bringing up the rear—squeezed right in the tail, his long legs tucked underneath him—sat Frank.

"Okay, boys," Captain Resnick's voice crackled over the intercom, "let's do the tests. Is everyone's throat mike working?"

One by one the crew reported in, then briefly they put on their air masks to ensure the oxygen supply was coming through.

When the preliminaries were done, Jimmy Resnick drummed his fingers on the instrument panel and waited for the all-clear from the weather boys.

Sitting at the radio operator's small table, Angelo hooked Daniel's teddy bear onto the bulkhead, where Tex used to watch over him, and he placed Ted in the corner beside the log book.

"Okay, you little furry guys," he told them, "I'm expecting you to be just as lucky as Tex was, so you got a tough act to follow. Stay sharp."

"There she goes," the captain's voice informed everyone. "Green flare. The mission's on, boys."

Slowly, the B-17s taxied to the runway, and with much roaring and shaking, they lurched into the air.

In the tail, Frank gazed out as the ground suddenly dropped below him, and soon he could see only the open sky as *The Kismet* steadily rose.

The tail gunner closed his eyes. He had been dreading today's mission as much as Angelo, and he hoped he wouldn't let the rest of the crew down.

"Sure would like to see Kath again," he murmured wistfully.

From his position on the radio table, Ted watched and waited as the aircraft assembled in formation then joined up with other groups from different airfields.

Eventually, they were flying over the English Channel. Each man was now wearing his oxygen mask, for *The Kismet* had climbed to twenty thousand feet and the air was thin and freezing.

Gazing up at Angelo, Ted could see the sweat had already frozen into beads of ice on his brow, and he knew that the danger was only just beginning.

An escort of smaller fighters flew in front of the huge box formation, but the range of those planes was slight and soon they would fall back, leaving the bombers vulnerable and exposed to attack.

"Is it colder today or is it just me?" Angelo spoke over the intercom.

"Reading fifty below," the captain told him, "and falling. Hey, Voo, why don't you magic up some heat in here?"

"You think I haven't tried?" came the quick response. "'Fraid my talent only runs to cigarettes and aces. Tried to pull a live rabbit outta my sleeve once, though. Would'a worked, too, if the danged critter hadn't died of fright up there."

"That ain't true!" the bombardier's voice buzzed.

"Don't you believe nothin', Dyson?"

"Not when it comes from your mouth, Signorelli."

"Wish I could make you disappear. Hey, Dyson, when we get back to base, what say I try an' saw you in half? Figure that'd impress you."

"Haw haw!"

Listening with amusement, Frank peered out of the

tail window at the bombers flying behind and around them.

"On our own now," the captain told everyone. "There go the P-47s. Bye-bye, boys."

With a pang of sadness, knowing they were now at the mercy of the Luftwaffe, Frank watched as the escort planes dropped out of formation and headed back to England, leaving the Flying Fortresses undefended.

A horrendous feeling of insecure isolation shivered down his spine, and he gritted his teeth, taking deep breaths of oxygen through the mask.

"You there, Voo?" Frank blurted.

"This is Mr. Signorelli's answering service," squeaked a falsetto voice. "The lieutenant just bailed out."

Frank relaxed and chuckled at this nonsense. "Shoulda let me know," he said. "I'd have jumped with you."

Suddenly, the drone of the surrounding engines was interrupted by a fierce spitting of gunfire, and Frank twisted his head to see a cloud of German fighters storm overhead like a swarm of furious hornets.

"Goering's flying circus, boys!" Captain Resnick rapped. "Don't spare the lead!"

At once, the waist gunners sprang into action, and their guns juddered as streams of flaming bullets shot into the sky. In the top turret, the flight engineer gripped the trigger of the gun, quaking as the weapon spouted out a trail of death. Under the belly of *The Kismet*, the ball turret rolled around, shooting into the empty sky below, not waiting to see if there were any fighters beneath.

Frank's gloved hands squeezed the tail gun desperately as he scanned the air for enemy planes. The Messerschmitts were no longer in his field of vision.

Then, without warning, one of them came swooping down, the shadow of its left wing passing right over his head. Straight for the Fortress following *The Kismet*, the fighter dived—its crackling guns streaking toward the flight deck.

To Frank's horror he saw the pilots jerk in their seats as the bullets ripped through them, and the bomber began to fall from the sky.

Arcing around, the Messerschmitt disappeared out of sight once more, and Frank could only watch as the B-17 dropped gracefully into the sea of clouds below.

Quaking, he took his hands from the tail gun and hugged himself desperately.

"Fish in a barrel," the bombardier quipped. "They're jus' pickin' us off one at a time, whenever they feel like."

"What else is new?" Angelo asked dryly.

But with a final burst of gunfire, the fighters wheeled away, and soon the bombers were left in peace.

"Hey!" Patrick Dyson cried. "What gives? Where'd they go?"

"Maybe they saw your mug gapin' at them," Angelo answered, looking around at the bullet holes punched through the fuselage. "We sure were lucky that time."

Unhooking Daniel's teddy, he gave it a kiss then returned it. "You did good, pal," he said, "but we still got a ways to go. Don't think you can take it easy from now on."

For nearly an hour the formation flew in untroubled skies, then, as they approached Germany, a second wave of fighters came spitting from the clouds.

Sitting on the table, Ted winced as three more bombers were hit. In the tail, Frank clung to the gun, screaming in abject terror as the dark shapes soared past and gripping the trigger so tight that his hand locked and cramped around it.

Then the air exploded.

A burst of black smoke thundered into existence as, far below on the ground, the antiaircraft guns spluttered into life.

"Here's the flak!" Dyson observed unnecessarily.

Angelo gave Daniel's teddy a warning tap to make certain he was on the job. Flak was even worse than the fighters—there was no one you could shoot at.

Violent eruptions flowered everywhere, and in a matter of minutes the sky had grown dark.

"God Almighty!" Captain Resnick bawled. "I can hardly see up here. You could get out and walk on this stuff."

"I ain't never seen it this thick before," the bombardier breathed.

With a booming roar, one of the Fortresses nearby took a direct hit, and rupturing into two flaming fragments, it plummeted out of the sky.

The noise of the exploding shells was deafening. Angelo covered his ears, and in the tail, Frank squeezed his eyes shut, unable to witness any more horror.

In the middle of all this confusion and fear, Ted screwed up his face and tried to remember what happened all that time ago—how did they get out of this? But no matter how hard he tried, the answer eluded him.

"What happened back then?" the bear murmured frantically. "Geez—why can't I remember?"

Suddenly, a shell detonated almost overhead.

A blasting gale tore through *The Kismet* as flak ripped

apart the fuselage as if it was tinfoil, slashing a two-foot hole horrendously close to Angelo's head.

Everything not fixed down was snatched up by the rampaging windstorm and sucked out into the freezing sky. Papers, log books, compasses, pens, even empty brass cartridges were flung through the jagged rent, and with a frightened wail, so was Ted.

Unable to stop himself, the bear was plucked from the desk and sent spinning through the air.

"Whoa!" Angelo cried, rushing forward.

But the gale was too fierce. Ted slipped through the American's fingers and was hurled out of the plane.

"Hey, how 'bout that?" Angelo yelled, peering out of the yawning hole.

Clutching hold of a sharp piece of ripped metal just outside the rent, Ted had managed to save himself. But the blistering, flak-filled air tore at him, and as his paws gradually lost their grip, he knew he would soon be ripped to shreds in the bomber's propellers when he fell.

Oily black smoke stung Angelo's eyes as he leaned recklessly out of the fissure and dragged Ted back inside the aircraft.

"This guy must have some luck," he called to the waist gunners, waving the bear at them. "He snagged on the fuselage."

Wedging Ted into the gap between the radio and the inside of the plane, he tweaked his furry cheek, saying, "You stay put from here on in."

When the man's eyes left him, the bear shook his head and let out a yelping groan. "That was too close," he moaned.

The heavens were black as ink now. Five more

Fortresses succumbed to the antiaircraft guns, their raging fires bursting briefly through the smoky darkness as they plunged downward.

"I never been on no mission like this," Angelo muttered. "What gives here, Captain?"

The B-17 lurched as another shell exploded close by and the wings were peppered with holes. A pall of smoke blew through the gun ports, and for a hideously long time, no one in the bomb bay could open his eyes.

Somewhere ahead another bomber caught fire, and when its fuel tank ignited, the flash of its demise lit up the whole fume-choked sky.

Flaming rags of metal spat toward *The Kismet*, and as Frank dared to brave the ghastly spectacle, he saw a piece of the aircraft's tail go rocketing past his window, with its gunner still screaming inside.

The clamor of two more B-17s spiraling out of control resounded through Frank's head, and he curled into a ball, unable to move a muscle.

As *The Kismet* plowed through the dense, violent bursts, Angelo held grimly to the desk, rocking with the turbulent motion of the aircraft.

Above the din of the rupturing shells the sky was filled with the uproar of dying engines as yet more Fortresses flared with ghastly brilliance. Flying blind through the blanketing smoke, two bombers collided with one another, and *The Kismet* pitched alarmingly as she flew straight through the outskirts of the ensuing holocaust.

Ravaging flames scorched the olive hull, and the picture of the woman painted on the nose bubbled and blistered.

Within the aircraft, a fireball came blasting through

the gun ports and roared the length of the bomb bay as the crew buried their faces in their gloved hands until it rumbled past, thundering toward the tail.

Hearing the noise, Frank turned, and his vision was filled by the inferno blasting straight for him.

"Cover your face!" Angelo bawled.

But all Frank could do was stare. The tremendous heat burned his skin and his eyebrows smoldered, but he was too petrified to save himself.

And then it was over. With only a foot to spare before the furnace enveloped him, it was gone, dissipating into the oxygen-starved air and leaving only a reek of burning fuel and smoke in its wake.

Frank slumped against the window, too frightened to be relieved.

"No way can we survive this," the captain murmured, the view from the flight deck a swirling chaos of black fog. "If the flak don't get us, one of our own Forts will."

Pressing his throat mike he barked to Angelo, "What does the lead plane say? This is a coffin trip."

"Don't know which is the lead plane!" the radio operator called back. "*Sweet Sue* was torched ten minutes ago, then *Naughty Katy* was grilled. All I'm gettin' is static and lotsa screamin'."

Angelo adjusted the dials, searching for a voice in the tortured ether, but his ears heard nothing. Glancing up at Daniel's bear, he was suddenly horrified to discover that the toy had been sliced to ribbons by a piece of flying shrapnel. Only a scrap of gray fur and a quantity of tattered stuffing was left on the hook, and the lieutenant trembled at what this omen portended.

"Knew it would be today," he whispered fatally.

Holding his head in his hands, Angelo waited for the end to come. Then, very faintly, a warbling voice spoke in his ear, and the airman sprang up hopefully.

"Mission aborted!" he hollered into the mike. "The *Helldragon*'s in charge now. She's tellin' everyone to turn about. Get this crate outta here!"

Slowly the formation veered around, suffering four more casualties as they blindly made the maneuver in the impenetrable fumes.

Presently, glimmers of daylight began to appear ahead as the shells fell, and with grateful sighs from all her crew, *The Kismet* sailed out of the infernal, fiery clouds and into clear skies.

"How many did we lose?" the captain asked.

"Reports just coming in," Angelo replied. "Thirty-seven B-17s missing."

"Damn."

"Let's just hope them Nazi bandits don't want us for dessert," the bombardier said grimly.

Crouching in the tail section, Frank rocked backward and forward, tears streaming down his face and freezing before they splashed onto the floor. Never in his entire life had he been so terrified, and he knew nothing would ever compel him to board another aircraft. They could court-martial him or throw him in the slammer—he didn't care. The horrific memories of this raid would plague him for the rest of his life. No, he was going to make sure that he would never fly on another mission.

"Don't feel right goin' home with all these bombs still in place," Angelo declared. "We really fouled up this time."

"Least we didn't buy the farm," Jimmy Resnick

answered. "Anyone want to know how cold it is out there? It's reading sixty-five below."

"That dial only goes down to sixty-five!" Angelo shouted back.

"What do you expect at twenty-eight thousand feet?"

Jammed beside the radio, Ted looked up at Angelo, and a faint smile appeared on the bear's face. They might be returning with their tails between their legs, but at least the crew was still alive.

"Enjoy this moment while you can, Voodini," the bear said to himself. "You got a big day ahead of you tomorrow. That's when the real trial begins. Don't you worry none, you got me with you this time."

Ted's musings were cut short as he noticed a startling change come over the radio operator's face.

Angelo coughed into the air mask, and his breathing became increasingly labored.

"Damn sup-supply," he gagged, reaching for the auxiliary oxygen bottle. But before he could make the switch, Angelo's eyes bulged and he collapsed, senseless, against the table.

In bewildered distress, Ted saw the other airmen fighting for breath, and one by one they blacked out, dropping to the floor of the bomber.

"Hey!" the bear cried, feverishly trying to dislodge himself from beside the radio. "What in Sam Hill's going on? This ain't right, it didn't happen—I was there!"

Hopping over the desk, he knelt beside Angelo's head and wrenched the air mask from his face.

"Line's damaged," he said. "They been suckin' in lungfuls of fumes. He'll never be able to breathe without an air line this high up, none of them will."

Slapping the airman's cheek, Ted yelled, "Don't flake out on me, pal! Hang in there. Wake up, Signorelli! Wake up!"

But Angelo did not move, and at that moment the bear was thrown from the table as the bomber dipped and the drone of the engines became a dreadful whine.

"The captain, too?" Ted shrieked, scrambling to his stumpy feet and hurrying to the flight deck. "Oh, no! This ain't happenin'! Tell me it ain't!"

Over the radio, the anxious voice of the lead plane called to *The Kismet* as it did a nosedive from the rest of the group, but the *Helldragon* received no answer.

In the cockpit, Ted leaped over the slumped body of the flight engineer and jumped onto the pilot's lap, ripping their masks from them as he went.

The Flying Fortress was plunging downward now, screaming through the clouds as it hurled headlong to destruction.

"Come on, Resnick!" Ted screeched. "You gotta pull her outta this dive!"

Leaping across the co-pilot, the bear tried to rouse him too, but it was no use. The whine of the engines was unbearable, and the bomber shuddered perilously. Rushing white clouds smothered the windows, and staring helplessly at the altimeter as it jerked ever downward, Ted reached for the steering column.

Growling in anguish, the bear pulled as hard as his paws could manage, but his puny strength was no match for the colossal forces that now controlled the aircraft.

"It didn't end this way!" he raged. "These men survived this mission. I oughta know!"

The gauge was reading fourteen thousand feet, and

the bear's impotent shrieks were drowned out by the blaring noise of the plane's breakneck descent.

"Help me!" Ted howled, throwing his head back and screaming until the fur stretched around his mouth. "It can't finish like this! Help me! Pleeeaaaase!"

"Don't grovel, Edward," a stern female voice suddenly commanded. "It's quite out of character for you."

Goggling in disbelief, the bear whipped around and let out a mad, joyous laugh.

Sitting where only a moment ago the unconscious body of Captain Resnick had sat, and looking exceedingly bizarre dressed in his flying suit, flak jacket, Mae West, and parachute, was Miss Ursula Webster.

Before Ted could say anything, he jumped in surprise as the co-pilot's knee gave an unexpected jerk, and gazing upward, he found that he was staring into the white-powdered visage of Miss Veronica, whose charcoal eyebrows had been drawn higher than ever.

"Good afternoon," she said with a giggle.

"Coooeee!" called a third voice. "Isn't it a lovely day for March—most bracing! I do hope there won't be any rain later."

Ted stared past the chalk-faced co-pilot to where the flight engineer was clicking a pair of knitting needles.

"Do excuse me," Miss Celandine whistled through her buck teeth. "I know I should offer you my hand in greeting but I'm afraid I simply cannot put this down. Too important, Ursula says. Isn't that lovely, to do something important again?"

The walnut-faced woman gave a merry chortle as she diverted her attention back to her knitting, and the bemused bear stared at Miss Ursula incredulously.

"Get that ridiculous look off your face," she told him. "You do want our help, I trust?"

"B . . . bbb . . . sure," he gabbled.

"Oh, Ursula!" her co-pilot twittered, gazing with pure delight at the instruments and looking even more absurd in the flying outfit than her sister did. "Isn't it splendid? Let me press a button, oh, do! Just a teeny one."

"Veronica!" the other sharply rapped. "Stop that foolishness at once. I need your assistance to pull us out of this hazard. Now, copy my actions exactly."

Taking hold of the steering column, Miss Ursula began to drag it back, and obeying her sister, Miss Veronica did the same.

"If you want to make yourself useful," the white-haired lady told Ted, "you had better remove all the masks from the rest of the crew. If it's your intention they should live, that is. We can't do everything for you, Edward."

Not waiting to answer, the bear leaped from Miss Veronica's lap, tripped over Miss Celandine's ball of dark green and silver wool, much to her tittering amusement, and obediently bounded through the bomb bay, hauling the air masks from his comrades.

Back on the flight deck, the two elderly lady pilots gradually hauled the Flying Fortress out of its momentous dive, and the plane gently leveled out.

"A fraction over a thousand feet," Miss Ursula primly observed. "They shall be able to breathe quite normally when they come around."

"Oh, Ursula!" Her raven-haired sister beamed, her eyes shining. "That was fun. May we do it again? Just once? I did enjoy it so."

"Patience, Veronica," came the instant rebuke. "Must I send you back?"

The co-pilot wriggled in her seat and folded her arms sulkily as she stuck out her garishly daubed bottom lip.

Glancing up from her knitting, Miss Celandine cooed with relish. "Is the deadly, awful danger over?" she asked salaciously.

"For the moment," her sister replied, "but now I would speak with Edward. Where is he? Has he not finished that simplest of tasks?"

Puffing, the bear returned to the flight deck, nimbly avoiding the length of wool that the peculiar flight engineer had negligently allowed to stretch across his path.

Miss Celandine pulled a disappointed face then scratched her straw-colored hair with one of the needles.

"I gotta hand it to ya!" Ted thanked the Webster sisters. "You dames really know how to get a guy out of a jam!"

Miss Ursula turned an imperious, oddly daunting face on him. Half closing her near translucent eyelids, she contemplated the small, grubby bear, then her thin mouth curled into a ghostly smile.

"Well, Edward," she uttered in a crisp, businesslike tone, "I imagine that, for you, these years of waiting have been all too long."

Ted scrabbled up onto the instrument panel and sat down before answering. "There were times when I thought I was gonna go nuts cooped up in that glass box," he agreed. "It ain't no picnic down in that room, you know. You got a lot o' kooky stuff in there. You listen to what I'm sayin' and chuck it out."

"Oh, it wouldn't be safe to throw anything away," Miss Veronica piped up, "would it, Ursula?"

Her sister shot her a warning glance then let go of the controls and spoke earnestly to the bear.

"A wearisome wait you have had since first our bargain was made," she said.

"Too long," Ted replied. "When you made that promise, I never figured it would take forever."

"You were grateful enough at the time, as I recall, only too eager to comply. I stated from the beginning that it would not be accomplished overnight. An endeavor such as ours cannot be rushed into."

"I know, I know," the bear muttered. "I just hated coolin' my heels fer fifty years, that's all. Oh yeah, what's the idea putting me back too early? I never said anything 'bout that—it hasn't been no barrel of jollies."

Lifting her wrinkled face from her knitting, Miss Celandine looked at him in astonishment. "But you had to go that far," she cried indignantly, "didn't he, Ursula? How else could it have worked? You really are an awful silly sometimes, Mr. Edward."

"What's the pickled munchkin squawking about now?" Ted asked.

Miss Ursula's smile widened, and her mottled teeth appeared below her thin lips.

"For once Celandine is speaking perfect sense," she blithely told him. "Tut, tut, Edward, can't you see? We knew all the time that you were going to go back early. It wouldn't have done at all for you to return to the point just before you died, now would it?"

Ted's forehead puckered into a frown. "Run that by me again," he said, beginning to feel uneasy.

Putting her knitting down for the briefest of moments, Miss Celandine leaned forward until her braided hair dragged over the floor, and she gave a childishly smug snigger.

"This is where you were meant to perish," she clucked. "You were supposed to die in the crash along with all the others."

Miss Ursula nodded briskly. "That was the original design of your destiny, but because of the honor you paid us with the dedication of this vessel and the libations you gave us, we decided to intervene—just once more. So we permitted you, in your present form, to return to this hazard and save yourself and the rest of the crew. You were here to accomplish it then, and now you have done it again."

Ted reeled backward. "I never knew," he whispered. "I always thought we came outta this mission on our own. Why'd you never tell me this before?"

"Personally," Miss Celandine said, harking back to the libations, "I was the only one who liked the beer. Ursula and Veronica had no taste for it, did you, dears?"

"And so," Miss Ursula continued firmly, "our part of the bargain has been kept, has it not?"

"Wh . . . what do you mean?"

"We promised that you could save yourself, Edward— this you have just done. We have given you all the assistance we are willing to give. One chance was all you asked for, and that is what you have had. Don't be greedy and ask for more."

"Refusal might cause offense," gurgled Miss Veronica, who was busily trying to glimpse her reflection in the window.

His head still spinning from what he had learned, Ted quickly grew angry.

"Hold on!" he cried. "That ain't fair. You tricked me!"

"Go on!" Miss Celandine urged excitedly. "Say it! How fickle we are—everyone does!"

"Can't you muzzle that one?" he snarled. "You're nothin' but a pack of lyin', cheatin', chiselin' weasels."

"Take care," Miss Ursula cautioned. "If you do not curb your tongue, then we will see to it that the ones you really want to save are killed again."

Ted looked at her hopefully. "You mean there's still a chance?" he cried. "I thought you was breakin' yer promise."

"Oh, there's always a slight possibility for threads to slip from the tapestry," she replied. "It would never be entertaining if there was no prospect of that."

"I adore it when a stitch goes astray," Miss Celandine broke in. "Sometimes I drop them just to see what'll happen."

"She's talking about stitches?" Ted asked wryly.

"Exactly," Miss Ursula concurred. "That really is the correct description of you, Edward, a dropped stitch in the fabric of our weaving. You are a stitch in time. But you may not count on our help again. The ordeals that lie before you must be resolved on your own merit. The lives of those you hold dear depend solely on how sharp your wits are."

The bear leaned confidently back against the instrument panel with his paws behind his head. "Then it'll be a piece of cake." He grinned. "I can do that blindfolded."

"You might not find it quite so easy as you think," she snorted, "for a circumstance has occurred that could prove ruinous for us all."

Startled by the gravity of her voice, Ted blinked at the white-haired pilot and sat bolt upright.

"It is entirely your fault, of course," Miss Ursula scolded him. "You were slipshod and careless."

"What'd I do?" he muttered, unsettled by her censorious gaze.

"The gateway," she said scornfully. "Did we not instruct you in its ways and what had to be done?"

"That daffy gizmo was all over the place!" he cried defensively. "I know it made a mess and broke a few things, but you can't—"

"I am not talking of broken furniture!" she proclaimed.

"What a topsy-turvy mess there was!" Miss Veronica butted in.

Her eldest sister glared at her. "Edward," she said, summoning her dwindling reserves of patience, "you were not alone when you journeyed back."

"I know. That Neil kid—he ain't so bad—"

"I do not refer to the Chapman maggot," she breathed. "Then what?"

Miss Ursula narrowed her eyes. "Something that should have been banished from this world in the great long ago, along with the lords of the ice," she uttered mysteriously. "Something that must never be allowed its freedom. That is why we were entrusted with its keeping, to ensure that it could never harry the living land again."

"One of your Separate goodies," he groaned. "Am I right?"

"Celandine, show him."

The flight engineer unfurled the prodigious length of knitting that was folded on her knee and held it up in front of her face.

Within the enchanted depths of the raveled wool, the livid shades of green swirled and pulsed as the strands of silver tinsel sparkled and shimmered. But as Ted stared, he saw that two ugly, ragged holes had been cut into the knitted cloth and Miss Celandine's beady, black eyes peeped through them sorrowfully.

"The pattern is marred," Miss Ursula said. "The weave is no longer perfect. For each of those holes there was a life, yet those lives have been ripped from Celandine's web and there is nothing we can do to retrieve them."

"You sayin' that what I brought back did this?" Ted swallowed. "The thing from your collection? Which . . . which one was it?"

Miss Ursula fixed him with her gaze and said quite simply, "Belial."

"Aw, geez!" the bear moaned, smacking his head with his paw. "Why couldn't it have been the frog bones? You tellin' me this critter's got outta his box?"

"Most assuredly," she replied. "The demon is loose, and if he is not dealt with, then Celandine's labors will become nothing more than a few straggling threads."

"You're not suggestin' I bump him off?" Ted asked suspiciously.

"Don't be absurd," Miss Ursula snapped.

"You can't kill him!" Miss Veronica laughed.

"He must be returned to the casket," her sister said. "That is your only hope. His dark essence can never be utterly vanquished. It is written that Belial shall one day pour fire down upon the earth and destroy its foundations. All you have to do is ensure that the day in question is delayed for as long as possible. That must not happen until after the remaining root is destroyed and the cold returns."

"Wait a minute!" the bear cried, defiantly waving his arms in the air. "This wasn't part of the deal. I ain't messin' with no thousand-year-old boogie man."

"Oh, he's far, far older than that," Miss Ursula informed him. "Older even than us. *Beli ya'al*—whose name means 'without worth.' He is an unclean spirit, and his continued freedom is an incident that shouldn't have occurred and cannot be tolerated. It is up to you to secure his return to us."

"No way. You gotta be off your rocker, lady!"

"Then both the woman and her child will die," she said.

Ted glowered at her then hung his head in defeat. "What've I gotta do?" he burbled.

Miss Ursula clicked her fingers, and Miss Celandine took from her knitting bag a tiny vial of pale green glass.

"Here are the last drops of the divine water drawn from my well before it was drained," Miss Ursula said, taking it from her sister and passing it to the bear.

"Do not waste it, for the liquid is exceedingly precious. The world-tree itself was nourished by the same water."

"Root beer, eh?" Ted murmured, raising the small bottle to his nose and giving it a wary sniff. "Has the critter gotta drink this?"

"Sprinkle but a drop upon the demon and he shall be rendered harmless," said Miss Ursula.

"Yeah," Ted muttered sarcastically. "All I gotta do is get close enough."

"You will find a way," she assured him. "Belial must be returned to the museum in the prison fashioned for him by the fathers of Israel. Now, our time with you grows short. You must guard that vial at all costs."

"Where am I s'posed to stash it? I ain't got no pockets!"

Miss Ursula reached over and took hold of the bear's soft body. Deftly she searched through his fur for the seam and, with her fingernails, snapped a thread.

"Hey!" Ted yelled as she unpicked the stitches. "Ya could've asked. Ouch, that smarts!"

"Until you find him," she said, pushing the vial down into the bear's stuffing, "let that remain hidden. Veronica, attend to Edward's seam."

Scowling, Ted stood on the instrument panel while Miss Veronica took out a needle and thread and zealously sewed up the fluffy gap.

"I feel as though I swallowed a baseball bat," he complained, prodding his lumpy stomach.

"Now we must return," Miss Ursula declared.

The faces of her two sisters fell in unison. "Oh, Ursula!" they whined. "Just a little longer."

The woman ignored them and, with a parting glance at Ted, said, "Remember, he who is without worth is sustained by feeding on human souls. Two he has devoured already, and he is not much stronger than when first he crept from the casket. This is a perfect moment in history for him, and one that he shall use to his best advantage. What better time could he have escaped into? A world torn by war. That is a condition he knows only too well. You, Edward, are not immune from his appetite. On the contrary, the fiercer the soul burns, the more palatable Belial will find it. A tasty morsel indeed would you make. Be careful when you encounter him. He is a lord of deceit and wears many guises."

"Mebbe ya shoulda rammed some garlic in with that bottle," the bear joked feebly, but already the Webster sisters were gone.

Captain Jimmy Resnick gave a retching cough as he sluggishly came to.

Suddenly his eyes snapped open.

"What the hell?" he bellowed, seizing hold of the controls and staring out of the window at the fields and hills below. "What happened? What's goin' on here?"

Bounding through the plane and clambering over Angelo's body, up to the desk, Ted paused to whisper in the ear of the stirring radio operator.

"Well, Signorelli," the bear hissed, "it's up to you an' me now." Groggily, Angelo shook his head and peered around him, looking for the person who had spoken, but he saw no one except the rest of the slowly recovering crew.

In the tail section, Frank Jeffries lowered his eyes and gritted his teeth vehemently. He had come around more swiftly than the others, and to his dismay he had beheld Angelo's teddy bear come hopping from the flight deck.

"Lord in heaven!" he whimpered pitifully. "I'm goin' crazy. Oh, Kathy, I gotta see you again. I can't go through this again! I just can't—I gotta get out, I gotta get out!"

CHAPTER 17

ABSENT WITHOUT LEAVE

Covent Garden market was still quiet when Kathleen Hewett stole up Long Acre, past the empty crates and carts that rustled with starving rats out on scavenging excursions. The alarming shadow of a solitary market porter carrying a teetering stack of baskets on his head loomed unexpectedly from the dark, and she quickened her steps to avoid speaking to him.

Into a pinched, cramped alleyway she hastened, keeping the pathetic beam of her flashlight trained on the ground.

A lithe, furry body suddenly darted into her path, and the girl drew her breath as the slimy rodent dove into a pile of boxes, wriggling inside their cozy shelter.

Kath cursed herself for being afraid of the creature then peered into the darkness. The doorway was around here somewhere.

Jerome's All-Night Snackery was a greasy, unhealthy little dive. The faded sign outside the shuttered windows declared to the world that it regularly opened at eleven o'clock at night and closed at seven the following morning, but during those bleary-eyed hours it was never frequented by more than a few shady customers. The proprietor always chuckled to himself when some uninformed fool strayed inside and asked for something to eat.

Not one of the market porters ventured through the putrid café's unwelcoming door, for the tepid brown water served up as coffee swam with globules of unidentifiable oil, and the origin of the snacks was even more dubious.

Yet night after night, Jerome's was open, sitting quiet and unobtrusive in the deep blackout like a slowly rotting apple hidden among a barrel of sweeter, incorrupt produce.

Sneaking a furtive glance around her, Kath strode up to the grimy door, pushed against the peeling paint, and slipped inside.

The interior of the café was a poky little cesspool, dingily illumined by two naked lightbulbs that appeared to discharge a dirty brown glow over every smudged and fat-spattered surface. A row of three tables, strewn with cigarette ash and circled with old mug stains, led to the serving counter, where a hulking Neanderthal brute leaned over a newspaper, not bothering to raise his eyes when the girl entered.

At the middle table a hunched, ferret-faced old man wearing a cap and scruffy coat stared up from the dregs in his cup and directed a loathsome leer in Kath's direction.

Ignoring him completely, but aware of his ogling eyes

following her every move, she ducked under a string of ancient and crowded flypapers that hung from the mildew-spotted ceiling and walked to the counter.

The proprietor continued to read the newspaper. He was a huge tank of a man who resembled a slothful animal kept in too small a cage. His shiny black hair was scraped flat against his big-boned skull and gave off a scent that suggested there was as much lard groomed into it as masked the crusting tiles behind him.

The sleeves of the thug's shirt were rolled up past his fat elbows, revealing badly drawn tattoos that blotched and discolored his skin. An unwashed apron was tied around his waist, abstractly besmirched with untold slops and spills. On his right hand he wore a viciously spiked ring that had slashed many a face in the scuffles and brawls that regularly found him.

But this intimidating subspecies of humanity did not daunt Kathleen Hewett. Slapping her hand down on the newspaper to gain his attention, she returned the ruthless glare that burned out at her from beneath the apelike brow until the man averted his eyes and gruffly jerked a dirty thumb toward a door at the back of the café.

"In there," his voice rumbled from some unknown region deep in his chest.

Without thanking him, Kath pushed through the hinged section of the counter and passed into the room beyond.

The green room, as it was euphemistically termed in the director's coded analogy, was mostly dark. A single shaded bulb blasted a circle of brilliant light onto a plain wooden chair in the center of the space. Before this spot-lit seat was a tidy office desk, identical to those used by lawyers and accountants throughout the city, and sitting with his hands clasped between the in and out trays was a small, bespectacled man in a gray flannel suit.

"Close the door behind you," his clipped, disparaging voice commanded.

The girl did as he instructed and crossed to the chair, where she sat blinking in the harsh overhead light.

Mr. Ormerod, although that was not his real name, was an insignificant squirt of a man, as unremarkable and unassuming as any thousand you might pass in the street. This mundane and commonplace quality made him an ideal choice for the role his superiors had selected him for, and the prosaic creature took great pleasure in wielding this delicious authority.

His face and hands were as pink as a piglet's, and his thinning gray hair was trim. Unlike the oaf in the other room, this man had anointed his hair with a tonic that smelled incredibly sweet and fragrant—like pulpy raspberries mingled with cherry blossom.

He was a methodical man, and this was shown in various ways—from the fastidious manner in which he folded his spotless handkerchief and placed it in his breast pocket to the neat arrangement of pens and pencils laid out in regimented lines on the desk.

When he spoke, a tire of babyish skin alternately bulged and contracted over his tightly buttoned collar, and at times of extreme concentration or effort, his reptilian eyes had been known almost to protrude from their lashless lids and push against the glass of his half-moon spectacles.

"You're punctual tonight, at least," he commented,

glancing at a pocket watch and leafing through a sheaf of papers. "What have you got for me?"

Closing her eyes to visualize the details more clearly in her mind, Kath collected the relevant files she had committed to memory and began speaking in an educated, cultured voice, totally alien to the chirpy cockney character that had been allocated to her.

First she related the gossip she had heard in the American nightclub she had visited that evening, however trivial it might have sounded. Reports of troop movements, rumors concerning weapons deployment, quartermaster's supplies, and numbers of men— Kathleen repeated it all and Mr. Ormerod jotted it down.

Then she told him everything she had learned during the past week at the munitions factory where she worked. Work rotas, the amount of explosives stored there at any one time, together with their possible destinations.

Page after page of Mr. Ormerod's notebook was diligently filled by his spidery handwriting. He paused only when his lip became too wet and droplets of sweat dripped onto the paper. During one of these intervals, when he was blotting up the trickling, salty moisture, Kath steeled herself and spoke the thought that had gnawed away at her all afternoon.

"Mr. Ormerod," she said firmly, "this week the transportation of another three consignments has been delayed. A considerable quantity of explosives and ammunition is now stored in the factory warehouse."

"I have already ascertained that from the rest of your statement," he replied coldly, peering over the rim of his glasses. "Have you any further information to add?"

The girl shifted in the uncomfortable chair and leaned forward, overcome by a patriotic fervor.

"Might I ask if this intelligence will be acted upon?" she questioned. "On the last occasion when I told you of a similar delay, nothing was done about it. These occurrences are extremely rare, the timing could never be better. All I need is your authorization and I shall undertake the task myself. There are enough explosives there to rip a vast chunk out of the landscape."

Mr. Ormerod's antiseptic gaze left her, and he meticulously aligned his papers. "You are too anxious to prove yourself," he said. "It is not up to you to dictate which is a valid stage and which is not."

"But in this I am certain!" she hotly answered. "The factory is surrounded by residential buildings. Think of it—the number of civilian casualties would be phenomenal. What a blow that would be to British morale. If no action is taken soon, then it will be too late!"

"Then so be it!" he argued, his voice rising to a piggish squeal. "You are only a common little prompter! Collect and pass on information, that is the sum of your function. Nothing more!"

Kathleen pushed the table angrily, causing the man's pencils to go clattering to the floor, and she knew she had gone too far.

Not waiting to mop up the sweat dribbling from his top lip, Mr. Ormerod rose from his seat and rushed around the table, raising his small pink hand to bring it slapping down across the girl's cheek.

Kath withstood the pain and humiliation of the blow in shamed silence, defying her stinging skin and forbidding her eyes to moisten. When she looked back at her stage manager, a livid red mark of his child-sized palm was already throbbing on her cheek.

Panting unpleasantly, Mr. Ormerod wiped his entire face with the handkerchief before returning it unfolded to his breast pocket.

"Do not overreach yourself!" his shrill voice shrieked. "Many others have attempted that most unwise policy. They were dealt with in the same fashion as the ones from whom they took their identities. Do I have to impress it upon you in plainer terms?"

The girl sullenly shook her head and, in the clipped German of her native tongue, apologized to him.

"I don't think you would find it agreeable to join the poor little girl who was the real Kathleen Hewett in an unmarked grave, would you?"

Flushed with the unaccustomed outburst of emotion, he returned to his seat and took deep breaths, putting considerable strain on the top button of his shirt.

"Never forget," he hissed in a repugnant breath, "that without me, you are nothing. None of you, not even the leading roles and star turns, can perform without me. I am the stage manager, the only one who can assimilate and organize. How long have you been in the profession?"

"Almost two years."

"I have lived here for twenty-one," he bragged, "and in that time I have become a respectable, conservative citizen of the Empire. Why, in the district where I now reside, I'm even an active member of the Home Guard. So I don't need a hotheaded novice like you, who hasn't even made it to the chorus, trying to tell me my responsibilities. I shall be here long after your useful days either have come to an end or have been brought to a rather swifter conclusion by either faction."

Kath bore this tirade in meek servility, and when Mr. Ormerod was done, she asked if she was free to go.

"Usual read-through next week," he reminded her as she made for the door. "Oh, and before you depart," he added sourly, "the producers were greatly pleased with the information concerning this morning's bombing raid. A bouquet and a critics' award to you."

"My aim is to serve," she said. "There was not time to inform you."

"Was there not? Are you not familiar with the emergency contact number?"

"And the code."

"Then make certain you use them next time. I have always said that to give someone in the wings access to sound equipment is counterproductive. Only harm can come of such folly."

"I will remember on the next occasion."

"I do hope so. I have been compelled to alter the code word, or perhaps I ought to say words. It is now 'over-ambitious fraulein.' I'm sure you will not forget that."

Suffering the last insult, the girl forced a polite good-bye from her lips then walked out of the green room, leaving Mr. Ormerod hissing through his teeth.

* * *

Angelo Signorelli traipsed wearily through the deserted streets and gave a whistle of relief when he eventually found Barker's Row.

Jumping over the garden wall of the end house, and cussing when he realized he had leaped straight into a compost heap, he slowly made his hurdling way to number twenty-three.

A perfect peace lay over the garden of the late Peter Stokes. In their tiny hut the chickens dozed serenely, not waking even when the American lost his shoe in the potato patch and took his irritation out on the woody stalks of last year's Brussels sprouts.

Brushing the soil from his trousers, Angelo crept toward the mound at the bottom of the garden where the ghostly tendrils of the strawberry plants hung over the entrance to the bomb shelter.

Stealthily, he descended to the doorway and hissed softly, his breath gushing from his mouth in clouds of steam.

"Jean," he called. "Jean, you in there?"

The lieutenant waited a moment, then called her name again.

Inside the shelter there came the sound of disturbed sleep as Jean Evans turned drowsily and murmured to Daniel to keep quiet.

"No, Jean," Angelo said a little louder. "It's me."

The woman's dazed voice floated to him from the snug dark. "What're you doing out there?"

"Mind if I come in?"

"Wait," she answered huskily. "I'll come out."

In a moment, she appeared dressed in a siren suit, over which was pulled a large and baggy sweater.

Rubbing the sleep from her eyes, she stared at the American in disbelief. "What time is it?" she asked.

"'Bout three o'clock."

"In the morning?"

"No, some wise-guy warden's blacked out the sun."

"What are you doing here?" she asked, still not convinced that this wasn't some peculiar dream.

Angelo pulled the collar of his flying jacket a little higher. "It's my buddy, Frank," he told her. "I was wonderin' if your friend has seen him."

The woman regarded him frostily as her muddled wits cleared. "It's the middle of the night," she said, "and you're asking me about Kath's love life? I don't know who's madder, you for asking or me for listening."

"You don't understand!"

"Hush, my Daniel and Neil are in there. I don't want you wakin' them up. Things are bad enough."

"Frank's gone AWOL," he told her. "The mission was a total screw up and it got to him real bad. When we returned to base, first chance he got he took right off."

"And you went straight after him?"

"He had a coupla hours lead on me, but I guessed where he was headin'. He's gonna be in deep trouble if I don't take him back to the camp—we both will. The guys are coverin' for us, but if we ain't back by tonight then we're in for it."

"Why didn't you go straight to Kath's?"

"Couldn't recollect the number," he said. "I wasn't exactly payin' attention to much else them nights. Didn't want to wake up the whole neighborhood."

Jean suddenly felt sorry for the anxious-looking airman and remembered her harsh treatment of him at their last meeting.

"Well, you can't go around there now," she sighed. "Let's go inside and I'll put the kettle on."

"Aw, I couldn't put you to all that trouble," he began.

"Well, I'm having one, anyway," she said, climbing out of the trench and hurrying through the garden.

In the kitchen, Jean lit the stove and warmed her hands on the gas flame before placing the kettle on it, then showed Angelo into the living room.

"Cozy," he said, gazing at the Stokeses' clutter, then for the first time he noticed how worn and drained the woman looked. "You okay, Jean?"

"A lot's happened since I saw you," she told him. "First, the woman across the road was found murdered, then yesterday morning my dad never came back from his ARP. They looked for him all day but didn't find him. I don't know what to think. He wouldn't just go off like that. Something must have happened to him. My gran keeps saying he's been got by the person who killed Mrs. Meacham. I've tried not to listen to her, but what other answer can there be?"

"Hey," Angelo muttered, "you really have been through a lot. I thought I had troubles. I brought a present for you!" he said, jerking his head up again.

"I don't want any nylons," she said wearily, trying to prevent the tears from falling as she thought about her father.

The American fished inside his flying jacket. "Hey, I wouldn't bring you none of those," he cried. "Here, look who I brought home!"

In his hands, Angelo flourished Ted, and Jean managed a faint smile. "Oh, that's marvelous!" she thanked him. "Neil's been so upset. Daniel will be so happy to get his back, too."

Angelo cleared his throat, and his irreverent face assumed a guilty air.

"You have got Daniel's teddy, haven't you?" she asked.

"Weren't enough of him left to bring back," he told her. "The varmint didn't make it through the mission."

"Oh, well, Daniel seemed to like Neil's better anyway. I'd better just go and see to that kettle."

When he was alone Angelo settled down into an armchair, yawning continuously.

"Why don't you get some sleep?" the woman asked, returning with two steaming cups. "There's nothing you can do till the morning anyway."

Angelo nodded. "When you're right, you're right," he drawled, unzipping his flying jacket and covering himself with it like a blanket.

Jean folded her arms and looked at him wryly. Unprotected by his veneer of brash impudence, Angelo reminded her of a small, vulnerable child. Snuggling into the sheepskin lining of his flying jacket, he was just a boy in a grown-up's uniform, and she realized, with a start, that she had missed him.

Sitting on the other chair, where he had been discarded, Ted's eyes were gleaming.

"Always wanted to be present at a birth," he chortled mysteriously to himself as he sensed a familiar presence waft into the room.

Jean covered Angelo with a comforter, then she stiffened as some will outside her own took control of her.

Stepping mechanically from the room with her eyelids fluttering down over her eyes as the possession overwhelmed her, she searched through the drawers in the kitchen and brought out the charred head of Angelo's old mascot.

Returning to the living room, moving like one in a dream, she gently pulled the flying jacket from under the comforter. Then, her eyes closed, the woman set to work with her grandmother's sewing basket, goofily resting her top row of teeth upon her lower lip and humming a waltz tune.

CHAPTER 18

SNORTIN' AROUND ITS BOUNDARIES

Wandering cautiously through the bomb site, Edie Dorkins was feeling wretched and alone. For most of the day she had lain hidden under a sheet of corrugated metal like a snail under a stone, only daring to venture out when the light began to fail. Yet, ever since that time, she had been aware that a grotesque change had transformed her once beautiful and secluded domain.

The whole atmosphere was different. The night was charged with a hideous, pervading terror that thrummed in the air and coursed through the ground like the pulse of some foul and evil heart. In certain areas of the desolation, close to the place she had considered to be her inviolate sanctuary, the ghastly veins of mindless terror were too powerful for her to approach. The spritelike girl had been forced to skirt around the ruins, searching constantly for the companions she so desperately wished to find, but as yet she had uncovered no trace of them.

Scampering lightly over the familiar, ragged terrain, Edie leaped onto a fragmented wall that was broken in such a way as to resemble, and serve, as a flight of extremely narrow steps.

Up this precarious staircase she ran, for it commanded an excellent view of her barren kingdom, and this was now the fifth time she had scanned the gloom from this vantage point.

Hopefully she trained her almond-shaped eyes, trying to see beyond the deep, shadowy gulfs that stretched below the demolished houses around her.

But no, not one single ghostly figure could she spy, and she skipped unhappily back to the ground.

Edie missed the souls she had restrained and kept bound to herself and the earth. It was a frightening, confusing time for her, for she knew the nature of the dark one that had come among them and turned her joyous, firework-filled world on its head.

Trailing morosely past the flattened remains of a collapsed house, where only a segment of burned-out hallway was still standing, she wiped her sprouty nose and sniveled into the pixie hat that she had dragged from her head.

"Miss Edie!" called a terrified and unexpected voice.

The girl whirled around and peered into the shadow-filled hallway.

From the darkness flashed a pale, pudgy hand, and the stubby fingers beckoned her nervously.

"In here!" the specter cried. "Quick!"

Jubilant, she sprang across the rubble and stared up at the quivering, rotund features of Arnold Porter.

Cringing as far into the shadows as possible, the

phantom warden sobbed with relief when she joined him.

"Bleedin' Nora!" he whispered in a tremorous breath. "Thank the stars you're safe an' sound. I thought you was a goner—so help me, I really did."

Shaking with fright, he almost hugged her before realizing how futile that would be and instead held the sides of his head as though it were about to explode.

"You been lookin' for the others?" he asked. "Well, you needn't bother no more. I seed it all, I was there. It nearly got me as well. Oh, strike me pink! It were the most terrible time of my life—beggin' your pardon, Miss."

The girl scowled at him, her expression demanding to know more.

Arnold's shade crumpled up his face when he thought of it and begged her not to make him tell, imploring her instead to leave the bomb site without delay. But Edie's mad mind was still too masterly to be denied and so, with many a shiver, he complied.

"After that nasty business last night," he yammered, "when poor Peter Stokes was taken, as you know, everything grew pretty quiet. Until the early hours of the morning, after you'd gone to sleep. I was over by what used to be Snickets Corner when all at once we knew. That . . . that thing were on the move again.

"Black as me hat, an' blacker it came, stalkin' us through the night. Like rabbits caught stupid in the light, the first ones were got, and you know what it did to them, that . . . that foul filth? It ate 'em, sucked them poor beggars down like they was mother's milk.

"Then how the rest of us took off. Terrified we was and terrified I still is. It liked that, it did, it liked the sport we gave it, havin' to chase us like some cat. I was lucky I escaped. Jus' when I thought my turn had come it gave up. Awful big it got, Miss Edie, and with each and every one of us it got bigger an' bigger.

"Can't you feel how strong it's grown? All day long it's holed up in your old place, asleepin' it off like a big Sunday dinner. But it's stirrin' now, an' it's hungry again. There ain't nothin' can stop it, Miss. Not a bleedin' thing."

The phantom covered his mouth with his hands as the full horror of what he had said scared him all the more. His overweight shape twitched, and a spasm of fear rifled through his vaporous body.

Edie shuddered, as she too felt the horrendous atmosphere of malevolence increase in intensity.

"It's full awake now," Arnold murmured tearfully. "That house can't contain it no more; it's grown too big. Hark, Miss Edie, it's leaving that place. It's prowlin' over the wasteland, on the hunt fer more souls to feast on."

Shrinking into the hallway, the girl tightened her fingers around the incendiary she wore about her neck and listened as a distant, lumbering pounding was carried to them on the chill night air.

"Snortin' around its boundaries," Arnold remarked with a whimper, "that's what the brute's doin'. Like a dog sniffin' fer scraps. Oh, no—listen!"

To her distress, Edie heard. The fiend was coming closer. The noise of its trampling was growing steadily louder, and abruptly a thunderous trumpeting blared into the sky.

"It's on to somethin'!" Arnold wailed. "An' that means us!"

Biting her lip, the girl cringed next to the last member of her spectral family and waited breathlessly as a deep shadow came stealing toward the ruins where they cowered.

A vile, heinous laugh came echoing to mock them, and the ancient force that was Belial poured into the fragmented hallway as a pool of black despair.

Clutching the incendiary to her chest, Edie Dorkins screamed. Rising over her a formless, dark mass splayed itself wide, blocking one end of the ruin with ravening, whiplike tentacles, as a grotesquely distended mouth bore down on her.

"Watch out, Miss!" Arnold Porter yelled, stumbling forward, placing himself between the snapping jaws and their helpless prey.

"Get back—you ruddy 'orror!" he bawled, uselessly flailing his ghostly arms before the demon's savage maw.

Relishing the amusement this paltry soul afforded him, Belial let out a malignant cackle. Then the darkness of the hall was dispelled as an infernal glare came bubbling up from the gaping throat. From the ghastly jaws a greedy tongue snaked out, lashing around Arnold's waist and dripping with hellish flame.

"Aaaiieeee!" the specter screeched as the demon dragged him toward his waiting mouth.

"Run, Miss Edie!" Arnold cried in his terror. "Run! . . ."

With a final howling shriek, the ghost of Arnold Porter disappeared when the terrible jaws closed over him, and the light from the dribbling flames was extinguished.

Racing from the ruins, Edie fled the hideous scene, the dead warden's tormented shrieks reverberating in her head.

Over walls and hills of debris she pelted, not daring to

turn back. The air was trembling as Belial gloated in the dark, allowing her a head start before he came thundering after.

Then, with a low, rumbling chuckle, he came—rolling over the bomb site.

Hearing the rumor of his swift progress, Edie squealed. She would never escape. Soon those jaws would come snapping for her and she too would be dragged into the fiery maw and down into oblivion.

Stumbling through the night she ran, till her heart raced and the metallic tang of blood danced in her mouth.

Suddenly, tearing blindly down a scree of brick and timber, the girl blundered into a tall, dark shape.

Screaming, Edie was plucked from the ground and thrown in the air by a pair of strong hands, and no matter how much she kicked and fought, her captor would not let go.

"Hey now," an astonished, buttery voice called, "cut that out, will ya? You nearly had m-my eye out."

So taken aback was she by the warm friendliness of that sound, Edie stopped struggling and gazed down at the man who held her.

"What you do-doing out so late, sweetpea?" Frank Jeffries asked. "Does your momma know where you are?"

Edie stared at the kindly face that beamed up at her. Behind those soft blue eyes she could see the turmoil that haunted him, and she sensed the affinity between them. He, like her, was also on the run. With an impulsive grin, she found that she liked the gawky American—then the girl remembered the danger she was in.

Turning her wild, frightened eyes away from him, she stabbed an urgent finger into the darkness behind.

"What is it, honey?" Frank asked, lowering his arms and placing her upon the ground. "You look scared half to d-death. Believe me, I know what that's like."

Edie caught hold of his hand and tugged it fiercely.

"Can't you speak?" he asked. "What're you so scared of? Hey, that g-gadget around your neck, it kinda looks like . . ."

The girl glanced fearfully past him, dreading the spectacle that would swiftly come rearing over the rubble heap.

With renewed vigor, she tore at his fingers, and almost as soon as a weak smile spread over his face the airman heard.

Coming from behind the ridge was the unmistakable roar of an aircraft.

"What's that?" he murmured as the din grew louder. "What's g-goin' on here?"

To the girl's dismay, Frank clambered up the slope and stared at the tortured landscape beyond.

Speeding over the waste ground, with its engines whining and every gun turret spitting out flaming streams of death, the vast shape of a B-17 came lurching toward them.

The nightmare that Frank Jeffries had fled the base camp to escape from plunged through the ruins, crashing over the remaining walls, smashing the fallen beams, unstoppable in its horrible majesty.

"Can't be," the American muttered as his fear mounted. "This ain't happenin'."

A whirling cloud of dust spiraled around the bomber's propellers as it stormed onward, rising clumsily into the air, its Plexiglas nose questing for him.

Rooted to the spot, Frank couldn't move. The clamor of the engines was deafening and his eardrums thumped, but still he remained, his eyes fixed on that terrible sight.

"It's g-gonna get me," he breathed. "It followed me here."

At that moment, Edie's small figure scrambled beside him. Not pausing to look on the rampaging nightmare below, she gave the airman a rough shove that sent him blundering back down the hill.

Frank let out a distraught howl as he skidded and staggered, but the action had revived his senses.

"You—you saw it, too?" he cried. "I—I thought I was seein' stuff again. Heck! We gotta get outta here! Come on, sweetpea!"

Snatching her up once more, he tore from that evil place as fast as his long legs could carry them. His mind was racing, nothing made any sense—the sight he had just witnessed was impossible. How could a B-17 be in an East End bomb site?

Cradled in his arms, Edie stared over his shoulder. Above the heap of rubble the Fortress rose, its landing gear dragging through the wreckage and inflaming the night with its crackling gunfire.

Tearfully the girl slapped the American's back, urging him to go faster.

Frank hurtled through the shadows. One more high hill and they would be out of the barren landscape, then he could seek refuge from the atrocity that hounded them.

Edie turned to see where they were going and immediately pulled on his collar. This way was treacherous, the ground was not safe. Beneath the ruins of this demolished building there was a large and unfilled cellar.

But Frank was too absorbed in his own fears to take any notice of her.

Leaping onto the slope, the American tore upward, but, without warning, a slab of concrete tilted beneath him and he lost his balance as a section of the cellar ceiling ripped open.

Shrieking, Edie was thrown from his arms, and they both plummeted into the sudden chasm that now yawned below.

Toppling down through the filth and plaster, Frank struck his head against a rafter with horrible force and his skull gave a sickening *crack.*

As he hit the submerged floor, his legs buckled under him and he rolled sideways, a shower of stones and dirt pouring over him.

Groaning with pain, he spat out the dust and shakily tried to stand.

Close by, Edie was nursing a bloody knee and staring up at the fissure above her head, but she forgot all about it when she saw the American peer at her drunkenly and put his hand to his forehead.

"S-sorry, swee-peeaa . . ." he muttered, as a bristling blackness closed over his vision and his legs turned to water.

As he flopped unconscious to the floor, Frank Jeffries's thoughts went drifting out into the void.

At once, Edie sprang across to him. Shaking the airman by the clothes and pummeling his face, she desperately tried to wake him, but it was no use.

Overhead, the noise of the berserk bomber steadily drew closer.

If only Arnold Porter had been wrong, if only the demon did not hunt by scent. Perhaps, if they cowered out of sight quieter than mice, it would pass over them.

Taking hold of the American's shoulders, she vainly tried to drag him out of the dim light that filtered through the ruptured ceiling. When she realized that she wasn't strong enough, Edie cast around for something to cover him with. Then she found a battered door that had followed them into the abyss, and she quickly scurried over to it.

Sharp splinters drove into the girl's palms as she trawled the door toward the American and propped it gently against his body, shielding him from any curious eyes that might stare hungrily into the cellar.

When she was satisfied that Frank was completely obscured by her deception, she darted into the farthest corner and huddled into a small, terrified ball.

In the world above, the horrendous roar of the demonic B-17 was painfully loud. A winged darkness came sweeping over the ruined cellar, plunging it into absolute night.

Edie shivered and covered her pounding ears as the blaring engines whined directly overhead and the basement shuddered beneath its awful weight. Walls buckled and the plaster crashed down in ragged sheets, then the concrete floor cracked as the foundation shook. Trapped in the middle of the calamitous tumult, the small girl screamed.

* * *

It was eight o'clock when Angelo awakened.

Stretching his arms, he gave a yodeling yawn and blinked. Then he blinked again.

"Geez," he mumbled, "I'm seein' double."

Sitting on the other armchair were two teddy bears, identical in every detail except that one of them was noticeably shabbier than the other.

Then he saw the scraps of sheepskin littering the floor, leading off to the dining table where . . .

"What the! . . ."

Leaping from the chair, the American rushed to the table, where his beloved flying jacket was lying leather-side down. Aghast and dumbfounded, he stared at the awful holes that had been snipped out of the fleecy lining.

"Ah," Jean said, standing in the doorway. "I see you're awake. I'm so sorry. I really don't know what came over me. It was so weird—one minute I was covering you with the comforter, the next thing I knew I was putting the sewing basket away."

Angelo gawked at her. He lifted the jacket in his hands, only then realizing that a tiny circle had been cut out of the leather as well.

"I think I must've used that bit for the nose," she admitted sheepishly, "but to be honest, I really can't remember. I must've been half asleep or something. Maybe it was worry about Dad—I just don't know."

Passing a critical eye over her handiwork, she had to confess that the new teddy bear was rather good.

"Isn't it a fabulous match?" she asked. "They're like two peas in a pod—even the eyes are the same! I must've got really carried away, 'cuz I even used some of the stuffing from the comforter. There's a big hole in it, too."

Angelo looked from the new teddy bear, back to his mutilated jacket, then repeated the movement.

"You, you hacked up my number-one lucky piece," he stammered in a careful voice, "the thing that's kept me alive through thirteen missions, to make . . . to make a doll!"

"Teddy bear!"

"Yeah, a teddy bear."

The airman was so shocked by what she had done that he didn't know how to react, and then, to his complete amazement, he laughed. Sitting beside his new twin, Ted watched as the woman became infected by Angelo's laughter and tutted to himself as they collapsed in a fit of hysterics.

Presently the mirth subsided, and Jean led the American into the hall. "Sometimes you gotta laugh before you cry," Angelo sighed, pulling the breezy jacket on.

Jean put her hand to her mouth shamefully. "I'm so sorry about that," she declared. "God knows what possessed me."

"The really weird part," Angelo said, "is that I ain't sore at all."

"Does that mean you'd forgive me anything?"

"Don't get carried away."

Smiling, Jean led him to the hall. "I'll come with you to Kath's," she said, "but I mustn't stay long. Daniel and Neil are still in the shelter."

And so, together, they left the house.

Alone with his duplicate, Ted gave it a cautious prod in the tummy.

"Jus' makin' sure which one of us is me," he

explained. "You know, I think it's true what they say, you do get better lookin' as time goes by. You ain't got that lovable, sat-on look yet. Now, if you'll pardon me leavin' you so soon, I got a little sunshine to bring to a kid's face."

Bouncing off the chair, Ted scurried through the house and ran into the garden.

Neil had spent a miserable night in the shelter. It had been numbingly cold, and his bunk was the most uncomfortable bed he had ever slept on.

"Hey, kid!" a voice called in his miserable dreams. "You down there, it's reveille!"

Standing small in the entrance, Ted tried to wake the boy, but it was Daniel who heard him.

In the bottom bunk, the two-year-old squirmed around to discover that his favorite teddy bear had magically come to life.

"More!" he cried, clapping his hands together excitedly.

"Oh, brother," Ted grumbled. "I woke up the king of the slobberers. Hi there, Danny boy—how's it goin'?"

Daniel gave a squawk of joy, the shrill sound waking the occupant of the top bunk more effectively than a bucket of ice water ever could have.

"What . . . who?" he mumbled, sitting upright and banging his head on the corrugated roof.

"Up an' at 'em!" Ted called, jumping aside as Daniel reached down and made a grab for him.

"Where've you been!" Neil cried, hastily climbing out of the bunk. "I thought I was stuck here forever!"

"That could still happen," the bear told him. "You an' me got our work cut out for us."

"Quiet, Daniel," Neil told the infant, who was still swiping the air with his hands in his unsuccessful attempts to snatch Ted and yelling with the full force of his lungs.

"It's today, isn't it?" Neil asked. "I'm fed up with you not telling me what's going on."

The bear nodded. "Yep, tonight Joshy'll be comin' through the gateway."

"I can hardly believe it," Neil said. "Tonight I'll be going home!"

"Hold on, kid," Ted interrupted. "Didn't I just say we had work to do?"

"I'm not going to like this, am I?" Neil groaned. "What is it, then?"

The bear patted his furry stomach thoughtfully. "It was all gonna be so sweet an' easy," he murmured. "Not anymore. You see, kid, the original deal went like this. I jus' wanted to come back an' save the lives of three people—well, four, counting slobberpuss there."

Sitting down with a gentle bump, Ted leaned back and let the sunlight play on his face before continuing.

"Frank, Jean, and Angelo Signorelli," he said quietly. "That's all I wanted. Save them, an' I would be the happiest piece of merchandise since Pinocchio. Now the whole darned ball game is loused up."

"What's the matter?" Neil asked. "Won't you be able to save them? I'll do whatever I can to help her."

The bear smiled and hugged his fluffy knees. "Oh, I could save them all right," he muttered, "if that was all I had to do."

"What else is there?"

"First let me tell you the original plan. At exactly

thirty-seven minutes to ten this very night, one mighty mother of a parachute mine is gonna come floating outta the great blue yonder—right on top of this shelter."

"Jean and Danny will be inside it by then," Neil spluttered in horror.

Ted nodded significantly. "No one ever found enough pieces to identify them. The mine made a crater forty feet wide, bringing half the street down."

"That's horrible. We've got to warn her."

"Sure. She'll have to go to the Underground station with the old witch, if you can convince her, that is."

"I'll make sure I do."

"That's not all," the bear said, signaling for Neil to remain where he was. "I ain't finished. While all this is goin' on, there's another ticklish problem we gotta solve."

"What's that?"

"Angelo and Frank."

"Are they back here?"

"Ain't no such thing as a homing bear, kid. I hadda hitch a ride off someone."

"So what happens to them?"

Ted wrinkled up his nose and rubbed one of his ears with his paw.

"Well," he began, taking a deep breath, "forty-five minutes before the mine falls, farm boy Frank gets stabbed."

"By the one who killed Mrs. Meacham?"

"No, though I never did work out who did it."

"And Frank dies?"

The bear gazed up at the boy's face, a strange light glinting in his glass eyes. "Yeah, but he ain't alone. You see, that Signorelli guy comes wadin' in like the born fool he is, and while he's grievin', his back gets perforated by a whole lot o' lead."

Neil sat down on the bunk beside Daniel. "How can we stop that?" he muttered softly.

Ted shifted on his bottom, feeling the vial of sacred water budge within his stuffing, but even as he opened his mouth to tell the boy about Belial, he clapped it shut again. Why should he help the Webster sisters? They didn't play straight with him—their motives were never his own. His main priority was saving the people he cared about. No, this time he wasn't going to be anyone's patsy.

Neil shook his head. "You didn't tell me where," he said at last.

"Where what?"

"Where is Josh going to appear?"

Ted slouched wearily and murmured something under his breath. He knew the boy wasn't going to like it. Ted felt wretched and ashamed to have to tell him after all he'd been through.

"I didn't hear that," the boy said firmly.

"All right, all right," the bear admitted guiltily. "Okay, Joshy is gonna come poppin' outta that gateway right over our heads."

"Here?" Neil cried. "At what time exactly?"

"Oh, about when the parachute mine hits," came the subdued reply.

CHAPTER 19

LOSING CONTROL

Angelo and Jean returned from the Meacham house with no news of Frank—Kathleen Hewett had not seen or heard from him.

"I was sure he'd have gone straight there," the American muttered. "The only thing that pulled him through that last raid was the thought of that airhead dame. I just don't understand it. Where is he?"

Jean looked at him thoughtfully, her green eyes gleaming as she considered this strange man who had wisecracked his way into her life.

"You're a funny one," she said. "You spend all your time pretending not to care about anything and spin lines left and center, but you're not like that at all, are you? Under that tough exterior you might even be quite nice."

Angelo returned her gaze and smiled. All he wanted to do was hold her, and he knew she felt the same.

Unexpectedly, the back door was flung open and Neil came storming inside. "Jean!" he cried urgently behind her. "There's something I've got to tell you."

The moment was gone. Jean whisked about and ran into the garden, leaving Angelo to cool his heels.

"Don't sleep in the bomb shelter tonight!" Neil called after her. "It's too dangerous!"

"Nice goin', kid!" Angelo said tersely.

"I've got to warn her," Neil mumbled. "She's got to listen."

"Yeah, sure. Hey, how's about me givin' you a stick of gum and you get lost?"

"Er . . . no thanks," the boy returned.

The American groaned at the ceiling. "Trust me to find the only kid in this whole darned country who don't like gum!"

A look of blank astonishment flooded Neil's face as he recognized something familiar about Angelo's voice. He stared at Ted incredulously.

Making certain that Angelo's eyes were off them, a cheesy grin stole over the bear's face and his fleecy brows jiggled in mild amusement at the boy's sudden realization.

"Took you long enough, kid," he mouthed.

Neil wrenched his eyes away from the softly chuckling toy and made his excuses to Angelo.

"Excuse me," he muttered. "I've got to go and explain to Jean. She mustn't stay there tonight. I've got to make her listen."

As the boy ran toward the garden, Angelo sauntered into the living room. "Well, Signorelli," he sighed. "I think the girl's weakenin'."

* * *

Waddling like a carrion crow on stilts, Old Mother Stokes entered Barker's Row. She had spent a most agreeable night in the Underground station at Bethnal Green. All her subterranean acquaintances had been most sympathetic with regard to the disappearance of Peter, her son, and she had wallowed in their compassionate concern.

With her beaky nose pecking at the brisk morning air and the feathers of her great hat springing insanely over her head, she trundled along, her mind seething with the plans she had been hatching.

Bearing in mind the murder of her despised neighbor, Ma Stokes doubted if her son would ever be seen alive again. Though that prospect had given her a momentary pang of sorrow and remorse, she could not be expected to grieve forever.

Without his ridiculously generous nature getting in the way and thwarting her more malicious schemes, Mrs. Stokes anticipated a far sunnier future ahead for herself.

First of all, she would have to get rid of that idiot boy her son had brought into their lives, and perhaps Jean could be persuaded to move out with Daniel.

Envisioning the whole house to herself, the harridan cackled gleefully.

In this most gratifying of humors, she continued past her home and veered instead toward the abode of the late, and in no way lamented, Doris Meacham.

Raising a bony fist, Mrs. Stokes rapped on the front door.

"Frank?" Kath called from inside as she pattered down the hall. "That you?"

As soon as the entrance was opened, Ma Stokes barged her way inside and made a beeline for the parlor.

"'Ere!" Kath cried, as the old woman bustled past her. "What you doing? You can't go in there. I was just on me way to the factory."

"You'd better get off then!" the intruder advised. "Now, where did she keep that cream jug with the picture of the cat on it?"

Leaving the front door open, Kath trotted after the unwanted visitor and found her opening the deceased Mrs. Meacham's china cabinets.

Years of stored-up resentment and jealousy were now released as Jean's grandmother poked and pried her way through the cupboards, sneering at most of the pieces on display.

"Never did know quality from junk," the geriatric thief proclaimed, turning from the cupboards and shambling out into the hall, where she began to climb the stairs.

Stupefied by this outrageous behavior, Kath chased her to the main bedroom, where the old woman was already ransacking the drawers and flinging sensible unmentionables behind her with disdain.

"You stop that!" Kath warned. "You got no right to come takin' poor Mrs. Meacham's lovely things."

Ma Stokes stared at her in surprise, her magnified eyes blinking in confusion.

"I'm only takin' what's mine by right," she declared with brazen indignation.

"How do you figure that?"

"It's what Doris would have wanted," the old woman replied, spurning the contents of the drawers and gravitating toward the wardrobe. "She always promised I could have whatever I fancied. A dear friend she was, said she wouldn't like her things to go to no stranger. These dresses aren't great, are they? Not as much as I thought there would be," she griped. "What's in the other bedroom?"

"Just my stuff!" Kath told her.

Mrs. Stokes regarded the girl suspiciously. "Bet you've been through all this already," she accused. "I know your type—out for all you can get. Had the best of the pickin's, have you? You shouldn't even be livin' here no more. Well, I'll just go and see what you've helped yourself to."

Kath leaped to the door of her bedroom and barricaded it with her body.

"Get out!" she yelled, her face suddenly disfigured with a desperate anger.

"Something to 'ide, 'ave we? I knew it, I knew it! You're a filchin' little urchin, when all's said and done, aren't you? Let me by, I won't let you get away with it."

Using her overflowing bag as a battering ram, she tried to push the girl out of the way, but Kath's temper was flaring now. Wrenching the bag away from Mrs. Stokes, she flung it down the stairs, then caught hold of the crone's arms and twisted them behind her back.

"Listen, you old hag!" she shrieked, frog-marching the caterwauling woman up to the banister and forcing her head over the edge. "If you don't get down those stairs right now, I'll throw you over this and say it were an accident!"

Mrs. Stokes jabbered and squawked. The spectacles fell from her nose and went clattering down the stairs as the girl hitched her scrawny arms painfully behind her.

"Aaargh!" she squealed. "You're hurtin' me! I'll have the law on you, I will."

Kath lowered her face to the old woman's ear.

"Don't think I won't do this!" she snarled menacingly. "You're a fine one to talk, aren't you? You're nothing but a vicious old shrew—a poisonous witch no one likes. What loss do you think you'd be to anyone? The day you die, the street'll throw a party and I'll come to dance on your grave. You know what I had to do to poor Mrs. Meacham's dog? I'd do that again and worse to put an end to your nasty, small-minded existence. You just provoke me one bit further and it'll start the day off lovely."

"No!" Mrs. Stokes blubbered, frightened by the callous savagery in the girl's voice. "Let me go. I'm seventy-five!"

"Aged bones snap more easily than young ones, don't they?" Kath ranted. "Shall we see how true that is? Do you think tired old hags like you bounce when they fall?"

"Leave me be!" the old woman screeched.

Kath held her over the banister a moment longer, then snorted in disgust and shoved her away.

Mrs. Stokes squeaked and whimpered like a timid mouse. For the first time in her life, her belligerent and spiteful spirit was utterly crushed. She pulled away from the girl, frightened and alarmed, fumbling blindly over the landing.

"I'll fetch a policeman," she cried, retreating to the safety of the stairs. "See if I don't!"

"Go ahead!" Kath bawled back. "I'll tell him what you were doing here in the first place. You know what they do to looters, don't you?"

Mrs. Stokes's shriveled mouth opened, but she thought better of whatever she had been about to say. Kathleen Hewett had scared her. For one awful moment she really did think the girl was going to hurl her down the stairs.

Muttering impotent threats in an inaudible monotone, she descended to the ground floor in defeat, retrieved her spectacles, and slammed the front door behind her.

Leaning against her bedroom door, flushed and trembling, the woman masquerading as Kathleen Hewett battled to regain her composure. Never before had she come so close to jeopardizing her position. An uncontrollable urge to lash out and kill had overwhelmed her. She was beginning to lose control, succumbing to the tantalizing waves of violence that now pervaded the atmosphere, and she shivered as she struggled to master her base, cruel nature once more.

* * *

At the edge of the bomb site, a shaft of light streamed into the ruined cellar, glittering with the dust and tiny stones that rattled through the slanting rays as a pair of small feet came dangling down.

Edie Dorkins dropped onto the basement floor and scampered over to her airman.

Frank Jeffries was still unconscious. An ugly, bruised lump had risen on his forehead, and his short hair was matted with a clot of blood that had oozed from the broken skin.

Edie had tried to make him as comfortable as possible. Crawling out of their hiding place at dawn, she had gone scavenging and brought back a filthy cushion and a blanket stolen from someone's washing line.

After dragging the battered door off him, she laid the American's head on the grimy pillow, brushed the dust from his face, then covered him with the blanket.

It had been a terrifying night. For nearly two hours Belial had raged around the wasteland wearing the shape of the Flying Fortress, reveling in its might and destructive potential. But eventually the bomb site had grown quiet, and Edie sensed that, for the time being at least, the demon had stopped searching for them.

Now Frank's face was gray with a ghastly, deathly pallor, and apprehensively the girl reached out to touch him.

Edie uttered a cry of dismay—the airman's skin was horribly cold and clammy.

Fearing that it was too late, she took out a cracked bottle she had found and put it to his parched lips.

The water Edie had taken from the drinking fountain of the Wyrd Museum spilled from the bottle's neck and flooded into his mouth.

When all the liquid had gone, the girl rocked back on her knees and held out her hands, drawing a curious branching symbol in the air above Frank's head.

Very slowly, the American's corpselike appearance faded as the faintest bloom of color returned to his flesh.

"Kath," he croaked, stirring in his stupor. "I don't want to die . . . Kath . . . help me . . . the bomber . . . she's burning . . ."

Heartened by the results of her nursing, but realizing the patient needed more help than she could give, Edie glanced up at the broken ceiling. Frank ought to be taken from the bomb site, to be cared for and made well in a proper hospital. Yet what could she do? If she went for help the tin hats would catch her. In the confused tangle of her fey mind, the girl did not know what to do, and huddling next to the stricken airman, she prepared to sit out the rest of the day, watching and waiting.

CHAPTER 20

AN UNHOLY ENCOUNTER

Old Mother Stokes stomped into her home and gave the umbrella stand a peevish kick.

"Who does that little hussy think she is?" she grumbled. "Threatenin' a frail old woman like me."

With a face that could sour milk, she tramped into the living room and prickled with outrage at the sight that met her eyes.

There, crawling around on the floor, an American was giving rides to her great-grandson, and watching him from the armchair, Jean was laughing happily.

"What's going on here?" she demanded.

Angelo blinked up at her, and Jean's laughter died.

"Jean!" the old woman barked. "Who's this you've brought into my house?"

"Name's Signorelli, ma'am," Angelo said, rising from the carpet and extending a hand to her. "Mighty nice to see you."

"Senior what?" she rapped back. "Did I hear that right? He's a ruddy Italian! Jean, how dare you bring an Italian into my house!"

"I'm American, ma'am," the lieutenant persisted,

withdrawing the hand that had deliberately been ignored.

"You're a dirty cat, Jean Evans," her grandmother spat, "entertainin' a Yank while your poor father's prob'ly met with a 'orrible end—murdered for all we know. 'Aven't you got no shame?"

Taken aback by the fury of her outburst, Angelo was at a loss for words, but Jean wasn't.

"You've got a filthy mind!" she said forcefully. "He's only here because his friend has gone missing!"

"Likely story," came the snorting and unconvinced reply. "Won't find no missing Yanks here!"

"Beggin' your pardon, ma'am . . ." Angelo began.

"Get him out of 'ere!" she told Jean. "Don't want his sort in decent people's houses."

"I will not!"

"You do as you're told—I won't have you bringin' shame on us! And where's that dirty urchin that Peter dragged home?"

"Neil's upstairs."

"He can get out, too!" Mrs. Stokes rattled. "Peter was a fool for bringin' him here. I'm takin' the nasty devil straight to the town hall. Let them feed an' clothe him. I've had enough!"

"You wouldn't!"

But her grandmother's mind was made up, and she strode into the hall and thumped on the banister.

"Get down here, you little beggar!" she cried.

Wondering what all the shouting was about, Neil had already opened the door of the bedroom and stood gazing out at her.

"Get down here!" she told him. "Move yourself. It's time you were gone!"

"Gran!" Jean called, hurrying to her side. "This isn't what Dad would want!"

Mrs. Stokes huffed and stuck out her chest impatiently. "It don't matter what he'd want, does it?" she sneered. "Not with him gone forever by the looks of things."

"But I can't go!" Neil shouted down. "I've got to stay here!"

"You ungrateful upstart!" the old woman snarled, clambering up the stairs and clamping her bony claws about his ear.

"You'll come with me and like it!" she snapped.

"Get off!" he protested, wincing as she twisted his earlobe and propelled him downstairs. "I've got to get Ted!"

"Stop it!" Jean told her grandmother. "Let him go!"

"You'd best bite your tongue, madam!" the old woman screeched back. "This is my house now, and if you want to have a roof over your baby's head, then pipe down."

Jean glared at her and knew that she meant every word. "Why are you so foul?" she cried. "For as long as I can remember you've been nothing but a hateful old misery! I don't know how Dad stuck it out all these years."

"Right!" Mrs. Stokes roared. "You can pack your things and go as well!"

"I would if I had somewhere to go!"

Her grandmother regarded her as though she were a pile of stinking dung. "You've always been trouble, Jean Evans!" she said. "I knew it and so did your father. Too willful, you are, and you've got an evil mouth. It was Billy my Peter loved best. I know what was going through his mind when he got that telegram. He'd rather you were the one that died, not his son. Billy was worth ten times you. Peter knew it and so does I!"

Shaking with anger, Jean clenched her fists, but Angelo was at her side and he pulled her gently away.

"Leave it," he said. "She ain't worth the trouble. You know that ain't true. She's just a twisted refugee from Halloween."

"I hate her!" Jean yelled. "She's like a poisonous old snake!"

"You gotta move outta this place," he said tenderly. "It's drivin' you crazy. Let the barracuda grouch all she likes and leave her be."

Mrs. Stokes pulled open the front door and with a vicious shove pushed Neil through it.

"Good riddance!" she spat.

"Jean!" the boy cried. "Promise me you won't sleep in the bomb shelter tonight." But the door slammed in his face, and he stepped out into the road to stare up at the window of the small bedroom where Ted was still shut inside.

"I'll just have to wait till the old bag goes to the Underground tonight," Neil muttered as he dragged his feet down the road and wandered aimlessly out of Barker's Row.

Inside the hallway of number twenty-three, Mrs. Stokes turned to her granddaughter with a malicious sneer on her hatchet face.

Jean looked at her coldly. "I'm going to move in with Kath," she informed her. "I'll pack up my and Daniel's things. We'll be out of this place before tonight."

"I won't miss you," the old woman said, "but I expect I'll be able to hear the brat bawlin' all the way over here."

Jean bristled, but before she could say anything Angelo took hold of her hand and pressed it gently. "Pack your things, Jean," he said. "I'll help you take them across the road."

Ma Stokes glowered at the pair of them. She could see how much the American cared for her granddaughter, and she despised the thought of her finding any kind of happiness. Then, like the blossoming of a black, venomous weed, a horrible idea occurred to her, but she suppressed the unpleasant grin that threatened to steal over her sharp features.

"I'm glad your father ain't here to see this," she growled. "You're as bad as that Hewett trollop! Well, you've made your bed now. I'm going to the Underground, and when I come back tomorrow you'd best be gone. If I find any of your things, they'll be burned."

With a strangely triumphant smile on her shrewish face, the old woman left the house and trotted lightly down the road.

"It's too early for her to go to the shelter," Jean muttered curiously. "She's up to something."

"Aw, who cares," Angelo said. "Let the old wasp hum some. There ain't nothin' she can do to hurt you no more."

"You don't know her," Jean muttered. "Well, I'd best start packing my things."

* * *

As the afternoon wore on, a white mist rose steadily into the cold evening air until it filled the streets of the East

End, hanging in ghostly skeins across the rooftops and enshrouding the bomb sites in a dense, milky vapor.

As the shadows lengthened in the foggy world above, Frank Jeffries moaned dismally and winced as he tried to move.

"What hit me?" he uttered groggily. "A coupla freight trains b-by the feel of it. Ouch!"

Gingerly he raised his hand and felt the great lump on his head with cringing fingertips.

"I g-got me a buffalo egg up there," he said with a shudder. "Where the heck am I?"

As he turned his head sideways, his bleary eyes swam into focus, and there before him, with her face lit by a brilliant grin, was Edie Dorkins.

"Hello, sweetpea," the airman said. "What happened?"

The girl narrowed her almond-shaped eyes, and the fearful memories of the previous night sparked and kindled in Frank's mind.

"Yes," he cried, "that's right. There was a Fort—comin' right at me."

Sucking the air through his teeth as the bump on his head throbbed painfully, he let out a chastising groan.

"I been workin' too hard," he said. "I'm g-goin' screwy. Gee, Frank, you sure got a lively bag o' tricks in that head of yours. Imagine, a B-17 tearin' around here!"

Suddenly another image reared in his dazed thoughts, and the American whistled softly. "Kathy," he breathed. "I came to see Kathy. I g-gotta go to her."

Lurching to his feet, Frank staggered and swayed, clutching hold of the cellar wall.

Edie leaped up to steady him, and the American put his hand on her shoulder.

"Whoa," he cried, "the legs've turned to J-Jell-o. No, no, I'll be all right in a minute. I just g-gotta take me some real deep breaths."

Waiting for his strength and balance to return, he gazed around at the basement, peering up at the hole in the ceiling through which a turgid stream of mist was pouring, like a snowy waterfall tumbling in slow motion.

"Hold on, now," he mused. "What g-goes on here? Looks like another day's g-gone by up there. That right, sweetpea?"

Edie nodded solemnly.

"No wonder I feel so hungry!" he exclaimed. "There, I figure I can fly solo now."

Lifting his hand from the girl's shoulder he took a shuffling step forward.

"Not bad," he said brightly. "Now all I gotta d-do is find a way outta this dungeon."

Edie scuttled to where a beam had fallen at a steep angle out of the ragged fissure in the ceiling and skipped the length of it.

"No need to show off, sweetpea." Frank laughed. "Okay, here I come."

After several minutes and some loss of patience, the airman finally managed to lumber out of the cellar and stood wreathed in the fog.

"G-gonna be a cold night," he told his spritish friend. "You better get back to your folks."

Edie pouted sullenly and dragged her toe through the dirt.

"Ain't you got no one?" Frank asked sorrowfully. "Gee, that's too bad. Hey, why d-don't you come with me? Kathy won't mind."

Pursing her lips and withdrawing farther into the mist, the girl shook her head.

"You can't stay out here," Frank told her. "Come on."

Sadly, Edie spun around and flitted through the fog, vanishing into the ether like a specter.

"Wait, sweetpea!" the airman called, but the girl did not reappear.

Frank shivered as the icy damp seeped into his flesh, and he felt his pulse beating in the broken skin of his forehead.

"Kathy," he repeated, to himself. "I gotta g-get to her."

*   *   *

Twenty minutes later there came a frantic knocking on the door of number twenty-three Barker's Row, and both Jean and Angelo hurried into the hallway to answer this fervent summons.

To their astonishment, they discovered Mickey Harmon standing on the doorstep with his bicycle propped up against the gate. The gossipy adolescent's face was full of excitement, which visibly doubled when he saw the American standing beside Jean.

"Is Neil in?" he asked eagerly, trying to peer past them and staring intensely at the bulging suitcase that had been placed at the bottom of the stairs.

"I'm sorry," Jean told him, "I'm afraid Neil's gone. Was it something important you wanted him for?"

Mickey wiped his nose on the entire length of his arm and took a deep breath before launching into a rapid and emphatic chatter.

"I was only going to tell him what I'd just seen," he babbled garrulously. "A huge fight it were. I never thought she was so mean, really told him what fer, she did. Told him to clear off, that he were a snivelin' coward and she never wanted to see him again. You shoulda seed his face—looked like a smacked puppy he did. He had a massive lump on his head, real nasty that looked. I was just on my firewatch round, Albert Fletcher bein' off again tonight, then this poor bloke staggers past, real upset he was—ooh it were awful, and real excitin'."

Jean and Angelo looked at each other, neither one comprehending a word of what the lad was babbling about.

"Well?" Mickey cried in delighted enthusiasm. "What are you going to do about it?"

"Do about what, kid?" Angelo laughed, tickled by this talkative, gauche teenager. "I can't make head nor tail of it."

"But he's your friend, ain't he?" Mickey blurted. "Don't you want to know what the argument was fer? He didn't look at all well."

The amusement drained from Angelo's face. "You mean Frank?" he demanded.

"The other GI." Mickey nodded. "That's what I've been saying. He had a fight with Miss Hewett."

Angelo pulled on his flying jacket. "Which way did he go?" he asked.

The boy pointed into the mist. "Toward the main street. Do you think he'll do somethin' stupid? He was real upset."

Angelo looked anxiously at Jean. "I gotta find him," he told her. "I'll catch you later, but we'll have to return to base before the MPs get on our tail. You'll be at Kath's, yeah?"

"The packing's all done," she answered.

Angelo hurried to the gate, pulling his collar up against the damp fog. As she watched him, a twinge of dread and misgiving troubled Jean. On an impulse, she darted back to the house, returning with the bear she had made for Daniel.

"Here," she said, pressing it into Angelo's hands and squeezing them tightly. "For luck."

The airman accepted it with a grin. "See you soon," he promised, and with that he hastened into the swirling mist.

Jean stared into the blank, milky vapor until her eyes ached. The pang of foreboding that had nettled her was swiftly developing into an unpleasant melancholy, and she shook herself in an effort to dispel it.

"What's Kath gone and done now?" she murmured. "Hasn't got any sense, that girl."

"Been a thrillin' few days, ain't it?" Mickey burbled as he took up his bicycle. "What with Mrs. Meacham and your dad goin missin'—it's been great!"

Unable to find any fitting response to the lad's ridiculous words, Jean turned and entered the Stokeses' house once more, closing the door behind her.

Mickey Harmon climbed onto the saddle, and his bicycle lumbered farther down the road. Pedaling through the clinging fog, he pretended that his bicycle lamp was a powerful searchlight and his rickety steed an airplane plunging through the clouds over enemy territory. Then, suddenly, he pulled on his brakes and the machine juddered to a halt.

Streaming from the house of the late Mrs. Meacham was a river of fog-diffused lemon light that poured over the road, audaciously breaching the blackout.

A joyful chortle issued from Mickey's lips as he tried to guess what else had happened for Kathleen Hewett to leave the door open like this. Had she darted after Frank to apologize, or had he come storming back and smashed his way in?

Dismounting, he knocked on the door but received no answer, and so, yielding to his own inquisitive nature, Mickey stepped inside and called out tentatively.

When there was still no answer, the baker's son made a furtive search of the ground-floor rooms before directing his gaze upstairs.

"Hello?" he sang out cheerily. "It's Michael Harmon. Is anyone up there?"

A mawkish thrill tingled through him as he ghoulishly savored the feeling of being alone in the house where the murdered Mrs. Meacham had lived. Perhaps the killer and the airman were one and the same. Is that what the huge fight had been about? His adolescent imagination rocketed.

What if Kathleen Hewett had discovered his heinous secret and threatened to tell the police? Maybe the despicable assassin had returned to chop her to bits.

"Miss Hewett?" Mickey called excitedly. "You in there?"

Stepping up to one of the bedroom doors, Mickey rapped on it lightly then pushed it open, preparing himself for the hopefully foul and grisly sight that might await him.

With much disappointment, he found no blood-drenched corpse in the room. Still, there was one other he hadn't checked out.

The bedroom of the late Doris Meacham was now tidy after the assaults inflicted upon it by the dead woman's spiteful neighbor.

Dejectedly, Mickey stared around at the humdrum daintiness of it all, from the lacy coverlet to the photograph of the pet dachshund positioned beneath the bedside lamp.

"Not one decent mutilated carcass," he grunted in disgust. "What a gyp."

As he turned to leave, the bloodthirsty boy's attention was caught by a wooden box sitting on the dressing table. Unable to stop himself, he wandered over to investigate.

"Wow," he breathed, lifting the lid and discovering that it contained a headset and a small microphone. "Hang on—what is it?"

Delving inside, he twiddled one of the dials, and a low, crackling hum began to splutter from the headphones as the machine warmed up.

"Smashing!" he breathed. "It's a radio—*and* a transmitter."

As he fiddled with the unfamiliar contraption, a wild and exhilarating idea struck him.

"Golly," he jabbered. "Old Meacham must've been a secret agent. I've got to show this to Dad. He'll know what to do with it."

Quickly, Mickey bundled the equipment under his arm, and fizzing with delirious excitement, he hurried from the room and ran to the stairs.

Abruptly he stopped, for there, standing on the lower steps, was Kathleen Hewett. An expression of complete and utter contempt was etched on her face.

After telling Frank to leave her alone, the girl had

stumbled out into the night to try and cool the fierce turmoil that was seething in her mind. An almighty dark force was coursing through the atmosphere, and within her callous soul it resonated and was already threatening to overwhelm her.

Yet the cold mist had managed, to some degree, to calm her wits. She returned to the house and was disturbed to find she had left the front door open. When she saw the delivery bicycle propped against the wall, an ember of panic scorched inside her.

Whispering a curse into the swaddling night, she had glared up at the darkened windows in suspicion, then crept silently up to the open door.

"I did knock!" the lad explained, misinterpreting that despising look. "You'd left the door open, I had to check. Ah, you've shut it now, that's good."

Kath's eyes glared at the radio, whose wires were trailing at the intruder's feet.

"I found it in Ma Meacham's room," he told her, disconcerted by the unwavering malice directed toward him. "I was just going to show my dad . . . it's a radio set."

"I know what it is," the girl hissed at him, "and the reception is far better in that room."

Mickey nibbled his top lip. "It's yours then," he realized. "Wow! And are you really a secret agent?"

A frightful slit opened in Kath's face as she smiled menacingly and mounted the next stair.

"You could say that," she breathed, "but not quite the sort you mean."

Mickey's face was blank as he tried to work out what she meant, and then, with a sickening spasm tightening his stomach, it dawned on him.

A malevolent, curdling laugh issued from her lips as she ascended, her eyes fixed on his rapidly whitening face.

"Poor little baker's boy," she chanted softly. "What will they think when they find you tomorrow, lying out there in the wasteland with a broken neck? What will your dear father think? That craven traitor who forsook his fatherland to come and live with the custard-livered and degenerate English. How will he react to your wrenched and twisted body? What a tragedy for you to have fallen so very badly in this terrible fog."

Mickey backed away from her, but he knew he was cornered. "You're a Nazi sympathizer!" he blurted. "A dirty Nazi lover!"

"Oh, no," she reveled, sniggering hollowly, "I *am* a Nazi."

In despair the lad stumbled against the landing wall as she mounted to the topmost step and bore down on him.

In his desperation, Mickey hurled the radio at her with all his might.

The wooden box slammed into Kath's stomach, and she reeled sideways as the breath was punched from her lungs.

Dodging past her, Mickey fled down the stairs and reached for the front door.

A furious yell rang from Kath's lips as she staggered after him, clutching her abdomen.

Still fumbling with the catch, Mickey wailed in terror as the girl came stomping down, her face a distorted mask of murderous wrath. An infernal light shone in her wild eyes.

"Help!" he shrieked, scrabbling at the lock. "Help!"

Suddenly he managed to pull the door open, just as Kath lurched at him.

Howling, Mickey tore out of the house and dove into

the waiting fog. He leaped over the gate and clambered onto his bicycle, but in his fear his foot slipped from the pedal and he almost toppled to the ground. Then he plunged the clattering machine down the street, slicing through the circling mists that thickly twirled and billowed behind him.

Growling through clenched teeth, Kathleen came speeding after him. Through the gate she sprang, glaring right and left, unable to see which way the wretch had fled. Then she heard the rattle of the old bicycle, and like one possessed, she bolted into the suffocating clouds.

Mickey was pedaling for his life. If he could only get home, if he could only tell someone. Over the pavement the bicycle bounced and jarred as he sailed into the alleyway leading to the main street.

Then, to his horror, the strident sound of urgent footsteps rang in the mist behind. She was gaining on him swiftly.

Pumping the pedals as fast as his legs could go, Mickey heard the clopping clamor grow steadily louder, and he cursed the ancient contraption, wishing it could go faster—and then he was caught.

Flying out of the blinding fog, Kathleen saw his shape grow ever closer, becoming more solid as the veils of vapor were rent aside. Screeching, she lashed out with her hand and grabbed Mickey by the collar, and for a moment they were traveling as one, gliding along in tandem. Then, making a ferocious effort, she leaped aside and hauled the squealing lad from the seat.

Riderless, the bicycle continued on its breakneck journey, emerging with a whirring burst onto the main road, where, the momentum gone, it careened against the far curb, somersaulted, and crashed with a resounding jangle and clanking of metal.

Lying facedown where he had been thrown, Mickey moaned pitifully and scrambled to his feet.

But Kath was there, standing over him.

The girl was breathing hard, fatigued and panting from her exertions. Yet now she was utterly possessed by the ancient evil that pulsed through the night, and her eyes flashed with hellish fires.

Feeling terribly alone and defenseless, with the impenetrable fog concealing his plight from any benevolent eyes, Mickey looked into the awful face of the unscrupulous and desperate female, and his heart quailed.

A base madness was animating Kathleen Hewett. A deep, unseated veneration for destruction drove her, and in her contorted, repellent countenance, there was only hatred.

Making a final bid to escape, Mickey lunged to the left, but this time she was ready for him.

"Oh, no!" she yelled, her hands snaking out and catching him by the throat. "You're not going anywhere, baker's boy!"

Mickey's screams were brusquely curtailed as she slapped her hand tightly over his mouth and thrust him roughly against the wall.

"Did you really think I'd let you go?" she spat, pressing her strong fingers into his throat and crushing his windpipe. "I haven't drudged away my time for a common little half-breed rat like you to spoil it all."

Choking and fighting for breath, the lad squirmed and flailed his arms, hitting Kathleen's side, thumping her with his thrashing fists.

"See where your prying snout has brought you!" she hissed, relishing her victim's agonies as the glare from her eyes burned into him. "So may all enemies of Germany perish."

Mickey's struggles grew weaker, and realizing that he was no longer capable of crying out, she took her other hand from his mouth and efficiently throttled him.

A dry, croaking breath whispered from his lips as his eyes rolled in their sockets, until only the whites were visible below the lids—and then his body went limp.

Snorting with immeasurable contempt and quivering from the intensity of her grisly labors, the girl released her grip, and Michael Harmon slumped, dead, to the ground.

Gazing down, with no emotion except relief in the comforting knowledge that she was now safe, and tinged with a measure of pride in the swift execution of her duties, Kathleen turned the body over with the toe of her shoe.

Mercilessly she gave the dead adolescent a despising kick, then looking upon Mickey's inert features, she saw with some amusement how innocent and angelic he appeared in death.

A malicious snigger shook her as an odious thought suggested itself.

"You should not have been so insolent, baker's boy," she murmured resentfully.

Grubbing in the dirt, she scraped up a smear of oily grime and daubed a neat square over Mickey's top lip.

"Heil Hitler," she chuckled horribly.

Suddenly Kath stared and rose to her feet, her sharp ears detecting a shambling movement just outside the mist-filled alley.

Cautiously she moved away, trying not to make a sound.

"Stay!" commanded a hollow, gurgling voice.

The girl shuddered at the sound of it and pushed through the fog more quickly.

"Hold!" the uncanny voice called again. "This is a most succulent kill."

A horrendous lapping noise trickled from the blank gloom, and Kath hesitated, curious to know who had spoken but unwilling to take a step nearer. Why was the mysterious stranger not horrified and outraged at what she had done?

Presently the slobbering ceased, and she heard a scratching clatter beetle over the ground.

"Who is it?" she snapped. "What do you want?"

"I desire only to applaud this delicious deed born of my dark thought," the unseen enigma told her—in a voice that was now rich and barbed, like poisoned honey—"and show my gratitude for the sweet nourishment you have bestowed upon me. The life essence of this whelp was fierce indeed—most sustaining."

Kath screwed her face up, becoming at first irritable, then angry. She did not understand what kind of game the hidden man was playing.

Yet she knew that to remain would certainly prove dangerous. So far, the stranger had not seen her, and that was exactly how she wanted it.

"Linger a while longer." The voice drifted through the mist, reading her thoughts. "Who is there to see us two in this captivating murk? Let us speak together."

"What is it you want of me?" she repeated coldly.

A guttural sigh came to her, as if the man was savoring

her scorn. "Long have I been withheld from this world," the prickly, syruped tone muttered. "Ages uncounted have I spent languishing in the fetters of mine enemies, whose bitter chains did bind me close and made me weak. But now I am released from their shackles. I, who sired the first grain of misery when the world was young; I, who nurtured the seeds of enmity and discontent and watched that harvest burgeon across the land, am free once more."

Kathleen peered through the obscuring vapor as a powerful desire to know the identity of this man was inflamed in her breast.

"Who are you?" she murmured.

"One of the legion who descended from on high," came the treacling answer. "Archduke of we who waged war about the throne of the Beginning. I am the mightiest under the fallen Lord of Light."

The girl frowned. The man was obviously unhinged, yet there was a compelling quality to his voice that fascinated her.

"Much do I know of your cause," the sour, sugary voice continued, "and great is mine knowledge of those you loyally serve and hold in high esteem. A blessed creed and purpose is theirs; to conquer and subdue the lesser species, destroying the impure strains—that is a glorious aspiration. You cannot imagine my gratification in knowing that there are still in this world such strong and ruthless leaders. For they are undoubtedly the fruit of my toil, the flourishing offspring of my will and mind."

Steadily, Kathleen fell under the stranger's spell. Enchanted by the mellifluous thorns of his speech, she edged a step closer to where she had left Michael Harmon's body.

"A common bond do we share," the melodic voice jarred. "There is in you an unquenchable thirst for the spice of glory, a wanton hunger for destruction and death."

Kathleen's skin pricked and needled as an unholy numbness stole over her, and she took another pace forward.

"Yes," she said thickly, from the depths of her trance.

"Unbridled should be your ambition," he vaunted, "yet why keep it shuttered and constrained? Give vent to your longing. Follow me, and I shall shower you with all that you crave. Serve with unswerving fidelity, and under my guidance you shall become mighty, a tyrant to rival the governors of ancient realms long despoiled. I it was who set them upon their thrones and anointed them with blood. Upon the graves of their vanquished foes were their kingdoms founded, with the bones of the slain were the palaces raised, and with terror did they reign."

An indistinct shape was now visible in the heaving mist. Twelve feet tall it stood, blocking the entrance to the street, its vague form writhing within the gloom.

Kathleen's breath panted with mounting excitement as triumphant visions for her beloved Germany were unfurled before her. No longer would she be an insignificant player in the mighty theater of the Führer's design. Now she saw herself standing at his side, spreading his doctrines of hate over the globe.

"Please," she begged the sinister, alluring shadow, "tell me who you are."

With a haughty, rumbling growl, the dim shape reared up, and two points of crimson fire came blasting through the mist.

"Beli Ya'al am I!" he cried arrogantly. "The worthless one, the arbiter of conflict, parent of despair, cultivator of all deeds deceitful and without mercy. Cain was my first disciple. I it was who steered his hand to spill the first blood and tasted the sweetness of the human soul.

"Behind the armies of the forgotten wars did I hoist my standard, and greatly did I feast on the battlefield. Ever was man ready to harken to my guiding counsel, and mighty did I become, till the ancients of the loathsome race we both revile did assail my towers and throw them down."

"Beli Ya'al . . ." the girl echoed. "Let me look on you, let me see your face."

A discordant, evil cackle blared from the mist-mantled demon before her, and the fiery eyes blazed round and wide.

"My face?" he hissed. "The aspect I choose depends on the company I keep. Already I have worn the raiment of many diverse forms, yet there is one that I found most pleasing and entertaining. Perhaps you shall also, for it contains an element you will surely recognize."

Kathleen watched as the dark figure in the fog shimmered and warped, assuming a different shape, one with long segmented limbs. Then, to the girl's insane elation, Belial came forward and the mists parted.

With her eyes mirroring the light emanating from those of the demon, Kathleen Hewett stared in awestruck wonder at the imposing, distorted image of the squander bug.

Larger now than when he had first escaped from the casket and probed the thoughts of Doris Meacham, the cockroachlike creature reached upward, standing on its powerful splayed legs, whose curved talons gouged deep into the ground.

Raising her eyes past the mottled, leathery belly, which was freckled and blemished with marks resembling swastikas, Kath gazed on the demon's face and fell to her knees with a gasp of devoted reverence.

Centered in the sagging flesh, housed beneath the tortured horns, which disappeared into the darkness above, the gross parody of her leader's face appeared to Kath, and she was filled with doubt and terror.

The looming nightmare hissed with ecstasy. "Such charming prostration," the squander bug savored. "In the days of my previous existence, before I was tethered and sealed within the confines of my casket, temples were built unto me and amusing sacrifices burned upon the altars. Worshipped and prayed to was I—it will be agreeable to be so again."

Staring down at the stricken girl, Belial ordered her to stand. "This is a strange new time for me," he proclaimed. "A prince cannot reclaim his fiefdom without loyal servants. You shall be my priestess, my honored slave, the first to be gathered back into my dark service."

Intoxicated by his grotesque grandeur, Kathleen readily consented.

"What do you ask of me?" she asked. "What is your will?"

The travesty of her Führer's face grinned hideously. "My wants are simple," the demon instructed. "I desire only the death of thousands. Then shall my strength be as of old, and my greatness shall resound over the circling seas once again."

The girl let out a shrill, boastful laugh. "I know exactly how you can begin!" she told him.

CHAPTER 21

THE SEVERED THREADS

Clambering over the garden wall behind the Stokeses' house, Neil Chapman strode purposefully up to the back door and rattled the handle.

The boy had spent a long, tiresome afternoon aimlessly wandering the streets and waiting for evening to fall before daring to return to number twenty-three. He had no wish to run into Mrs. Stokes again and had deliberately delayed his reappearance until the time when he was sure she would be in the Underground station.

The door was locked, so he hunted through the garden for a tool he could use to break his way in, dwelling on the wonderful prospect of returning to the future and seeing both Josh and his father again. Soon all this would be behind him and back in the past where it belonged.

To his surprise the kitchen door suddenly opened, and armed with a poker, Jean appeared and called out into the fog, "Who's there?"

"Jean!" Neil cried. "What are you doing here? You

promised to go to the Underground with your grandmother!"

The young woman groaned with relief, put the poker down, and ushered him inside.

"Neil, love," she said, delighted to find him there. "I didn't think I'd see you again. I thought that old battle-axe had frightened you off forever."

"I don't understand," he said. "You shouldn't be here!"

Jean laughed. "Don't start that again," she told him. "Ooh, you're freezing. I bet you haven't eaten anything either. There's some stew left, then I'll mash you up a boiled parsnip and put a drop of banana essence in. How does that sound?"

"Awful. Please, you must get out of here."

"I am. I was just about to go over to Kath's when I heard you trying to get in."

Neil relaxed and gave a grateful sigh. "Good," he breathed. "I thought for a minute you were going to sleep in the bomb shelter tonight."

"Well, I will," she replied. "The one in Mrs. Meacham's garden."

"That's all right. You'll be safe there."

Jean laughed at him. "You're acting strangely," she said. "I s'pose you'll have to come to Kath's as well. Hope there's room in that shelter."

"Er . . . no," he said quickly. "I'll be fine."

"But you've got nowhere to stay."

"I have," he answered, fumbling for an explanation. "I . . . I finally remembered where my dad lives. I only came back to pick up Ted."

Jean looked at him dubiously. "So where do you

live?" she asked, not satisfied by the clumsy statement.

"Oh, you wouldn't know it," he said. "It's over in Ealing."

"Ealing!" she repeated in astonishment. "Then what were you doing on the other side of London when my dad found you?"

"Sleepwalking?"

"I'm not stupid, Neil. Anyway, how are you going to get back there tonight?"

"Don't worry about it," he assured her, making for the hallway. "Do you mind if I go upstairs to get Ted?"

"'Course not. I don't care what happens in this house no more."

Assuming this to be a mere figure of speech, Neil hurried up the stairs and ran into the bedroom.

"Geez!" Ted shrieked furiously. "Where have you been? I been goin' nuts here. You know what time it is? You realize we only got a little over half an hour to fix everything! I told them screwy dames not to make me drag you along—I just knew you'd louse it up somehow!"

"What are you screaming about?" the boy cried. "Everything's fine. Jean's taking Danny to Mrs. Meacham's, so she won't be here when the bomb lands."

"And Angelo and Frank?"

Neil shrugged. "Umm, I don't know," he said.

"Angelo is still downstairs, ain't he? I mean, he ain't gone out yet, right?"

"I don't know, I came straight up here."

The bear pulled a ferocious face and shook his paw at him. "If he's gone . . ." he threatened. "I gotta go find out—come on."

Neil picked him up and leaped downstairs.

Jean was in the living room, fastening the catches on a suitcase and tying up the neck of a backpack. At her feet Daniel was sucking on a carrot lollipop that he waved in a mad greeting when Neil entered with Ted.

"Is the American here?" the boy asked.

"Did you want to say good-bye?" she said. "That's nice. No, he went out after his friend."

Neil flinched as Ted gave him a discreet kick.

"I see. Well, I better get going then," he babbled quickly. "Sorry to rush off. It was nice knowing you, Jean. P'raps I'll come back one day and say hello."

"Well, don't look for me here," she told him. "I'm not setting foot in this house again."

Neil wavered in the doorway as her words struck a dismal chord inside him. "You're leaving then?" he muttered.

"I am," she declared. "That evil old crab of a grandmother's gone too far this time. I can't take any more of her. As if things aren't bad enough, what with Dad still missing—heaven knows what's become of him. If it hadn't been for Angelo, I would've wrung that wicked old bat's neck."

"What do you mean, if it wasn't for Angelo?" Neil murmured, ignoring Ted's urgent pinching.

Jean flushed a little and looked away. "Take no notice of me," she sighed. "I'm just wishing for the moon, that's all. I could never be that happy. My life's never worked out like that."

Neil bit his lip and looked at the mantelpiece, where Jean's wedding photograph still stood in its frame. The woman followed his gaze and uttered a sorrowful gasp as she realized that she had not thought to take it with her.

Hurriedly, she took it in her hands and stared at it.

"Don't know how that happened," she muttered guiltily. "I've got too much on my mind, that's what it is. You do understand, don't you, Neil? I do still love my husband, it's just that I don't know if he's dead or alive and it's killing me. I can't go on anymore—I just want to get away. I know I sound stupid and selfish, but it isn't like that, it isn't. Is it so terrible to want a little bit of joy?"

Neil thought of his own mother and realized for the first time that the abrupt and severe manner of her departure was the only possible way she could have gone. She had seen her one chance of happiness and had seized it utterly. The complete and final separation from her former life was the only way she could escape and begin again.

"You like Angelo a lot, don't you?" he ventured.

Jean placed the photograph in her pocket and smiled. "I feel safe when he's around," she said simply. "Heaven knows why, because he's the most outrageous man I've ever met. I don't know what it is. I sort of sense that he'll always take care of me. What am I saying? I don't even know what he really thinks of me. I'm probably just the latest in a long line of girls he's sweet-talked."

Neil said nothing, and Ted softened, ceasing the violent nudging he had been engaged in.

"Got to go now," the boy finally told her. "Be happy, Jean, whatever you decide. Whatever happens, be happy."

"Don't go without giving me your address," she said. "I'll write to you."

"No," he replied. "The way things are, a letter would take years to reach me."

"Good-bye, Neil."

But the boy had gone into the hall and was already out of the front door.

"Did you really love her?" he asked, holding Ted before him as he paused by the gate.

"I wanted to take her to the States with me," Ted answered sorrowfully. "Her an' Danny. Only I never told her, I never once said to that lovely creature how much I adored her. What kind of a jerk was I? If there were ever two people in this crazy world who deserved a little happiness, it was Jean and Angelo."

The bear stared back at the mist-enshrouded house, and a fierce, determined scowl appeared on his furry face.

"This time I'm gonna make sure they do," he growled. "Hey! We gotta get with the program. I just hope we ain't been delayed too much. We don't have no time left, kid. The lives of two men are depending on us. You gotta turn right here and run as fast as you ever did. Please, I'm beggin' ya."

"'Course I will," Neil promised, and into the swirling curtain of fog he ran—into the night, where Belial was stalking.

* * *

"That's everything," Jean muttered, glancing at the bulging suitcase and backpack. "I think I'm going to have to make two trips with these, Daniel. Why don't I take you over to your Auntie Kath's, then I can run back for the rest?"

The two-year-old chuckled and nodded his agreement, so Jean picked him up and stepped into the hall, where the huge baby carriage was waiting.

Before she had time to lay him down, the air raid siren abruptly warbled to life.

"Flippin' nuisance!" she tutted. "Well, I'm not going to toddle across the street in the middle of no air raid. Looks like you and me'll spend one more night in the same old bomb shelter after all, doesn't it, Daniel?"

The infant gurgled, and Jean reached inside the carriage to take an extra blanket out into the garden.

As she hurried to the kitchen door, the thick cloth in her hand shimmered with countless shades of green and sparkled momentarily with threads of silver tinsel.

"Brrrrr!" she cried, wrapping herself and her young son in the blanket and running across to the shelter. "We could freeze to death."

* * *

As she made for the Bethnal Green Underground station, Old Mother Stokes was feeling extremely pleased with herself. She had seen to it that her granddaughter's happiness wouldn't last for long.

After leaving Barker's Row that afternoon, she had caught a bus and traveled to Central London to divulge some information concerning the whereabouts of a certain deserter from the United States Air Force. The Military Police had taken the matter extremely seriously and promised that they would apprehend Lieutenant Signorelli as soon as possible.

Enjoying herself, the vindictive old woman also told them that he had been most abusive and threatening in his behavior, adding that he seemed quite mad and that she was now too afraid to go back to her own house.

The MPs guaranteed that the airman would be severely dealt with, and hardly able to contain her malicious glee at this most splendid eventuality, Mrs. Stokes caught another bus and returned to the East End, munching her dripping sandwiches contentedly.

Outside the station's single entrance the mist was thinning, and only a few slender wisps lingered in the nearby park. The street was unusually busy, as a great many people were moving toward the Underground, and the old woman reminded herself that the numbers on the platforms had been steadily increasing in recent nights. The crowds who congregated there were noticeably jumpier than she had ever known them to be, and on three occasions to her knowledge, fights and scuffles had broken out among them.

Everyone was expecting some kind of retaliation to the raids that the Allies had been inflicting on Germany lately, and they all dreaded what could prove to be a devastating bombardment. As her shoes clopped over the road, Mrs. Stokes hoped the shelter warden had saved her regular bunk for her. If he had not, then she was quite prepared to do battle for it, and she steeled herself for this possibility.

Then, just before she reached the entrance, the siren sounded, wailing dismally overhead, and with a surge the people hurried forward.

Squawking insults at them as they overtook her, Mrs. Stokes scrunched up her hatchet face and waded through the throng, elbowing them sideways until she managed to barge onto the dimly lit stairway that led down to the platform.

Half a mile away, in Victoria Park, the new Z rocket

batteries spluttered into life against the as-yet-unseen enemy aircraft.

The noise of their sudden firing was tremendous. No one had heard such a deafening series of blasts before, and the frightened people trying to get into the Underground station looked up fearfully.

"What is it?" they shrieked above the terrible din.

Bulldozing her way down the steps, Mrs. Stokes was infuriated when she blundered into someone's back and could find no way of getting past.

Her pernicious mind thought quickly, and as the antiaircraft batteries exploded into the night, she screeched, "Land mines! They're dropping land mines on us!"

A wave of panic swept through the horde that impeded her progress, and they stumbled more swiftly down the stairs. Yet behind the cackling old woman, the multitude of terrified people had also heard her squawks, and as one they shoved forward.

Near the bottom of the steps, in almost pitch dark, a woman carrying a baby suddenly tripped and fell. At her side, an elderly man lost his footing and tumbled after her. Unable to stop, shunted along by the mass of panic-stricken people pushing behind them, a third, then a fourth stumbled, trampling over those already fallen.

In the dark, like a macabre line of human dominoes, men, women, and children fell and were crushed against the wall at the bottom of the poorly lit staircase, and ever the tide poured in.

In the midst of this suffocating terror, as those around her pressed and jostled and the clamor of those in front rang in her ears, Mrs. Stokes squealed as she trod over soft, breaking bodies, crunching a woman's hand under the heel of her shoe.

Horror and fear hung thick on the air, and the old woman tried to turn back, to escape the crushing nightmare that she was swiftly approaching. But her efforts were futile, and the river of people pushed all the more.

Suddenly a hand lashed out as a man tried to prevent himself from falling, and his fist viciously punched into her shoulder.

Howling, the old woman jerked forward, and her thick spectacles went flying from her nose to be crunched underfoot.

In another second, Jean's grandmother was thrown down upon a pile of compressed bodies, and almost immediately she was buried by two more.

Irene Stokes's final screams were smothered by the clothes of those who crushed the breath from her. Like a withered twig, the old body that had stored so much bile and resentment snapped under the oncoming waves of death. Interred in that dark, terrible place, the old woman perished.

* * *

On the main street, Frank Jeffries was too immersed in his own heartache to even hear the booming of the Z rockets overhead.

Cracking with emotion, his normally buttery voice came in gulping bursts as he tried to figure out what had happened.

"What . . . what have I d-done?" he wept. "How could . . . she treat me so bad? She was so changed—it scared me."

Shaking his head, he wiped his eyes and resolved to make amends.

"She can't . . . can't have meant it," he fooled himself. "My Kath wouldn't be so cruel. I g-gotta put her straight. When she understands, it'll be the way it was. I'd d-do anything for her—she's gotta know that. Yeah, that's what I'll do—g-go back and talk to her."

The street was still filled with obscuring fog, and as Frank smartened himself up, he heard the sound of a woman's footsteps clattering down the far side of the road.

In an ecstasy of anticipation, Kathleen Hewett hurried to the red telephone box near the Gaumont Picture Palace and squinted in the feeble blue light of the bulb above the phone.

Inserting her money, she dialed the number she had memorized and waited impatiently for the ringing tone to end.

"He must be there," she muttered. "He must be!"

Abruptly the telephone at the other end was picked up, and the unmistakable clipped tones of her stage manager said, "To whom am I speaking?"

Kath wanted to laugh out loud at his caution. There was no longer any need for his petty rivalries and vying for attention from "the directors and producers." All his ludicrously secretive euphemisms and clandestine rendezvous points were obsolete now, and she wanted Mr. Ormerod to be the first to know it.

"Over-ambitious fraulein," she said, trying to keep her voice level and serious.

There was a silence at the other end, and she could practically hear his well-ordered thoughts churning in surprise.

"What is it?" he demanded curtly.

Kath grinned. "Not over the telephone," she chided him.

"Where then?"

"Outside the entrance of my own little theater."

The girl knew he would understand what that meant and wondered if his lizardlike eyes had started to bulge yet.

"When?" he snapped.

"The curtain goes up in fifteen minutes."

The sound of Mr. Ormerod's startled coughing honked in the earpiece. "Impossible!" he snorted. "How am I supposed to reach you in time?"

"Oh, I'm sure you keep some emergency gas somewhere," she said. "The performance will continue with or without you to manage it."

The apoplectic jabbering at the other end brought a satisfied smile to her lips.

Without warning, a loud tapping on one of the small windows made her whirl around. The glass of the telephone booth had been painted black, but one of the panes was broken, and there, peeping fearfully in at her, was Frank.

Hastily, Kath turned her back on him and muttered into the mouthpiece before slamming the receiver back into its cradle.

"What do you want?" she cried, pushing open the door and rounding on the airman.

Frank looked at her questioningly. "Kathy," he said miserably, "I only wanted to explain. Whatever it is I d-did to make you like this, to make you not like me anymore, to make you so cruel, I wanna make it right."

"Make it right?" she repeated mockingly.

"'Course I d-do!" he insisted. "I know it can be done, too. You're 'shamed of the way I acted up in the Fort; well, it won't be like that no more. I d-done a whole mess of thinkin', and I know that you're the most important woman in my life. If I don't g-got you, then I don't have nothin'. Don't you see? I'd rather face a pack of them Messerschmitts and fly straight through a sky full of flak than live my life without you by me. What d-do you say, Kathy? We can find a way to be happy. I'll hightail it back to base and you can be p-proud o' me."

The girl's eyebrows arched in amusement, and for an instant she glanced past him into the fog above.

"You really don't see, do you?" she said.

Frank put his hands on her shoulders and gazed desperately into her eyes. "Please, Kathy!" he begged. "You frightened me back there, but I love you so much— I ain't afeared of d-dyin' no more if you'll stand by me."

The corners of her mouth twitched as she smiled ruefully, and Frank wept with joy as he believed she had forgiven him.

"Oh, Kathy!" he cried, hugging her tightly. "You an' me, it'll be j-just like in the movies—a happy ending. Only our love won't never end, it'll just go on and on, getting bigger and stronger every d-day."

With her chin pressed against his shoulder, the girl parted her lips and whispered into the American's ear. "Lieutenant Elmer Burakoff," she hissed. "Sergeant Hank McCall, Private David Johnson, Sergeant Ralph Driberg . . ."

Frank leaned backward. "What's that you're saying, Kathy?" he asked timidly.

"I'm simply telling you about the others." She laughed with derision. "You wouldn't believe the information I managed to get out of them—or what I did to get it. Of course, there's lots more, but it's so difficult remembering all of their names when I can't even remember their faces. There was one who had the most awful breath—I won't forget him in a hurry, but then he was the only one who seemed to know anything vital that particular weekend."

Frank stood as still as stone while she continued to taunt him.

"As for you," she spat, "you were the easiest of them all! Stupid Frank Jeffries—was there ever an idiot to equal you? You were so gullible and lapped up everything I said. And how you sang. You'll never know how saddened I was to learn that you'd survived that mission. I had hoped the guns of the magnificent German air force would rip through your skinny body and send your wretched aircraft plummeting to the cold, hard ground."

Unable to utter a sound, the American felt his entire world drop away, and an empty, raw grief howled inside his soul.

Starting to shake, he tried to pull himself from her, but Kath would not let him go.

"Oh, no!" She laughed. "You can't g-g-g-g-go yet, Frank d-d-d-d-darling! There's something I want you to see. The nights I spent listening to crass, dull-witted bores like you are finally ended. I shall never have to humiliate or sell myself again, for now I have a power of my own."

Stupefied and aghast, Frank stumbled backward, but

the girl clapped her hands to the sides of his face and cried, "Turn, my poor pathetic sweetheart. Look on the new object of my affections. See his might and majesty!"

Too weak to resist her scratching fingers, the airman slowly twisted his neck and stared back at the awful shape that had been towering over them the entire time.

Rearing from the mist, the huge, demonic form of the squander bug filled Frank's vision, and his legs buckled when the horrendous glare from those fiery eyes burned through the fog and ripped into his frail spirit.

"What . . . what is it?" he yelled, tripping over himself, unable to tear his gaze from the ghastly spectacle.

Above them, Belial let loose a bellowing roar, and Kath's exulting voice joined it.

The twin evil sounds cut right through the American, and he covered his face with his hands.

"See the doom that awaits you and your kind!" she shrieked at him. "The Archduke of Demons will lay your fat, idle land to waste and spill fire upon your corrupt cities."

Bathed in the harsh crimson light, Frank tried to escape, but Kath grabbed his arm and dragged him back to her.

"Isn't that what you wanted, beloved?" she sneered. "To hold me forever in your embrace?"

"No," he whimpered, still staring up at the mind-numbing horror that was Belial. "Let me g-go, please!"

"Just one f-f-f-final kiss," she teasingly implored, "for old time's sake."

The petrified airman was powerless to stop her, and Kath hauled his head down to her mouth. With a sadistic snigger, she pressed her lips against his, while at the same time plunging the blade of a long knife between his ribs and twisting it into his heart.

Recoiling from her, Frank uttered a dismal, agonizing cry and lurched into the road.

Kathleen watched with delight as he fell to the ground.

"Accept this offering, my lord!" she crowed to the grotesque creature at her side.

Belial glared down at her, and the repugnant face glowered with malice.

"This is not what you promised," he growled menacingly. "What is one base life when you vowed I could feast on hundreds? The night is full of death, it floats thick and close, pervading every drifting air. A hundred murdered souls and more have I sensed near to this place, and yet you would throw me scraps."

Kathleen glanced up fearfully. There was a terrible edge to his rumbling voice, and she was quick to appease him.

"Follow me!" she beseeched. "I swear that we are close to that place. Come, it is not much farther, and your hunger shall be satiated."

The baleful eyes fixed on her suspiciously. But Kath took a step forward and beckoned the demon on.

The clawed limbs of the squander bug raked through the mist as the demon lumbered after her, dragging the sagging belly of his loathsome raiment over the ground. Into the dense fog they went, Belial's forked, scorpionlike tail lashing the vapor to shreds behind him.

Close to death, Frank Jeffries lay in the middle of the road, clutching the handle of the knife that was still firmly lodged in his chest.

Using the last remnant of his ebbing strength, he tightened his fingers about the weapon and slowly drew it out, screaming as the unbearable pain jolted through his body like lightning.

The instant the blade was loose, a fountain of blood pumped up from the ugly wound. Cascading over his body, it flowed in a steaming river across the road and into the gutter, where it formed an ever-widening lake.

In the veiled sky above, the drone of the Luftwaffe grew louder, and Frank whined piteously as his head lolled feebly to one side. Now, beyond despair, the gentle American ironically reflected that the ominous noise of the enemy aircraft was the last sound he would ever hear. Then his eyelids fluttered shut.

Angelo was not far away when he heard Frank's anguished scream. For a dread-filled moment he hesitated, then charged toward that curdling cry, his heart thumping.

"Frank!" he yelled, stampeding through the fog that separated them. "Frank!"

From the dense, blanketing cloud the airman came, his dark eyes burning with anxious concern. Then the final, hazy curtain was ripped aside and Angelo saw him.

"No!" he bawled, rushing to the wounded man's side and gazing in horror at the waning spout of blood.

"You'll be okay!" he cried, covering the gash with his hand and trying to staunch the dwindling flow. "Don't you worry now, Frank, Voodini's here. He's gonna make everything all right. You just hang in there!"

Jerking his head around, Angelo stared into the foggy street and called out desperately. "Help!" he roared. "Help us, someone! For God's sake help me!"

The flow of blood had become a seeping trickle, but still Angelo tried to stop its escape from the airman's chest.

"Come on, Frank," he urged, "listen to old Voo.

There'll be a medic here any time now. You gotta hold on till then."

A pitiful moan drifted from Frank's lips, and his eyes trembled open.

"That's it, pal!" Angelo cried, lifting his head and cradling it in his arms. "You'll be fine, just fine."

The ghost of a smile flickered about Frank's mouth, and gazing up into the tear-brimming eyes of his friend, he died.

"Fraaaaaank!" Angelo howled, hugging his buddy close and rocking him like a baby.

For several minutes, he held him and cried desolately. Then Angelo turned to the knife that was still clenched in Frank's hand and gently took it from him.

As the airman raised the gore-covered blade before his face, his tears subsided and a bitter anger welled up in their stead.

"Why wasn't I here when you needed me?" he muttered thickly. "Don't you worry now, Frank, I'll find whoever did this. I swear to the Almighty I will. If it costs my immortal soul, I'll avenge you. Trust your old Voodini, I won't never rest, I won't never give up till I find out who did this to you."

The first of the German bombs erupted in the distance with a dull *crump*, and throwing his head back, the lieutenant called upon heaven to witness his oath.

"You hear me?" His defiant cry challenged the powers of the world. "Whatever it takes!"

Sorrowfully he closed Frank's blank, staring eyes, then took off his own flying jacket and placed it under his dead comrade's head.

Tumbling from the chopped-up garment, Daniel's new

teddy fell at his feet, and Angelo snatched it up, smearing the fur with blood.

With a tremendous roar, the ground quivered as a parachute mine exploded three streets away.

Angelo stared at the bear in his grasp, and his horror plumbed new depths as a hideous premonition seized him. "Jean," he murmured. "Oh, no!"

Suddenly, two circles of light came sweeping through the mist, accompanied by the fierce rattle of an engine.

Heading for number twenty-three Barker's Row, the jeep containing two military policemen had swerved aside when they heard Angelo's lamenting screams.

Bouncing over the road, the vehicle plowed through the fog, its hooded headlights straining to see the way ahead.

Leaning forward in their seats, the MPs looked aghast at the gruesome sight unexpectedly captured in the soft beams.

Standing over the blood-drenched corpse of a GI was a lieutenant of the American air force. The murder weapon was still in his hands, and the face he turned to them was wrung with guilt.

The driver of the jeep slammed on the brakes, and the tires skidded to a halt.

"Drop it!" he hollered, leaping from his seat and reaching cautiously for his baton.

Angelo stared at them in bewilderment as they prowled closer, their white belts and gaiters shining in the lights.

"Frank's dead," he called dismally.

"The knife!" the driver repeated angrily. "I said drop it!"

Angelo stared at the blade in his hand and realized what they were thinking. Hastily he threw it down.

"You got it all wrong!" he cried.

"Reach!" the other MP shouted, sliding the handcuffs from his belt.

"Lieutenant Signorelli?" the driver barked.

The airman nodded, puzzled as to how they knew his name.

"The old dame was right," the MP whispered across to his partner. "The guy's bats—look what he's got in his other hand."

"Better be careful," the second MP hissed back. "Ain't no telling what crazies'll do."

"Listen to me," Angelo cried as they drew near.

"Quiet!" the driver yelled. "You're gonna fry for this, flyboy."

At that moment, another bomb landed, and its shivering violence jolted through the street. To Angelo's dismay, the explosion seemed to have come from the vicinity of Barker's Row, and consumed with fear for Jean, he panicked.

Lunging forward, Angelo pushed the nearest MP sideways, and the man went flying into his partner.

Bounding over them, the airman pelted into the fog. He needed time to think. If he could only get back to Jean, if he could just be sure she was safe.

Behind him he could hear the MPs' frantic, furious voices ordering him to freeze. His mind a turmoil, Angelo raced deeper into the enveloping vapor. They'd never catch him; in a moment he would be invisible in the mist.

Darting past Frank's body, the driver pulled out a gun and bawled, "Hold it, Signorelli!"

Tearing down the street, haring toward the desperate

commotion, came the figure of a boy, upon whose shoulder sat an anxious teddy bear.

"We're too late!" Ted shrieked at Neil. "It's just as it was!"

Leaping from the boy's shoulder the bear sped forward, cupping his paws to his mouth as he shouted at the top of his voice. "Stop, Signorelli! Stop!"

For an instant, the concealing fog was drawn aside, and Neil saw the running figure of Angelo shudder as a burst of white light flared behind him.

With the gun shot still resounding through the mist, Angelo glanced down and saw a blossoming circle of red soaking through his shirt.

The pistol blazed three more times, and Angelo screeched as the bullets blasted and ripped clean through his flesh.

Gasping, the airman toppled backward to the ground, clasping his hands to his perforated chest.

"No!" he choked, convulsing with shock. "Oh, Lord, no—I ain't ready. Hell, I *weren't* ready."

His frantic movements began to slow, and Angelo rolled onto his front.

"Jean," he groaned, as a blackness closed over his eyes.

The lieutenant's fingers clenched, tightening around the soft, fleecy toy in his hand.

Before the darkness took him, Angelo Signorelli gazed into the furry face of the bear that would house his soul for the next fifty years—and then it was over.

CHAPTER 22

THE DECREES OF FATE

"No-o-o!" Ted caterwauled, speeding over to the bullet-riddled, motionless body. Stroking Angelo's hair, the bear glared upward, then shook his fists.

"This can't be!" he raged. "Not after all these years of waiting! It ain't fair! You hear me? It ain't fair!"

Stepping awkwardly up behind the disconsolate bear, Neil crouched beside him and stared over to where the figures of the military policemen were advancing.

"We've got to go!" the boy urged.

"Who's that?" the driver of the jeep demanded, keeping the pistol trained on the dim shapes ahead. "Stand up and keep your hands where I can see 'em!"

The boy rose and gave Ted a nudge with his foot, but the mourning bear ignored him.

Neil rubbed his eyes, for the billowing haze had blurred the two figures, distorting and shriveling them.

Through the swirling murk the MPs came, staring dispassionately down at Angelo's body and not in the least surprised or disturbed to see a teddy bear standing guard over him.

Tilting back his white hat, the driver returned the gun to the holster, and Neil shook his head incredulously.

"Edward," said a sad female voice, "you have our sincerest condolences."

Ted raised his glass eyes.

Looking more absurd than ever dressed in the uniforms of the military policemen were Miss Ursula Webster and her sister Veronica.

"I truly am sorry, Edward," Miss Ursula said. "I wish it had been possible for you to save both yourself and your friend."

The bear scowled at her. "You knew all along, di'n'tcha?" he demanded angrily. "You never had the slightest intention of letting me do it. This is what you wanted!"

Miss Ursula looked at him pityingly, a single diamantine earring glittering on one of her ears. "It is never a question of what we desire," she said sensitively. "The path we all follow is already woven for us."

"That's a crock and you know it!" he ranted back. "You're the ones who do the weaving! What difference would it have made for these two guys to live? You promised me! You said there was a way!"

With her raven hair piled underneath her tin hat, Miss Veronica peered down at the airman and cooed softly, a forlorn expression on her chalky face.

"Oh, Ursula," she tutted. "See how young and dashing Edward was. What a pity Celandine isn't here to see him. How she used to admire the pretty gentlemen who came to call on us, all that time ago in Askar."

"The toy," her sister instructed.

Stooping awkwardly with her stiff leg, Miss Veronica took the bear's twin from Angelo's fingers. "I rather think we had better wash this before it joins the collection," she twittered. "The poor dear's covered in blood. It would never do for him to wake up and find himself in such a state, now would it?"

"Right from the start," Ted spat, "right here—you tricked me!"

Miss Ursula nodded in confirmation. "I did, yes."

"Why?" he shouted.

"There really was no other way," she replied.

"So it's all been for nothing. I wait fifty years, fly back to here, haulin' the kid with me, and for what?"

Miss Ursula cleared her throat as a sign that she was growing tired of the bear's complaining.

"Do cease your grizzling, Edward!" she snorted, a degree of the familiar irritation creeping into her voice. "You appear to have forgotten the other matter we spoke of, or did you deliberately disobey my decree?"

Ted grunted disparagingly. "Yeah, well, I figured the critter from the box was your problem, not mine."

"There is still time to deal with him."

The bear scoffed and waved a dismissive paw. "You gotta be crazy, sister!" he cried. "I ain't doin' nothin'."

Neil had been staring at the Websters in amazement and listening to Miss Ursula's discourse with Ted in fascination, but now he felt it was time to butt in.

"I'm sorry," he said, "but I think we ought to be getting back to the Stokeses'. It won't be long before Josh and the gateway appear . . ."

Miss Ursula turned on him with a disdainful glance.

"The maggot speaks!" she announced. "And what does he have to say for himself? Not a word of apology for breaking into our premises and trespassing where he was strictly forbidden to enter."

"Hey!" Ted yelled. "Let him alone. Grouching at him won't make me help you."

"Then I wonder what will?" she asked, eyeing the bear intently.

"I know! I know!" her sister piped up.

"Quiet, Veronica. Now, Edward."

"Will you stop calling me Edward? The name's Angelo!"

Miss Ursula turned on her most dangerous smile. "Angelo, then, if you prefer," she humored him, "are you not anxious to go back and save the life of the Evans girl?"

"Jean," the bear growled. "What's she got to do with this? There's nothing you can do to her—at least that's something I got right this time around. She's safe in the shelter at number thirty."

Miss Ursula turned to her sister, who was tittering, and let her explain.

"Oh, no," Miss Veronica simpered. "Both she and her little boy are still at home. They never went across the road. Isn't it awful? In—how long will it be, Ursula?"

"A little over thirty minutes."

"Oh, yes, in thirty minutes time the bomb will land just as it did before. Won't that be a splendidly large bang?"

Both Ted and Neil stared at her, appalled.

"Then I ain't changed nothin' yet!" the bear muttered. "Kid, we gotta get back there, now!"

"Oh, no!" Miss Ursula told them. "If you attempt to rescue the young lady and her son then I shall surely see to it that your efforts fail and they suffer the same . . . fate, as before."

Ted glared at her.

"You know I am more than capable of that," she said.

"Please," he cried, "don't do this!"

Miss Ursula laced her fingers together and revealed her brown teeth in a triumphant grin. "I believe you will find Belial at the . . . er . . . munitions factory, is it? Even now he is approaching the gates. Very great has he become. I hope for Jean's sake you will be able to dispatch him in time."

"The factory?" Ted cried. "I don't know where that is!"

"I do!" Neil answered. "I was around there today, after I got away from Mrs. Stokes."

"Under thirty minutes left," Miss Veronica chirruped.

The bear glared desperately at Miss Ursula. "You promise I can save Jean and little Danny if I pull this off?"

"You have my solemn word."

"Right!" Ted roared at Neil. "Kid, we ain't got much time—we gotta steal that jeep."

The boy gaped at him. "Who's going to drive it?" he asked.

"I'll tell you how!" came the confident reply.

Hurrying over to the abandoned vehicle, Neil and the bear jumped into the seats, and Ted barked out his instructions.

With a lurch, the jeep sprang backward. Then, with a screech of burning rubber, it plunged through the fog.

Glancing behind them, the bear saw the shapes of the

• 367 •

Webster sisters shimmer and vanish to be replaced by the bodies of the real MPs, who shook themselves and wondered what had happened.

* * *

Outside the entrance to the munitions factory, Kathleen Hewett peered into the mist as a small black car came chugging into view.

Mr. Ormerod stepped from the automobile, looking unusually flustered and mopping his perspiring lip with his handkerchief.

Furtively glancing around, he strode up to her, his babyish face flushed and trembling.

"This had better be of the utmost necessity!" he snapped. "Should I find that you have falsely used the emergency code then you will be struck from the company."

To his surprise the girl was laughing at him.

"Don't worry, little piggy!" she jeered. "None of that matters anymore."

The meticulous man gawked at her. "Are you crazy?" he began to squeal.

"There's something I think you should see," she told him. "A vision so magnificent you will no longer have any use for any other performer. The whole production has been canceled, and in its place a drama, the likes of which you have never dreamed, is about to unfold."

"You're drunk!" he glowered, his lashless eyes beginning to swell.

Kath ignored the remark and pointed to the indistinct bulk of the factory rising behind the high walls.

"Hush," she said. "The overture commences."

Mr. Ormerod quaked with rage. "If you have dared to bring me here merely to plead yet again for the destruction of this place, then you have overreached yourself for the last time."

Sliding a hand into his jacket, he pulled out a stubby pistol, but Kath was unconcerned.

"Now shall this grubby little country and its dithering population know that they are beaten!" she cried. "Arise, my lord, the time is upon us!"

Mr. Ormerod thought she had gone completely insane. Then his froggish eyes saw a large shape rear up behind the high brick wall, and he noticed for the first time that the iron gates of the factory had been thrown down and were lying buckled and twisted on the ground.

Framed within the demolished entrance, the indistinct figure of the monstrous squander bug wavered for a moment, its terrible eyes gleaming thirstily. Then, with a thrash of its powerful segmented limbs, it veered around and clawed its way toward the vastness of the munitions factory.

"What . . . what is that?" Mr. Ormerod's strangled whisper asked.

Kathleen hooted exultantly. "It is a sign," she cried, "in which all our dreams are made manifest. A divine testament to the excellence of the Reich. A thousand years and more shall our dominion be, for with Beli Ya'al as our guiding beacon, our enemies shall be utterly defeated."

As she spoke, inflamed by her madness, there came a violent, thundering din of crashing bricks as the demon's talons went crashing through the factory wall.

Mr. Ormerod turned a scared face to her as the

squander bug smashed his way into the munitions building, and his pink face quivered like an unset strawberry mousse.

"What is it doing?" he cried shrilly.

Kathleen began to step away from the entrance and in a jubilant voice said, "Why, he's going to detonate the stored explosives! How else can he feed and grow strong?"

Guffawing, she turned and began to run for cover, tearing through the mist and leaving her former superior to slowly realize the mortal danger she had placed him in.

In a sweating fluster, the man ran back to his car, fumbled with the door handle, then scrambled inside.

Through the fog there came the chilling roar of the demon's laughter, and the hideous sound made Mr. Ormerod drop his keys on the floor.

Groping for them in the darkness and whining pathetically, he finally turned the ignition, and the automobile coughed and spluttered to life.

Wrenching the steering wheel around, Mr. Ormerod pressed his foot down—but it was too late.

With a tremendous, bone-jarring boom that pounded and echoed in the man's chest, shattering the windshield into a million fragments, the buildings of the factory flew apart.

Into the troubled fog-filled night, a dazzling flash of brilliant white flame suddenly erupted. Expanding to a gargantuan ball of ravaging force, the fire flowered blindingly in the milky fog, piercing its smothering ceiling and scorching up into the plane-filled heavens.

Mr. Ormerod's car was flung across the street as the perimeter wall was hurled down. Smashed and dazed, he emitted jolting screams, which were silenced only when the shattered vehicle was engulfed in the ensuing shock wave. A second, smaller explosion resounded through the streets as the car detonated with such ferocity that it was propelled forty feet into the air, executing a perfect fiery arc over the roof of a shuddering rowhouse.

The houses that had surrounded the factory were utterly destroyed, flattened before the savage might of the lethal, obliterating energies.

Foundations were laid bare and ripped from the earth, while an immense black cloud of choking debris was cast into the tormented air.

Huddling in the shelters, the terrified inhabitants were either crushed beneath the tons of collapsing rubble or shaken to death by the ghastly unleashed forces. Many fell headlong into the massive pits that gaped greedily open in the rupturing ground, their bodies never to be recovered. Into these splintering gulfs buckled roads and burning trees tipped and slithered, and the night was rent with despair.

Within the smoking ruins, unharmed by the rending blast and rearing up from the crater that was once the factory floor, Belial stretched his cockroachlike limbs up to the churning sky.

The once dense fog was now ragged, and it swirled around the horrendous destruction in tattered shreds. Within the fine, lacerated threads of vapor rising sluggishly from the fresh graves, other forms were moving.

Into the night the souls of the dead ascended, mingling ethereally with the eddying, melting mist.

Yet Belial was aware of them. His lusting eyes peered through the haze, and a ravenous skirl rumbled from his scabious guts when he beheld the countless victims of his unhallowed appetite.

Drawing his foul lips back over his fangs, the demon gulped down deep, insatiable, gluttonous breaths.

Drawn into the powerful, devouring gale, the misty souls were sucked down into his blistering gullet, and with them came the delectable, nourishing morsels he so avidly coveted.

* * *

Bouncing through the streets, the military jeep had braked sharply when the factory exploded.

"Watch out!" Ted cried, as the fierce glare shone through the fog and the ground shuddered.

Neil shielded his eyes from the intense light, then threw his arms over his face as a hail of stones and smoldering chunks of timber came battering from above.

Over the road the splintered wreckage fell, ricocheting off the jeep's hood and drumming on the rooftops of the trembling houses nearby.

"What was that?" Neil gasped, shaking the grit from his hair. "It didn't sound like a bomb—it was too big!"

"That was your factory!" the bear told him. "Step on the gas, kid. I got a feelin' this ain't gonna be as easy as those sisters said."

Over the rubble the jeep charged, kicking out a plume of dust in its wake.

Swiftly they reached the outskirts of the devastation, and somberly they gazed on the battered ruins of the once populated row houses.

Winding between fallen telegraph poles and crackling

rafters, Neil drove the vehicle more slowly, until at last both he and Ted beheld the source of the sickening violence and their courage left them.

"Heaven help us!" the bear murmured.

Gorged upon the souls of the recent dead, Belial had grown to a fearsome height. Retaining the shape of the squander bug, he was now taller than the factory had stood, and his immense lobster-red limbs were the size of great trees, their cruel hooked talons slicing through the air like tremendous scythes.

Above the bloated expanse of his blemish-ridden abdomen his misshapen, poisonous features were now repulsively distorted. From his jaws rivers of wrathful flame dripped through the night, and his burning, swollen eyes stabbed through the gloom, brimming with unquenchable rancor and cruelty.

Casting back his monstrous head, ripping the atmosphere with the pinnacles of his twisting horns, the demon bellowed, trumpeting his glory out over the wasteland of his diabolic creation.

"Now am I returned to my former majesty and splendor!" he rumbled. "The worthless one has cheated the old fathers and is once more free to harry the unhappy world. Thus shall a new age of darkness and death begin!"

Cowering in the jeep, Neil turned a stricken face to Ted.

"You said it was just an imp!" he muttered. "How are we supposed to deal with that . . . that thing?"

Grimly the bear stared past him at the nightmarish spectacle and reached for the seam at his side.

"We gotta do something—and quick," he said, pulling

open his stitches and searching inside the stuffing with his paw. "Get us as close to that big desperado as you can, kid!"

Reluctantly, Neil drove the jeep up to the side of the demolished factory, pulling up just before a heap of bricks that blockaded the road.

"I'm sorry I got you mixed up in this!" Ted growled, a fierce look of determination stealing over his face. "This ain't your problem. I gotta do this on my own!"

"What exactly are you going to do?" Neil hissed as the bear jumped from the vehicle.

With the unpicked hole in his side still gaping, Ted held up a small vial of green glass. "I'm gonna make the big lug take his medicine!" he answered cryptically.

"You'll never make it!"

The bear grinned at him and saluted with his paw. "So long, Neil!" he cried, darting over the debris and into the factory ruins.

Neil stared up at the titanic horror that reared against a sky filled with the frantic sweep of searchlights. Never in his life had he seen anything that inspired so much dread and fear, yet as he watched the small, insignificant figure of the teddy bear leaping into the demon's vast shadow, he knew what he had to do.

Into the smoking wreckage, hopping over sizzling embers, Ted hurried.

Belial towered above him like a giant looming over an insect. Undaunted, the bear rushed on.

From his lofty height, the Archduke of Demons sensed his presence. The tantalizing essence of the defiant soul that possessed and animated the toy fascinated his dark mind and tempted his jaded palate.

Rolling his fire-brimming eyes, Belial stared down at the trifling shape that scuttled toward him and cackled raucously.

"What new manner of beasts do they breed in this age of the world?" he mocked, lowering one of his tremendous segmented limbs and scraping the great claw through the rubble.

Ted leaped aside as the hideous talon plowed straight for him, then ran quickly in the other direction as it bore around, chasing him over the wreckage.

With his gaze fixed on the infernal vision above, the bear raised the paw that held the vial and, judging that he was close enough, prepared to throw it.

Before Ted knew what had happened, the massive claw flew into him, flicking him helplessly aside.

Yelping, the bear was tossed through the air, and the vial went spinning out of his grasp.

"As a flea in the sand are you to me!" Belial thundered. "What madness is it that brings you raving before my grand majesty? Are you so weary of existence you must flee unto your destruction, for assuredly that is what you have found."

Sprawled on his back, where the brutal blow had knocked him, Ted clambered to his feet then stared in horror at his paws. Where was the vial?

Despairing and defenseless, the bear searched through the mortar dust and pulverized brick, but no trace of the glass vessel could he find.

High over his head, he heard the rumble of Belial's scorn as the demon lumbered forward.

"Easy, big fella!" the bear called. "You know, you oughta sweep up around here, it really is a mess. I'd love to stay and have a few beers, but I gotta make tracks."

Backing away as one of the legs of the horrific squander bug came crunching into the rubble, Ted suddenly caught a glimpse of something glittering in the darkness.

Half-buried in the dirt, lost in the gloom of the demon's shadow, was the tiny bottle of green glass.

The bear's face lit up, but even as hope kindled within him, the demon dragged his sagging, distended belly right on top of it.

Glaring upward, Ted looked into the frightful countenance and stifled the qualms of panic simmering in his kapok.

"Okay, blubbermountain!" he cried. "You want some sport? You gotta be in better shape than that to catch a flyboy of the Mighty Eighth!"

Tearing over the ground, Ted nimbly dodged the claws that came razoring down for him. Like a demented cricket he bounded from one heap of bricks to another, always a mere instant away from the barbed talons that came diving after him.

Over the rim of the crater he sprang, his stumpy legs aching with fatigue. Roaring in amusement, Belial waved his massive limbs in the air, lashing them in the stuffed toy's path.

As he gargled with hellish mirth, flaming strings of saliva came dribbling from his awful jaws, erupting in loud bursts when they hit the ground.

"How long can you continue to flee?" the demon asked with a laugh. "Already I sense that you are weakening, your energies are nearly spent!"

Taunting him, the hulking fiend spat out a stream of fire that raged through the night and exploded a mere hair's breadth behind the puny quarry.

Howling, Ted lurched on. A patch of fur on his back was scorched and smoldering, and wherever he ran, more flames leaped up, blocking the way.

Cackling malevolently, Belial watched him scamper to and fro, like a vicious cat idly playing with an exhausted mouse. Then he grew bored of the game. The attraction of the bear's in-dwelling spirit was too strong, and when the claws next came snaking after Ted, they were driven by a deadly purpose.

Stumbling through the ruins, Neil Chapman stared at the terrible scene before him. The bear was still jumping from one spot to another, and though his movements were slowing and becoming labored, with every bound he was heading back into the deep shadow, drawing ever closer to the now uncovered vial.

Anxiously, Neil watched as Ted scooted toward it, when suddenly he saw one of the segmented limbs come swooping unerringly down.

"Ted!" the boy yelled. "Look out!"

For a moment the demon wavered, his cruel eyes glinting across to the edge of the crater where Neil was standing. With a ghastly roar, a torrent of flame went streaking from his slobbering mouth and struck the ground just feet away from the wretched boy.

But Neil's distraction was just enough. Vaulting one of the bitter talons, Ted reached the vial at last and snatched it from the dust.

"Okay!" he cried, kissing the glass and scowling up at the pale, blemished belly. "The party's over."

Raising his paw, the bear leaned back and hurled the tiny vessel straight at the glistening, leathery hide.

Through the fume-filled air the vial soared, turning over and over until, with a sharp tinkle of shattering glass—it smashed.

From the broken vial, the water taken from the sacred well of the Nornir, which had once fed the mighty world-tree of ancient legend, splashed onto the demon's foul, rippling flesh.

At once the liquid frothed and seethed, eating into the infernal, crusting scales of skin like acid.

A deafening screech issued from Belial's jaws as a searing pain stabbed into him and a pall of oily black smoke came gushing from the dark, festering wound.

"That's it, baby!" Ted crowed. "Bawl your last! This is the Signorelli Exterminating Service—let us splat your roaches!"

The gigantic squander bug thrashed his misshapen limbs. Inflamed by agony he staggered from the crater, his talons raking enormous trenches in the rubble.

Chuckling gleefully, Ted scurried over to Neil.

"Them sisters sure know how to brew up some powerful hooch," he said, laughing.

But the boy did not glance down at him. His eyes were still fixed upon Belial, and to Ted's dismay he realized that the shrieks were dwindling.

Whipping around, he saw that where the vial had smashed and the water ate into the bloated hide, the wound was already beginning to close.

"It weren't enough!" the bear cried in woeful realization. "Them screwy broads didn't give me enough!"

Swaying unsteadily while he recovered, the towering demon tore his twisting horns through the dark, reeking clouds that had poured from his own flesh, and his eyes swiveled down, overflowing with malice.

"Geez!" Ted yelped. "It's really hit the fan now."

With ravaging flame dripping from his screaming jaws, Belial lumbered forward, his malignant mind bent on vengeance.

"Kid!" Ted cried, waving the boy away. "Get outta here—I'll keep him busy."

Neil took one final look at the nightmare that stormed toward them and blundered back through the demolished entrance, flinging himself into the driving seat of the jeep.

The roar of the boundless squander bug split the heavens with boiling savagery. Only once before had his demonic majesty been assailed with mortal agonies. Then he had been vanquished and consigned to the casket, but now his rage was terrible to witness.

Fleeing across the barren destruction and waving his arms over his head, Ted tried to divert the monster's attention from Neil.

"Hey!" he yelled. "Dogbreath—over here!"

Intense as the beams of searchlights, Belial's evil glance glared into the shadows and saw the bear sprinting below him.

Snarling with immeasurable hatred, he lunged with his claws, and Ted let out a terrified wail.

Turning the jeep around, Neil stared wretchedly back at the hellish spectacle, and his spirits sank.

All over London the bombs were falling. The flare of their explosions burning angrily in the misty sky created a perfect backdrop for the Archduke of Demons. It was like stealing a glimpse into Hades, and the boy turned away, aghast.

With a start, he whirled around again and peered at the murky horizon. Beyond the stretch of fallen houses a familiar sight was standing quiet and sedate in the gloom, its spikes and pinnacles pricking the cloudy vapor.

A desperate, wild idea jolted through Neil as he remembered the harsh, accusing words Miss Ursula Webster had once addressed to him, and a glimmer of hope ignited in his heart.

Shouting at the top of his voice, the boy sprang from the jeep and raced back into the wreckage.

As Ted galloped through the shadows, vainly trying to evade the demon's piercing glare as he scrambled over the ruins, his flight was suddenly curtailed when three ferocious claws plunged into the rubble around him.

A victorious roar blasted from Belial's lips as he plucked the yowling bear from the ground and lifted him high into the air.

Dangling helplessly by his right arm, Ted kicked and jerked, but his paw was impaled upon the sharp talon, and though he continued to squirm and fight, he knew there was no escape.

Past the putrescent abdomen, peppered with a foul rash of swastikas, the struggling bear was hauled. Up past the blighted ridges from which the enormous limbs radiated out in mighty branching sections he rose, until, finally, he was brought up to the demon's face.

The abhorrent folds of undulating, scaly skin that stretched across either side of the hideously grotesque features pulsed and throbbed as the bear's singed, jiggling figure was swung close to the yawning jaws.

With his free paw, Ted covered his eyes. The immense head of the deformed, distended squander bug was too horrendous to look at.

Every feature of the revolting countenance was a separate nightmare in itself. The ghastly downturned mouth was rimmed by folds of clammy, twitching flesh, as pale and gray as that of a waterlogged cadaver.

From the rotting gums in which the jagged yellow fangs were rooted, a stomach-curdling stench of death and decay gusted up into the bear's face until he gagged and balked.

The mustache that had once parodied the leader of the Third Reich now sprouted wildly in the dark crevices of the wart-ruptured cheeks and bristled up over the snorting truncated snout.

Yet even though these foul, diabolic features instilled equal measures of terror in Ted's fluffy heart, none of them frightened him as much as the demon's eyes.

The garish, baleful glare of these huge lamps that blazed with undiluted malice burned into him, steeping the bear in a glow of pure evil. Dangling forlornly by his paw, he could feel the virulent stare penetrating his soul, slicing right into the very essence of him.

"Give thanks unto the profane glory that is Belial," the repellent mouth thundered, "for by his impenitent grace the trials of your unhappy existence are over."

To Ted's terror, the frightful jaws lolled open, and deep in the echoing throat, a ruddy light welled up as the fiery caverns of his gullet rumbled to be fed.

"All souls are my nourishment," the demon gloated, "and upon your tender succulence shall I sup most readily."

Cackling, Belial put forth his malevolent power, and the bear, suspended from his claws, shivered uncontrollably, racked by fierce, rifling spasms.

From Ted's fleecy skin, seeping with painful inevitability through the grubby fur, threads of glimmering shadow were gradually drawn toward the waiting maw.

The shade of Angelo Signorelli was dragged and ripped from the stuffed toy, while behind it the battling bear abruptly went limp and lifeless.

A trickle of flame splashed from Belial's tongue as it flicked out to receive this delectable and most sustaining of souls.

CHAPTER 23

A DESTINY FULFILLED

Into Belial's monstrous jaws the shimmering wisps of the airman's spirit were drawn—down into the enormous, hell-reeking throat.

Suddenly the demon was pelted with a flurry of stones and bricks, and to his irritation, something was striking against one of his huge, cockroachlike legs.

His concentration broken, Belial glowered down, and there was Neil, with a length of railing in his hands, hammering furiously upon the steel-strong segmented limb.

Immediately, Angelo's soul snapped back into the bear's body and Ted shook himself, feeling horribly sick.

Defying the booming roars above him, Neil continued to smash the railing against the squander bug's powerful leg, oblivious to the claw that was reaching down to seize him.

"Kid!" Ted yelled. "Get away from there!"

The boy glanced up and flung himself aside as the talon cleaved the air.

"Not without you!" he bawled back.

Swinging from the demon's grasp, Ted thought frantically for a way to free himself, but there was only one thing he could do.

As Belial stooped to try and snatch the boy again, the bear fumbled with the stitches in his shoulder and pulled them out with a wrench.

Warbling, Ted tumbled down, narrowly avoiding the cascading spouts of flame that flowed from the demon's mouth. With a jarring bump, he landed on the ground, and the force of the impact catapulted a wad of stuffing from the ragged tear in his shoulder.

Not pausing to retrieve it, he flipped himself to his feet, and at once Neil's fingers closed around his middle.

With Belial pounding after them, the boy fled as fast as he could through the ruined entrance and back to the jeep.

"Take us outta here!" the one-armed bear yelled.

Neil hesitated, turning to see the towering horror of the squander bug come lurching over the wreckage, the forked tail switching angrily behind his vast and loathsome body.

To Ted's amazement, a grim smile appeared on the boy's face.

"What you waiting fer?" he hollered.

His eyes shining, Neil delayed a moment longer. Then, just as Belial's flailing claws came reaching for them, the jeep screeched out of his grasp.

Bellowing in thwarted rage the demon tore after, the violence of his wrathful pursuit shaking the surrounding rubble.

Bouncing on the passenger seat, Ted tugged at Neil's

clothes. "Where you takin' us?" he cried. "This ain't the way we came."

The boy only laughed in reply, even when the road burst into flames behind them and the heat scalded their backs.

Veering recklessly around fog-hidden bends, the jeep careered and bounced, crashing through a garden hedge when Neil misjudged a particularly sharp corner.

"You can't lose him!" Ted cried, staring fearfully back.

"What makes you think I want to?" the boy replied wildly.

Into a narrow street the jeep sped, until at last it spun to a halt—at the end of Well Lane.

Ted stared up at the fastness of the Wyrd Museum, its darkened windows gazing morosely out at the war-torn world.

"You're crazy!" he shouted at Neil. "What'd you bring us here fer? This ain't gonna help us, kid! Them daffy sisters won't be here!"

Within the blacked-out panes of the museum's Georgian windows an infernal glare welled up as Belial came rampaging around the buildings behind them.

"It's not the Websters I'm thinking of," the boy answered, scooping Ted up in his hands and tearing into the dingy, fog-filled road that lay behind the museum. "Besides, you and me don't need them, do we?"

Waiting a moment to make certain the demon had seen him, Neil hurried to the large gate that barred the entrance to the cramped yard and pushed it wide.

Over the top of the encircling wall the hellish glow rose, and the grotesque monstrosity of the squander bug lumbered into view.

The dismal yard was flooded with a bloody light as the demon's eyes hunted for its prey, and with a deep gurgle of treacherous joy, it saw that they were trapped.

Staring up into the venom-filled, merciless face, Neil stumbled back until the museum wall prevented him from going any farther.

"Hope you know what you're doing," Ted muttered, sitting on his shoulder.

As Belial came crashing through the entrance, battering the gates off their hinges, his claws gouging into the concrete, Neil whispered, "So do I."

Into the courtyard the indomitable demon came, the tempest of his boiling fury screaming around the walls, rattling the windows and gushing flame over the ground.

The chase was over, and as he glowered down at the puny creatures cringing below, his accursed spirit squalled with supremacy and doom.

From this point on, his blasphemous glory would spread over the land. Into the hearts of mankind would he sow yet more hatred and aggression, until a new pandemonium would be born from the burning desolation. The true age of war was only just beginning. Horror and chaos would overmantle his death-drenched realm, and he, Beli Ya'al—mightiest of the fallen host— would cruelly govern all despairing souls. The time that was prophesied had come at last.

The titan's odious braying laughter tore malignantly into the night as he bent his baneful anger upon Neil and Ted.

Staring up at the pestilential face, the bear cowered back. "Nice while it lasted, kid," he burbled.

Neil shivered as three malformed talons came plunging

through Belial's fiery breath, ready to kill him.

"Hope I guessed right," he murmured.

With a yell, the boy leaped away as the vicious claws came grinding and slicing.

Even as they swooped after, he dashed to the place where the drinking fountain stood and, using all his strength, kicked and battered the pipe that fed it from the wall.

At once a deluge of rushing, icy water shot into the sky as the liquid blasted out under pressure.

Grabbing the broken pipe with his hands, soaking himself and Ted to the skin, Neil wrenched it down and directed the deluge straight at Belial.

The demon roared in mockery as the splashing jet hissed toward him. Too late, his repugnant mind clouded with doubt. Then the fierce flood struck him full in the face.

With a deafening peal of anguish, Belial recoiled from the maelstrom that devoured and burned him. Black smoke flooded the air as the hideous face started to melt, and the squander bug's enormous limbs flailed insanely before him in a futile attempt to ward the deadly liquid off.

But the segmented legs dissolved in the streaming spray, withering like wax in a flame.

Screeching, the demon was wreathed in a noxious cloud, whipped by his massive horns, which pounded with such agonized force upon the walls of the museum that the building rocked and the slates rattled from the roof.

Dripping with water, Ted punched the air with his paw and gave a whooping cheer. "You did it, kid!" he crowed. "He's shrinking!"

Racked with blistering torments, the towering squander bug was diminishing. Down into the engulfing smoke his liquifying head plummeted, and the tremendous shrieks lost their thunderous resonance.

Pushing the pipe still lower, Neil followed the demon's descent, and Ted leaped from his shoulder to scamper closer to the churning plume of poisonous fumes.

Writhing within the stinging, choking smoke, Belial felt his might and strength flood from his being. With a rush of shimmering shadow, the many souls he had ingested flew from his bubbling, molten mouth, rising through the billowing black reek. Scintillating like dim stars, they soared upward, free at last of the living world, and without them the demon was nothing.

Unable to maintain it, he cast aside the shape of the squander bug as down he dwindled, snorting and squealing like a stuck pig. All his splendor, all his foul majesty was ripped away, yet even as the sacred water tortured and consumed him, his vile mind knew that there was still a slender chance.

Looking away from the curling pall of smoke, Neil saw that the water pressure was dropping.

"That's all there is!" he cried in disappointment.

Ted watched as the powerful jet swiftly became an erratic spurting spout before it spluttered into a dribbling trickle.

Glancing back at the dark, swirling smoke, the bear saw that it too was failing.

"That oughta have done it!" he said.

Through the damaged gateway a strong breeze suddenly gusted, and the reek was borne away, leaving only dark shadows in the waterlogged courtyard.

"Is it over?" Neil murmured. "Is the demon dead?"

Ted paddled into the gloom, rubbing his ear thoughtfully. "I don't get it," he said. "They told me it weren't possible!"

At that moment, with a yammering squeal, a stunted, bristly shape came leaping from the shadows.

The gnashing, deformed imp was only as tall as Ted's shoulder, but its unexpected appearance startled him and he gave a cry of alarm.

"Geez!" he wailed.

Splashing through the wide puddles, the peevish little demon scampered around the yard, trilling a high-pitched, angry cheep like a frightened gerbil. The shrill shrieking was so ridiculous that Neil almost laughed.

Belial's beady red eyes hunted for a way to escape them, alighting finally upon the gaping entrance. Quacking sharply, he scudded through the tainted waters toward the battered gates.

"Don't just stand there, kid!" Ted shouted. "Catch the little varmint!"

To the frenzied, grunting demon's dismay, the bear lunged across his path, and careening over the slippery concrete, he was unable to stop himself.

Squealing, Belial cannoned straight into Ted's sopping body, and the two went tumbling head over heels in the muddy puddle.

Angrily the bear sprang to his feet, showering a spray of water all around as he shook himself and cast about for the imp.

The bristle-covered demon was retching and spitting out the mire he had swallowed when Ted came stomping up to him.

"I might only have one paw left," he snapped, "but it sure makes a heckuva fist!"

Spinning on his legs and swinging his body around, the bear slugged Belial right on his quivering jaw.

With a piercing yowl, the demon toppled backward into the water again.

"Boy, that felt good!" Ted jeered.

Simmering with impotent fury, the imp glared past the obstructing body of the bear and prepared to spring.

"Always did have a mean left hook," Ted called over to Neil.

Spitting with rage, Belial launched himself from the puddle and catapulted past the one-armed bear.

Ted whirled around in surprise.

"Stop him!" he cried.

Neil watched the jabbering imp race toward the entrance and shook his head. "Let him go," he said. "What harm can he do now!"

"You outta your mind?" Ted yelled, crashing through the water. "If he gets loose, then it'll start all over."

Fearfully, Neil darted after him, but it was no use. Belial scrabbled over the broken gates and leaped into the street beyond.

"No!" Ted wailed.

Seething with glee the imp danced in the gloom. Soon he would be mighty again.

Even as he jigged and capered, out of the darkness a child's hand came swooping down, and Belial was captured.

Lifting her wriggling pixie hat before her face, Edie Dorkins grinned. Tiny claws were already ripping at the wool, tearing it to shreds, but she was prepared for that.

Champing his needlelike teeth, the pugnacious imp finally ripped through the woolly hat and hurled himself out.

Into a wooden box he fell, and as soon as the demon was inside, the girl slammed the lid down tightly.

Taking the Casket of Belial in her hands, she raised it and laughed out loud.

Standing in the entrance to the courtyard, Neil and Ted stared in bewilderment at poor, mad little Edie Dorkins.

Then a cold horror crept over the bear, and he gazed despairingly up at Neil.

"Jean," he cried.

Neil's hand flew to his mouth. "Josh!" he howled. "We're too late!"

Not wasting any more time, the boy grabbed Ted and they tore from the yard and into Well Lane.

Into the jeep they leaped, and the vehicle went scorching out of the narrow street.

The time was nine forty-five. The parachute mine, which had previously killed Jean Evans and her young son, had fallen from the sky nine minutes before.

* * *

Into Barker's Row the jeep roared, plowing through the fog that still covered the houses.

With a quaking heart, Neil stamped on the brake, and the vehicle screeched to a tire-melting halt.

In dreadful silence, the boy and Ted gazed up at number twenty-three.

"It's still here," Neil whispered.

"Not for much longer," the bear yelled, hopping from the jeep and running to the front door.

A sheet of milky mist was spread over the Stokeses' garden. Slowly shifting and curdling, it was like the calm surface of a silver lake from a romance of the middle ages. The woody stalks of last year's Brussels sprouts that rose from the tranquil, ghostly pool were the towers of wizards, and the tangle of strawberry plants that crowned the bomb shelter was an island forest inhabited by the wild fairy folk.

Such was the fluttering, merry fancy of the one who gazed on the harmonious scene. Then, abruptly, both the peace and the pretty illusion were shattered.

With a juddering slam, the back door flew open and the skeins of mist fled. A frightened clamor squawked out of the chicken house as Neil and Ted burst into the garden.

Hurtling toward the shelter by the far wall, they suddenly stumbled and tripped over one another as they beheld the figure standing in the potato plot.

"Good evening, dears," she chortled. "I was beginning to think you were never going to arrive."

Dressed in her shabby nightgown, with an eager, expectant look on her crinkly, toothy face, was Miss Celandine Webster.

Both Neil and the bear stared at her, but before either of them could utter a sound they saw the large, sinister shape behind her.

Suspended in the empty air, hanging impossibly in the ether, with the mist curling over its smooth metal surface, was a bomb.

Lifting his gaze, Neil saw the unfurled parachute

hovering over the garden, frozen in the final seconds of its descent.

Miss Celandine followed their eyes and turned to the great sea mine while she fiddled with the knitting in her hands.

"Isn't it a big one?" she observed. "Will it make such a very large hole? Ursula said it would—isn't it marvelous what they can do these days?"

Ted gave an admiring whistle that the elderly woman mistakenly thought was meant for her, and she blushed coyly.

"Oh, Mr. Edward," she giggled, still pulling at her knitting, "you are a gallant, aren't you? No wonder you charmed old Ursula. I almost wept when she told me that she had decided to spare the woman and the little boy, really I nearly did. She can be so very mean and stingy most of the time, but I am so happy for you, I am, I am."

Neil took a pace closer to the suspended bomb as Miss Celandine prattled on.

"Amazing," he breathed. "I mean . . . how?"

"Still, you cut it awfully fine, didn't you?" she gabbled. "When ten minutes had gone by I nearly despaired. Oh, it was thrilling—I mean, there's so little of it left. How daring and rash you pair are."

Only then did Ted notice what she was doing. Miss Celandine had removed the needles from her knitting and was busily unraveling the stitches. On the soil about her feet she had already discarded a great snarl of twinkling wool, and in her flickering fingers only about a foot of her once prodigious handiwork remained.

"Wait a minute," the bear cried, "you mean that deadly

can of beans a-dangling there can stay up only as long as that knitting holds out?"

"Well, naturally," she tittered. "You are a silly, Mr. Edward. Why else would Ursula let me out of her sight?"

Frantically, Ted ran to the shelter and called Neil over. "You better get Jean outta there and quick!" he told him. "That screwball's web's nearly undone. Take her and Danny to the wardens' hut, they'll be fine there. You should have enough time."

As Neil clambered into the trench, Miss Celandine piped up behind him, "Hurry, hurry—the gateway will be here presently. Ursula was very strict that the woman should not see it!"

"Go on," Ted urged. "And hey, Neil—I'm glad you tagged along. You did real good back there, I'm proud of you. If I'd ever had a son, I wish he'd been like you."

There wasn't time for the boy to question the finality that rang in Ted's voice when he said that. Hastening into the dank bomb shelter, Neil found Jean and her son fast asleep.

"Wake up!" he cried, shaking them roughly.

Grumbling, Daniel whined drowsily, but Jean was soon wide awake and comforted him in her arms.

"Neil?" she muttered. "What's the matter—what is it? Is it Angelo?"

"Yes," the boy found himself saying. "He wants you to go to him."

"But the raid's still on—where is he?"

"In the wardens' hut."

Worriedly the woman looked at Daniel and shook her head. "I can't go now," she said. "It's too dangerous."

"But you have to!" he ranted, desperate to get her out

of there. "Angelo's been injured. If you don't go now then it might be too late!"

Jean's face turned pale, and she lifted her son to give him to Neil.

"Take him with you," he shouted. "Hurry!"

Anxiously the woman left the shelter and climbed into the garden.

Close on her heels, Neil stared around for Miss Celandine, but both she and the parachute mine were completely hidden behind a curtain of thick fog.

With Daniel in her arms, Jean ran into the house, and the boy followed her.

Down Barker's Row they hurried, and through the little park, until finally the sandbagged hut of the ARP wardens' post emerged out of the swirling mist.

Jean quickly ran inside.

"Angelo!" she cried. But the hut was empty.

The woman turned around in confusion. "Neil?" she called. "He isn't here! Neil? Neil, where are you?"

The boy was nowhere to be found, and outside the wardens' post she could see only the cold, flowing vapor.

In the garden behind number twenty-three, Miss Celandine gave a ticklish cough and stepped from the choking fog that had concealed her.

"Oh, there you are," she said, welcoming Neil back as he came tearing from the kitchen. "Look, only a few inches left. It's all spun out perfectly."

Resting her buck teeth on her lower lip, she beamed at him as she continued to unravel the sparkling wool, then nodded toward the bomb shelter.

Above the mound, where the straggly strawberry plants hung limp and lifeless, the mist began to move.

Gently at first the dense, milky haze rippled and turned, then it began to revolve more violently until the air itself was twisting and wheeling.

Through the torn vapors a raging vortex whipped into existence, drilling and spiraling deep into the night.

The reeling darkness stretched wider at the center of the tumult, and from its black heart vivid bolts of lightning came crackling over the garden.

With a flash of purple light, the insanely spinning rim of the gateway blazed with fire, and blinding sparks went hissing through the surrounding, whisking fog.

"What a pretty thing!" Miss Celandine declared. "It really is too mean of Ursula not to let us play with them more often. But then all the water is gone, and without it these will be no more. How sad."

As the violet glare played over Neil's face and the lightning erupted from its fathomless depths, he heard, in the far distance, the piteous howls of a small child.

"Josh!" he shouted excitedly. "It's Josh!"

Within the twisting helix, a pajama-clad figure appeared, rocketing through the darkness at an incredible speed.

Whirling above the shelter, the vortex churned thunderously, and Neil gazed in wonder as his younger brother came shooting toward them.

Josh's screams were now ringing out over the garden, and then, with a terrific shower of sparks, he was flung over the fiery threshold.

The four-year-old's screams were brusquely silenced when he landed softly among the strawberry plants, and with a trembling bottom lip, he surveyed the misty scene before him.

"Josh!" Neil cried, lurching forward.

"Keep back!" a harsh, savage voice suddenly snapped.

Reaching from the shadows behind the shelter, a scratched and bloody hand made a grab for the youngster's arm, and Josh screamed again when he was dragged backward.

"No!" Neil bawled.

Stooping over his brother's prostrate form, with her singed hair hanging in matted clumps about her cut and bleeding face—was Kathleen Hewett.

Wrenching the boy to his feet, she crooked her bruised arm about his neck and held a jagged piece of broken glass to his throat.

"If anyone makes a move," she warned, the garish purple flames of the gateway reflected in her mad, staring eyes, "then we all get to see what little boys are really made of!"

Snarling, she glanced up at the twisting vortex and pressed the glass to Josh's skin.

"What is that?" she demanded.

"Don't hurt him!" Neil bawled. "I'll tell you! It's an entrance—a gateway to the future!"

Kath bared her teeth like a rabid dog. "I'll ask you once more!" she raged menacingly.

"It's true!" Neil cried. "I wouldn't take risks with my brother's life. Just look at it. Have you ever seen anything like it before?"

The girl stared at the whirling portal then let out a horrible laugh. "A doorway!" she hooted. "Then I can escape!"

"I do apologize!" Miss Celandine interrupted urgently, having witnessed the girl's arrival with mounting alarm and astonishment. "But who are you? I'm afraid Ursula never mentioned anyone else would be here. I'm most certain she never did. Oh, I hope I haven't gone and forgotten a piece of the pattern again. It's so difficult to remember, you see. It's all so intricate and complicated. That's why, when the loom was broken, Veronica and I were secretly relieved."

Holding up the remains of her knitting, she said, "There are only six rows left!"

Kathleen eyed the elderly woman uncertainly before fixing her hate-filled gaze on Neil.

"I saw you!" she spat. "I saw what you did to him—to Beli Ya'al. It was you who ruined my one, fabulous chance. His magnificence was a blessing, a divine sign that the Third Reich would succeed. Beli Ya'al was the embodiment of all our aspirations, all our dreams. A glorious vision revealed to me alone for the greater renown of the Fatherland. It was to me he came, I was the first one to worship him. But now all that is finished! Finished!"

"Belial was very naughty!" clucked Miss Celandine tersely. "He knew it wasn't time for him to be free. Oh dear, there are only four rows now."

Kath glared at Neil, then roughly pulled Josh over to the brink of the twisting gateway.

"I'm afraid that I shan't be able to keep the bomb in the air for very much longer!" Miss Celandine told them. "This chatter is all very pleasant, but don't you think you should hurry up and jump through the gateway? We can talk later, over some sherry and a little cake if Ursula allows. Perhaps she will let us have a teeny party—won't that be nice?"

Peering through the mist at the large parachute mine that hung in the air, Kath snorted. "You can stay here to die!" she yelled venomously at Neil. "Here! Take your brother and make the most of his company before you both get blown to pieces!"

With a violent shove, she thrust Josh from her and lunged toward the churning gateway.

A bolt of ferocious energy lashed from the portal's spiraling center, snaking about Kath's waist and lifting her slowly from the ground.

Laughing, she saw the fiery entrance rear over her and the yawning tunnel stretch way back into the whirling distance.

Suddenly, onto the bomb shelter leaped a small figure that raced through the tangle of withered plants, screaming shrilly.

As the gateway dragged her into its depths, Kath turned at the shrieking interruption—and there was Edie Dorkins.

Removing something from around her neck, the fey girl threw it at her, and without thinking, Kathleen caught it automatically.

Then it was her turn to scream.

The incendiary burst into flame as white-hot phosphor splashed over the woman's arms and body. Hurling the spluttering device from her, she screeched and thrashed her burning hands, but it was no use. Her clothes ignited, and as she began her journey down the wheeling tunnel, Kathleen Hewett became a living torch.

Writhing in torment, her face and hair blazing with ravaging fire, she went spinning into the future, illuminating the dark depths of the gateway until she became only a bright, flickering speck in the immense distance.

With her anguished screams still echoing from the crackling entrance, Neil ran over to Josh and hugged him tightly.

"Quickly!" Miss Celandine urged. "You must follow her. Both of you!"

Neil took his brother's hand and prepared to leap, then he whisked around and stared fearfully at the old woman.

"Where is he?" the boy shouted. "Where's Ted?"

Miss Celandine turned her toothy smile on him and sighed. "Edward is not fated to return with you," she said gently.

"That's not fair!" Neil cried. "What have you done with him?"

"Oh, I assure you it was his own idea," she replied. "Edward ran to the wardens' hut before you took that pretty woman and her son there. He wants to stay. This is where he belongs now. His time of waiting is over, don't you see? There is nothing left for the poor dear to fulfill. He must rest now. This is all about who belongs where. Didn't you know?"

"But I didn't . . . I didn't say good-bye to him!" Neil blurted. "I didn't tell him . . ."

Miss Celandine peered at the meager line of knitting in her fingers. "The final row," she said.

With tears brimming in his eyes, Neil turned back to the gateway. Suddenly, he and Josh were snatched by the lightning and went hurtling through the darkness.

Leisurely unpicking the wool, Miss Celandine raised her eyebrows at the figure standing on the bomb shelter.

"Will you come with us?" she invited. "All of this, the gateway, my weaving, it was entirely for your benefit, after all. You do know why, don't you? I can see that you do."

Edie Dorkins considered for a moment, and her silvery-blue, almond-shaped eyes sparkled in the darkness. Suddenly she ran to the chicken house and released the madly clucking birds, shooing them from the garden.

Then, with a puckish grin, the girl nodded and capered back up the slope, where she retrieved something from the strawberry plants before springing into the air.

With a roar, the gateway dragged her inside and immediately collapsed with a flurry of sparks.

Contentedly humming a waltz to herself, Miss Celandine unraveled the last of the stitches then spun on her toe, throwing the final strand of wool away into the mist.

The ragged lace of her nightgown furled around her for an instant, and then she was gone.

Down came the parachute mine, and with a horrendous boom, the Stokeses' house was utterly destroyed and the garden annihilated.

* * *

Sitting in the wardens' hut, Jean Evans heard the terrible blast and grimly held on to Daniel, praying that they would not be hit next.

"Jean!" a voice called from outside.

The woman looked up sharply. "Angelo?" she cried, recognizing the voice. "Is that you?"

Leaving her son behind, she stepped cautiously outside and peered into the blank, blanketing fog.

"Angelo? Where are you?"

"Stay there, Jean!" the airman's familiar voice told her. "Don't come out here. It's too dangerous!"

"Well, you come inside!" she said. "Did you find Frank? Are you both going back to the base now?"

A little distance away, standing upon a low wall, the small shape of a teddy bear could see the outline of the woman he loved as she stared into the thick, rolling cloud, straining to find him.

"I won't come in, Jean," he said shakily. "I . . . er . . . I can't stop."

"What's wrong?" she cried, sensing the turmoil he was in.

"I love you, Jean Evans," Ted told her. "Do you know that?"

"Yes," she answered, "I truly do."

With his glass eyes gleaming, the bear gazed sorrowfully at her, yearning for what never was. "I love you more than life itself, Jean!" he called. "More than you will ever, ever know. I really do. I love you so much it hurts."

"Angelo," she said worriedly, "you're making me nervous. Please, let me see you. Come in. Are you in trouble?"

"I can't be with you, Jean."

The woman shuddered at his words and hugged herself bitterly. "What . . . what are you saying?" she murmured.

"I been doing a lotta thinking," the bear went on. "An awful lot."

"Don't frighten me, Angelo."

Ted pressed his paw into his forehead as her injured tone stabbed into his soul.

"You an' me don't stand a chance," he eventually answered. "Never did and never will."

Jean leaned against the doorway of the hut. "You . . . you're leaving me," she muttered. "Angelo, why?"

"Lady Luck just ain't willin' to smile on me no more," the bear told her, cursing himself for the pain he was inflicting. "Your husband's alive, Jean, believe me—I know. He's gonna come back to you some day, and you gotta wait for him, Jean. Right now the thought of you waitin' here is the only thing that's keepin' the poor Joe alive. I . . . I can understand that—boy, do I ever."

The tears were streaming down the woman's face.

"I know it's stupid," she wept. "I've only known you a few days, but, Angelo, I really don't know what I'll do without you."

"You'll learn to live without me," Ted murmured. "It'll work out how it's supposed to."

With his head in his paw, the bear spurred himself on for the final moments. "It's time now, we gotta say good-bye. Unlike the song, we won't never meet again. All I wanna tell you is that, though this lousy war'll come to an end someday, it'll always be waged in my heart."

Ted stared across at the woman he adored, remembering every contour, every detail of her lovely young face.

"Whatever you might hear about me in the days to come," he said thickly, "I want you to remember this, Jean Evans. I did all I could to save Frank, but like everything else, I failed. You . . . you were the one shining light of my miserable existence, and without you, there's a mighty dark emptiness. Don't you ever get to thinking that Angelo Signorelli was a bad man. He just met the dearest, sweetest soul of his short life a coupla years too late. It just weren't meant to be. The fates were arranged against us from the start."

As the wretched tears threatened to overwhelm her, Jean wiped her eyes and somehow managed to stem the mounting tide.

"That's my girl," Ted encouraged. "You don't need a bum like me around, anyhow."

Jean battled with her voice, defying it to break into racking sobs. "Well," she uttered in a hoarse, rasping tone that Ted loved her all the more for, "so that's . . . that's it. I see. . . . Before . . . before you do your last trick for me, Voodini, and disappear, can't I see you one last time? Is that really too much to ask?"

"Yes," the bear said forlornly. "I gotta go now. Remember the night we danced under the moon, Jean? That's the moment I'll treasure for the rest of eternity. I . . . I . . . I'll leave you something to remember me by— as a kind of token of my love. If you ever wanna think of me, if for some mad reason you still want to, after what I've put you through, then look at this, and I promise, I swear, that wherever I am, I'll know about it."

"I'll always love you, Angelo," she cried. "Always and forever."

Staring solemnly at her, the bear shivered. "I know that," he whispered, before adding in a faltering, failing voice, "good-bye—I love you, too."

"Angelo?" she called. "Angelo?"

But the bear spoke no more and went limp as the soul of Angelo Signorelli finally departed and was at last able to rest, his torments over. Running into the fog after the airman, Jean found the toy lying motionless on the ground.

"Angelo!" she wailed, crying into the darkness. "Please!"

Finding no trace of her lieutenant, Jean picked up the teddy bear and understood that here was the American's gift to her.

The woman hugged the scorched, mutilated toy tightly and kissed it in utter despair.

Then, distraught, she ran back into the ARP shelter and threw herself onto the stool beside her son as the grief burst from her heart.

In her grasp, Ted's glass eyes were fixed and still. Angelo's soul was finally at rest, and the bear never moved or spoke again. Yet in that terrible bleak hour, when Jean mourned for the lost love of her life, the fur around the toy's staring eyes became damp, and as if the airman's departed spirit had placed them there, two great, weeping tears went splashing to the floor, where they mingled with hers.

The Separate Collection was dark.

Over the shattered wreckage of the glass cabinets and display cases, the ponderous shadows that lay heavily in the Wyrd Museum scattered into the dark corners.

In the dank air above, a fierce crackle of energy signaled the reopening of the gateway. Suddenly the shards of glass that littered the floor winked and flashed as the purple lightning rampaged once more around the ceiling and the vortex ripped apart the atmosphere.

Into the debris two figures came tumbling, and Neil Chapman and his brother, Josh, sprawled headlong into a heap of blackened ashes.

The whirling portal flared, and gurgling with excited joy, Edie Dorkins came spinning into the shadows.

Staggering to his feet, Neil stared groggily at the young blonde-haired girl.

"What are you doing here?" he mumbled. "You don't belong in this time!"

Edie ignored him and glanced up at the gateway. The churning rent sprayed a hail of glittering sparks and then imploded.

At Neil's side Josh was bawling his head off, and the older boy tried his best to comfort him.

Then, without warning, the lights were snapped on, and standing in the doorway were the Webster sisters.

They were all dressed in their nightgowns. Miss Celandine looked just as she had when they'd last seen her, over fifty years ago. Her sister, Miss Ursula, had her hair tied in curling papers and covered with a fine net, while Miss Veronica's face was thickly plastered with beauty cream.

Sternly, Miss Ursula surveyed the mess, snorting at the damaged exhibits and twitching her eyebrows at the branches that now grew from the oak panels. Eventually, her vexed and irritated gaze came to rest upon Neil.

"Well, Maggot," she said, "I see your father will certainly have much to do in the coming weeks."

Neil opened his mouth, but her eyes had already left him.

"Welcome, Edith," she said with a rare measure of genuine warmth. "A long, long time have we awaited your arrival."

The girl waded through the rubble toward her and the others, and when she reached them she bowed low before taking out the bulky object she had stuffed inside her coat.

Reverently, Edie Dorkins lifted the Casket of Belial and gravely presented it to Miss Ursula.

The old woman received it with equal gravity. "I shall see to it that he is sealed inside for a great many more years," she said before turning to her sisters.

"Let me give it to her!" Miss Veronica begged.

"Will not!" Miss Celandine answered.

"Ursula, tell her I want to!"

"But I made it!"

"I cast it on for you and measured the thread!"

Miss Ursula primly clapped her hands for them to stop squabbling.

"Celandine," she commanded archly, "surrender it to me."

Pouting, Miss Celandine handed over the scrap of knitting she and her sister had been fighting over.

"Blood and sand," a man's voice exclaimed behind them. "What's been going on?"

"Dad!" Neil yelled, rushing past the Webster sisters and flinging his arms around Brian Chapman, much to the gangly man's embarrassed discomfort. "Oh, Dad, I'm sorry I said what I did. I'm glad Mom left me behind—I am, really."

Miss Ursula's thin lips curled into a smile, and she knelt down and placed her sister's gift upon Edie Dorkins's head with the utmost ceremony, as though she was crowning a princess of a rare and sacred lineage.

The girl gurgled happily as the green pixie hat, shot through with strands of silver tinsel, was pulled down over her hair.

"There," Miss Ursula said firmly, "now are the three fates of the unhappy world contented. Behold, my sisters, the daughter that should have been ours is finally come among us. Now the Nornir are four in number and the hope of the land is renewed, for the days ahead shall be dark indeed. Edith, dear, you are joined with us, we who walked under the youthful stars and heard the chorus of the wind in the branches of the world-tree are now your family. You are one of us, Edith, and a great yet deadly destiny awaits. Speak your thoughts, child."

Edie stared around her, from the face of the imperious old woman to her two twittering sisters, at the unfamiliar man pinching the bridge of his nose while hugging his children, and then, finally, at the jumbled devastation that was The Separate Collection.

Taking a deep, thoughtful breath, Edie Dorkins gazed

back at the women who were so eager to adopt her and, in a slow, considered whisper, said, "Oh, yes, I know I shall like it here. This is where I belong."